MW01259485

CROOKS

CROOKS

A Novel About Crime and Family

LOU BERNEY

WM
WILLIAM MORROW
An Imprint of HarperCollins*Publishers*

HarperCollins books may be purchased for educational, business, or sales promotional use. For information, please email the Special Markets Department at SPsales@harpercollins.com.

hc.com

FIRST EDITION

Designed by Michele Cameron

Library of Congress Cataloging-in-Publication Data

Names: Berney, Lou, author.
Title: Crooks : a family story / Lou Berney.
Description: First edition. | New York, NY : William Morrow, 2025.
Identifiers: LCCN 2025000399 (print) | LCCN 2025000400 (ebook) | ISBN 9780063445574 (hardcover) | ISBN 9780063445567 (paperback) | ISBN 9780063445550 (ebook)
Subjects: LCGFT: Thrillers (Fiction) | Novels.
Classification: LCC PS3552.E73125 C76 2025 (print) | LCC PS3552.E73125 (ebook) | DDC 813/.54--dc23/eng/20250107
LC record available at https://lccn.loc.gov/2025000399
LC ebook record available at https://lccn.loc.gov/2025000400

ISBN 978-0-06-344557-4

25 26 27 28 29 LBC 5 4 3 2 1

For Sarah, Lauren, and Kayla

CROOKS

PART I

Buddy and Lillian
1961–1972

CHAPTER 1

I t's in his blood.

You don't believe him? Listen to this.

Buddy Mercurio's father worked for the Chicago Outfit during the Depression, running a network of books and keeping the local precinct cops in line. Before that, Buddy's grandfather handled Al Capone's bootlegging operation. Yes, *that* Al Capone. Before that, back in Naples, Buddy's great-grandfather was capo for the preeminent Camorra clan in Campania. Before that . . . who knows? A Mercurio probably sold counterfeit Michelangelos to gullible popes. A Mercurio probably supplied dice to the Roman legions and took a healthy cut of the action.

Mercurios don't play by the rules, Buddy tells anyone who will listen. Mercurios make up their own rules, follow their own laws. They're born pirates, outlaws, rogues, and desperados. It's in their blood.

Buddy's father is killed in the Ardennes, the Battle of the Bulge, when Buddy is six. His mother remarries and moves the family to St. Louis. Those aren't happy years for Buddy. The family bounces around from cold-water flat to cold-water flat, each one smaller and more squalid than the last. Buddy's stepfather drinks away whatever money he manages to earn burning trash or hosing down slaughterhouse walls. A real bum, a loser, so Buddy's mother beats Buddy and his brothers. Does that make sense? Not to Buddy it doesn't. His mother hammers them with a wooden spatula until the bruises bloom on the backs of their thighs. She goes about it solemnly, devoutly, daily, like she's saying the rosary.

Buddy's almost expelled freshman year of high school for breaking into gym lockers, but he talks his way out of that jam. He is almost expelled sophomore year for losing his temper and breaking a punk's nose. But he talks his way out of that jam too. The principal likes him. Teachers too, even though Buddy barely squeaks by in most of his classes. Buddy knows when to crack wise and when to shut up. You have to pick your spots.

Expelled senior year for smuggling booze onto campus and selling it to the freshmen. Buddy doesn't bother trying to talk his way out of that. By this point Buddy has taken the measure of secondary education. A textbook can't teach you anything about life.

He has to get out of St. Louis. The dreary winters, the air gritty with coal smoke. It's going to kill him. He gets a job setting up pins at the local bowling alley. The owner of the alley, when he's busy at the bar, lets Buddy count the night's receipts. A grave error. Within a month Buddy has enough money for a bus ticket. He's read about Las Vegas in a copy of *Life*. He's gawked at the photos. A place like that can't be real.

And now, 1961, here he is: the top of the world. Vegas is everything Buddy imagined and more, the city a convertible speeding down the highway, a soft whisper in your ear, a pounding heart. At night the glow from the Strip can be seen from miles and miles away, as if a flying saucer from some distant planet just landed in the desert. Maybe it has!

Vegas is an open city, a peaceable kingdom, a miracle of criminal cooperation. The New York families, the Chicago Outfit, the New Orleans mob. Los Angeles, of course. Cleveland, Detroit. It's the United Nations of crime. Buddy, twenty-two years old, works for the man himself, Sam Giancana. Well, Buddy works for Vincent Salvo, who reports to Pete Bommarito, one of Sam Giancana's top guys. The Outfit, when it comes to corporate structure, is as stiff and rigid as IBM. But Buddy is climbing the ladder fast, building a reputation for himself. Sam Giancana has an eye on Buddy. Whenever their paths cross, Sam winks and says, *Heya, sport.*

Buddy gets a prime booth at the Golden Steer. He sits next to the stage when Louis Prima plays the Casbar Lounge. When Buddy steps up to a table at the Stardust, the dealer slides over a stack of chips. Not bad for a kid who—just a couple of years ago—climbed off the bus with a cardboard suitcase coming apart at the seams.

What Buddy loves most about Vegas is how brand-spanking-*new* it is.

Bright, clean, hardly anything more than a few years old. Buddy drives a Jewel Blue Chevrolet Biscayne straight off the dealer floor. He rents an apartment with air-conditioning, an electric range, paint so fresh you can still smell it. St. Louis was old and crippled and dying. Vegas squeals like a brand-new baby, big deep breaths and the blood pumping.

The work is right up Buddy's alley. He's a talker the way Gene Kelly is a dancer. Vinnie Salvo, his boss, always sends someone along with Buddy, but Buddy usually tells the gorilla to wait in the car. Honey catches more flies than vinegar. "We've got a problem," Buddy will say sadly, earnestly, like he and the guy late with the dough are in this together.

Buddy isn't what you'd call classically handsome. Not quite enough forehead, not quite enough chin, a bit too much nose. But he's got a nice head of hair and his dark eyes hint at intriguing depths. And don't forget: he's a silver-tongued devil.

He dates showgirls from Lido de Paris, Les Folies Bergere, Holiday in Japan. He dates backup singers for Nat King Cole and Frankie Vaughan, cocktail waitresses from the high-roller rooms. A different girl, or two, every weekend. His social calendar is full. A gentleman, he always brings flowers. He opens doors, lights cigarettes, never misses a beat.

Vinnie Salvo's wife tells Buddy he needs to find himself a nice girl and settle down. Settle down? Fat chance, Mrs. Salvo, fat chance.

• • •

May of '61, balmy and sweet, the mountains softening and the hotel pools opening. A rumor reaches Buddy: a girl at the Hacienda so beautiful she'll stop your heart. Buddy scoffs. The Hacienda? Nobody worth knowing spends a minute at the Hacienda. It's a dud, a snooze, the only hotel and casino in Vegas without mob ties. The crowd: families, tight-fisted yokels. There's a go-kart track, a miniature golf course, and (get this) a puppet show.

Still, Buddy's philosophy, when it comes to the ladies, is to leave no stone unturned. He rolls down in his Chevy Biscayne one Wednesday afternoon to have a look at this alleged Greek goddess. She works in the lobby dress shop, the only salesgirl on duty at the moment, and . . .

She's a looker, sure. Not bad. But his heart doesn't stop. Buddy, don't forget, dates the crème de la crème. This girl is tall and lanky, no curves to speak of, with blond bangs and a ponytail. Nice legs, blue eyes. Not bad at all.

That's his first impression from across the shop, watching as she steers a grumpy matron from the dressing rooms to the floor-length mirror.

"Be right with you, sir," she calls.

He pretends to browse. She leads her customer back to the dressing room. Buddy eases around so he can peek down the hallway. The girl is rummaging through the customer's purse.

"Take your time, ma'am," the girl calls over the curtain. She finds the wallet and plucks out a couple of bills, leaving the rest of the cash so the customer won't notice anything missing. "Would you like me to bring you the one with the cap sleeves?"

The girl glances over, notices Buddy. She's caught red-handed, but she doesn't blush, doesn't rattle. Instead she just gazes coolly back at Buddy. *Now* his heart stops. *Now* he's in love. Because he can see, plain as day, glowing like Vegas in the night, the truth about this girl:

It's in her blood too.

CHAPTER 2

Lillian Ott grows up poor, lonely, and bored in Oklahoma City. Her father flies the coop when she's six. Her mother dies when she's seven. A strict spinster aunt raises Lillian. So many rules! Don't run in the house. Don't laugh too loudly. Don't get mud on your shoes. Don't wear lipstick. Don't talk to boys. *Don't, don't, don't.*

She learns to use her angelic blue eyes, her impeccable manners. When Susie Minton's favorite bracelet goes missing freshman year of high school, no one would *dream* of suspecting Lillian. When the clerk at John A. Brown can't locate the watch he just showed Lillian, he interrogates the lady next to her, who smells like onions.

California beckons. She leaves home at age seventeen and makes it as far as Las Vegas. Good enough. In Las Vegas she's still poor but rarely bored. She lives in a two-room apartment with four other girls. They share custody of three nice dresses. On weekends, the lucky three live it up at the Dunes or the Sands. Lillian takes a job in the dress shop at the Hacienda. Any casino in town would hire her to run cocktails, but Lillian doesn't have the patience or inclination to flirt with drunk ass-grabbers and sweaty low-rollers. The Hacienda will do for the time being.

"My name's Buddy Mercurio," the guy says after Mrs. Ferguson—who finally decides she can't decide on a dress without her husband present—leaves. "Enchanted to meet you."

"Buddy Mercurio?" she says. "That sounds like something you made up."

"My real name is Raymond. You like that better?"

"No. My real name is Lillian. How may I help you, sir?"

"Let's make a deal."

"A deal?"

"Have dinner with me this weekend and I'll show you the time of your life."

She laughs. If Lillian had a dime for every two-bit hood who's asked her out in the past year and a half . . . but this particular two-bit hood does have a certain panache. His eyes twinkled with amusement when he caught her lifting the bills from Mrs. Ferguson's purse. He might be full of shit, he might be an inch shorter than her, but Lillian senses that Buddy Mercurio won't be boring.

"Pick me up Friday," she says. "I get off at seven."

Friday night arrives and . . . what do you know? Raymond "Buddy" Mercurio does show Lillian the time of her life. She doesn't let him know that, of course. At the Starlight Lounge, where Rosemary Clooney greets Buddy by name, Lillian pretends to hide a yawn with the back of her hand. At the Golden Steer, she eats a few bites of her tomahawk steak, the biggest piece of meat she's ever seen in her life, and pronounces it "Fine." At the late performance of Lido, their booth practically on the stage, Lillian leans over to whisper in Buddy's ear: "Is this the best you can do?"

After Lido, he gets them into the Laundry Room, the coziest lounge in Vegas, verboten to the general public. Buddy points out the infamous John Roselli, Handsome Johnny himself, noodling on the house piano. The bartender confides that Howard Hughes just left, not ten minutes ago.

"Well?" Buddy asks.

"It's late."

He twinkles. He thinks she's pulling his leg, but he can't *quite* be sure. "All right," he says after a second. "But I need to make one stop before I take you home. Don't worry, you'll be perfectly safe. You can wait in the car if you want."

The nerve of the guy, trying to turn the tables on her. But Lillian is curious despite herself. "Did I say I want to wait in the car?"

"Come on, then."

The El Marrakech, still buzzing at two in the morning. Buddy strolls through like he owns the place. He nods at a bruiser and the bruiser opens a door marked PRIVATE. Buddy leads Lillian down a hallway. A second bruiser opens a second door.

"What?" The man behind the desk glares at them. Jet-black hair and eyes dead for centuries. "You're not supposed to be here till tomorrow."

"And yet here I am," Buddy says, amiably. He turns to Lillian. "Meet Angie Pappalardo, honey. When he's not looking for a dog to kick, he runs this joint for us."

The smoky air in the office crackles with electricity. Lillian hears the bruiser pop his knuckles, each crack like a gunshot.

"I don't have it," the man says.

Buddy unbuttons his suit coat and pulls over a chair. He takes a seat without asking permission. "I can wait," he says.

In the car, Buddy opens the paper sack and dumps the pile of dirty, sweet-smelling bills onto the seat between them. "Shame if a few bucks fell on the floor," he says, "but we earned it, don't you think?"

Lillian leans over and kisses him, long and hard.

• • •

Three months later they're engaged. Six months later they're married. Sam Giancana sends a wedding present, a gorgeous hostess trolley. Lillian quits her job at the Hacienda. Vinnie Salvo puts Buddy in charge of the crew and starts paying him a piece of the action. Buddy and Lillian move into a three-bedroom split-level modern in Beverly Green. The house is less than a year old, wall-to-wall cream-colored carpet, picture windows.

When are they actually home, though? Not often. Almost every night is a night on the town. Shooting craps at the Dunes, drinking champagne at the Laundry Room, skinny-dipping at the Flamingo pool. Lillian charms the movers and shakers of Vegas's underworld. Moe Dalitz, Big Ed Zingel. She picks their brains. Explain to me how that works, why you bought that property, why you parked your money there.

Oklahoma City could be another planet, as far as Lillian is concerned. A dream too fuzzy to remember.

Lillian and Buddy fight. Sure. What married couple doesn't? Lillian gives as good as she gets. They always screw afterward. Sometimes they screw during.

Raymond Jr. is born in 1963. Eleven pounds, three ounces. Lillian has never experienced true pain before. The doctor calls in his colleagues to get a load of this heavyweight, this goliath. By the time Ray is nine months old, he's bigger than some kindergartners and could probably help you move your sofa. He doesn't speak, doesn't smile, but Lillian isn't concerned. Ray behaves, never fusses. Sometimes Lillian forgets he's even there.

Jeremy comes next, in 1965. Now we're talking: he's a beautiful baby, golden and pink, with a smile that melts hearts. Lillian wants to eat him like a piece of cake. Sometimes she can't resist and takes a—gentle!—bite.

Ten months later Alice arrives. Stern Alice, wary Alice. She does a number on Lillian's nipples. Even less pleasant is the way Alice observes Lillian from the crib, like she's evaluating her mother's performance, noting pros and (mostly) cons. Hey, cookie, Lillian tells her, I'm doing the best I can here.

Honestly, Lillian finds motherhood more or less a snap. During the day the maid helps keep an eye on the flock, and for evenings out Lillian hires Mormon girls from the college to babysit. In general, Lillian keeps the supervision to a minimum. She will not, will never, become her aunt. Kids need freedom. They need to learn how to fend for themselves, the sooner the better. *Do*, not *don't*.

In 1967, Buddy comes home one day with a little brown Choctaw baby, wrapped in a blanket. "Her name's Tallulah," he says. "She's ours now."

She's *what*?

Buddy tersely explains that the baby is a favor to Joey Aiuppa, who now oversees the Outfit's operation in Vegas. Terse is the last thing Buddy usually is, and Lillian understands this isn't the kind of favor—Joey Aiuppa isn't the kind of man—you can refuse.

"Well, hell," Lillian says with a shrug, a sigh, a splash of vodka in her glass. "The more the merrier, I suppose."

CHAPTER 3

The sixties were good to Buddy. The seventies, from all indications, will be even better. Vinnie Salvo has a stroke, so Buddy moves up a slot, sliding in right behind Pete Bommarito. Opportunities abound and Buddy puts together a few discreet projects on the side. A pinch of off-the-books bookmaking, a dash of low-risk, high-vig loans. He's a Mercurio. What is luck good for if you don't push it? Lillian agrees. She comes up with some of Buddy's best ideas, he's the first to admit.

Family life is harmonious too, even though there's always a kid underfoot, a kid making a racket, a kid knocking over a lamp or spilling the orange juice. We need a bigger place, he tells Lillian, and she starts scouting out homes in the Scotch 80s, where some of the houses have swimming pools. What's money good for if you don't spend it?

Buddy is a good father. He never lays a hand on his children. Never. Once in a while, when Buddy happens to be around for bedtime, he'll read a story to them. The kids love it. Buddy does all the different voices and juices up the action. Sometimes he points out the mistakes made by various characters. The Big Bad Wolf in "Three Little Pigs," for example. The Big Bad Wolf tips his hand too early, comes on too strong. He needs to play it cool, wait for the right moment to pounce. That's what a Mercurio would do. Huffing and puffing is for amateurs.

Summer of 1972, dusk, hot but invigorating. Buddy and Lillian sit on the patio, drinking highballs and waiting for the babysitter to show up. The kids splash around in the pool.

"Ahh," Buddy says, and Lillian smiles.

That night the phone in the master bedroom jangles. Buddy, jolted from a sound sleep, picks up his watch. Three o'clock in the morning. Who the hell is calling at three o'clock in the morning.

"Hello?"

"Go," says a gravelly voice. At least that's what Buddy thinks it says. There's an odd wobble to it, a bend in the pitch, like the guy's tongue is too big for his mouth. "Now."

"Who the hell is this?"

"Me."

Me? Then Buddy realizes—it's Vinnie Salvo, Buddy's old boss. The stroke has done a number on him. The line clicks dead before Buddy can ask any more questions.

Buddy doesn't need to ask any more questions. The details don't matter. It's Bommarito. He's found out about Buddy's side projects. Or it's Joey Aiuppa—he's in trouble with Chicago and needs to put a pin in somebody. Doesn't matter. Buddy has to *go*. *Now*. God bless Vinnie Salvo.

"Wake up, honey." Buddy gives Lillian's shoulder a shake. "Get dressed. Put the kids in the car. Leave anything we can live without. Thirty minutes."

She's up and moving almost before he is. Good girl. Buddy pops out the false bottom of the diaper drawer. Some cash, a .38. Why didn't he put aside more cash for a day like this? Don't worry about it now. He checks the .38 to make sure it's loaded. He's fired a gun once in his life, at the literal side of a barn, and missed. But don't worry about that now.

He hears Lillian waking the kids, her voice low and calm. He hears the word *adventure*.

Buddy's best guess, now that he's had time to think: Bommarito feels threatened by Buddy. Buddy sparkles and in this business that can be dangerous.

"In, in, in. Hurry, hurry, hurry."

"But why, Daddy?" Alice asks, skeptical as always. "Where are we going? Why are we leaving in the middle of the night?"

"Shh, honey, not now. In, in, in."

Enough room in Lillian's Chevrolet Kingswood station wagon, just barely, to pack everyone in, plus a few suitcases full of clothes. Buddy takes one last look at the house, then backs down the driveway.

They barrel southeast on the Boulder Highway and leave Las Vegas behind. No moon, just stardust and black velvet. The kids fall back asleep, all except for Alice. Buddy gives her a Texaco road map so she can follow along.

Boulder Highway is utterly deserted this time of night. Where do they go now? Vegas is over, forever. The thought sinks in. Buddy has no idea where they'll go now. But look at the bright side. At least they're safe. They've . . .

Headlights behind them, flashing in the rearview mirror, a sedan coming up fast. Buddy's heart jumps. He counted his chickens too fast, didn't he?

Buddy stomps the gas. The Kingswood's V8 growls and the headlights behind drop back, but only for a second. The sedan has a V8 too. The Kingswood is too heavy, loaded with sleeping kids and suitcases. Buddy won't win a race. The .38 is in the back, with the suitcases. No time to grab it.

He's smart enough to sweat. Bommarito's gorillas are the meanest in the business, connoisseurs of inflicting pain. Oh, the stories Buddy has heard. They'll run the Kingswood off the road. They'll take Buddy somewhere nice and secluded where they can go to work on him and take their time.

And the kids, Lillian. Buddy's shirt is as wet as a dishrag now. Bommarito's gorillas will shoot the kids and Lillian right here. That's if they, and Buddy, are lucky.

Lillian knows that too. Buddy glances over. She's rolling down her window. She's got an empty Coke bottle in her hand. Buddy doesn't have a better idea.

The sedan closes in, maneuvering for position on Buddy's side. One good bump in the right spot and the Kingswood will spin out of control. Buddy jockeys—speeding up, slowing down, weaving across both lanes. A spark twangs off his side-view mirror, followed instantly by a bang. Gunshot. The boys in the sedan are getting impatient.

"What was that, Daddy?" Alice says, lifting her disheveled head over the seat, groggy.

"Just a bug," Buddy says. He keeps his cool. He can't afford to lose it. "A big bug hitting the car."

"Why are we going so fast?"

"Lie back down, Alice," Lillian says, cool too, "right this second."

"On three," Buddy tells Lillian.

The timing of this dance step has to be perfect. The two partners have to move as one.

On the count of three—the sedan creeping up on his left, an inch away from the angle it needs—Buddy guns the Kingswood. He clears the nose of the sedan, cuts the wheel left, then right. Lillian flings the empty Coke bottle.

The bottle hits the windshield of the sedan, dead center. *Boosh!* The sedan wags and skids and dives into the ditch next to the highway. Flip, flop, and fly. Buddy steadies the Kingswood and slows to the speed limit.

Alice lifts her head again. "Daddy, where are we going?"

Lillian rolls her window back up and smooths into place a strand of hair blown awry by the wind. She's wondering the same thing.

"What about Oklahoma City?" Buddy says. Lillian's aunt died a few months ago and left her the wreck of a house. They haven't gotten around to selling it yet.

"No," Lillian says. "I'm not going back there."

Buddy isn't any more delighted by the prospect of Oklahoma City than Lillian. Shitty St. Louis is the Pearl of the Orient compared to Oklahoma City. But what are their options? They'll be safe in Oklahoma City, hours from Dallas, the nearest real city. No one from Vegas will ever think to look for them there.

"It's just for the time being," he says, "till we get back on our feet."

A new set of headlights behind them, flashing in the rearview mirror. Another sedan coming up fast. And then . . . the sedan zooms around them, rockets away, disappears into the night.

Lillian, in the darkness, finally nods. "I'm pregnant, by the way," she says.

PART II

The Mercurios
1976–1978

CHAPTER 4

Alice, as always, devises the plan. She broods, she brainstorms. Next, she dispatches her older brothers to scout the alley behind the TG&Y discount store, to determine when *exactly* the lady who works at TG&Y steps out back to smoke a cigarette. Individually, Alice's brothers can't be trusted. Ray is dumb and Jeremy gets distracted. Together, though, they usually provide accurate information. Usually.

Tallulah, Alice's little sister, *can* be trusted. Alice sends her to the top of a towering tree. Lulu is fearless, nimble, a pint-sized Tarzan. She reports back that there's some kind of metal ventilation dealie on the roof of the shed behind TG&Y.

Interesting. Alice scraps her first plan. Not good enough. She starts again from scratch. Even though she's only ten years old, Alice is confident that nobody in Oklahoma City is more careful, more meticulous than her. If there's someone in Oklahoma City more careful and meticulous than her, Alice would like to meet them.

"What are we waiting for?" Jeremy says. "I'm bored. Let's do it."

He's eleven. He and Alice, born ten and a half months apart, look almost exactly alike. The only difference between them is that Jeremy glows and Alice doesn't. He has blonder hair and bluer eyes, and his smile makes other people smile too. He's like the color funnies on Sunday and Alice is like the black-and-white comics that run in the daily paper. Her face at rest is a frown, because her mind is always working, working, working.

"Not yet," Alice says.

But Jeremy gets to make the final decision because he's ten and a half months older than her. It drives her nuts.

Let's get this show on the road, Jeremy thinks. He balances on one leg and spins slowly on the merry-go-round, a rusted metal disc that wobbles and screeches. He likes the merry-go-round: the world moving toward him, then moving away, the future, then the past. It's like he's flying, but through both space and time. And all he has to do is stand there.

But he's getting bored. "Let's get this show on the road," he says.

"Not *yet*," Alice says.

His sister can be a pain in the butt. She racks her brains about stuff three times longer than a brain needs to be racked. But Jeremy admits she does come up with some cool ideas. Sneaking through the parking lot at St. Francis during mass on Sunday and swiping hood ornaments from the cars was fun. Exploring that abandoned house on NW 36th Street. Climbing a construction fence and rolling the giant pipes around.

The merry-go-round spins and Jeremy strikes a kung fu pose. He's watched every episode of *Kung Fu* on TV and is learning fast. Kung fu, like almost everything Jeremy tries, is no sweat for him.

Jeremy is good at baseball. He's good at swimming and singing and making people like him. Actually, he doesn't *make* people like him—they already do, even before he says a word, kids and adults both. Jeremy just has to stand there and fly through space.

His mom promises him he'll be a famous movie star someday, or a rich and powerful businessman. Why can't Jeremy be both, plus a master kung fu fighter too? He strikes with his leg, then his hand. He moves faster than lightning.

"We have to have the perfect, perfect, *perfect* plan," Alice says.

Because, Alice knows, this is the prize of a lifetime. She discovered it accidentally: a long, low-slung cinder-block addition behind TG&Y, next to the dumpster. Her jaw dropped, all their jaws dropped, when Ray dragged open the heavy metal door and sunlight spread across . . . *treasure*.

Expired cartons of candy bars, stacks of paperback books with the covers ripped off, bundles of T-shirts and embroidered jeans, popcorn poppers and Crock-Pots. And more! A mannequin with broken-off fingers, a heap of tangled Christmas lights, a brand-new Schwinn Junior Sting-Ray, still in the box.

But just then the TG&Y lady came outside to smoke a cigarette. "What are you kids doing back here? Get out of here."

Alice put one fist on her hip and narrowed her eyes and pretended the lady didn't scare her. "It's just trash," Alice said.

"It's not *your* trash." The lady streamed smoke down at Alice. "Now beat it before I call the cops."

An hour later the lady was gone, and the coast was clear. But now the door to the treasure was locked. Ray yanked and yanked, but it didn't budge.

"It's an okay plan," Jeremy says. "The one we already have."

"The one *I* already have," Alice says.

Tallulah listens to them argue. They can argue like this for what seems like hours, so Tallulah darts away. She can't stay still for more than a few minutes, like a hummingbird whose wings have to keep beating. If she stays still for more than a few minutes, the blood inside her begins to boil and churn. Her ears buzz. Her lungs shrink. She has to *move*.

She darts around the slide and across Memorial Park and back again, bounding from sandstone boulder to sandstone boulder, trying to match each landing to the rapid *thwock-thwock-thwock* of balls from the tennis courts.

Sit still! Alice or their mom will say, at the dinner table or watching TV, and Tallulah will be surprised. She thought she *was* sitting still!

This year in school Tallulah learned that the Earth is always moving too, spinning, and spinning *fast*, just like Tallulah. That's just about the neatest thing Tallulah has ever learned in school.

She darts around the park again, another lap, racing the Earth. When she gets back to the playground, Alice and Jeremy are still arguing. Piggy is still swinging in his swing. He's very mellow for a two-year-old. He's content to hang out and observe, which makes him easy to keep an eye on. His real name is Paul, but he's called Piggy because he's the fifth kid, the little toe, the one that goes wee wee wee all the way home.

"What do you think, Tallulah?" Alice asks her.

Tallulah doesn't like to take sides. She wishes everyone, meaning Jeremy and Alice, were on the same side. So she just shrugs.

Alice, exasperated, kicks at the dirt. A sharp chip of sandstone flies up at Jeremy, perched on one leg. He shifts his hips gracefully at the very last second, without losing his balance, and the rock misses him.

Ray stands with his arms folded across his chest, awaiting the final verdict. Alice doesn't bother asking his opinion. Ray will do whatever he's told. He prefers it that way. At least Alice believes so. It's impossible to tell what Ray is thinking, or if he's thinking anything at all. Alice kicks the dirt again.

Jeremy has hopped off the merry-go-round and is walking away. Ray follows, with Piggy on his back, then Lulu. Alice sighs and follows too. What choice does she have? One day, when she's grown up, *she* will be in charge. She will *always* be in charge.

CHAPTER 5

Up Classen Boulevard, past the laundromat and Baskin-Robbins. They swipe a shopping cart from IGA. This might be their only crack at the shed behind TG&Y. They need to be able to grab as much treasure as possible.

"You have to think about every angle, especially the ones you don't think about." That's what Dad says. He always pointed out, when he read "Hansel and Gretel" to her, that the witch should have been ready for those kids to pull a fast one on her. She should never have fallen for that chicken bone trick, never should have ended up in that oven.

The lady is in the alley behind TG&Y. When she grinds out her cigarette and goes back inside, Jeremy will go around to the front. He'll go inside too, pretend to shop, and keep an eye on the lady. If she starts to come back outside, he'll distract her.

How exactly will he distract her? Alice has several suggestions, but Jeremy doesn't want to hear them. "I can handle it, no problem," he says. "I'll figure it out."

And he probably will, Alice knows. It drives her nuts.

Jeremy isn't thinking about the lady who works at TG&Y. He's thinking instead about the bike in the shed. The second he saw the picture of that Junior Sting-Ray on the box, he fell deeply in love. Banana seat, ape-hanger handlebars, gleaming chrome fenders. *Flamboyant red.* That's the color, according to the label on the box. The Sting-Ray is so much foxier than the secondhand clunker he rides now.

Tallulah bounces on her toes, practically dancing, ready for action. Ray waits for orders. Piggy sits at their feet, scraping gravel around with his hands and placidly watching them.

"You're the lookout," Alice whispers to him, exasperated. "Look at the street, not us."

Piggy nods. He keeps looking at her, not the street.

The lady grinds out her cigarette. The door clunks shut behind her. It's time. This is the moment Alice loves, when her plan becomes real, when it goes flapping out of the nest and into the world.

Jeremy saunters off toward the front entrance. Ray boosts Tallulah onto the roof of the shed. Will the metal ventilation dealie be locked? Will Tallulah be able to open it? Alice's whole plan depends on that. She holds her breath.

Tallulah disappears. A few seconds later, the door to the shed swings open. The treasure is theirs! They start loading the cart.

But then Jeremy appears in the alley. *Jeremy!* He's supposed to be inside TG&Y, making sure the lady doesn't catch them!

Screw that, is Jeremy's thinking. He wants to make sure they don't forget the bike and accidentally leave it behind or something. *His* bike. He tells Alice to cool it. Everything's fine.

There's a problem, though. The bike hasn't been assembled and is still in pieces: the wheels, the frame, the seat, the handlebars. So Jeremy can't ride it home and the cart is already almost full. They'll have to leave the Sting-Ray behind.

"Nope," Jeremy says. He crouches, digs the baggie full of bolts and screws out of the box, and patiently slides a wheel into the front fork.

"You dumbbell!" Alice says.

Jeremy ignores her. Tallulah bounces on her toes. Ray awaits instructions. Piggy toddles gazes at Alice. The lady steps outside again to smoke and they're busted.

• • •

Well, Ray is busted. Alice is sorry, but somebody has to take one for the team and let the rest of them escape. Ray, big and slow, is going to get caught anyway. He stays obediently behind while Jeremy and Alice bolt, while Tallulah scoops up Piggy and bolts.

The store security guard marches Ray inside. Ray doesn't squeal. "It was just me," he says, over and over. The store manager and the store security guard wonder if Ray is "special." Ray hears that a lot. He's not sure if it's true or not. Maybe? Why else would so many people say it?

In the end, the store manager calls Ray's mom and dad instead of the police. Dad shows up and—when he figures out the store manager thinks Ray might be special—lays it on thick. *The poor kid! You're scaring him to death! Because of some junk you're going to throw away anyway? I ought to call a lawyer!*

Ray watches the store manager wilt like honeysuckle in the heat. Dad can make just about anybody wilt. The store manager lets Ray off with a warning.

Back home, Dad makes a drink for himself and one for Mom. Alice explains what happened. Dad wants to know why they, the kids, can't go two minutes without giving him a headache.

"What the hell were you thinking?" Dad asks, turning to Jeremy.

Jeremy shrugs. "I wanted that bike."

Mom shrugs too. "He wanted the bike."

Dad lets Tallulah up onto his lap. He lets her have a sip of his drink.

"It wasn't the world's worst plan," Dad says, and Alice feels her heart melt like a pat of butter on toast.

CHAPTER 6

The two-story Prairie Foursquare on NW 34th Street—deep porch with columns on stacked-stone pedestals, a center attic dormer—would have been a jewel back in the day, but now it's slouching, sloughing, sinking, rotting. The foundation's cracked. The siding springs loose. A brick tumbles off the chimney and almost brains the mailman.

Inside, everything creaks, even when nobody moves and the wind doesn't blow. The rafters, the floors, the walls. No creak in the same key. It's like the orchestra in hell, says Buddy. Then fix it, says Lillian. Fix it? Where would he even start?

The plumbing isn't great either. And don't use the toaster if the fridge is running.

The neighborhood is more respectable than the house, though not by much and growing iffier by the day. Families who can afford to move are fleeing to the suburbs. Potholes go unpatched. Drug deals go down after dark in Memorial Park. A pawnshop replaces the menswear store on Classen.

The Mercurios can't afford to move. The nest egg from Vegas is long gone and now money is tight. None of Buddy's previous experience, his sharply honed professional skills, count for anything in a place like Oklahoma City. He's forced to take whatever demeaning, poorly paid civilian job he can find. Car salesman. Appliance salesman. Hotel night manager.

Hotel night manager! Buddy can barely look himself in the mirror some days. The longest he sticks in a place is five, six months. His pride gets the best of him, his hot temper when some punk of a boss tries to show him up.

Buddy's latest gig is assistant manager at the Long John Silver restaurant. He despises the job more than all the others combined. By the end of every shift his skin glistens with grease and he's ready to murder the lazy, pimple-faced teenage hippies who work for him. And the customers! They demand and whine and threaten to report Buddy to corporate HQ if he refuses to bow and genuflect, to kiss the hem of their robes.

He doesn't blame Lillian for his misery. He blames her for remaining as beautiful as she was at nineteen. He blames her for getting a part-time job at the ladies' shoe store on Classen, for making a big deal about her "sacrifice" for the family. He blames her for cheating on him with the dashing local real estate bigwig who handled their refinancing. How could she? Buddy cheats too, but he's only had luck with wallflower cashiers and anemic secretaries.

Lillian is just as unhappy as Buddy. The boredom is killing her, Oklahoma smothering her with a pillow. No glitz, no glamour. There's a church on every corner. Once a year the State Fair comes to town and the line for the egg roll stand is a mile long. That's as exciting as this place ever gets.

The children, when they're around, exhaust her. They're always bumping into you, bouncing off you, always grabbing at you with grubby little hands. *Mom Mom Mom Mom Mom.* The shoe store is a grind, and the real estate bigwig soon loses his luster. He's really not that dashing at all, and once, during sex, he asks her to check his back for suspicious moles.

Lillian and Buddy bicker. They drink. They brood. Lillian throws a glass ashtray at the wall. Buddy stomps out to the porch to sweat (summer) or shiver (winter). They ignore each other for days at a time or whip-crack snide comments back and forth across the dinner table.

Dinner: cans of Chef Boyardee, Hamburger Helper light on the hamburger, tuna casserole with cornflakes on top, Swanson's Hungry-Man TV dinners. Lillian glares at Buddy. She wants him to remember the rib eyes at the Golden Steer. He glares back. He remembers just fine.

Divorce is out of the question. Lillian and Buddy are both Catholic. More importantly, neither one of them wants to get stuck with five kids.

She's only thirty-four in 1976. He's only thirty-seven. They're both baffled by the same thing: This is it? This is how the story ends?

August, Long John Silver's, the six o'clock dinner rush. A kid drops a large Dr Pepper on the floor. *Kaboom!* A lake of Dr Pepper. A customer demands to know why Buddy has skimped on her deep-fried cracklins.

Buddy bites his tongue. He's been tinkering with a scheme, you see. Buddy's boss goes on vacation next week. Meaning: Buddy will be in charge of the deposit bag. Meaning: what a terrible shame if Buddy gets "robbed" on the way to his car after he locks up for the night.

The cops will buy Buddy's story because—here's the most elegant part of the scheme—Buddy will have a couple of eyewitnesses with him, a couple of his darling innocent children. Alice and Jeremy, or Alice and Tallulah. Buddy knows they'll stick to the story and sell it—they're Mercurios, after all.

If Buddy hits the night deposit on a Saturday, he figures that's enough dough to . . .

A man pushes through the door of the restaurant. He's wearing a red, white, and blue ski mask and waving around a gun. For a second Buddy is confused. Is he imagining this? Or did the imaginary robber in his mind somehow become, magically, a real one?

"On the floor!" the robber yells. "Everyone! Keep your heads down!"

Screams. Moans. People tumble like dominos. Buddy grimaces. He uses a napkin to mop grease off his forehead. You've got to be kidding me.

The robber points his gun at Buddy. A .38 revolver. Same model, Buddy notes, as the piece he keeps in the top drawer of his bedside table. He doesn't need a gun in Oklahoma City, but the old .38 reminds him of Vegas, of the life he used to lead.

"Open the register!"

The guy's a clown. Who wears a wool ski mask to a robbery in August? But clowns can be more dangerous than professionals. They lose their heads. They start pulling the trigger and can't stop.

"Okay, okay." Buddy opens the drawer. The clown can have the money. Buddy doesn't care. "Take it easy."

"I said open the register, motherfucker!"

"It's open, it's open. Look."

"Open the register!" a customer on the floor says. The lady who was complaining about her cracklins. "Or he's going to kill everyone!"

Thanks, lady, for giving him the idea.

What are the odds? What are the odds that this clown walks in here today and screws up Buddy's scheme? Long John Silver's can't get robbed *twice* in the same month. And now Buddy might get shot in the bargain.

"Give me the cash, motherfucker! Or I'm gonna kill all of you!"

Buddy should hand over the money, soothe the guy's nerves, talk him down. But Buddy's temper is coming to a slow, rolling boil. The universe isn't compassionate. Buddy accepts that. He'd just like a fair shake.

"Who the hell wears a wool ski mask to a robbery in August?" he says.

"What?" the robber says.

"I bet you're almost out of gas too, your getaway car."

"What the fuck did you say?"

The robber takes a step to his right. Maybe he's nervously shifting his weight; maybe he's edging away toward the door; maybe he's lining up the gunsight between Buddy's eyes, his finger tightening on the trigger. No one will ever know because his foot hits the puddle of spilled Dr Pepper and he slips. Down he goes. His head thumps against the floor and the .38 spins away.

Buddy climbs cautiously over the counter. The robber doesn't move. Buddy picks up the .38. Customers begin to lift their heads and look around. A teenage employee peeks over the counter.

"Whoa," he says. "You took him down, Mr. Mercurio."

Buddy thinks about it. In a general sense he did take the robber down, didn't he? You could easily make the case.

"I had to do it," Buddy says. "He was going to kill everyone. Leave no witnesses."

"Whoa."

Customers weep with relief and hug Buddy. The cops, when they get there, shake his hand. *Nice work.* A crew from Channel Four arrives soon after, followed a few minutes later by Channel Nine. In front of the cameras, Buddy is halting and humble. He's Gary Cooper at Yankee Stadium. He considers himself the luckiest man alive.

"I had to protect my employees, my customers," Buddy says. "That's all I was thinking."

CHAPTER 7

Buddy takes every advantage of his newfound celebrity. He meets the mayor and cuts the ribbon at a new IGA grocery store and goes out drinking every night with fat-cat oilmen. One of the fat cats, Ronnie Hinkle, offers to bankroll Buddy, ten grand for whatever business Buddy wants to start. Buddy gives it some thought. He comes up with the perfect play.

A *disco*? Lillian has never heard a more harebrained idea in her life. A disco in Oklahoma City? Where the biggest draw of the year is the National Finals Rodeo?

Just listen. Buddy himself can't stand disco music. All that throbbing and wailing is like having a seizure. But he and Ronnie went down to the disco in Dallas last weekend and . . . holy shit. The dance floor was so crowded you couldn't move, chicks in spaghetti-strap dresses ordering $4 cocktails, a line just to enter that stretched four blocks on a Saturday night. A place like that, the only game in town, must be printing cash.

"Disco is the future," he tells Lillian. "And here *we'd* be the only game in town."

"Why don't you just set that ten grand on fire?" Lillian says. "Or use it to go buy some magic beans?"

"The beans in the story *were* magic," Buddy fires back. "Ha!"

And then they just glare at each other silently, because neither of them can remember how "Jack and the Beanstalk" plays out. In the end is it good the beans are magic? Or not good?

"Think about the possibilities, honey," Buddy says. "You know what I'm saying? The opportunities that come with running a club. This is what we should be doing, me and you. It's in my blood. It's in yours."

"Jesus, Bud." But Lillian is starting to come around, a little. If nothing else, Buddy's harebrained idea isn't *boring*. And he's probably already dipping into the ten grand anyway.

"This town needs some pizzazz. And Ronnie Hinkle is a rube. His father made all the money. Ronnie doesn't have a brain in his head. He's a gift, honey."

Fine. If the disco fails, Lillian will be there to enjoy the disaster, will take great pleasure in telling him, *I told you so.*

Buddy leases the old Lakeside movie theater, which went out of business a few months earlier. Now it's full steam ahead. He puts Ray to work unbolting all the theater seats and dumping them out behind the theater. He applies for a liquor license and buys the biggest, loudest sound system he can find. He amazes Ronnie Hinkle with the new sound system and convinces him to double his initial investment.

Buddy has plenty of expertise in basic business principles—skimming the take, keeping two sets of books, paying off the right people and watering down the booze just enough, not too much—but he doesn't know anything about the creative side. Buddy remembers a guy at the car dealership where he used to work, a mechanic in the service department. The radio in the guy's bay was always thumping and wailing, intolerable.

Ronnie Hinkle's eyes go wide when he finds out the guy, Warren, is black.

"But," Ronnie says, "we can't . . ."

"Can't what?"

Buddy's been prickly ever since he and Lillian adopted Tallulah. He doesn't like the idea that a Mercurio might be discriminated against because of the color of her skin. So he's had to accept that he doesn't like the idea that *anybody* might be.

Ronnie clears his throat. "Warren could be okay."

"You want to make money?" Buddy says. "We'll hire a goddamn Martian if he helps make us money."

At first Warren in the service department assumes this is a put-on. A middle-aged white dude wants to open a disco?

"What's hot right now?" Buddy asks, testing him. "Who are some acts you like?"

Warren studies Buddy, still trying to make sure he's serious, then names a few acts. Silver Convention, Rufus and Chaka Khan, the O'Jays. Buddy's never heard of any of them. That's good.

Buddy shows Warren the big auditorium at the old Lakeside, the sound system. Warren examines the floor, cleared of seats now but still sticky with spilled soda pop.

"This here the dance floor?" Warren says. "It slopes."

"So?" Buddy says. Of course the floor slopes. The place used to be a movie theater. The floor slants up from the screen so people in back can see. "Is that a problem?"

Warren considers. "Maybe you make it a thing. You know what I'm saying? Something special."

Buddy has his man. He offers Warren full creative freedom, within budgetary limits. Warren will have final say on paint colors, furniture, mirror ball, everything. He'll pick what music gets played and when. And Warren, if he doesn't mind, will give Buddy some tips on how to update his wardrobe.

"Y'all for real?" Warren says, studying Buddy. "Juan didn't tell y'all to do this?"

"Juan?"

"My boyfriend. One of them."

"Your . . . what?" Warren is a big guy, six-foot-two, with broad shoulders and thick ropes for muscles, like Jim Brown in *The Dirty Dozen*. He's got a mustache like Burt Reynolds in *Gator*. Buddy would've never guessed he was light in the loafers.

"That a problem?" Warren says.

"I don't care if you're a goddamned Martian."

Buddy invites Warren and Ronnie Hinkle over for dinner. Lillian finds Ronnie Hinkle insufferable, a spoiled little boy who can't take his eyes off her tits. But she confirms for herself what Buddy said: Ronnie *is* a rube, a gift from heaven.

Warren is a delight. Lillian loves his style. A gorgeous canary-yellow shirt over tight flared slacks, canary socks, and white loafers. He treats Lillian like an actual human being, not just "the wife." *Where you from? What kind of remodel you want to do? You like selling shoes?* He seems to understand, his glance sliding over to her now and then, that Buddy is a bullshitter extraordinaire.

After dinner Buddy plays a forty-five he picked up at Rainbow Records. "Muskrat Love," by the Captain and Tennille.

"It's a good tune, right?" Buddy asks Warren. "A hippie at work recommended it."

"He was putting you on, man," Warren says.

Buddy frowns. But he sticks to his word, whenever possible, and he promised Warren creative control. "Your call," he says.

As Warren is leaving, Lillian takes him aside. "This is going to be a complete disaster, isn't it?" she says.

Warren clears his throat. He scratches his mustache.

Lillian gives his elbow a friendly squeeze. "Better not quit your day job, honey."

CHAPTER 8

Over the next three months, Buddy throws himself body and soul into Club Mercurio. He's always on the phone, always on the move, taking notes, poring over blueprints and estimates, pounding away at his adding machine, meeting with people at the crack of dawn and late into the night.

Lillian has to admit, though she would never admit it, that Buddy is working his ass off. Who would have guessed he could be so focused, so dedicated? Who could have guessed he could work his ass off?

Buddy is going to make this fly. He *has* to make it fly. Either that or he spends the rest of his life standing over the deep fryer at Long John Silver's, or worse.

The old Lakeside auditorium is transformed. Not just one mirror ball—three of them, gigantic. Velvet drapes and colored spotlights, comfy love seats in secluded corners and old black-and-white Busby Berkeley movies playing on the movie screen. Movies playing at the same time as the music? Won't that confuse people? Buddy doesn't get it, but he defers to Warren, as promised. Warren designs the look for the bartenders and the cocktail waitresses. Shiny red vinyl jackets, epaulets, lots of heavy eye shadow. Buddy thinks they look like . . . he doesn't know what the hell they look like. He prays Warren knows what he's doing.

Buddy squeezes another five grand out of Ronnie Hinkle and buys TV time on Channel Four. Buddy doesn't want to pay for an actor, so he puts eleven-year-old Jeremy in platform shoes, striped pants, and a turtleneck. Warren teaches Jeremy how to dance—one called the Bump, another one called the Electric Slide. At the end of the spot, rainbow-colored words flash:

Limited Admission! The commercial starts running the first of December, after the local news and right before the *Tonight Show.*

The big day arrives. Opening night: Saturday, December 4. Buddy turns the houselights down and Warren drops the needle on the Commodores. Tallulah and Alice stand ready to fling confetti at everyone who boogies through the doors.

Nobody boogies through the doors. Club Mercurio is, as Lillian predicted, a complete disaster. A few of Warren's light-in-the-loafers friends show up, peek inside at the deserted lobby, then scram. A young couple thinks the Lakeside is still a movie theater. "We've got movies!" Buddy tells them. "And dancing! Come on in!" They scram. Ronnie Hinkle sits slumped at the bar, a glass of Jim Beam in one hand and his head in the other.

Lillian makes her entrance at midnight. She swans around, admiring the sconces and epaulets, nodding her head to the beat. Buddy trails her, talking and talking and talking, like his life depends on it.

Opening night is always a dud . . . once word gets around, Lil . . . the important thing to remember is . . . big picture . . . forest and trees . . . sprints and marathons . . . you'll see . . . I guarantee . . . just wait . . .

Warren hides in the projection booth before Lillian can get to him. She sips the glass of champagne Buddy pours for her. He's finally run out of words.

Lillian has anticipated this moment with relish. The twist of the knife, the *I told you so.* She'll never, ever forgive Buddy for blowing the money from Ronnie Hinkle, for moving them from Vegas to Oklahoma City, for everything.

But now, as she watches Buddy struggle to maintain his confident smile, she's more sad than vindictive. She feels—almost—sorry for him. He tried, didn't he? She supposes that should count for something. Not enough, but something.

The taste of the champagne, the bubbles, stirs old memories. She remembers the twinkle in Buddy's eye when he caught her dipping into that purse, back at the Hacienda.

Ronnie Hinkle, down at the other end of the bar, blows his nose. Is that idiot crying?

"A toast," Lillian says.

Buddy eyes her warily. "Sure."

Tomorrow, at home, in the more cheerful light of day, after Buddy's had a little time to lick his wounds and pull himself together, Lillian will twist the knife and tell him, *I told you so*. But not tonight.

"To the big picture," Lillian says, and clinks her glass against his.

• • •

The lease is already paid through the end of the month, the bartenders and cocktail waitresses work for tips, and the power bill is getting tossed in the trash either way. So why the hell not keep Club Mercurio open for another weekend? That's Buddy's attitude once he recovers from the punch in the nose of opening night. *Fuck you, universe. I'm not dead yet.*

Friday night the weather is a mess. Sleet, wind that slices you thin like deli meat. But would you believe it: a handful of actual customers actually turn up. Warren's friends return, guilty for abandoning him the previous weekend. A group of dolled-up dolls, driving by and desperate for fun, notice the marquee and pull in. They end up staying till the club closes at two. So do Warren's friends, and some friends of the friends. Warren's selection of music is tight, man. That's what everyone tells Buddy. Buddy gives the okay for heavy pours.

It's still a disaster, but not a *complete* disaster. Saturday night the chicks are back, two cars full of them this time, and even more of Warren's friends. Some of Ronnie Hinkle's country club buddies deign to make an appearance. A few oil and gas landmen migrate over after steak dinners at Junior's. Their waiter, a friend of Warren's, tipped them off.

The next weekend draws an even bigger crowd. Word has spread that there's finally a real party in town. And the TV commercial has become a sensation. Longtime viewers of News 9 and 5 Alive switch over to Channel Four so they won't miss Jeremy bumping and electric-sliding to "Gimme My Mule." The song grooves and Jeremy can really move. With his blue eyes, his smile, his confidence, his feathered blond wings of hair—the camera loves him. That's no surprise to Lillian. Jeremy, her beautiful baby boy, is the only child of hers who inherited Lillian's golden nimbus, her charm. She's been whispering in his ear since he was born: *You're going to be a star.*

On New Year's Eve the line stretches all the way across the parking lot. Club Mercurio does gangbusters business the rest of the winter. Buddy's timing, as he'd hoped, is flawless. Disco is catching on everywhere, even Oklahoma, and Club Mercurio is the only game in town. Plus, the oil business is booming, cash filling Oklahoma City and spilling over. Buddy doubles the cover charge, and the lines just get longer. Everyone wants in. Jeremy's second commercial, showcasing a new dance called the New York Hustle, makes him a local celebrity, in the same starry constellation as Barry Switzer and Linda Soundtrak.

Buddy feels alive again, first time since Vegas. The dancing and the pulsing lights, the drifting clouds of smoke and perfume. This is where Buddy is meant to be. This is *who* he is meant to be. Every night, all night, he circulates through the club, schmoozing and slapping palms. *What's shakin', man? You enjoying yourself? Look at you!* And his eyes never stop roving, they never miss anything. *Clean up those ashtrays. How long they been waiting for their drinks? Smile, honey, this is the best job in the world.*

Buddy's houndstooth fedora is ancient history. Warren has guided him toward three-piece leisure suits in various shades of powder blue and blood orange, wide lapels and spread-collar shirts, stylish but classy. Zip-up Cuban-heel boots, gold cuff links. Buddy lets his hair grow long—well, long for him, an extra inch spilling down the back of his neck. One of Warren's friends suggests he grow a mustache, but Warren puts the kibosh on that.

Lillian is back in her element, the foxiest lady in the hottest club. This isn't Vegas, and she's no longer twenty-three, but close your eyes and it almost feels that way. Lillian's an even better schmoozer than Buddy. When she makes the rounds, the cocktail waitresses can barely keep up with the drink orders. When she hits the dance floor—for just one song a night, her favorite, Gloria Gaynor's "Honey Bee"—the mirror balls seem to spin faster, the temperature spikes.

Her ideas for maximizing revenue always deliver. Caribbean Night: a smash. Amateur dance contest: another smash.

Buddy and Lillian get along better than they have in years. No more big fights, hardly any bickering. For Valentine's Day, Buddy buys Lillian a diamond bracelet. Lillian makes sure Buddy's suits are pristine, his coffee piping hot in the morning. For his birthday she buys him a twenty-five-inch RCA ColorTrak TV in a genuine pecan veneer cabinet. Sometimes they sneak up to the projection booth and make out like teenagers.

"This is just the beginning," Buddy says. "You know what I'm saying?"

Lillian knows what he's saying. "This place is the golden goose."

CHAPTER 9

When their dad first mentions his idea, the Mercurio kids aren't sure what a disco actually *is*. Late at night in Alice and Tallulah's room, they discuss. Jeremy claims that of course he knows: a disco is a place where people go to dance. No shit, Sherlock, Alice says.

Tallulah hopes Club Mercurio will have lions, like at the zoo, or acrobats, like at the circus, or go-karts like the Cannady family two blocks over have. The possibilities make Tallulah's head spin as she takes a puff of Dad's cigarette. Sometimes he falls asleep with a Camel still burning. If Tallulah is daring and stealthy, she can swipe it right from between his fingertips.

Ray sits quietly, patiently, perched on Alice's tiny desk chair. He doesn't have an opinion. Well, he doesn't have an opinion yet. That's how his brain works. His brain takes its time. By the time he has an opinion, everyone is already talking about something else and his opinion doesn't matter anymore. Probably his opinion didn't matter in the first place. That's fine with Ray.

Piggy should have been in bed hours ago, but he's here too, gnawing on a Stretch Armstrong action figure.

"A disco," Jeremy says, "is a place that plays disco music."

"No shit, Sherlock!"

Once Club Mercurio opens, Dad puts the kids to work. "When I was your age!" Dad says. And "All hands on deck!" And when Warren worries that the kids should be home doing homework or getting a good night's sleep, "Homework? A good night's sleep? That's for squares. We're Mercurios!"

They're free labor too, Alice recognizes. At the age of ten, though, she's already reading grown-up books from the library (Dickens is okay, Homer is better, Machiavelli is the best) and can finish her fifth-grade homework in about half a minute. The club is much more interesting than idiotic little math problems. *If a train carrying 100 people* . . .

Dad parks Alice in the back office of the club. At first, she's just in charge of sorting and organizing all the paperwork. Receipts, bills, invoices, canceled checks, tax forms, permit applications, pay stubs, bank statements, night deposit slips, time cards. Not to mention the less official documents too: scraps of paper torn from phone books and old issues of the *Daily Oklahoman* with scribbled numbers and initials in the margins.

Now *this*, unlike junior high, is fun, a giant complex jigsaw puzzle. Alice moves pieces around until she discovers relationships, studies numbers until they make sense.

See? Buddy charges X for a Stolichnaya and tonic (Y number of ounces), but a wholesale case of Stolichnaya only costs Z. And if you have the bartenders pour Smirnoff instead of Stolichnaya when the customers are too drunk to notice (those are the little stars the bartenders jot on the tab, next to the price), that's extra profit.

On credit card receipts, on the line for tips, the cocktail waitresses sometimes turn a one into a four, or a five into an eight. See? The pen stroke is just a shade darker and heavier. The bartenders sometimes clock in or out for each other. That's harder to catch, but if you examine each card carefully you see the disruption in the usual pattern. Each person's punch is uniquely individual, like a fingerprint or a snowflake.

Alice doesn't squeal on the cocktail waitresses or the bartenders. Number one: a Mercurio never squeals. Number two: the pleasure for her, the payoff, is discovering a mystery, then solving it. After that, who cares? Number three: the things she knows about the cocktail waitresses and bartenders might come in handy one day, you never know.

Pretty soon Dad lets Alice handle The Bible all by herself. That's the spiral notebook where they keep track of what Dad calls the real numbers—the money coming in that's nobody's business. Also, donations are recorded in The Bible. As in, Dad will pop his head in the office and say, "That damn fire marshal is going to bleed me dry." And Alice will say, "How much?" And Dad will say, "Four front-row tickets to Led Zeppelin at the Myriad. Eleven bucks apiece." Alice will make a note in The Bible and say, "Done."

Once or twice a night Dad stows cash in the floor safe. There are two safes: one in the floor, hidden under the carpet, and the other one by the door. Only Dad and Alice know about the hidden safe. And only Dad knows the combination. He makes Alice turn her back when he dials in the numbers.

"You don't trust me?" she says. "I'm your daughter!"

He chuckles. "You think I don't know that?"

When he leaves, Alice presses her ear against the door of the floor safe, the cool metal grained like the skin of an orange. She turns the knob very slowly and listens for a *click*. One of these days, if Alice is just patient enough, she knows she'll hear it.

Dad stations Ray out front, to oversee the velvet rope. Ray is only thirteen going on fourteen, but he's already more than six feet tall, built like a tank, and still growing. He has the temperament for the job too. Ray never loses his composure. He never raises his voice. He never deviates from the instructions he's been issued.

"What do you mean? I'm not drunk!"

"You need to leave now."

"I'm not fucking drunk! Look. You want me to walk a straight line?"

"You need to leave now."

"Listen, pal. Let's just have a fucking conversation for two seconds."

"You need to leave now."

It's like trying to reason with a brick wall, Jeremy says, except a brick wall is smarter. Tallulah defends Ray's intelligence. No one really knows, she says, what's going on in Ray's head. Jeremy rolls his eyes. "Or *isn't* going on," he says.

Every now and then, not often, someone tests Ray. A weight lifter in a tank top, showing off for his girlfriend. Ray always takes the first shove. That usually ends things, when Ray doesn't budge an inch, and the weight lifter comes to his senses. If he doesn't, if he shoves Ray again, Ray puts the guy on the ground.

Ray doesn't enjoy when he has to put a guy on the ground. He doesn't not enjoy it either.

No one ever shoves him a third time.

"Okay, okay, okay, okay. I'm sorry. I'm leaving right now."

Even though Jeremy is a celebrity now, Buddy puts him to work too. "Work?" Alice says. "Is that what you call it? Ha. Ha. Ha."

Jeremy helps out at the bar, running to the back for fresh ice or more limes whenever needed. It's an okay job. He likes, during the rush, when he returns from the supply room with some box or bucket or tub and everyone cheers for him. Mostly, though, he just hangs out with the cocktail waitresses. They explain the signs of the Zodiac to him and play with his hair to see which style makes him look most like Shaun Cassidy. He's so cute. He's so cool and debonair. Some girl in a few years is going to be so lucky. Jeremy knows all that already, but it's nice to hear.

The cocktail waitresses talk to the customers one way and to the bartenders a different way. Because he's in with the cocktail waitresses, Jeremy also observes how they talk to each other. Girls, he learns, are both tougher and more vulnerable than he thought, both meaner and sweeter, both simpler and a lot more complicated. He senses that this understanding might come in handy someday.

Lots of customers recognize Jeremy from his TV commercials. He signs autographs on cocktail napkins and Club Mercurio matchbooks. One night a lady asks Jeremy to sign her actual bare skin, just below her collarbone. She has to slide a spaghetti strap off her shoulder so he can get to the spot she wants, right above her heart. The bartenders crack up laughing. The lady's date glares at Jeremy.

"If you were a few years older . . ." the lady whispers in Jeremy's ear.

Jeremy isn't sure what she means. He's happy now. He'll be happy when he's a few years older. He'll be happy for the rest of his life. Why is he so certain? He just is.

Tallulah would die if she was stuck at the bar or the front door or in the back office. She would wig out. So, Dad keeps her moving. Dad gives her a message for Mom, or Mom gives her a message for Warren, or Warren gives her a message for Dad, and Tallulah has to deliver the message as fast as possible. Seconds count! That's what Dad says. Time is money! Go, go, go!

Go, go, go! Those are Tallulah's three favorite words. She is a speed de-

mon, a roadrunner, faster than the Flash from comic books. She jukes and
dodges and slips gracefully past dancers, invisibly *between* them. When the
dance floor is crowded, it's a maze that shifts and bulges, spins and contracts,
impossible to navigate unless, like Tallulah, you're able to see everything one
split second before it happens. Sometimes Tallulah pretends she's liquid—
but not water, something more sparkly and golden, like champagne.

Go, go, go! Tallulah leaps down the stairs, using the handrail like a pole
vault and ducking under the time clock at the last second. Depending on the
song Warren is playing, and how crowded the dance floor, she can usually
make it from the top of the auditorium to the farthest VIP sofa in under fifty
deep, thumping beats. That's less than a minute. A lot less!

"You got to slow down, sister," Warren says.

Tallulah likes that Warren calls her *sister*, just her, nobody else. "I can't!"
she says.

She also helps deliver the candy. It's grown-up candy, not kid candy, like
the powder in Pixie Stix but white, and in tiny little packets instead of straws.
Mom will give Jolene the shoeshine girl a packet, then Jolene will give Tallulah the packet and tell her which customer to find. "Guy in a green shirt
with dragons on it." "The tall chick with the short chick." And then Tallulah
will *go go go*.

When she's not go-go-going, Tallulah has to watch Piggy. Mom makes
all the kids take a turn watching him, all except Jeremy. Tallulah tries to teach
Piggy to flow like champagne. But he's only three years old and hopeless. He's
like a dog who looks at your finger instead of wherever you're pointing.

"See how it's like a maze?" she says. "See that opening? You have to go
before it closes."

"Yes."

"Go!"

"Go?"

Alice cheats. If she's in charge of Piggy, she sticks him in the sarcopha-
gus. That's—Alice named it—the old movie theater's box office, where the
cashier sold tickets, a closet with a window that looks out at the front entrance. Ray can keep an eye on Piggy this way.

"Make sure he doesn't die or anything," Alice tells Ray.

Ray nods. He takes his assignments very seriously.

Hunched on the stool behind the box office window, Piggy looks like a little old man. Cheeks chubby, eyes sleepy. Dad thinks he looks like a coin-operated fortune teller you'd see in an arcade. He wants to put a turban on Piggy and have him hand out Tarot cards for a quarter a pop.

CHAPTER 10

The money pours in, a deluge of biblical proportion. Buddy buys a new floor safe, twice the size of the old one. "We need a bigger boat!" he says, quoting his favorite line from his favorite movie. He loves *Jaws* because Roy Scheider, who happens to look quite a bit like Buddy from certain angles, is an underdog who saves the day. In *Jaws*, the little guy comes out on top.

Buddy shoots a new commercial with Jeremy—twice the original budget, with backup dancers and special effects added in postproduction. Peels, flips, strobes.

In September, to celebrate Buddy's birthday, Club Mercurio hosts the biggest blowout Oklahoma City has ever seen. Buddy books a fire-eater and a snake charmer, installs a champagne fountain, orders truckloads of balloons and streamers. People drive in all the way from Tulsa, Little Rock, Dallas. Barry Switzer takes a chauffeured limousine straight up from Norman, right after the game between the Sooners and Vanderbilt. He doesn't want to miss the fun.

The fire marshal is in Buddy's pocket, but he finally has to say enough, no more guests. If you're not a very VIP, Ray escorts you to the door.

• • •

By October of '77, disco is officially a craze. It's everywhere: malls, high school pep rallies, progressive churches. At health clubs you can hit the Nautilus machines and then take a class in the Hustle, the Rollercoaster, the Funky Chicken.

And now the Mercury Club has competition. Disco 36 opens on the corner of NW 36th and Shartel. Buddy scoffs. The place is less than half the size of the Mercury Club. And only one mirror ball! But it's new, it's fresh. And so are Michael's Plum and Pistachio's, opening one right after the other.

The line outside Club Mercurio shrinks. Lillian gets nervous. Buddy doesn't panic. People will be back. They'll take the new joints for a spin and realize Club Mercurio is the Cadillac of discos.

Buddy gives Warren lists of popular songs to play. Warren bristles. He's proud of his talent to break songs *before* they're hits—that's what makes Club Mercurio *cook*. You're right, you're right, Buddy says. He slaps five with Warren and promises a raise, a big one, right around the corner.

Warren is a nag about the kids too. He thinks kids that age shouldn't be around all the drinking, the smoking, the various other activities. What the hell does Warren know about kids? What the hell does he know about *Mercurio* kids?

Buddy worries that Warren's more flamboyant friends are scaring off the mainstream clientele. The towering wigs, the false eyelashes, the prizefighters in miniskirts. Buddy tells Warren to spread the word: cool it, a little, with the homosexual shit. A reasonable request. Warren glowers. No. He will not. They will not.

What's Buddy supposed to do? This is his club, his and Lillian's. Warren is a valued employee, but that's all he is: an employee. *No.* Right to Buddy's face! Buddy gets hotter and hotter. "You're fired," he tells Warren. "Get the hell out of here and don't ever come back."

Lillian is in the ladies' room, when all this goes down, touching up her makeup with Jolene. She's furious that Buddy fired Warren. "You idiot!" she says. "What are you thinking?"

"I'm thinking someone needs to save this business!" he says. "Before it all goes up your nose!"

"Up *my* nose?" She throws a highball glass at him. It shatters against the wall, and Tallulah, who Buddy didn't even realize was there, gets sparkling shards in her hair.

Buddy hires one of the hippies from Long John Silver's to DJ. The hippie plays the songs Buddy tells him to play, in the prescribed order. Warren, the traitor, goes to work for yet another new disco in town, Clementine's in the basement of Penn Square Mall.

Some good news, though: for the one-year anniversary of Oklahoma City's very first disco, Channel Four and the *Daily Oklahoman* plan big stories about Club Mercurio. It's the kind of free advertising you can't buy—the kind of attention, Buddy promises Ronnie Hinkle, that turns fortunes around.

A chilly, drizzly Monday morning in early December. Trees have dumped their dead leaves and whitecaps corrugate the iron-gray surface of Lake Hefner.

Channel Four sends a reporter and a cameraman. The cameraman grabs some B-roll while the reporter lobs a few softballs at Buddy. Then everyone goes outside, under the marquee, and the reporter asks Buddy about the drugs.

"What?" Buddy says. "Are we rolling?"

The reporter, a freckle-faced Howdy Doody barely out of college, pushes the microphone closer. "There are reports that illegal drugs can be easily purchased at Club Mercurio."

"What the hell are you talking about?" Buddy says. "Turn off that camera, please."

Lillian sees Buddy's face flush. When he's about to blow, she knows, he smiles like he's smiling now. She eases herself into the frame, laughs gaily, and grips Buddy's arm so tightly she can feel the bone.

"Oh, Michael," she tells the reporter, "that's such a silly question. If illegal drugs were available here, do you think our dance floor would be crowded every Saturday night with Oklahoma City's most reputable politicians and businessmen and owners of local television stations?"

It's that easy. The reporter nods. Then *nods*. Lillian catches a smirk from the cameraman. All Buddy has to do now is keep that big mouth of his shut for once.

"That's not what this story is supposed to be about," Buddy says. "Turn off that goddamn camera right now."

"Buddy," Lillian says under her breath. "Cool it."

Cool it? After all the dough Buddy has paid Channel Four for the TV spots? But it's not just Howdy Doody and his libelous allegations. It's yet another disco opening up. It's the line out front of Club Mercurio shrinking, shrinking. It's Warren, that traitor. The movie can't end this way, with Roy Scheider losing everything, with the shark biting him in half. Buddy's fury builds. His vision pulses.

Lillian says something. Buddy doesn't hear it. Howdy Doody pushes the microphone closer, closer . . .

• • •

Buddy barely touches the reporter. The camera distorts. The camera gets it all wrong. Buddy isn't *dragging* the kid back to the van, he's escorting him firmly but politely. The kid trips and stumbles. That's on the kid, not Buddy! The microphone . . . okay, Buddy takes responsibility for that. He shouldn't have grabbed the microphone. He shouldn't have hammered it against the side-view mirror of the van until they're broken and dangling, the mirror and the microphone both.

The clip plays at six and ten. Jack Ogle, Channel Four anchor, shakes his head and calls the reporter courageous, the experience terrifying.

Howdy Doody doesn't press charges. Why would he? He's a star. But Buddy has to start considering his options. All of them. Club Mercurio is in a dire situation. Buddy, on the other hand, has a secret safe full of cash that he's skimmed, that Ronnie Hinkle knows nothing about. A fresh start for Buddy and Lillian, the kids. They can move to the East Coast, maybe. Atlantic City?

Or . . . just Buddy could move to Atlantic City. A wife, five kids . . . Buddy would need *two* safes full of cash to support a crew that big. Fresh starts are expensive. And you could argue that Lillian and the kids might be better off without Buddy around.

But no, no, no. He hasn't made up his mind. He's just *considering* options. He'll give Club Mercurio another month or two. If he can get the club back on its feet, all's well that ends well.

CHAPTER 11

Early in January, Ronnie Hinkle's rich daddy storms into Club Mercurio. Ronnie Hinkle follows meekly behind. The rich daddy is big and husky, his heavy belly hanging down over belted Wranglers. He backs Buddy up against the bar. It's Friday afternoon, hours before the club opens, and Ray isn't there to restore order.

"I want me some answers," Larry Hinkle says. He's right up in Buddy's face, his nose an inch from Buddy's nose. "And I want 'em right doggone now."

Buddy has no idea what this is about, but he's confident he can talk his way out of it. Larry Hinkle is sharper than his son, but only in the sense that a butter knife is sharper than a spoon.

"Calm down, Larry," Buddy says. "I'll tell you anything you want to know."

"You're cheatin' my boy, aren't you? You're cookin' the books and stealin' money."

The heat is cranked to seventy-five, the club warm and stuffy, but a chill sweeps through Buddy. How does Larry Hinkle know that Buddy's been skimming? He *can't* know. It's impossible. Ronnie hasn't asked to look at the books once. He's shown not the slightest hint of suspicion.

"What?" Buddy says. "That's ridiculous. Cheating him? Stealing? You're way off base, Larry. Ronnie? What's he talking about?"

Ronnie, brow furrowed, pours himself three fingers of Jim Beam. "Let's just hear his side of it, Buddy. I'm sure it's just a mix-up."

"How much a profit've you turned on this place so far, you sonofabitch?" Larry asks Buddy. "Since this place opened."

"Ronnie already knows," Buddy says. "We've cleared around thirty, thirty-two thousand the first year. I don't have to tell you, Larry. That's an excellent return on—"

"Thirty-two grand my shiny red *ass*," Larry says. "I bet you've made double that. More, probably."

A lot more, definitely. But Larry Hinkle *can't* know that. It's impossible. "Now, just hold on a second," Buddy says, "let's all just—"

"Shut your mouth, you sneaky Italian sonofabitch. Ronnie, how much *return* you seen so far? Actual cash."

Ronnie gulps. "Well, not too much yet, if you're talking actual *cash*. But . . ."

"Dog*gone* it, Ronnie. Shut your mouth." Larry points a finger at Buddy. "Open the damn safe. Now."

They march back to the office. Buddy opens the dummy safe. He never keeps more than a couple of grand in it.

He throws up his hands. "That's it, Larry. Hand to my heart. We've been running on fumes for the last two or three months. Ever since those other discos opened."

"Give me that," Larry says.

Buddy hands over the couple of grand. "Give me a few days," he says. "I'll call in some markers and see what else I can get you. Good faith effort. Okay?"

"You got till Sunday morning, ten o'clock. I want Ronnie's twenty thousand dollars by Sunday morning or you're going to jail. I'll make doggone sure of it."

Larry Hinkle storms back out, Ronnie hurrying after him. At the door, Ronnie pauses to look back at Buddy. He smiles apologetically, shrugs helplessly.

• • •

This is a pain in the ass Buddy doesn't need right now. Larry might not be bluffing about the cops. Will another two or three grand calm him down?

We'll see. Over Buddy's dead body will he give that rube a penny more than he has to.

In the meantime, Buddy needs to relocate the cash in the secret safe to a more secure location. Hinkle Dee and Hinkle Dum might figure out that Buddy keeps his eggs in two baskets. They might come back Sunday and tear the office apart. Better safe than sorry.

Buddy has plenty of time before the bartenders and cocktail waitresses show up for their shift, before the kids get home from school, before Lillian finishes at the hairdresser, her usual Friday appointment. He locks up the club and speeds down May Avenue to North Park Mall. At Kamber's he splashes out for a sturdy and capacious American Tourister suitcase, gold, scuff-resistant vinyl. From there he speeds back to the club and packs the suitcase—close to seventy grand from the secret safe.

Home. Buddy circles the block a couple of times to make sure the coast is clear. Inside, he searches for a good, temporary hiding place. What about the laundry chute, which runs from the top floor to the basement? Tie some twine around the handle of the suitcase, lower it halfway down . . . No, too complicated. Buddy tries the attic, up in the rafters. No. He humps the suitcase down to the basement. Here we go. He sticks the suitcase in a moldy cardboard box, then stacks jars of Lillian's late great-aunt's fruit preserves on top. The jars are crusted, seeping, in a murky, muddy rainbow of troubling colors. No one in their right mind would go near those jars.

Driving back to Club Mercurio, Buddy whistles along to the song on the radio. The Bee Gees, "Stayin' Alive." Staying alive, you better believe it. Try to match wits with a Mercurio, you'll lose every time.

Sunday morning, ten o'clock sharp: Larry and Ronnie Hinkle arrive at Club Mercurio. Buddy is waiting. He's brought along Alice and Piggy. He figures they might help melt Larry's heart, two adorable kids. At the least, they'll keep Larry from getting rough.

Larry spots the kids and frowns. Alice is reading a book. Piggy, God bless him, is watching her read a book.

"Where is it?" Larry says. What he really wants to say, but can't, is "Where the hell is it?"

Buddy opens a drawer, takes out an envelope, slides the envelope across to Larry. "This is the best I was able to do, Larry. Call the cops if you have to, but I'm doing the best I can."

"Dad," Ronnie Hinkle says. "I just think—"

"Shut your mouth."

The weather has turned nasty outside. Buddy listens to the sleet clatter against the roof and watches Larry count the money in the envelope. Two grand. Along with the original seventeen hundred from the dummy safe, that makes close to four grand. Larry is trying to decide if that's enough for now. He's wondering, Buddy guesses, if maybe the dirty little Italian really is doing the best he can.

Larry counts the money again. Buddy keeps his mouth zipped. Never interrupt your enemy when he's making a mistake. Napoleon said that. He was an honorary Mercurio.

"Hell," Larry grumbles finally, and Buddy relaxes. "Now you better listen to me."

"All right, Larry."

"I want another two thousand by the end of next month."

"Sure thing, Larry. You've got my word."

They shake hands. Buddy has to fight the urge to grin. He walks Larry and Ronnie to the front door of the theater. The sleet rakes the parking lot. Everyone shakes hands again. Drive safely now.

Back in the office, Buddy kicks his feet up onto the desk and basks in the glow of victory. The glow fades, though. Four grand down the drain is *not* a victory. Getting his business partner stirred up is not a victory. From now on, Buddy will have to be more careful about covering his tracks.

And the fact remains: Club Mercurio is wobbling. Buddy should never have fired Warren. He sees that now. What if Buddy can lure Warren back to the fold? Or what if Club Mercurio starts booking live acts? Risky, and expensive, but Buddy has to make some bold moves, or else.

Or else. He circles back to his original thought. He could muck a questionable hand and leave the poker table—take the seventy grand in the suitcase and start over somewhere new. Or even go back to Vegas! How's that for an idea? It's been five and a half years. Buddy might be welcomed back with open arms.

Buddy loves Lillian, loves his kids, sure, but the prospect of a grand new adventure makes him tingle. He's a Mercurio! And, you know, he could send for Lillian and the kids once he gets established, his feet on the ground. Maybe Buddy will take Alice with him. Alice has Buddy's brains. Maybe . . .

He can't concentrate. It still irks him that Larry Hinkle suspected Buddy was skimming money. Who the hell put the idea in that rube's head? Not Ronnie, that's for sure. *Why* would someone put the idea in that rube's head? That's the better question.

The oxygen in the office dwindles. Buddy's hand begins to tremble and the ash from his cigar crumbles into his lap.

Next thing he knows, he's in his car, driving too fast in the sleet. Alice is sitting in the passenger seat, Piggy on her lap. Did Buddy tell Alice and Piggy to come with him? He must have, but he doesn't remember doing it. Buddy's brain is fogged over, his heart thundering.

No, no, no, no, he thinks. It's all he can think. No, no, no, no.

CHAPTER 12

Lillian grabs a flashlight and checks the attic first. Nothing. She peers down the laundry chute. Lillian remembers the time she caught Jeremy and Alice about to drop Tallulah (or was it Piggy?) from the top floor down to the laundry basket in the basement. "It's an experiment!" Alice said.

Nothing in the laundry chute. Buddy probably deliberated, but then decided too much effort was involved.

The basement! Lillian hurries downstairs. She hates the basement, damp and dark and pungently ripe. Buddy knows that. Sure enough, she finds a suitcase in a box, under jars of old preserves. This is the story of her husband: smart, but not quite smart enough. At least not quite smart enough for Lillian.

Lillian didn't need the combination to Buddy's secret safe. She just dropped a few hints to Larry Hinkle and let Buddy do all the heavy lifting for her.

In the kitchen, Lillian wipes down the golden vinyl before she unzips the suitcase. Ah, yes. There's even more money than she anticipated. Oh, Buddy, you devil you. This is why she loves him.

Jeremy is in the bedroom he shares with Ray, practicing new dance moves in the mirror. Ray sits like a lump on one of the twin beds, waiting expressionless (always expressionless) for God knows what.

"Hi, Mom," Jeremy says. "Get a load of this move. It's called the Snap."

"Ray," Lillian says, "go up to the attic for me, will you? See if you can find my aunt's old patchwork quilt. I know it's up there somewhere, in one of the boxes."

Ray stands, lumbers out. That should keep him occupied for a good hour or two.

Lillian snaps her fingers in Jeremy's face to get his attention. "Pack some clothes."

Reluctantly he draws his gaze away from his own reflection. Lillian can't blame him. When she was his age, young and beautiful, nothing made her happier than a mirror. People go to museums and stare at paintings, don't they?

"Huh?" he says.

"Pack some clothes and whatever else you want to take. Hurry. We're leaving in ten minutes."

"Where?"

She doesn't have time to explain. "Do you want to come with me or not?"

"Yeah. Sure."

"Okay, then. Ten minutes."

It only takes Lillian five to pack. Her jewelry, some clothes. In New York City or Miami or Los Angeles or maybe even Vegas—she hasn't decided yet—she'll buy whatever she needs. She'll buy whatever she wants.

She throws her bags and the golden suitcase in the trunk of her Buick. The sleet drums against the skin of her umbrella. She will not miss Oklahoma City in January. She will not miss it any time of the year.

Yes, of course, Lillian feels a twinge of guilt for abandoning Buddy and the other kids, a faint but persistent ache of sadness. But get real. Club Mercurio has already sunk beneath the surface and it's only a matter of months before the business, and all she's invested in it, settles at the dark bottom of the ocean. Lillian can't, she *cannot*, go back to the life she lived before. And she can't trust Buddy with the money in the golden suitcase. Who knows what harebrained scheme he'll throw it away on?

"Hi, Mom. What are you doing?"

Lillian, startled, practically jumps out of her heels. It's Tallulah, arms spread wide like she's flying, and one leg hooked through the back porch railing.

"Nothing." Lillian slams the trunk shut and hurries back to the porch. She shakes out her umbrella. "Go inside. Go watch TV."

"Where are you going?" Tallulah says. "You have suitcases. Are you going on a trip? Are we going with you? Where's Dad?"

Shit. Tallulah's curiosity, Lillian knows from long experience, is voracious. She won't be quickly or easily distracted like Ray was. And she'll blow Lillian's head start. When Buddy gets home, Tallulah will spill the beans. Lillian can't ask her to lie. Tallulah is a mediocre liar, by Mercurio standards. Buddy will see right through her.

"Yes, you're coming with me." The more the merrier, Lillian supposes. "You and Jeremy."

"Where?"

"You'll see. Go find Jeremy. *Hurry.* Tell him we're leaving *right now.*"

• • •

The sleet has turned to freezing rain, and in the time it takes Lillian to get Jeremy and Tallulah in the Buick the driveway is a sheet of ice. She backs out slowly. At least the weather will keep people off the road. There's no traffic on 34th, no traffic even on Classen. Lillian is almost all the way to Northwest Expressway when she encounters her first car, coming from the opposite direction. A cherry-red Camaro, the same model Buddy drives.

"There's Dad!" Tallulah calls from the back seat.

Lillian's hands tighten on the steering wheel. She sees Buddy's face, when he recognizes her, go slack with surprise. She supposes her face does the same. They float past one another, the freezing rain creating a soft-focus scrim between the two cars.

And then Lillian hears the shrill rubbery *squeeeeeeee* of Buddy's tires as he slams on his brakes, as the Camaro fishtails.

Lillian hits the gas. "Hold tight," she tells Jeremy and Tallulah.

CHAPTER 13

"Hold tight," Buddy tells Alice.

She props a foot on the dashboard to brace herself and hugs Piggy to her chest. Buddy yanks the steering wheel.

No, no, no. But now he means it differently: he's driven now by resolve, not despair. *No, no, no, you are* not *getting away with this.*

A Buick is no match for a Camaro. But the goddamn ice, the patches of asphalt that look dry but aren't. Buddy's Camaro weighs less than the Buick, a tank. He slips and slides. A couple of times the car spins all the way around the clock dial, from twelve o'clock high and back again. He doesn't run off the road. That's the main thing.

Jeremy's in the front seat with Lillian, Tallulah in the back, turned around and waving through the window.

"Lulu!" Piggy says, waving back at Tallulah.

Buddy waves back too. They're on deserted Western Avenue now, barreling past McGuinness High School, barreling under the concrete bridge covered with graffiti. Buddy is furious, heartbroken. How could Lillian do this to him? She probably didn't even leave a note. Buddy would have left her a note, at least.

He gains ground on the Buick until they're neck and neck. Buddy pounds his horn, jerks his arm. *Pull over, goddamnit!* Lillian is as stubborn as the day is long. Buddy noses the Camaro in front of her and she's forced to brake. The Buick drifts sideways on the ice and off the road, throwing up a sparkling sheet of gravel and grinding to a lopsided stop, half on and half off the Britton train tracks.

"Wait here," Buddy tells Alice. He leaves the car running so the kids will stay warm and leaps out. The back tire of the Buick spins helplessly as Lillian tries to launch herself off the tracks. No chance, honey. Buddy has the spare key to the Buick on his ring. He inserts it in the lock and pops the trunk. *Yes, yes, yes.* His suitcase, his money.

A crack of thunder splits the heavens. What the hell? Buddy looks up, over, around. And there stands Lillian, Buddy's .38 revolver in her hand, pointed right at him.

"Did you just try to shoot me?" he says, flabbergasted.

"That was a warning!" she says. "Get away from the car!"

"That's my gun! And it's my goddamn money!"

"It's *our* goddamn money!"

"That's exactly my point! You're stealing *our* goddamn money!"

"You don't get another warning!"

Buddy takes a step toward her. She won't shoot him in cold blood. Will she? He decides not to take another step, just in case. "Honey. What are you doing?"

"Tell me you didn't think of it first," she says.

She's got him there, so he dodges the question. "Remember that first time? At the Hacienda?"

"We're meant for each other. Is that what you're going to say?"

He doesn't know what he was going to say. Buddy usually doesn't know what he's going to say until he says it. But it's true. They are meant for each other. Or at least they're not meant for anyone else.

"That was a helluva smart play," he says. "Tipping off Larry to flush the money. That was my girl."

She lowers the gun. An ambush? Buddy takes the risk. He moves closer. Somewhere, far off, a train whistle wails.

"I know it was smart. How much else do you have squirreled away?"

"Wouldn't you like to know?"

He takes her in his arms. She bites the lobe of his ear, hard, then kisses him. They kiss and they kiss, and they kiss, like the ending to a beautiful movie. The freezing rain pelts them, they're drenched and icing over, but they don't care. The train whistle wails again, louder, closer than Buddy realized.

CHAPTER 14

Carpool on Monday is Mrs. Dillon. After school, everyone packs into her station wagon: Alice and Katie Dillon, who is in Alice's grade; Tallulah and Kenny Dillon, who is in Tallulah's grade; Jeremy and Sean McCall, who is in Jeremy's grade. Ray has to ride next to Mrs. Dillon. He takes up two-thirds of the front bench seat.

"You get bigger every week, Ray," Mrs. Dillon says cheerfully.

The entire ride, Kenny Dillon yammers on and on. He will *not* shut up about *Star Wars*. Isn't it the greatest movie ever? Isn't Han Solo the greatest? What is Tallulah's favorite part? The cantina, maybe?

Tallulah squirms. She doesn't understand why they have to carpool, why they can't just walk or better yet run home. Tallulah bets she could make it home just as fast as the car. She wouldn't have to stop for stoplights like Mrs. Dillon does.

Jeremy's mind drifts pleasantly. It's cold outside, but the car is warm. Who would Jeremy rather make out with—Marcia Brady from *The Brady Bunch* or Lori Partridge from *The Partridge Family*? That's easy. Both of them. Katie Dillon turns in her seat, pretending to listen to Kenny, and gives Jeremy a shy smile. He smiles back.

"What's wrong?" Tallulah asks Alice. Alice hasn't said a word since yesterday, when Mom tried to shoot Dad but then they made up and kissed.

"Leave me alone," Alice says.

Mrs. Dillon drops them all off at the end of their block so they can pick up Piggy. Mrs. Snyder watches Piggy at her house during the day, while the older kids are in school.

When they get home, the kids tromp inside, kicking filthy slush off their shoes. They all head straight to the den. Jeremy turns on *Gilligan's Island*. Who would Jeremy rather make out with—Mary Ann or Ginger? That's easy too. Both.

"Do you think Mom was really going to shoot Dad?" Tallulah asks.

"Of course not," Jeremy says. "Probably not."

Tallulah turns to Ray. "Ray. Ray! What do you think?"

Ray blinks. "I don't know," he says.

"What's wrong with you?" Jeremy asks Alice. "Usually, you're the complete expert on everything."

"Leave me alone," Alice says.

"It was so exciting," Tallulah says. "It was like being in a movie."

"We're Mercurios," Jeremy says, shrugging. "It's in our blood."

PART III

Jeremy

1984–1985

CHAPTER 15

Jeremy is propped comfortably against the wall of the service bar, chatting with the new chick, when Scott, one of the other waiters, blows past on his way to the kitchen.

"Table twelve is *not* happy," Scott says.

The new chick is cute. With her messy blond bangs, Jeremy thinks she looks—from certain angles—a little bit like Madonna. She's a senior at OCU, three years older than Jeremy who is eighteen, but he's the wise old veteran here. He's worked at Wellingford's since he graduated high school, back in May.

"So, what do you want to do when you're done with college?" he says.

"I might apply to law school," the new chick says. "I hear it's so hard, though, law school. I'm kind of scared."

"Don't be scared!" Jeremy says. "You should totally apply. Follow your heart, you know? You only regret the things you *don't* do."

Scott blows back past with a tray of sizzling appetizers. "Did I mention that table twelve is *losing* their *shit*?" he says.

Table twelve. Oh. Jeremy forgot that was his four-top.

"I'll be back to check on you," he tells the new chick. "Pinkie swear."

She laughs and hooks her pinkie through his. She's definitely cute. He likes the way she looks at him, the tilt of her face and the light swimming in her eyes.

Jeremy grabs his order from the pass-through and runs it out to the dining room. Scott wasn't exaggerating: table twelve is losing their shit. The two men are puffed out and scowling. The two women are drumming their fingers on the table. Jeremy glides up and pops open the tray stand.

"I'm really, really sorry about the delay with your entrees," he says.

He means it. He's not faking. That's something Jeremy can do. He can create, out of thin air, a temporary but true feeling in himself. Five seconds ago he was unconcerned about the people at table twelve. And he'll be unconcerned again when he turns his back and walks away. In this one moment, though, here and now, a firefly flickers to life in his chest, and he genuinely is really, truly sorry about the delay with their entrees.

The men stop scowling. The women smile.

"It's just fine, sugar," one of the women says, reaching out to touch Jeremy's forearm. "Don't you worry about it."

Alice says Jeremy is . . . what is it his sister says? She says Jeremy is an empty vessel, without normal human emotions. But Jeremy disputes that. He has lots of emotions, ready to go whenever he needs them.

"The shit you get away with," Scott murmurs as he and Jeremy slide sideways past each other in the narrow alley between tables. Scott shakes his head and sighs with disgust, with admiration.

• • •

It's true. Jeremy can't explain why, exactly, but he does get away with a lot of shit. He never studied in high school, never turned in his homework, but his teachers always let him slide. They just shook their heads and smiled. *Oh, Jeremy.* At Wellingford's, the fanciest restaurant in Oklahoma City, which usually only hires professional waiters with a ton of experience, Jeremy's boss never busts him. When Jeremy "forgets" to inform parties of six and eight that the tip is already included in their bill, the boss, Gerhardt, just shakes his head and smiles.

And the chicks! Jeremy has juggled three, four girls at a time ever since seventh grade. In high school, he was the first freshman boy to lose his virginity, and junior year he dated—simultaneously—the homecoming queen at his high school *and* the homecoming queen at the rival high school across town. Eventually the two girls found out about each other, but neither got mad at Jeremy.

Jeremy appreciates the charmed life he leads. He does. He appreciates when, for example, a friend of his mom's gives him a sweet '64 Karmann

Ghia convertible that her husband never drives anymore. But a charmed life is still just a life, you know? *His* life. You get used to it. Alice, when she's not calling him an empty vessel, tells Jeremy he's like a spoiled Greek god, like Apollo lounging on Olympus, serenely accepting all the gifts and offerings piled on his altar.

Okay, but Jeremy can't understand why that's so terrible. What is Apollo *supposed* to do?

The next morning, bright light and a sharp chill wrenches him from a sound sleep. Jeremy tries to burrow deeper beneath his blankets. But wait . . . where are his blankets?

"Wake up." Alice stands next to the bed, his blankets piled at her feet. "You promised to drive us to school."

He reaches for a blanket. Alice slaps his hand away. "What time is it?"

"Seven thirty," she says. "We're going to be late."

"Seven thirty in the *morning*?" Unacceptable. Inconceivable. "Go away, Alice."

"Get up!" Alice says. "You promised."

So what if Jeremy promised? A promise is just hypothetical. It's a *possibility*, subject to change, a statement from the past about the future that has no actual bearing on the *present*.

"And put some clothes on," Alice says.

"Okay. *Okay.* Jesus, Alice!"

They squish into his Karmann Ghia, Tallulah sitting on Alice's lap. Tallulah cranks the heater, then dials through every single radio station on the dial once, twice, three times until she finally finds a song ("Little Red Corvette") she likes. But then thirty seconds later she gets antsy and starts dialing through stations again.

The ice is even nastier this morning than it was last night. Jeremy doesn't sweat it. Every time the road swishes out from under him, the tires catch, and the car straightens back out.

Alice reaches over and pokes him in the shoulder. "Are you listening to me?" she says.

He's vaguely aware she's been talking, but no, he has not been listening. "Sure."

"You should take Classen. It's sanded."

"When are you going to get your own car and drive yourself to school?" he says. Alice is a tightwad, saving every penny she makes from babysitting and tutoring for college next fall.

"When are you going to move to Los Angeles like you keep promising?" she says.

Not soon enough, Jeremy thinks. Oklahoma City isn't a place for someone like him. That's what Mom says. That's what everyone says. In LA, Jeremy will be able to spread his wings and fucking *soar*. He's going to be an actor. Or a producer. Maybe both, if that's a thing. He can't wait.

Jeremy has an epiphany. His plan was to live at home for a year after high school and save up a ton of money, but . . . why not go ahead and move to LA *now*? Why wait another five or six months? He's got some money, plenty of money. Things will work out for him. They always do.

CHAPTER 16

Jeremy doesn't waste any time. He buys some new Polos, an Omega Seamaster watch like John McEnroe wears, and a brand-new Alpine tape deck for the Karmann Ghia. That takes a fairly huge chunk out of his savings, but he still has more than four hundred dollars cash, plus the hundred Mom sneaks him when he tells her he's leaving. She warns Jeremy, like always, not to mention the money to Dad or the other kids.

Gerhardt isn't thrilled when Jeremy quits Wellingford's without notice, but then he snaps his fingers. It turns out that Gerhardt's grandparents live in Los Angeles, in Santa Monica. Gerhardt calls them up and they say Jeremy is welcome to stay in their guest suite as long as he likes. Very cool. Jeremy won't have to burn money on a motel or youth hostel while he looks for an apartment. Gerhardt's grandmother, Gerhardt says, is a tremendous cook.

On the big day, another cold January morning, gray sky and skeleton trees, Jeremy loads up the Karmann Ghia. The family gathers to wish him bon voyage. Well, most of the family. Tallulah has Saturday detention at school because she's skipped so much class and Dad left for work earlier. He either forgot that Jeremy was leaving today or never knew it. That's Dad for you. If a tree falls in a forest and Dad's not there? The tree and that forest don't exist. Mom, to be honest, is kind of the same way, at least with all the kids but Jeremy.

Alice gives Jeremy a hug, which is a strange development. She's in a strangely good mood, serene and smiling. "Goodbye forever!" she says.

Piggy shakes Jeremy's hand. His lower lip trembles with emotion. Piggy worships Jeremy, which makes Jeremy like him the best of all his siblings.

He tries to think of some words of wisdom for his little brother, but it's obvious that Piggy will be a complete nerd for the rest of his life. "Follow your dreams," Jeremy says. "Know when to fold 'em, know when to hold 'em."

Piggy's eyes get big. "Will you write me lots of letters? Will you tell me everything you're doing?"

Jeremy is more than happy to promise he will.

Mom is the last one left in the driveway. She slips another twenty bucks in Jeremy's pocket. "You're going to have everything you ever wanted, baby," she says, kissing his cheek so hard he can feel her teeth. "I wish I was you."

The first stretch of the trip is boring. Oklahoma City to Amarillo, into New Mexico. This is the first time Jeremy has been away from home by himself. So far, so good. He likes making all his own decisions. The first morning, in Gallup, he sleeps until almost noon—his decision! In Kingman, Arizona, he glances at the map. Las Vegas is just a short detour up Highway 93. Jeremy's brother Ray moved to Vegas two years ago, when he graduated from high school, and has gone to work for a friend of their dad's. Jeremy can crash with Ray and is curious to see the city where he was born, but he sticks to the plan. Vegas can wait. He'll check it out when he can afford a penthouse suite, a limo to drive him down the Strip.

Kingman to Barstow. California! Rancho Cucamonga. Asuza. Jeremy isn't blown away by California yet. It's greener than Oklahoma City in January, and a lot warmer. He spots a few palm trees, but nothing you'd really stick on a postcard. Traffic on the freeway is nuts, bumper to bumper but booming along at seventy miles an hour. The sky is slightly yellowish, like fingertips stained by nicotine.

And then the landscape changes, the slant of the sun as it drops toward the horizon. Suddenly the breeze blowing through his open windows is sweeter, fresher. Flowers spill off white stucco. Jeremy can smell the ocean. Traffic still sucks but who cares? He's in Los Angeles. He has arrived.

The steering wheel jerks in his hands. Did the Karmann Ghia hit a pothole? Jeremy hears a *thuh-wunk*, followed by high-pitched *zzzzzing*, like a bullet in a comic book ricocheting off a metal door. He smells smoke now, and burning oil. The Karmann Ghia slows to a crawl. Cars blast their horns at Jeremy as they swerve around him. He gives the Karmann Ghia more gas. *Thuh-WUNK.* It lurches to a complete stop. Smoke seeps from the seam around the hood.

Jeremy's not sure what to do. He had a flat tire once, but Ray was with him and knew how to put on the spare. Maybe the Karmann Ghia just over-heated? Jeremy shifts to park and turns off the ignition, waits a minute, horns blaring and cars whizzing past, so close the Karmann Ghia rocks back and forth. When he restarts the car and shifts to drive, the engine sounds like a broken bottle in a washing machine. Jeremy shuts it off.

Okay. He can handle this. He'll find someone to handle this. There are two lanes of whizzing cars between him and the shoulder of the freeway. He waits for an opening and books across as fast as he's ever booked in his life.

He climbs a scrubby berm of weeds and trash, then walks to the nearest surface street. Boxy little apartments balanced on top of carports, a laundromat, a liquor store, another liquor store. Jeremy notices the bars on the windows, the graffiti everywhere, the coils of barbed wire on top of the laundromat. This is not, he realizes, that great of a neighborhood.

He spots a pay phone outside one of the liquor stores. But when he searches his wallet, he can't find the piece of paper he's looking for—the one with the phone number and address for Gerhardt's grandparents.

He's absolutely sure he has it. He remembers very clearly folding the piece of paper in half and sticking it in his wallet. At least he remembers very clearly folding the piece of paper in half. After that, he's fuzzier. Possibly he only *intended* to stick the piece of paper in his wallet and instead put it . . . where?

Huh. He looks around. It doesn't make any sense, he knows, but he can visualize a person—maybe one of the guys standing on the corner, or the lady leaving the liquor store—coming over to him and handing him the lost number and address. *Here you go.* For a second that scenario seems completely believable and imminent.

It's Monday. Wellingford's is closed, so he can't get in touch with Gerhardt until tomorrow. Jeremy guesses he'll call a cab, find a motel. He has plenty of cash. Except now the two guys on the corner are watching him. They don't seem particularly friendly, even though they're smiling.

Jeremy starts walking back to the freeway. The two guys on the corner stir. Are they following him? They could be headed toward the liquor store.

The ocean breeze has died. The light has shifted again, dusk spreading and color draining. Jeremy feels weird, a strange new sensation he can't identify, a tightening of muscles in his stomach. Is this freaking out? It's never happened to him before, not that he can remember. Other people freak out. The point guard on Jeremy's team before he shot a free throw to win or lose a game. Kids at a party when the cops showed up. But not Jeremy.

Jeremy realizes he doesn't know a single person in Los Angeles. Which means there are *millions* of people here who don't know him. Why hasn't that occurred to him until just now? The enormity of this imbalance, the wrongness of it, makes him dizzy.

The two guys are following him, still smiling. One guy is holding a bottle. Did he just pick that up or did he have it all along?

Jeremy is on the sloped berm now, but it feels flat. When he gets to the flat shoulder of the freeway, it feels sloped. Cars thunder past. His Karmann Ghia is a hundred miles away, the hood still smoking. What are you supposed to tell someone who is freaking out? *C'mon, man*, Jeremy told the point guard that one time, *nail this fucking shot and we win, man*. But that doesn't work here, obviously. His forehead is damp. He can't stop picturing the millions and millions of people in Los Angeles who don't know him.

A ruby-red convertible Mustang pulls onto the shoulder and slows to a stop a few yards away from Jeremy. Three chicks, about his age, wearing bikini tops and big hoop earrings. A blonde, a brunette, a redhead.

The two guys following Jeremy stop, then fade back away into the dusk.

"Hi!" The blond chick, the driver of the Mustang, is a total babe—and not just compared to what Jeremy is used to in Oklahoma City, but a total babe by the standards of the world, of MTV. Her smile is a bright, exploding skyrocket. She points to the Karmann Ghia. "Is that your poor car?"

"That's my poor car," Jeremy says.

"We can give you a ride," the brunette says. She's almost as hot as the blonde. So is the redhead. "What's your name?"

"Jeremy."

"Come on, Jeremy," the blonde says. "Hop in."

"Oh, we'll give you a ride!" the redhead says, and all three chicks howl with laughter.

Jeremy laughs too. He feels the ground shift again beneath his feet, the universe straightening itself back into the correct and familiar position. "Very cool," he says.

CHAPTER 17

Jeremy grabs his stuff from the Karmann Ghia and abandons his car in the middle of the freeway. It will probably cost a fortune to fix the Karmann Ghia, and he needs a more reliable ride now that he's in LA anyway. Something better is bound to come along soon.

The three chicks in the convertible are on their way home from a day at the beach. Tina, Tammy, and Dawn. Dawn is the blonde. Jeremy will remember that no problem because *Dawn* and *blonde* kind of rhyme. She's the hottest, the most stacked, the leader.

When they find out he's from Oklahoma, they ask him if grew up on a ranch, if he has a surrey with fringe on top. The three of them burst into song. *Ohhhh-klahoma.* Jeremy doesn't mind. It's a good sign, in his experience, when hot chicks tease you.

"Don't worry," Dawn says, "we're all from nowhere too. I'm from Oregon." She reaches over to squeeze his hand as she says it. That's a good sign too.

Jeremy borrows the brunette's heart-shaped sunglasses and pops his collar like Tom Cruise in *Risky Business*. "I'm from LA now," he says, which cracks the chicks up.

They're renting a house in Encino, on Martha Street. It's sprawling and spacious, with a sunken living room and a wet bar and wallpaper flecked with gold. The pool out back throbs in the darkness, like some glowing green source of alien energy. You have to take your shoes off before you enter. It's a California thing, Jeremy learns.

"You can crash here tonight," Dawn tells him.

"Are you sure? I've got a place to stay tomorrow."

"It's no hassle. We have an extra bedroom."

While the chicks shower, Jeremy lounges by the pool and drinks a cold beer. For dinner the brunette mashes up fresh avocados for guacamole. The redhead makes a pitcher of margaritas. Dawn turns the stereo up so they can hear the music outside and lights a tiki torch.

The chicks are so sweet and funny and down to earth. They're not stuck up at all, even though—those faces, those bods—they have every right to be.

After dinner they smoke a joint and play Monopoly by the light of the tiki torch. The chicks aren't surprised when Jeremy tells them he moved here to become an actor. It must be obvious, he realizes. It must be the reason why they moved here too, right? All three chicks nod. But then Dawn sighs.

"I don't know how much longer I'll stick with it," she says. "It's been fun and all, but I'm thinking I might go back to college. I could be a nurse."

"Or you could just *play* a nurse," the brunette says.

The redhead laughs. "I've played so many nurses," she says.

"Really?" Jeremy says, impressed.

"Speaking of which." The brunette yawns and uncurls from her lounger. "I've got to be on set early. I'm hitting the hay."

"Me too," the redhead says.

The brunette and redhead go inside. Dawn and Jeremy sit side by side on a wicker love seat. She turns to give Jeremy a quizzical look.

"Jeremy," she says, "you understand what we do, right? The other girls and me?"

"Sure," he says. "You're actresses."

"We are." She waits, studying him as he works it out.

"Oh," he says. *Oh.*

Jeremy isn't naïve, but he's only seen one porn movie in this life. Junior year of high school, he and a couple of friends used their fake IDs to get into the Cinema Mayflower, a sleazy, sticky-floored place on 23rd Street. Jeremy can't recall much about the movie they watched. He just remembers how huge and overwhelming the screen seemed, how the sex was kind of gross, both too real and not real at all. Why did there have to be so many extremely close close-ups of penises and vaginas, so much thrusting and slurping?

"Some people are weird about it," Dawn says. He realizes she's been watching him closely. "Or creepy. Or judgmental. A lot of people."

"It's just your job," Jeremy says, trying to see the situation from Dawn's point of view. That's what he does whenever he has a serious talk with a chick. It's how he always knows the right thing to say. "It's not *who* you are."

She rests her head against his shoulder. She smells nice, like coconut oil and tiki smoke. "You can crash here as long as you want," she says.

CHAPTER 18

Jeremy eases right away into the flow of Martha Street. He waters the ferns when the girls forget and makes pancakes for breakfast on Sundays. He runs lines with Tammy when she has an audition for a low-budget slasher or a USC student film. He accompanies Tina to the dentist because dentists terrify her. Everyone agrees Jeremy doesn't need to pay any rent until he finds a job. He chips in now and then for food and pot.

He has his own bedroom, but most nights he crashes with Dawn. After a few weeks they transition naturally from friends to more than that. They don't put a label on it, though. They're with each other in what Jeremy discovers is a California way, in a way that just *is*, that you don't have to define or talk about.

"We are what we are," Dawn says, kissing him, pressing against him.

This is Jeremy's first adult relationship. He digs it. He digs Dawn. She shows him around LA. They hike up to the Griffith Park Observatory and ride the Ferris wheel on Santa Monica Pier. At the ring toss booth, Jeremy wins Dawn a stuffed panda. The carnival guy is pissed. He can't believe Jeremy's aim and suspects cheating. The carnival guy bans Jeremy from all future ring tossing.

"Well?" Dawn asks, teasing, as they walk away. "Were you cheating?"

"I'm cheating at life," Jeremy says, which is a joke but also kind of true.

Most evenings he and Dawn hang out at a club in Reseda, the Country Club, with other porn people—actors and actresses, directors, the guys who run the camera and the chicks who do makeup. Everyone in the business seems to know everyone else. After the club closes, sometimes a small crowd migrates to the house on Martha Street. Porn people, Jeremy discovers, aren't as wild as you might think. They do a fair amount of coke, but not significantly more than the waiters and line cooks back home at Wellingford's. An orgy breaks out once. Though does it count as an orgy when there are only four people involved? Jeremy's not sure.

Dawn tells Jeremy he can have sex with anyone he wants, it's cool, she doesn't mind. But here's the strange thing: Jeremy isn't really interested in having sex with anyone but Dawn. This is a first for him. When he's with Dawn, he's never imagining a different chick, the next chick, the even better chicks who are yet to come.

Jeremy wonders if he might be in love. How do you know when you're in love? It's a mystery to him.

Dawn isn't having sex with anyone but Jeremy, as far as he knows. He's cool either way. He's never been the jealous type. He's not even jealous when he goes to set a couple of times to watch her work. The fucking is just so *fake*, all the moaning and hair-flinging. Jeremy knows what Dawn looks like when she's having fun for real, and this isn't it, not even close. It's hard to be jealous when she's trying to keep from being jackhammered out of frame and a fake eyelash is coming loose and the director is eating a hoagie and Gordon, Dawn's co-star, is staring intensely down at his own dick and praying it stays hard.

When the director finally says cut, Dawn flops onto her back and pops her gum back in. She and Gordon continue the conversation they were having before the camera rolled. What's the best way from North Hollywood to LAX? Gordon has to pick up his mother at the airport tomorrow. Take the 405? No, not on a weekday. Take the 101. Or Laurel Canyon? It depends on what time of day.

The porn business, from what Jeremy can tell, is like any other business. Most people are cool. Maybe it's not *completely* like any other business. One day he's leaving a shoot—midway through because it's so boring—and he finds an actress named Samantha sitting on the curb, hugging her knees and sobbing. She's one of the youngest actresses Jeremy has met, just turned eighteen and starting out. Jeremy asks Samantha if she's okay, if she wants a glass of water or something. Before she can answer, a producer named Steve swoops in. Steve has Jeremy help him lead Samantha back inside.

"She just needs to rest for a few minutes," Steve assures Jeremy. "She'll be just fine."

Will she? Jeremy wonders if he should say something to Dawn, but then decides it's easier for everyone if he takes Steve's word for it.

Once in a while Dawn gets into a funk, after back-to-back-to-back shoots, for example, and just wants to soak in the tub with the lights off and a candle burning. When she finally comes out, Jeremy knows the right things to say and she bounces back pretty quickly. The next morning she'll be at the library, her usual cheerful self, researching nursing programs.

• • •

Jeremy blinks and, boom, already it's March. He's been in LA almost two months. He decides it must be about to happen soon, his career as an actor or producer taking off.

That night at the Country Club in Reseda, Jeremy crowds into a booth with Dawn and a few other porn people. He's listening to Gordon and Dawn discuss which Kinko's in the Valley is the best Kinko's (Gordon is possibly the most boring guy Jeremy has ever met), when the DJ plays a beat that sounds familiar. It takes a few bars for Jeremy to recognize "Gimme My Mule," by the Commodores, the song that made him a local TV star when he was eleven years old.

What a blast from the past. Jeremy still remembers his old moves. The Electric Slide! He remembers how his body would pulse with flecks of light from the mirror balls.

Everyone in the booth chips in for another pitcher of Bud. Porn people, even the actresses and actors, don't make much money. Jeremy was surprised how not much. He borrows three dollars from Dawn to pay for his share and offers to make the run to the bar.

While the bartender fills the pitcher, Jeremy scopes out the club. It's the same old crowd, the same faces and dance moves. After coming here three or four nights a week for two months, Jeremy feels like he's been coming here forever.

Except, wait—sitting in a booth, off in a shadowy corner of the club, is a group he hasn't seen before. Two guys and three chicks, all early twenties or so. The two guys, one black and one white, are wearing linen blazers with the sleeves pushed up to their elbows. One of the chicks has dark, dark lipstick. Another chick has blond hair cut in a glossy bob that reminds Jeremy of a movie star from the 1920s. The five of them are so sleek, so sophisticated, so effortlessly hip. Jeremy has a feeling the two guys wouldn't be caught dead in the plaid shirt Gordon is wearing, or maybe even the Polo Jeremy has on.

It's not just their looks, though. It's the way they're slouching and sipping their drinks and lazily checking out the room like—even though they've probably never been here before—they own the place.

Jeremy, who was always one of the cool kids growing up, recognizes his tribe. He's one of them.

He'll stroll over and say hi. That's the best approach, one that's never failed him: simple, direct, confident. Before he can make his move, though, one of the guys, the black dude, makes his way to the bar. Jeremy feels a pang of jealousy, how good-looking the dude is. He's Kevin Bacon if Kevin Bacon had light brown skin and sparkling green eyes. He's an even-better-looking Kevin Bacon, in other words.

"An Old Fashioned," the black dude tells the bartender. "With rye, of course, not bourbon."

The black dude glances over at Jeremy and lifts a skeptical eyebrow—like they're in this together, like they both understand how unlikely it is the bartender knows how to make a proper Old Fashioned.

"Good luck with that," Jeremy says.

The black dude smirks. When he smirks, his lips purse, a small perfect heart. "My thoughts exactly. And you are?"

"Jeremy."

"Cushing."

Cushing? Jeremy's not sure he's heard the name correctly, but he doesn't ask him to repeat it. That would be, he understands instinctively, a grievous faux pas. Jeremy would come across as a hick.

Jeremy, the first time Dawn brought him here, thought the Country Club was exciting and hip, so far removed from Oklahoma City it existed in a completely different universe. But now he sees the club through Cushing's eyes—the old-fashioned music, the painted cement floor and chipped wooden tables, all the hair and clothes and makeup that were on MTV *last year.*

"What brings you to the Valley?" Cushing says, giving *Valley* another heart-shaped smirk.

How Jeremy answers the question will determine if he's in or out. He considers various options. He has one shot. He has to say the right thing.

"My girlfriend is a porn star," he says. He shrugs. "What can you do?"

Cushing smiles and slaps Jeremy on the back. "Outrageous! I love it. Come join us, won't you?"

Jeremy glances over at Dawn. She's watching him, head cocked, wondering why he hasn't returned to the booth yet. He gives her a quick wave. She'll be fine. She's got Gordon and the others to keep her company for a while.

"Why not?" Jeremy says. He leaves the pitcher of beer on the bar and happily follows Cushing into the shadows.

CHAPTER 19

Jeremy gets back to the house on Martha Street just before sunrise. He strips off his clothes and slides into bed with Dawn. She stirs, lifts her head.

"Where did you go last night?"

"I met some people."

"You just disappeared. You didn't even say goodbye."

He concentrates, conjures, searching deep inside himself for exactly the right true emotion. Apologizing for something like this is completely different from apologizing for a missed shift at work or a small loan from your sister you can't pay back.

"I'm so stupid," he says. "Dawn, I'm sorry."

She pecks his cheek and wriggles deeper into her pillow. "It's fine."

He rolls onto his back and tries to sleep. What a night! Cushing and his friends are outrageous. At the Country Club, they took turns making predictions for the various patrons. *He* with the shag haircut will be a drive-time disc jockey in Omaha soon. *She* with the halter top will be pregnant, waddling around a double-wide while her husband sleeps off a bender. "We call this going on safari," Cushing confides to Jeremy. "It's amusing every now and then."

By midnight, the Country Club had ceased to amuse, so Cushing and his friends jetted to a birthday party in the Hollywood Hills. Jeremy came along—of course he did, it was just assumed. *He was one of them*. At the birthday party, Cushing introduced Jeremy to agents and producers. *Real* agents and producers, not porn ones. The house was mostly glass, with views of the city below that made Jeremy feel like he was upside down, whooshing through space, surrounded by stars. The coke Cushing shared with him, incredibly pure, made the experience even more vivid.

Late in the night, or early in the morning, Cushing led Jeremy deep into the house, up the stairs and down a series of hallways, to show him the birthday boy's walk-in closet. Wow. The closet was as big as, and better stocked than, C.R. Anthony's, the best place to buy clothes back home. A wall of shoes, a wall of blazers and shirts, everything color-coordinated, a glass case filled with watches.

"You're a forty-two regular?" Cushing looked Jeremy over and plucked a black linen blazer off a hanger before Jeremy could answer. "Try this."

Jeremy slipped on the blazer. It fit him perfectly, the fabric rough and rich and beautiful.

"He'll never know it's gone," Cushing said.

Cushing is witty, suave, and knows everything that matters—where Jeremy should get his hair cut, which hotel in New York City is currently *the* hotel in New York City. And like Jeremy, he's a self-made man. The rest of his crowd all come from money—Yvonne's mother is an actual countess back in England—but Cushing grew up in South Central Los Angeles.

"The bona fide *ghett-o*," he confided to Jeremy. "One day I looked around. I was only six, seven years old. This is the truth, cross my heart. I looked around and said to myself, 'I am *not* one of these people. I will *not* spend my life like this.'"

Jeremy has always pictured his life unfolding on sort of a *Donkey Kong–*esque scaffolding. Sometimes he walks along a plank and hops over a barrel, sometimes he climbs up a ladder. Every now and then, he takes a huge leap—*boing*—and makes a ton of extra progress. Last night was like that.

"I get it," Jeremy said. "I totally get it."

Cushing nodded. "You get it. I know you do."

• • •

A couple of days later, a little before midnight, Cushing calls. "I'll pick you up in half an hour," Cushing says. "We're going to be vampires."

They drive to Malibu in Cushing's BMW, past Point Dume, to a decrepit old motel on Pacific Coast Highway. A production company is shooting a low-budget horror flick and needs extras. It's a blast. Jeremy and Cushing are issued plastic fangs and blood-soaked concert T-shirts to wear (Kiss for Cushing, Judas Priest for Jeremy). They get to creep and hiss and claw at locked motel doors. The director singles out Cushing. "Very convincing, kid," he says.

After their scenes wrap, Jeremy and Cushing cross the highway to the beach with two sexy female vampires. They do some coke and fool around with the chicks as the sun comes up. The chicks write their phone numbers on a Ralphs receipt, but during the drive back to civilization Cushing tears up the piece of paper and lets the wind whip away the scraps.

"We can do better," he says.

Jeremy nods. He's thinking exactly the same thing.

Almost every night for the next few weeks Jeremy goes out with Cushing and his friends. Cushing knows all the hottest spots, the spots just coming to a boil. During the day they comb through the vintage stores on Melrose, like Flip and Aardvark's, looking for a vest that matches the one Bogart wears in *Petrified Forest*, or a driving cap like Belmondo's in *Breathless*. During long, traffic-clogged drives back and forth across town, Cushing points out the sites of various heinous crimes while Jeremy flips through the magazines Cushing has assigned him to read (*GQ*, *Interview*, *The Paris Review*).

Jeremy hardly ever sees Dawn anymore. He understands chicks and senses trouble brewing, so he invites Dawn to come out with him and Cushing on Friday night—to check out a new club on Sunset, it'll be a blast.

It *is* a blast. Cushing turns on the charm, just like Jeremy knows he will. Yvonne is kind of a snob to Dawn, and so is Lance, but that's just Yvonne and Lance. And Dawn is weirdly uptight with them, not making any effort to fit in. With people like Yvonne and Lance, you have to *try*. It's fine if you're from Oregon or Oklahoma, but you don't have to advertise it.

Dawn bails early and takes a cab back to the Valley. Jeremy isn't worried, though. Dawn loves Cushing. That's the important thing.

Except Dawn doesn't love Cushing. She can't even stand him.

"What?" Jeremy says the next morning, when she breaks the surprising news. "I thought . . ."

"He's so fake. Just so . . ." She shakes her head. "I can't explain it. I don't trust him. The way he was just telling me what I wanted to hear."

Why is telling someone what they want to hear such a terrible thing? Jeremy wonders. That's called friendly conversation.

"How can you not like him?" Jeremy says. "We could be brothers. We're so much alike!"

Dawn is studying him. "That's kind of true," she says, which makes Jeremy feel better.

CHAPTER 20

That afternoon Cushing takes Jeremy to the opening-day game at Dodger Stadium. A friend gave Cushing two tickets for seats right behind home plate. Jeremy and Cushing drink beer and look for celebrities in the crowd. After a couple of innings, Jeremy realizes that he and Cushing are getting some glances themselves. People think *they* might be celebrities.

After the game, they swing by Cushing's place. Jeremy hasn't seen where Cushing lives yet. He only knows that Cushing rents a room in Holmby Hills, in a house a few blocks off Sunset.

A wrought-iron gate swings open and Cushing pulls his BMW into a forest of towering trees. At the end of the drive is a rambling three-story house—a *mansion*, no exaggeration—with witch-hat turrets, multiple chimneys, bright purple shutters. Jeremy gawks. Three houses in the Valley could fit inside of this one. Four.

Cushing smiles. "Not bad, is it? Welcome to Chez Mais Oui."

"Mais oui?"

"It means 'but of course,' in French. The house philosophy."

Inside, the mansion feels both spacious—soaring wood-beamed ceilings; rooms that stretch forever—and cozy. Funky art hangs on the walls. A reproduction of a Warhol tomato soup can. Or is it a genuine Warhol tomato soup can? A leopard skin rug and a chandelier made from old fishing lures. Jeremy tries to identify the heavy but pleasant smell. Baking bread mixed with sandalwood mixed with pot. He searches for a word to describe the place. *Magical*.

Cushing's room is on the second floor. His *room*? Jeremy gawks. Cushing has an entire suite—a large living area; an even larger bedroom; a private bathroom with an enormous claw-foot tub; a second, smaller bedroom, filled with books, that he uses for a study. The study has a balcony that looks out over a vast, wild, overgrown garden.

"Wow. How much do you . . ." Jeremy says before he can stop himself. It's never cool to ask how much something costs. Cool people don't need to know how much something costs.

"Just a token payment now and then," Cushing says. "I do some errands for Anna."

"She owns all this?"

"Of course. You should meet her. What am I thinking? I need to introduce you."

Out back is a crescent-shaped pool, sunk deep in the shade of trees and climbing vines. A woman sits cross-legged on the end of the diving board, eyes closed. Her strawberry blond hair is epic—thick and riotous. She's wearing a flowing, gauzy, transparent sarong over a bathing suit and huarache sandals.

"Hi!" she says. She opens her eyes and stands. Her epic hair reaches all the way past her butt. She spreads her arms wide. "So, you're Jeremy!"

"So, you're Anna!" Jeremy says.

She walks the length of the diving board, bouncing with every step, and gives Jeremy a hug. Anna smells like the house, even better. Jeremy breathes her in. She places a warm palm against each of his cheeks and examines his face intently, like she's trying to memorize it.

"Jeremy!"

"Anna!"

She's about his mom's age, he guesses, or maybe a few years younger. Mid-thirties? Pretty in an ordinary sort of way, no makeup, a sunburned nose. Jeremy has seen photos of his mom in the sixties: sleek, glossy, a blond Jackie Kennedy. He bets Anna, in the sixties, was a hippie, a flower child turning happy circles at some music festival, her hair swirling.

The three of them go inside. Anna makes tea. "Cushing's told me a lot about you," she tells Jeremy. "Now it's your turn."

Jeremy gives her a few basic facts: where he's from, his plan to become an actor or producer or both, how his father used to be in the Vegas mob.

Jeremy doesn't usually mention that last part, but he wants to win Anna over, to make sure she finds him memorable. There's something mysteriously bewitching about her, but he can tell she doesn't want to fuck him. Her energy toward both Jeremy and Cushing feels extremely maternal.

When Jeremy asks Anna about herself, because usually that's what people like to talk about, themselves, she waves him off. "I'm boring," she says.

"Jeremy wants to move in," Cushing says. He's finished his tea and is rolling a joint.

What? But then Jeremy immediately realizes he absolutely *does* want to move in. Cushing plucked the idea out of his head the instant before he thought it.

"You don't want to stay in the Valley," Cushing tells Jeremy as he hands the joint to Anna. "Your porn star's a sweetheart, don't get me wrong."

Cushing leaves the *but* unsaid. Still, it rings out, echoing down the long hallways of the mansion. *But she's a* porn star. *She lives in the* Valley. *Don't let her drag you down to her level.*

"*Mais oui*," Anna says. "We'd love to have you."

She inhales, holds the smoke in her lungs, and waits for Jeremy to answer. Jeremy hesitates, but only for a second. He's genuinely happy in the Valley. He's genuinely happy with Dawn. But he'll be *happier* here. Decisions are easy when it's that simple.

"I'd love to be had," Jeremy says.

CHAPTER 21

Jeremy ends it with Dawn—gently, quickly, decisively. That's always the best approach. Her eyes water, but Dawn is a grown-up. She's tough. She won't fall apart just because someone breaks her heart. Jeremy appreciates that about her. She hugs him goodbye and tells him to please take care of himself.

Standing on the lawn with his suitcases and his box, waiting for Cushing to pick him up, Jeremy is a little melancholy. What if he *is* in love with Dawn? What if he's making the wrong decision here?

That's not a question he asks himself very often. Luckily, the thought is fleeting. By the time Cushing pulls up, a few minutes later, Jeremy is feeling just fine.

Anna situates Jeremy on the ground floor, the east wing. The digs aren't quite as deluxe as Cushing's, no living area and a small patio instead of a balcony, but they're still outrageous. A glorious sunset view; a massive canopied bed; an ornately framed mirror on every wall. The Reflection Rooms, Anna calls it.

Best of all, Jeremy's new quarters come with a set of wheels he can use whenever he wants, a classic 1968 Firebird with a metallic silver paint job and a bad attitude. Anna asks if he likes the car. *Mais oui.*

One other person lives in the mansion, Rex, on the second floor, west wing. Anna calls Rex, Cushing, and Jeremy her "kiddos." Jeremy likes Rex. He's freckly and not as good-looking as Cushing or Jeremy, so no competition there, and he's a hoot, always cracking jokes and doing celebrity impressions. Beautiful women sometimes prefer a guy like Rex, Cushing explains to Jeremy. Rex makes them laugh. He makes them feel safe.

A typical lazy day at Chez Mais Oui starts with breakfast around ten. Anna likes to cook. Omelets, crepes, exotic Middle Eastern spreads with mysterious ingredients. Afternoons, Jeremy hangs out by the pool with Anna. They smoke pot and chat. She's traveled almost everywhere—India, Germany, Argentina. And sure enough, just like Jeremy speculated, Anna was a total hippie in the sixties. She lived in a commune in the desert, hitch-hiked across the country, dropped acid a few times with Charles Manson.

"Before everything got so weird," she clarifies. "When he was just normal ol' Charlie. Before he let some destructive people into his life."

In the evening, Jeremy and Cushing hit the town. The '84 Olympics start in a couple of months and LA is pulsing with energy and excitement. Every night is an E ticket, thrilling and unpredictable. Anything can happen. Yvonne cranks the BMW up to 110 on Mulholland and nearly rear-ends a prom limo. A chick Lance picks up at a club passes out. He leaves her floating naked on a rubber raft in the pool of the Sunset Hyatt.

Jeremy doesn't have any illusions about Cushing and his crowd. They're not "nice" people. If Jeremy gets the flu, they won't make soup for him and hold his hand. But they're so much more fun and wild and glamorous than Dawn and her friends—never, ever boring.

• • •

A month passes. The June gloom creeps over the beach communities, the temperature climbs in the hills, and hordes of tourists descend everywhere, dressed head to toe in red, white, and blue.

Anna still hasn't informed Jeremy how he'll be earning his keep at Chez Mais Oui. No problem. What's the rush? Jeremy concentrates on his act-ing career. He practices different audition monologues (Brando from *On the Waterfront*, Tom Cruise from *Risky Business*) and thinks about taking some acting classes. He has coffee with a talent agent he meets at a party. Or the guy is almost but not quite yet a talent agent. Jeremy is fuzzy about that. Either way, he's very encouraging about Jeremy's prospects.

"I have a project for you," Anna finally says one evening. "Cushing will show you the ropes."

"Cool."

"You start tonight."

Anna leads Jeremy out onto the patio so she can examine him in the golden-hour light. Jeremy is wearing his best vintage velvet blazer, the color of dark wine, his best brand-new stonewashed jeans, spotless white Converse high-tops. He worked on his hair for half an hour upstairs. It's the perfect balance between shaggy and sculpted.

Anna nods her approval. "Just be yourself," she says.

"I can do that," Jeremy says. "My specialty."

The event is a fundraiser at the Los Angeles County Museum of Art. Very stiff, very sedate. A string quartet, the soft clinking of champagne flutes, nobody—other than Jeremy, Cushing, and the catering staff—a day under forty. A day under *fifty*.

Jeremy and Cushing grab some champagne and take a turn around the room. Jeremy tries to figure out what they're doing here. Whatever Anna has planned for him is probably illegal and possibly risky. You don't get to live in a magical mansion without a few strings attached. Which is cool with him. Jeremy isn't opposed to probably illegal and possibly risky, not as long as the payoff is worth it.

His best guess, until now, was that he'd have to move some drugs from Point A to Point B for Anna. But . . . *here*? Among a bunch of old folks shuffling around while a string quartet warbles?

"See her?" Cushing nods discreetly. "The woman over by the second-tier Picasso. With her hair up, the Oscar de la Renta dress."

"I see her."

"You're going to seduce her."

"Oh."

"You understand now?"

Jeremy thinks so. Yeah, of course. The pieces of the puzzle start clicking together—why Anna picked him, why she picked Cushing and Rex.

"She's rich," Jeremy says.

"Very rich," Cushing says. "And lonely. Anna's research is thorough and meticulous. I can vouch for that. Your lady's name is Dolores Green."

"So, it's like . . . blackmail?"

"No." Cushing scoffs. "Nothing like that. Nothing unsavory. Dolores has been divorced for fifteen years. Your lady falls in love with you. Or falls in lust, either way. You get access to her checkbook, her accounts. We help ourselves to a little off the top. She won't even notice it's gone."

Jeremy observes Dolores Green. "His" lady. She's probably around sixty-five but looks younger than that. An LA sixty-five, not an Oklahoma City sixty-five. Taut and tan skin, shapely calves, silvery-blond hair in a fancy bun. She is, he supposes, attractive for a sixty-five-year-old woman. But . . . *sixty-five*. That's—Jeremy does some quick math in his head—more than three times older than he is. She could be his grandmother. And he's supposed to . . .

"How much of it do I get?" he says.

"Ten percent, plus the room, board, et cetera."

"And how much is ten percent?"

"It depends. You won't be disappointed. It won't be less than five thousand."

"Five thousand?"

Cushing takes Jeremy's arm and steers him over to the bar so they won't get caught watching the lady.

"I'll share a few tips with you," Cushing says. "You're a natural, but you're in the big leagues now."

Five thousand dollars. At *least*. While he continues to live like a prince. Jeremy accepts a flute of champagne from the bartender and downs it in one gulp. An old man in a tuxedo hobbles up to them. He jabs his cigar at Jeremy.

"Where the hell's Roger?"

"Roger already left," Cushing says, not missing a beat. "He decided to go home early."

"Nuts!" the old man says, and hobbles away.

"Now listen carefully," Cushing tells Jeremy.

Get her attention. Let *her* come to you. Or at least make her think that's what happened. *Intrigue* her from afar. Never rush, but don't hide your desire either. Women that age, the women Anna finds, they're desperate to feel *heat* again.

Jeremy feels a pinch of annoyance. Cushing might know more than Jeremy when it comes to fashion and movies and where the best parties are, but Jeremy was *born* to do this. He was *raised* to do this. He's a *Mercurio*.

"Anna only has one rule," Cushing says. "Never, ever, ever go freelance. We work for Anna. *Anna* chooses the projects and supervises them. She's very serious about that."

"Got it."

"You're sure? You do *not* want to get on Anna's bad side. I cannot stress that enough."

Dolores Green is chatting with another older woman. The conversation is about to fizzle out—Jeremy can tell from the body language. He can tell from the body language that the other woman will turn left, Dolores right. A painting—a brown-skinned man with angel wings made from flower blossoms—hangs a few steps away. Jeremy can stand and admire the painting. Dolores will run right into him.

And she does.

CHAPTER 22

It sure beats waiting tables. Instead of hot kitchens and demanding customers, Jeremy gets shopping trips to Barney's, evenings at the ballet, and a weekend jaunt to Palm Springs. *He* can be the demanding customer now, at the best restaurants in LA. And Dolores is pleasant and intelligent. She's *lovely*. That's a word Dolores uses a lot. The view from the hotel patio is *lovely*. The chopped salad at La Scala is *lovely*.

Jeremy doesn't mind the sex. Dolores keeps her eyes closed the whole time so Jeremy can too. He floats in the darkness and imagines he's with Suzanne Somers or Yvonne, Cushing's girlfriend. Obviously, Dolores's body doesn't *feel* like a body that belongs to Suzanne Somers or Yvonne—it's too sharp and boney in some places, too pliant and fleshy in others. Jeremy's strategy, though, is surprisingly effective.

They don't have sex that often anyway, just once or twice a week. What Dolores really craves is Jeremy's company. She seems happiest when they're just strolling down Rodeo together or driving along PCH or sharing a dessert at an outdoor café, discreetly holding hands under the table.

Anna is delighted by how quickly and comprehensively Jeremy braids himself into Dolores's life. Jeremy sees the gleam of jealousy in Cushing's eye. Jeremy was confident he'd be good at this. Turns out he's *excellent* at this. With Dolores, Jeremy taps into that special talent of his. He finds a way to truly and genuinely *mean* it, in the moment, when he tells her how much he wants her, how much he loves her.

Barely five weeks after Jeremy bumps into Dolores at the LACMA fundraiser, she writes a first check to "Leo Maxwell," the name Jeremy is going by: ten thousand dollars to pay for an experimental leukemia treatment that "Leo's" sister, "Allison," desperately needs.

"Dolores, no, I can't, I can't take your money," Jeremy says. But she squeezes his hand and insists.

"Allison" improves dramatically, experiences a devastating setback, rallies heroically. Each time Dolores writes another check.

"Don't feel guilty," Cushing says. "These women have more money than God. They're giving us crumbs."

Jeremy doesn't feel guilty. Dolores is having a wonderful summer, the best summer she's had in years. How can you put a price on that?

By the beginning of August, as Mary Lou Retton wins the individual all-around gold medal in gymnastics, Dolores has signed over a grand total of sixty thousand dollars. Anna decides to call it. Dolores is good for another fifty or so grand, potentially, but the risk increases exponentially. She'll start to wonder. It's better to quit while they're ahead.

Jeremy argues they should keep going. He knows Dolores better than Anna does. Dolores won't get suspicious. She's good for another *hundred* grand, at least. Why not push this as far as it can go?

Anna pinches Jeremy's cheek affectionately. "Don't be greedy," she says. "The road to hell is paved with greedy."

So, Jeremy (Leo) exits Dolores's life. Leo moves back home to Iowa to help care for Allison. He'll call Dolores every day, twice a day. He'll return as soon as he can. Et cetera.

LA is a big city. Jeremy won't accidentally run into Dolores. If he does, he'll have a story ready to go, just in case. His sister's suffering and painful death crushed him. He can barely get out of bed in the morning. Et cetera.

A few days later, at breakfast, Anna presents Jeremy with an envelope. Inside are sixty crisp one-hundred-dollar bills, six thousand bucks, Jeremy's ten percent cut of Dolores Green.

"Nicely done, old chap," Cushing tells Jeremy. It's just the two of them now, sitting on the edge of the pool with their chinos rolled up, their bare feet stirring the water. "Very nicely done."

But Cushing's been cool to Jeremy lately. Jeremy thinks he sees it again, that gleam of jealousy in Cushing's eye.

"You taught me everything I know," Jeremy says. A lie, but Jeremy knows he should stay in the good graces of someone like Cushing.

"The pupil surpasses the master. Or so our dear Anna seems to believe. You're her new favorite."

Jeremy shakes his head. "That's absurd. You'll always be her favorite, Cush. There's no doubt."

Cushing claps a hand to Jeremy's shoulder and squeezes, a bit too forcefully. He smiles a bit too forcefully. "Right you are, old man."

CHAPTER 23

Lazy September. Lazy October. Jeremy experiences the Santa Ana winds for the first time—not as forceful as the wind in Oklahoma, but hotter and drier, with a strangely ominous aftertaste.

Anna hasn't found a new project for him yet. Jeremy hangs out mostly with Rex now, since Cushing started a new lady on Labor Day and isn't around much. Rex is fun enough, but he doesn't cover the tab like Cushing did when Jeremy was still an apprentice. Jeremy is amazed by how rapidly six thousand dollars can dwindle to almost nothing. Nights out, new clothes, more new clothes, a new watch, a new bumper for the Firebird when he gets drunk and clocks a telephone pole.

"Patience, kiddo," Anna says when Jeremy bugs her about his next assignment. "All good things come to those who wait."

Jeremy misses Dawn. Not all the time, but more than he expected. He can picture their future together. They'll be happy. They'll have kids. Jeremy will be a husband, a father. It's a truly great future!

But is it the *best* future? Jeremy's instincts say *no*. He trusts his instincts. They've always served him well.

A few days before Halloween, he and Rex crash a party in Bel Air. Rex heard about it from Cushing. Why is Cushing tipping off Rex and not Jeremy? Jeremy doesn't worry about it. Cushing, once he finishes his project, once he thinks he's Anna's favorite again, will come around.

The party is a wrap party for a music video, a band called Mr. Mister, a video for a song called "Hunters of the Night." Jeremy gives the party four out of five stars. No big movie stars, unless you consider Judge Reinhold from *Fast Times at Ridgemont High* and *Gremlins* a big movie star, but lots of drugs and people leaping naked into the pool. The two main guys from Mr. Mister mingle awkwardly. Jeremy is glad he's not them. This is it, probably, the highlight of their lives. Jeremy would not want this to be the highlight of his life.

Rex is talking to two chicks. They're way out of his league, but he's cracking them up. Rex's dream is to be on *Saturday Night Live* someday. He's more interested in trying out new material than getting one of the chicks in bed.

Jeremy's attention wanders. He notices a woman standing by herself. She's a lot older than everyone else at the party—in her sixties like Dolores, though not trying as hard as Dolores does to look younger. She's wearing a simple but classy white blouse, a simple but classy gray skirt, not much jewelry, none of it flashy. Her expression is stern, and she reminds Jeremy of Julie Andrews in *Mary Poppins* before Mary Poppins turned out to be fun. What's a woman like this doing at a wrap party for a New Wave music video? She seems bored out of her mind.

Rex has finished his set and the two chicks have wandered off. Jeremy pokes him with an elbow. "Who's that over there?" he says. "The lady by herself?"

"Her?" Rex growls. "Of all the gin joints in the world, she walks into mine."

It's a fairly excellent Bogart impression, but Jeremy's heard it a hundred times. "Rex, be serious for two seconds. Do you know who she is or not?"

"Sure. That's Penelope Schwartz. Sid Schwartz's mother."

"Sid Schwartz?"

"*You* be serious. Sid Schwartz the real estate tycoon? The movie mogul? The dark prince of—"

"Stop," Jeremy says before Rex spins off into some new long riff. "So her son is some rich guy?"

"Very rich."

Jeremy watches the woman, Penelope Schwartz, stifle a yawn. Her son is rich, which means *she* must be rich too. And Jeremy doesn't see a wedding ring. Hmm. What if Penelope Schwartz is rich *and* lonely?

"I might," Jeremy says, "go say hello."

It takes a second for Rex to catch Jeremy's drift. "No way, man," Rex says. "Don't even think about it. Anna will flip out. It's her one rule."

No freelancing. Yeah, yeah, Jeremy knows the rule. By carefully selecting and screening each candidate herself, Anna reduces the risks and protects her kiddos. Or so says Anna. Who, Jeremy has noticed, takes ninety percent of the profits while he and the others do a hundred percent of the heavy lifting.

And how long will Jeremy have to just sit around until Anna decides he's ready for his next project? Jeremy needs cash. At the very least he should be allowed, between jobs for Anna, to use his talents to support himself.

There are two kinds of people, his mom says. Those who do what they're told and those who get the most out of life. Jeremy loves the way his mom glides through any situation, past every expectation, bending the world toward *her.*

Jeremy is a *Mercurio.* And since when does a Mercurio follow the rules?

"Anna won't ever know," he tells Rex.

"She'll find out."

"She won't."

"You don't know Anna."

"I just want to test the waters. I'll give you a share if you don't say anything."

"She'll still find out. Jeremy, listen to me. Do not, I repeat do *not,* fuck with Anna. There was the kid who worked for her, before my time. He went behind her back and she got him arrested. He's in *prison* now."

Doubtful, Jeremy thinks. That sounds suspiciously like a tall tale meant to scare pussies like Rex. But Jeremy better be smart. Rex is such a pussy he'll probably spill the beans to Anna.

"You're right," Jeremy says. "It's a bad idea."

"It's a worse than bad idea. That kid is serving like twenty years in San Quentin."

"Okay! I agree. Forget I said anything. Can you manage that?"

"Yeah," Rex says. "Good. Now let's get out of here."

"Meet me out front," Jeremy says. "I just need to take a leak first."

• • •

No, of course, Jeremy doesn't need to take a leak. Only Rex would fall for that. Jeremy waits till the coast is clear, then moseys over to Penelope Schwartz.

"You're not enjoying this," he says.

Penelope Schwartz turns to regard him. She has large owlish eyes, dark and unblinking. Jeremy guesses her stare makes most people uncomfortable, but he's okay with it. Almost nothing makes him uncomfortable.

"Why *would* I be enjoying this?" she says.

"The hijinks? The major motion picture stars like Judge Reinhold?"

She snorts softly.

"My name's Jeff," he says. "Jeff Cushing."

"Goodbye, Jeff. I'm not interested."

She walks away before Jeremy has a chance to open his mouth again. Jeremy, surprised, watches her briskly circle the pool, dodging cannonball splashes, and enter the house. He replays the conversation in his mind, but it's like a movie that ends before the opening credits are over.

What just happened? He has no idea.

A Mr. Mister taps out a melody on an electronic keyboard. A few people gather around a stage that's been set up and applaud politely.

Jeremy follows Penelope Schwartz into the house. He only has a minute before he has to meet Rex out front. He doesn't see her anywhere. The living area of the house is massive and packed.

There she is. Working her way toward the door with steady, steely determination. Jeremy spots an angle, cuts over, intercepts her.

"You're not interested in what?" he says.

"Pardon me?"

"You said, 'Goodbye, I'm not interested.'"

"Jeff, is it?"

"Yes."

"You have a certain charm. And you're a very nice-looking young man. I'm sure you're a wonderful aspiring actor or director or screenwriter. But if you want to talk to my son, you'll have to find a different approach. Goodbye."

She turns away, but finds her path blocked by—God bless him—Judge Reinhold. Judge Reinhold is regaling a flock of chicks with an amusing story from the set of *Fast Times at Ridgemont High*. "And then Sean comes out of his trailer, and he's so pissed off."

"What if I want to talk to *you*?" Jeremy says.

Penelope Schwartz sighs. "And why would that be?"

"Because you're the only person here who seems worth talking to. You remind me of Julie Andrews in *Mary Poppins*, before Mary Poppins turns out to be fun."

Her gaze penetrates him again. This time, though, there's also the faintest curl of a smile. It's taken more effort than Jeremy is accustomed to, but he finally has her attention.

"You're suggesting I'm not fun?" she says.

"I'm suggesting you, like Mary Poppins, are not all that meets the eye."

The faint curl of a smile remains. "I *should* introduce you to my son. You're as full of shit as he is."

"Can I call you sometime?" Jeremy says.

Judge Reinhold shifts his attention toward a redhead who looks just like Molly Ringwald—there are at least three different redheads here who look just like Molly Ringwald—and Penelope Schwartz makes her move. She edges past him, toward the front door.

"You don't have my number," she calls over her shoulder to Jeremy, which he notes isn't a *no*. In fact, it's almost as good as a *yes*.

CHAPTER 24

Penelope Schwartz is going to kill Jeremy. She's prickly, perceptive, suspicious—nothing at all like Dolores, or really any woman Jeremy has ever met. She snorts when Jeremy tells her how lovely she is. She rolls her eyes when Jeremy tells her how smart and sophisticated she seems.

She's impossible to seduce!

Jeremy has to call her three times before she agrees to have coffee with him. Just coffee! And she only *grudgingly* agrees. They have coffee twice before she grudgingly agrees to lunch. They have lunch twice before they go on their first dinner date—and that's just hot dogs at Pink's, which doesn't really count as a dinner date at all.

Jeremy almost gives up at least once a day. Alice claims that he's never had to work for anything in his life. Well, he works his ass off for Penelope Schwartz. The biggest obstacle for Jeremy: Penelope is extremely difficult to read. Most chicks show him right away what they want. And Jeremy delivers the exact right flavor of himself—kind, aloof, edgy, passionate, cool, casual, serious, a touch of this, a splash of that. He's a bartender mixing a drink. Penelope is a customer who demands a delicious drink but won't give the bartender anything to go on. *Surprise me.*

It's exhausting. Every single conversation, Jeremy has to stay on his toes. He has to make sure Penelope stays on *her* toes. Because that's it, actually, he eventually realizes: she wants him to be *surprising*.

Why is Jeremy putting so much effort into Penelope Schwartz? He's not really sure. The potential payday is a big part of it, definitely. Suppose he makes sixty thousand dollars from Penelope like he did from Dolores Green. Jeremy's share will be *sixty thousand dollars*. It will probably be even more than that. Jeremy's done some (discreet) asking around, people he knows at clubs and parties, and Penelope's son, Sid Schwartz, isn't just very rich but very very rich, as filthy as it gets.

It's not just about the money, though. If it was, Jeremy would ditch Penelope and find an easier freelance project for himself, someone like Dolores. So . . . what then?

Their second dinner together, a real dinner this time, at a real restaurant. They're discussing countries of the world. Penelope asks Jeremy which country he'd most like to visit. He scrambles to think of a surprising, non-obvious choice. But not a *too* nonobvious choice either. He can't say something boring like France or Italy, but he also can't say, like, Pakistan. That would just be weird.

She sets her wineglass down and owl-eyes Jeremy. "Forget about that," she says. "Who are you? What do you want from me? Really?"

Caught off-balance, Jeremy has only an instant to decide on the best approach. Penelope Schwartz won't give him a second chance to get it right. Not now, not ever.

"You're driving me crazy," he says, going with the truth—which he hasn't realized is the truth until right this moment. "This is usually easy for me. It's *always* easy for me. But I'm, like, barely hanging on."

She nods. "Barely."

He might *not* hang on. He might fail, *lose*, for once in his life. Jeremy doesn't want to fail or to lose, but the possibility is kind of a rush. What a humiliation it will be if he can't manage to score with a pleasant-looking but not particularly beautiful sixty-five-year-old woman. What a triumph it will be if he can manage to score with *this* prickly, perceptive, and suspicious sixty-five-year-old woman.

"So, you enjoy a challenge," she says.

"Not really. Not usually."

"Do you want to know why I allow you to hang on? Barely? Even though I know I'm ridiculous?"

"I keep you on your toes."

Penelope considers that. "I suppose you do."

"But that's not the main reason?"

"No."

"What is it?"

She reaches across the table. She grips his thumb in her palm with surprising force and what he thinks might be actual affection, the first sign of it she's shown.

"I don't miss being twenty-one," she says, "but I'm ashamed to admit I do miss being fucked by a twenty-one-year-old."

They skip dessert and go back to her place—her gated estate—in Bel Air. The Mexican housekeeper bows and vanishes. Upstairs, Jeremy leans in to kiss Penelope, savoring the fucking *triumph* of this moment, and she pushes him away.

"None of that," she says. "Take your clothes off. Slowly. Stand over there."

He takes his clothes off. Slowly. Shoes, socks, jeans, shirt. Finally, he drops his boxers. He's already hard. His cock, Jeremy learned from Dolores, is always up for action, even if the action is three times his age.

After a moment, Penelope steps out of her shoes and unzips her dress. Underneath she's wearing . . . Jeremy's not sure what it's called. A slip, maybe? Like a second, shorter dress. Dolores wore normal bras and panties, so he's only seen a slip in old movies. She leaves it on.

"Put on a condom. In the bedside table. And I bought lubricant too."

"You've thought of everything."

"No talking."

She gets in bed. Jeremy eases himself on top of her, eases himself into her, taking it slow even though he's used a ton of K-Y. He's deciding which chick he'll imagine fucking—Suzanne Somers always comes through for him—when Penelope pinches his earlobe, hard.

"Keep your eyes open," she says.

"You can't just order me around," he says, only half-joking.

"No talking."

He picks up the pace, annoyed but also mysteriously aroused. Let's see how she likes what happens when she orders him around.

"Good," she manages to say between short, sharp breaths. "Harder. You're not going to break me."

CHAPTER 25

Anna doesn't have a clue about Penelope Schwartz. Neither does Cushing, or Rex. If anyone asks where he's going or where he's been, Jeremy always has a good lie ready to roll. He hooked up with a UCLA chick he met at a club called Fake. He's going to see a band at the Whisky. Which band? The Motels.

Jeremy does have one big problem, though. While he's giving Penelope what she wants, in and out of bed, he's not getting any closer to what *he* wants. She pays for their dinners out, but that's it. After six full weeks, Jeremy still hasn't been able to squeeze a dime out of Penelope. She snorts when he tells her his sister needs an experimental treatment. She changes the subject when he mentions he has to move to a new apartment and could use help with a security deposit.

It's a dilemma. Jeremy considers bailing. If Penelope hasn't written him a check by now, she never will. He's just wasting his time, heading deeper and deeper down a dead end.

Unless it's not a dead end. What if Jeremy is closer than he thinks to cashing in? Penelope's guard could be dropping. Her affection for him could be growing.

He can pull this off. He knows he can. He already did the impossible by seducing her. Now he just needs to be patient. He just needs to figure out some way to get a piece of Penelope's massive wealth. It would be stupid to give up now.

"I've decided to go to college," Jeremy says. He and Penelope are having Sunday brunch in the courtyard of a place on Montana Avenue, a few blocks from the beach. It's become their regular Sunday spot.

"You've decided to go to college," she says.

"But I can't afford it here. I'll have to move home to Nebraska. I'll have to live with my parents and take some classes at the community college."

Jeremy has spent a lot of time crafting this angle. It's a subtle but clear threat. If Penelope wants to keep Jeremy around much longer, she'll have to pay for the privilege. Plus, the thought of community college will horrify someone as rich as Penelope. The thought of Nebraska will horrify her even more. So if she cares for Jeremy even a little . . .

She lowers her fork and laughs. Jeremy has only rarely been able to make her laugh—rarely bordering on never—so this comes as a surprise.

"You? Moving back to Nebraska?" she says. "You expect me to believe that?"

"Yes. Why not? Yes." *Fuck.* Jeremy recognizes the flaw in his plan. She's right. She's called his silly bluff. It's totally implausible that he'd move back to a place like Nebraska, like Oklahoma.

"Don't sulk," she says. She calls the waiter over and tells him to bring Jeremy another mimosa.

"You like telling people what to do, don't you?" Jeremy says.

"Who doesn't?"

"I'll sulk if I want to."

She sighs. "You don't really want to go to college, do you?"

"No. I don't see the point."

"Good. It's fine for ordinary people."

The waiter brings Jeremy's mimosa. A spark of hope flares. Interesting. He notes that Penelope hasn't changed the subject or ignored, not exactly, his request for financial assistance. Has it occurred to her that while he'll never leave LA, he might leave *her*? Is he—finally, possibly—getting somewhere?

Jeremy debates whether it's smarter to keep pushing about the money, subtly, or drop the subject for the time being and follow up later. It's a coin toss. Penelope is so hard to read.

"Sid!" She's looking over Jeremy's shoulder. "You're late."

Jeremy turns. A short, heavyset guy in a suit strides up to their table and drops into an empty chair. Penelope's son, unmistakably. He has her build, her nose, her owlish eyes.

"I've got a goddamn business to run, Mother." He sticks out a hand for Jeremy to shake. "So, you must be Jeffrey. How are you?"

"Great, thanks." Jeremy shakes his hand. Penelope's son has a strong grip, an easy smile. Jeremy matches grip and smile both. Sid is good at making a stranger feel comfortable, Jeremy can tell right away. No, it's more than that. He's good at making a stranger feel like an old friend. Jeremy is good at that too. "How's your goddamn business?"

The son, Sid, laughs. "It's Sunday! I should be able to take one day a week off, don't you think?"

"You've never taken a day off in your life," Penelope says. She waves the waiter over again and orders a Bloody Mary, extra spicy and heavy on the vodka.

"I can order for myself, Mother."

"Why? Did I get it wrong?"

Sid grunts with pretend exasperation and leans over to peck her on the cheek. He turns back to Jeremy. "I see my mother didn't warn you. That I was coming to brunch."

"It's an excellent surprise," Jeremy says. His mind works. This *is* an excellent surprise. Penelope must be more attached to Jeremy than she's been letting on. Why else would she introduce him to her son? It's like a boyfriend meeting the parents, but in reverse. Now Jeremy just has to make a good impression.

That won't be easy. Sid is turning on the charm, but Jeremy suspects that deep down Sid can't be thrilled about his mother dating some kid young enough to be her grandson. Jeremy needs to win Sid over. No problem. Jeremy is up for the challenge. He's realizing more and more that's what was missing from his life back in Oklahoma City—challenges! Winning is always satisfying, but *more* satisfying when it's not guaranteed.

Sid snaps open his menu. "What are you having, Jeffrey?"

"The eggs Benedict, Mr. Schwartz."

"Good choice. And call me Sid, for fuck's sake. Let me tell you a story about this joint. I mean . . ." He stops, lets the comic tension build. "If my mother will allow it."

Penelope shoots him the bird. He grins.

"So, I was just getting started in the business," Sid says. "I'd been working in the mail room at Morris. They finally moved me onto a desk. Guess what my very first job was."

He tells a highly entertaining story—expertly polished to seem completely off-the-cuff—about tracking down an agent's stool sample that the doctor sent to the wrong lab. A coyote puppy ends up in the back seat of his car and the stool sample accidentally ends up in a take-out bag from this very joint.

Jeremy returns serve with the story about Club Mercurio (relocated to Omaha, renamed the Venus Lounge). A cocktail waitress's enraged ex-boyfriend shows up after closing, armed with a knife, and gets inside the club somehow. Jeremy the barback, eleven years old, stands his ground. He picks up the nearest weapon: a lime. A lime! "You better cool it," Jeremy tells the ex-boyfriend, trying to keep his voice from shaking. The ex-boyfriend can't take the absurdity of the situation. He shakes his head and leaves.

"Don't bring a knife to a lime fight!" Sid says.

The story is funny, but most importantly it sneakily illustrates Jeremy's loyalty, courage, and capacity for hard work at a very young age, qualities that Sid probably values. Also most importantly: Jeremy's story isn't quite as funny as Sid's. Jeremy is no fool.

The rest of brunch goes well too. Jeremy knows Sid is watching, so he pays just the right amount of attention to Penelope. Jeremy observes her, as she's talking, and finds fresh new things to like. A dimple when she smiles that he's never noticed before. The way she doesn't miss a beat when Sid discusses commission structures and gross points. Jeremy is a total gentleman, obviously—no hand-holding or shoulder-rubbing—but Sid can see he's genuinely smitten.

Jeremy offers, but Sid insists on picking up the check. He shakes Jeremy's hand again and this time also slaps him on the shoulder. "This was fun," he says. "Till next time."

Till next time. Good. Jeremy nailed it. He and Penelope drive back to her estate. Bring the money up again now? Jeremy decides to hold off a little longer. He'll let Penelope soak up the glow of brunch.

During sex, Jeremy has a new trick. He developed it because Penelope makes him keep his eyes open. He focuses tightly on her right pupil, so tightly all he sees is black, a black room, like a stage before the lights come on. And then he imagines the lights coming on and on the stage is a bed, and on the bed he's fucking (but also watching himself fuck) Suzanne Somers or Penelope's Mexican housekeeper or whoever. The Mexican housekeeper is in the bed onstage today, after brunch. It's a great trick. Penelope thinks he's looking deep into her soul.

"What did you think of Sid?" Penelope says, when Jeremy gets back from flushing the condom and getting a drink of water from the bathroom faucet.

"He's a really nice guy."

She watches Jeremy get dressed. Boxers, socks, chinos. He's halfway through the buttons of his dress shirt before she responds. "You're not joking."

"Joking?" He glances over at her. "No. Why would I be joking?"

"You think Sid is 'a really nice guy'?"

"Don't you?"

"Never mind."

Jeremy shrugs. There must be some complicated mother-son shit going on between the two of them that he's not aware of—and doesn't really care about. He finishes buttoning up his shirt.

"So, you never answered me." He takes a seat on the edge of the bed, next to Penelope, and traces a finger down her neck, along her bare shoulder. "About the college thing. About maybe getting a little help with that so I can stay in LA."

She reaches up and starts unbuttoning his shirt again. "Let me think about it. We might be able to arrange something."

Yes! Jeremy thinks as she pulls him closer, his lips to hers, and he gazes deep into the pupil of her right eye.

CHAPTER 26

Jeremy drives away from Penelope's estate high as a kite. Not drugs, not booze—it's the sweet rush of *success* that has him flying. *We might be able to arrange something.* That's a *yes*. Jeremy is a safecracker in a movie. Ingenuity, persistence, supernatural talent. The tumblers have dropped into place for him. The door of Penelope's vault is about to swing open.

He pulls into the parking lot of the YMCA on Santa Monica Boulevard. He always showers and changes before he heads back to Chez Mais Oui, with no trace of Penelope on him. Penelope wears a perfume called Shalimar, an old lady perfume, and Jeremy doesn't want to make Cushing or Anna suspicious.

"Hi, there," a guy leaning against a car says.

A gay dude, is Jeremy's first thought, hitting on him. It happens, no big deal. But, second look, he sees this isn't the kind of dude, gay or otherwise, who works out at the YMCA on Santa Monica. He's too old, needs a shave, wears JCPenney slacks that clash with the JCPenney blazer. Pale complexion, kind of grayish. He looks like a sitcom father gone to seed, like if Mr. Brady had a drinking problem and smoked two packs a day.

"My name's Carl," he says, smiling.

Jeremy gives him a curt nod and walks quickly past.

"I work for Sid Schwartz," the guy says.

Jeremy stops.

"Mr. Schwartz wanted me to discuss a couple of matters with you, Jeffrey." Carl lights a cigarette and takes a drag. "Is this a good time? Won't take a minuto."

A Santa Ana is blowing across the parking lot, hot and dry. The sweat on

Jeremy's forehead evaporates the instant it forms. He's not scared. Carl is not a scary guy. But why is he here? What so-called *matters* does Sid Schwartz want him to discuss with Jeremy?

"No problem," Jeremy says.

What pops into his mind is this: maybe Sid is informing Jeremy that Penelope has cancer, with only a few months to live. Penelope wants to keep it a secret, so Jeremy can't say anything. He needs to keep treating her like a queen, keep making her happy, and Sid will take care of Jeremy, financially, after . . . you know.

Okay, it's kind of a wild theory. But also plausible, right?

"Mr. Schwartz would like you to have no further contact with his mother," Carl says. "Starting immediately. No calls, no letters, no chance encounters at the supermarket. Understand?"

What? No, Jeremy doesn't understand. Sid liked him! The two of them hit it off! "Till next time." That was the last thing Sid said to Jeremy.

"There must be . . . this is a misunderstanding of some kind," Jeremy says.

"I'm afraid not, Jeffrey. You . . ." Carl lurches into a coughing fit, wet and grinding. He gives Jeremy a thumbs-up to indicate he's okay. When he finally finishes coughing, he spits a wad of phlegm onto the asphalt.

"Listen," Jeremy says. "If—"

"Jeffrey, Jeremy, Jiminy Cricket, whatever your real name is. Shut up, please. Let's cut to the happy ending. A man like Mr. Schwartz always gets what he wants. Simple as that. Trust me."

Jeremy blinks. How does Carl know his real name? And how did he know exactly where to find Jeremy? It's troubling. It's troubling that Jeremy read Sid Schwartz so completely wrong at brunch. But what really has the sweat popping (then evaporating) on Jeremy's forehead is the thought of *giving up*. Giving up *now*, just when he's cracked the safe and the vault door is about to swing—

"Are you listening to me?" Carl says.

"What's in it for me?" Jeremy says. He finally recognizes the opportunity here. Sid Schwartz always gets what he wants. Sid Schwartz is rich. One plus one equals . . . a hundred grand? More? "If I agree to all this."

Carl has already smoked his Marlboro down to the filter. He flicks it away and starts coughing again. No, Jeremy realizes, he's laughing, not coughing. The two sound almost identical, equally unpleasant.

"If you agree?"

"What do I get if I agree to Mr. Schwartz's terms?"

"Oh, muchacho. You're a hoot. You get everything. A life, a future, the whole enchilada. You get to forget this ever happened."

"I want a hundred thousand dollars. Cash."

Carl lights another cigarette. He pulls open the door of his car. "Stay away from her," he says. "Starting five minutes ago. You don't want to run into me again."

Jeremy takes a shower and changes clothes. As he drives home to Chez Mais Oui, his indignation burns. This is bullshit. Sid Schwartz has no right to tell Jeremy what to do. You know who gets to decide if Jeremy stays away from Penelope? Only Jeremy does. And Penelope, of course. But it's obvious she doesn't want Jeremy to stay away.

Screw Sid Schwartz. Just because he's some rich big shot, he thinks he can intimidate and bully Jeremy. Oh, yeah? Well, Sid Schwartz doesn't know Jeremy.

Anna is waiting for Jeremy on the porch, her arms folded across her chest. She doesn't look like the Anna he knows. Her face is stone, eyes blazing.

"Give me the keys," she says. "House keys, car keys."

"Anna, please, let me—"

"You've got thirty seconds to get off the property. After that I call the police."

"I'm sorry I broke the rule. I don't know what I was thinking. I—"

"You're sorry??" She slaps his face so hard his ears ring. He wobbles backward and almost tumbles off the porch. "This is why I have the rule. Sid Schwartz? Are you fucking kidding me? Do you know how badly you've fucked me?"

The front door is open. Cushing stands in the foyer, watching and smirking.

"Anna, come on," Jeremy says. She's overreacting. Where is he supposed to go, if she kicks him out? "I'll fix this. Sid Schwartz is a bully. He—"

"Fifteen seconds," Anna says.

"What about my stuff?"

"Start walking."

She's out of her mind. Jeremy has no choice. He trudges down the drive. The front door of Chez Mais Oui thuds shut behind him. At the gate, Jeremy stops. He's spinning. How can this be happening? Where is he supposed to go now? And everything in his room—he's got some very cool and expensive stuff. He can't just leave it behind!

His mom wouldn't leave behind *her* stuff. Jeremy decides he won't either. No way. He sneaks back through the trees. It's dark now and Anna won't be able to spot him from the house, even if she's looking for him. And she won't be. She'll be in the dining room, laughing and serving dinner. Anna, so full of herself, can't imagine the possibility that anyone would ever stand up to her.

Jeremy has that advantage, plus another huge one too. His room is on the ground floor, on the complete opposite side of the house from the dining room. Nobody, if he's careful, will hear him make a peep.

The garden is jungly, a little tricky to navigate in the night. Jeremy inches along the edge of the pool. This is the one place he might be spotted: the pool lights, the angle of the dining room windows.

But he's golden. He reaches his patio and opens the door, which he never keeps locked. Good thinking! Too risky to turn on the lights, so he loads up his suitcase in the dark. His favorite jeans, his blazers, his watches, a pair of pristine New Balance 1300s he knows Cushing covets.

Voices. Jeremy stops, listens. Voices? He's not sure. The gurgle of the pool filter, maybe. He finishes loading up the suitcase. He has to sit on it to make it latch. Two seconds later he's out the door, in the garden, a totally clean getaway.

• • •

Jeremy calls Dawn from the gas station on Santa Monica Boulevard. It's eight o'clock in the evening now. He crosses his fingers that she's home and not out with her porn friends at the Country Club or shooting a night scene somewhere.

"Hello?"

"It's me."

Silence. Then, finally, "What's wrong."

What's wrong is that he never should have left her. He never should have left the house on Martha Street. Fucking Cushing. Fucking Anna. They're not nice people. Jeremy knew that and followed them anyway. He wants to cry, how badly he's fucked up, how badly he's let down Dawn—the first chick he's ever truly loved, maybe the only chick he'll ever love.

"I miss you," he says, his voice hoarse.

She doesn't say anything. She doesn't hang up. So far, so good.

"I know you're not going to take me back," Jeremy says. "But I just . . . there's just so much I never told you. So much I want to say to you."

"Jeremy . . ."

"I don't know why it's so hard to open up. It's always been so hard for me. But with you . . . you make me want to open my heart, Dawn."

He means it. He truly does.

CHAPTER 27

That first week back in the Valley is fantastic. Jeremy and Dawn spend every possible moment together. It's like they can't survive unless they're physically touching, unless various parts of their bodies are smashed tightly together. On days Dawn doesn't have to shoot, they don't leave her bed until one or two in the afternoon. Love lifts them on the crest of a wave and keeps them suspended there.

One night Jeremy wakes up and discovers Dawn sitting on the edge of the bed, quietly crying. With joy? He guesses so. He runs his fingertips down her bare back, the spiraling constellation of freckles between her shoulder blades.

"I'm so stupid," she whispers.

"Why?" he says. "What do you mean?"

The next morning, that's all he remembers. He must have drifted back to sleep during the conversation, or else it was all just a dream. During breakfast, Dawn is her usual bright, bubbly, cheerful self. A dream makes the most sense.

Jeremy is so happy. Lying by the pool with Dawn, his right leg pressed against her left one—this is exactly what he wants; this is exactly what he *always* wanted and was just too blind to see.

Roll the credits. It's a perfect ending to the movie.

An *almost* perfect ending.

He was so close! Jeremy can't stop thinking about Penelope, about the hundred thousand dollars he could have made from her. He had Penelope in the palm of his hand. All he needed was a couple more weeks, a month tops, and then . . .

How can Jeremy turn his back on such a huge score? A hundred thousand dollars—or more!—will change his life. His and *Dawn's* life, that's what he means. She can quit porn and go to school full-time, for example. Or he'll get her a new car. First, of course, he needs a car of his own.

No way he can turn his back on such a huge score, Jeremy decides, especially not when he's put so much effort into it. Giving up now would be like . . . like playing a great game, then walking off the court right before the final buzzer, when all you need is an easy layup to win.

Okay, maybe this isn't an *easy* layup. Jeremy isn't scared of Lung Cancer Carl, but Sid Schwartz *is* a rich big shot. He definitely has ways to make himself a total pain in Jeremy's ass if Jeremy doesn't stay away from Penelope. Think about Jeremy's acting career, for example. But! There's a simple solution to the problem. Sid Schwartz *never finds out* Jeremy is still seeing Penelope.

Dawn has class Wednesday evenings from seven till ten. Jeremy drops her off on campus, then takes Coldwater Canyon over the hills to Bel Air. He's extremely cautious. He drives past Penelope's house a few times to make sure Lung Cancer Carl isn't lurking around. He parks a street over, down the block, walking past Penelope's house and doubling back only when he's absolutely sure the coast is clear.

Penelope answers the door. If looks could kill. "Where have you been?" she says.

"I'm sorry."

"You just disappeared. I don't appreciate that."

"Your son tried to scare me off. He sent some guy to threaten me."

Her expression shifts. A gleam in her eye dances. "And yet here you are."

Jeremy realizes that Sid Schwartz has done him a favor. "Are you going to let me in?"

They're upstairs, in bed, thirty seconds later. Penelope digs her nails deep into the grooves between Jeremy's ribs. The pain makes it hard to concentrate on the spotlit theater stage of her pupil. She smiles when he winces.

Afterward, she stays in bed while he slowly gets dressed. "What is it?" she says.

"Nothing."

"What?"

He sighs. "Sid got me kicked out of the place I was staying. I'm crashing with a friend for a few days. On his couch. I don't know what I'm going to do."

Penelope rises from bed, slips on a robe. Jeremy takes the moment to check the scratches on his rib cage. He knows he'll have to come up with an innocent explanation for Dawn. He will. Inspiration will strike at exactly the right moment. That's a nice feeling.

She takes a seat at her antique credenza and opens her checkbook. "Remind me. Your last name?"

"You can just make it out to cash."

"Of course."

She signs with a flourish. Jeremy crosses the bedroom to accept the check. Five thousand dollars. An excellent start. You see? Jeremy is so, so close.

"Thank you," he says. "I'll see you again soon."

"I expect so," she says.

•••

Penelope in Bel Air, Dawn in the Valley. It's tricky, but Jeremy quickly finds the rhythm and learns the steps, like he always does. He's eleven years old again and grooving to "Gimme My Mule," blowing Warren's mind with moves that no white kid should be able to master.

Two evenings a week with Penelope during Dawn's class, and a late lunch whenever Dawn has to work. Friday and Saturday night with Dawn while Penelope attends fundraising galas and dinner parties with fellow rich ladies. Penelope insists that Jeremy sleep over at least once a week, so he tells Dawn he landed a small part in a movie that sometimes shoots all night, a cheapo vampire slasher. She buys it—he sprinkles in details from his experience with Cushing that no one could ever make up.

Jeremy uses three grand from Penelope's first check as a down payment on an almost-new BMW 325es, the sports package. Every now and then, though, he still borrows Dawn's Mustang—to mix things up, to be as careful as possible.

The double life wears him down a little. His poor aching cock, for example. But he's getting two lives for the price of one. What bargain is better than that? Dawn gives him warmth, comfort, a bottomless well of unconditional love, and a rocking body. Penelope gives him a taste of real money, the promise of real money, the deep satisfaction of doing a job well, doing a job done *brilliantly*. Cushing wouldn't have been able to get this far with Penelope, not in a million years. Cushing will never have someone love him the way Dawn loves Jeremy.

"I think I'm done," Dawn says.

Jeremy looks at her plate. She's barely touched her caprese salad. This is a Saturday night, almost exactly a month since he left Chez Mais Oui, and they're at their favorite Italian place on Ventura, Sotto's. Penelope, on the other side of the hills, is at a fundraising gala for . . . some charity, Jeremy can't remember which one.

"You're not hungry?" he asks Dawn.

"The biz," she clarifies. "I think I'm done with it."

"You are?" This is news to Jeremy. Dawn hasn't even mentioned the possibility of quitting porn until now. He's pretty sure she hasn't.

"I want to do it. College, full-time. I want to finally do it. I want to be a nurse."

"Okay. Yeah!" Good for her, though Jeremy can't see the appeal—sick people all day, bleeding people, people with sores and constant needs.

"Porn has been fun," she says. "It's been fine. But at some point . . . I don't want to be doing this when I'm, like, twenty-five."

"You're only twenty-two," Jeremy says.

"It's not really fine anymore. I don't want to be doing this *now*."

Jeremy pours her more wine and thinks about their financial situation. His plan is to save the money he gets from Penelope. That's money for their future, his and Dawn's, not their present. How are he and Dawn going to live, in a decent house, eating out whenever they want, without Dawn's porn money coming in?

"Then you should definitely be done with it," he says. "One more year and you're done."

"One more year?"

"You want to have, like, a runway, like at an airport. Right? You want room to take off."

She sips her wine. After a second, she nods. "I guess so. I guess that makes sense."

"Go out on your own terms," he says. "You've totally earned it."

CHAPTER 28

Dawn has a boy-girl-boy scene the next afternoon. She kisses Jeremy goodbye, and he hustles over the hills to see Penelope. Sex, lunch, more sex. Jeremy can barely keep up with Penelope. She's the one who should be in porn, not Dawn. When they finish, he hustles back over the hills to the Valley.

Jeremy pulls up to the house on Martha Street. Dawn's Mustang isn't in the driveway, which means he beat her home. Perfect! He had a good lie ready, just in case. He was just driving around, checking out different famous movie locations for fun. Like Point Dume, where they filmed the end of *Planet of the Apes*.

He drops his keys in the bowl trimmed with seashells. A quick dip in the pool sounds good. Maybe a sandwich first. Jeremy notices that the stereo is on, the jingle for KIIS 102.7, followed by the opening guitar twang of Don Henley's "Boys of Summer." Dawn must be home after all. He wonders where her car is.

"Hey!" Jeremy calls as he steps into the living room.

Lung Cancer Carl, sitting on the sofa, turns and smiles. "Hey yourself."

What the fuck? How did he find Jeremy? Jeremy is confused, then annoyed that this jerk is making himself at home in Jeremy's house, then—finally, when he sees the gun in Carl's hand—Jeremy is nothing at all.

"What do you want?" Jeremy says. The words come lurching out of his mouth, the wrong rhythm. He tries again, makes it sound more casual. "What do you want, Carl?"

"Let's go for a ride. What do you say?"

Jeremy feels a flutter of nausea. But it's okay. He's going to be fine. He always is. Carl just wants to scare him. "No, thank you," he says.

Carl checks his watch. "Your girl gets home soon, doesn't she? I'd rather leave before she gets home. She'll be a hassle."

Don Henley sings. Jeremy loves the video for "Boys of Summer." Carl is just trying to scare him. Jeremy glances again at the gun in Carl's hand. Another flutter of nausea.

Carl starts coughing. He doesn't stop coughing until he lights a cigarette and takes the first deep drag. "Relax," he says, his voice hoarse and smoky.

"Okay."

"I'm driving you to the bus station. You're going to take a bus to Florida. My treat. You're never coming back to Los Angeles. You'll never contact Mr. Schwartz's mother again. How does that sound? Does that sound fair?"

It does sound fair. Jeremy feels lightheaded with relief. But what if Carl is lying? Is his offer *too* fair? Carl doesn't have any reason to lie, though. He could kill Jeremy right here and now if he wanted. Jeremy tries to think of reasons why Carl might lie, but he can't concentrate on anything but the gun. Jeremy doesn't understand how Carl found out he was still seeing Penelope. Jeremy was so careful!

"I need to pack," Jeremy says.

"Go right ahead. But hurry."

They take Jeremy's car. Carl drives. Jeremy sits in the passenger seat. He doesn't know where the gun is now. Under Carl's ugly plaid blazer, Jeremy guesses.

It's still hot at eight o'clock in the evening, but Carl keeps the air conditioner off, the windows rolled down. "You don't mind if I smoke?" he says.

"I don't mind," Jeremy says.

They were on the 101. Now they're on East 4th Street, past downtown, in a Mexican neighborhood Jeremy has never visited before. He assumed the main bus terminal was downtown. Maybe not. Or maybe they're looping back around to downtown. LA is a bowl of noodles, so many shortcuts and bypasses and alternate routes that sometimes you have to go west to get east. Like Columbus.

"What time does my bus leave?" Jeremy says.

"Don't worry about that," Carl says, lighting a new cigarette off the butt of an old one. "We've got plenty of time."

"Where's the bus station?"

"Don't worry about that either. We're going to make a quick stop first. Friend of mine."

At 4th and Soto, two cars block the intersection, one with a wrecked nose, the other with a wrecked tail. The asphalt glitters, broken glass and shattered ruby taillight.

The bar lights of a police car pulse soundlessly. Carl eases to a stop. He unbuttons his ugly blazer and shows Jeremy the gun in a shoulder holster.

"Just sit nice and tight," he says. "Do you understand?"

One cop is making a man touch his nose with his finger. The second cop is talking to an angry lady. The second cop is only a few yards away from the BMW. Jeremy can hear their conversation. The cop is patiently suggesting that the woman please calm down, ma'am. The angry lady keeps asking why. *Why? Why should I calm down?*

"Did you hear me?" Carl says, his voice low. "Don't move a fucking muscle. Don't make a fucking sound."

Carl's not taking Jeremy to the bus station. Jeremy understands that now. He understands the two wrecked cars, the cop, are a miracle, just for him.

Jeremy unclips his seat belt. He opens his door and Carl grabs his arm. He's stronger than he looks. More serious.

"Thanks for the lift," Jeremy tells Carl, loudly enough that the cop glances over. Carl releases Jeremy's arm. Jeremy climbs out of the car. "I can just walk the rest of the way."

"Lucky?" the angry lady says. She points to her wrecked car. "You call that lucky?"

"Ma'am," the cop says. "Please."

Jeremy walks past the cop and the angry lady. He puts one foot in front of the other—not too fast, not too slow. He's not in a rush, but he has places to be, people to see. Breathe in, breathe out. Don't look back. Carl won't shoot him, not with a cop standing right there. Right?

When he gets to the corner, Jeremy turns left and starts running.

CHAPTER 29

His sister Alice is the smartest person he knows. What would Alice do in this situation?

I'd never be in this situation, you moron.

Jeremy finds a cab. He takes it to Santa Monica. Why Santa Monica? It's the first random place that pops into his mind. He doesn't have any connection to Santa Monica. Carl won't look for him there.

Ha. You better hope not.

Cab fare just about cleans him out, almost all the cash he has in his wallet. Jeremy finds a pie place on Wilshire that's open all night. He gets a table far from the windows and orders black coffee.

His hands won't stop shaking. He clenches his fists. That helps. Holy shit! Jeremy knows how lucky he is. The miracle of that car wreck, those cops. He hasn't lost his magic.

But now he needs some more magic. Carl will be looking for him. Carl, Jeremy has a feeling, won't stop looking for him. So where can Jeremy go? Who can help him? Jeremy needs a place to hole up and hide out *immediately*.

Jeremy calls Cushing from a gas station pay phone across the street from the pie place. Luckily Cushing has his own line at Chez Mais Oui. Luckily Jeremy remembers the number.

Cushing answers on the ninth ring, just as Jeremy is about to give up and try again later. "At your service," Cushing says.

"It's me." Jeremy clears his throat. He's not desperate. He doesn't want to sound desperate. That won't work with Cushing. "Are you just coming in or just going out?"

Silence. Then, finally: "What do you want?" Cushing says. "I shouldn't be talking to you."

"I need a favor. Just a small one."

"A *favor*? After the shit you pulled."

"I know, I know. But—"

"You didn't just screw Anna. You screwed *me*. Did that ever occur to you?"

"I'm sorry about that. I am."

Silence again, but a shorter stretch of it this time. "A *favor*," Cushing says. "You've got balls, old chap. I'll give you that."

Jeremy covers the mouthpiece of the phone so he can take a deep breath of relief. He tells Cushing everything. Whatever friction exists between them, Jeremy and Cushing are still friends. They've been friends since the minute they met, two peas in a pod. Cushing will help Jeremy if he understands how much danger Jeremy is truly in.

Plus, Cushing loves drama. He loves a juicy situation.

"So, let me make sure I have this straight," Cushing says. "You got out of the car and just sauntered away?"

"More of a stroll. Until I turned the corner. That's when I ran like my ass was on fire."

Cushing laughs. "Well played."

A lone car drives past, down Wilshire. Santa Monica is dead this time of night. The gas station is a bright bubble of humming light and Jeremy feels completely exposed, naked.

"I need to get out of LA."

"I'll say."

Jeremy waits, eyes closed. Cushing, on the other end of the line, is imagining himself in Jeremy's predicament. No money or car or place to stay, no chance except Jeremy. Cushing is imagining himself having to make this call. At least Jeremy hopes so.

Finally, Cushing sighs. "Where are you?" he says.

CHAPTER 30

Cushing picks up Jeremy and drives him to a motel in Inglewood, near the airport. It's a bleak, crappy motel on a bleak, crappy block. The motel office appears to be closed, but when they get closer Jeremy sees that a light is actually on—the window has been broken and patched with cardboard.

"Wait here," Cushing says.

He's in the motel office for about five minutes. When he slides back into the car, he hands Jeremy a room key attached to a cracked plastic fob. Number 13.

"If I'm going to help you," Cushing says, "we're going to do it my way. I have to protect myself. You do exactly what I tell you to do."

"I understand," Jeremy says. They've been over this already. "Totally."

"Stay in the room. Don't use the phone. Don't open the door for anyone but me. There's a McDonald's down the street if you're hungry. Don't go anywhere else."

"I don't have any money. I only have seven dollars."

Cushing takes a twenty out of his wallet and hands it to Jeremy. "That'll be enough. I paid for the room. Three nights. I'll be back by then."

Hold on. What? Jeremy is supposed to stay in a bleak, crappy motel room for three days? But he doesn't say anything. He's in no position to negotiate.

"Got it," he says.

Room 13 is cramped and hot, the shag carpet crunchy underfoot. Jeremy locks the door behind him, pulls the curtains, turns on the air conditioner under the window. The unit shudders, exhales warm, bad breath—flat beer, rotting teeth. Jeremy turns it back off.

He takes a seat on the edge of the bed. For a long time, he just sits and stares at the bare wall. Hours? Maybe. The last of the adrenaline from earlier has drained away and now he's stupefied by exhaustion. Or he's just plain stupefied. How did this happen? More specifically, how did this happen to *him*? This can't be happening to him.

Jeremy closes his eyes for a second. The next thing he knows it's morning, or maybe afternoon, the room brighter and even hotter. He's sprawled out on top of the stained bedspread, his throat so dry he can barely swallow.

He drinks water from the bathroom faucet and splashes his face. He's starving, but he's too scared to leave the room. He's also too scared to stay in the room. But it's okay, he reminds himself. He's safe. Nobody knows where to find him except Cushing.

An hour goes by. Another. The TV doesn't work. Jeremy takes a rusty-smelling shower and finally works up the courage for McDonald's. He walks the two blocks quickly, eyes down, staring straight ahead. Not many fellow pedestrians, but a few. A lady emerges from the shadows, startling the shit out of him, and asks Jeremy if he has a light. He ignores her and hurries past.

He makes it safely back to the room with his Big Mac, large fries, large Coke. Now, though, he's lost his appetite. He can't keep this up for three days. He can't just sit here and wait for Cushing. It's the same ominous tingle he felt in the car with Lung Cancer Carl. Jeremy has to *do* something.

The phone in the room works. Jeremy has never been so happy in his life to hear the buzz of a dial tone. He places a call home. Alice answers. The operator asks if she'll accept the charges.

"Jeremy who?" Alice says.

"Jesus fucking Christ, Alice." Why couldn't he get Mom? Or Tallulah, at least. "Accept the fucking charges, please."

"Fine. Because you said please. I accept."

"Let me talk to Mom."

Mom will send him enough money for a fresh start somewhere else— San Francisco, maybe? New York?

"I'm very well," Alice says. "Thank you for asking. I'm starting to get my college acceptance letters and—"

"Alice! Let me talk to Mom. Now!"

"She's not home. What's wrong?"

Fucking Alice. How can she tell that something's wrong? Even the tiniest opportunity to torment him—Alice spots it, pounces. He pictures her back in Oklahoma City, twirling the phone cord around her finger as her eyes go slitty with suspicion and pleasure.

"Nothing's wrong," Jeremy says. "I just want to talk to Mom. *Please.*"

"If nothing's wrong, why are you in such a rush to talk to Mom? Hmm? Why are you calling collect?"

Fucking *Alice.* "Alice, I swear to God . . ."

"Whatever. I'll get her. Hold on."

Thank god. The wire wrapped around Jeremy's chest untightens, just a little. His lungs can expand again. Everything will be okay. Mom will send him money.

A minute passes. Jeremy stares at the alarm clock on the bedside table. Another minute passes. The digital numbers of the clock hum just before they flip. Hum, flip. Hum, flip. Three minutes, four, five. Where is Mom? Why is she taking so long to . . .

Finally, someone picks up the phone in Oklahoma. Jeremy hears breathing. "Mom?" he says. "Are you there? It's me, it's Jeremy."

"Jeremy!"

Jeremy recognizes the voice, the excitement. It's Piggy, not Mom. What the hell? *Where is Mom?* The clock hums and flips. "Piggy, I need to talk to Mom, okay?"

"Jeremy! It's like magic! I was just walking by the phone and it was sitting there and it was you! Do you love California? Is it the best ever?"

Jeremy grimaces. "Yes. It's the best ever. Piggy—"

"Are you coming home for Easter? You have to come home for Easter so the whole family is together. The whole family has to be together at Easter."

"Piggy! Listen to me! I need to talk to Mom. *Right now.*"

"Oh. Mom's not home."

"What?"

"She's eating lunch with Mrs. Downey. They might go to Dillard's after that."

Fucking *Alice*. Jeremy reads Piggy the number typed on the dial of the motel room's phone. "Have Mom call me the minute she gets home," he says, then hangs up before Piggy can grill him more about California or Easter.

Jeremy unwraps the Big Mac and forces himself to take a bite. Piggy is only ten years old, but reliable. He'll give their mom the message. But when? Every minute counts. Hum, flip. Hum, flip. Jeremy digs through his wallet, all the scraps of paper with the scribbled names and phone numbers he's collected over the last several months in LA. *Maria. Holly. Monique*. A different *Holly*. He digs more furiously. It has to be there. Please, please, please. There: his brother's number in Las Vegas.

Please answer. Please, please, please.

Ray answers. He accepts the charges.

"Ray!" Jeremy says. "Hey, man! How are you? How's Vegas?"

"Okay," Ray says, his usual chatty and eloquent self.

"I've been thinking about you a lot. You know, thought I'd drop you a line. Catch up. I'm in Los Angeles. You probably heard. It's amazing. You have no idea. I met Judge Reinhold. From *Gremlins*?"

"Okay."

That's the best he's going to get from Ray, so Jeremy cuts to the chase. He keeps it simple so Ray can follow. "I'm kind of in a bind, Ray. There's a guy here. He hired someone to kill me. I'm not kidding around. He already . . . I'm not kidding around, Ray. This is real. I don't have any money. I'm hiding out in a crappy motel. I have to get out of town."

"Okay," Ray says. His tone doesn't change. Jeremy could be telling him about the weather in LA. "What's his name?"

"I might come to Vegas and crash with you for a while. Maybe you could loan me a couple of bucks for a plane ticket."

"What's his name?"

"The guy who wants to kill me? Sid Schwartz. He's a big deal, a movie producer. The guy he hired is like a private detective. His name is Carl something. But that doesn't matter. If you can just send me—"

"Where are you? What's the name of the motel?"

"The Capri, on Airport Boulevard. That doesn't matter either, Ray. Focus, okay?"

"I'll be there by nine tonight."

What? No, no, no. Ray and his solid concrete-block head. Hasn't he been listening? Jeremy doesn't need Ray to come to Los Angeles. Jeremy needs to go to Vegas. Like, *now*.

"Listen, Ray, there's a Western Union down the street. Just send me money for a plane ticket."

"I'll be there by nine," Ray says, and the line goes dead.

CHAPTER 31

Jeremy hasn't seen Ray in almost three years, since Ray left home and moved to Vegas. He's even bigger than Jeremy remembers, at least six-five, six-six. One of Ray's biceps is the size of Jeremy's thigh.

Ray is wearing a navy-blue suit, a white shirt, a navy-blue tie, none of which fit quite right. Buttons strain, the tie comes up too short. White gym socks with black shoes. Jesus, Ray. What are you thinking? And what did he do to his hair? Ray's head is shaved down to the bone. It's not a bad look, actually. Ray has been going bald since he was fourteen.

"My favorite big brother!" Jeremy says. He sees Ray's forehead crease. Yes, Ray, you're my *only* big brother. That's the joke. "How are you, man?"

"Let's go," Ray says.

"Now?" Jeremy says. "Tonight?"

"Does anybody know you're here? This motel?"

"No. Nobody."

Ray waits.

Jeremy shrugs. "Just a friend of mine who helped me out."

"Let's go," Ray says.

It's strange, Ray taking the lead like this. Ray follows. That's what he's always done. But it's a relief, actually. Jeremy is exhausted. He'll sleep on the way back to Vegas.

They're not headed back to Vegas, though. Instead, Ray drives up the 405 and gets them a room at a different hotel, a nicer hotel, on the edge of Brentwood.

Ray orders room service for them, a couple of steaks and a couple of beers. Jeremy knocks back his beer in two gulps, but just picks at the food.

He doesn't know if he'll ever be hungry again. Ray makes Jeremy tell him everything. Dawn, Anna, Cushing, Penelope, Carl.

"What else?" Ray says.

"What do you mean?" Jeremy says.

"What else do I need to know?"

"Nothing."

And then before Jeremy realizes what's happening, his eyes are stinging. Tears. He honestly can't remember the last time he cried, or why.

"I'm in such deep shit, Ray," Jeremy says. He rubs the tears out of his eyes with a stiffly starched room-service napkin.

"Okay," Ray says. He stands. "I'm going to take a shower."

When Jeremy wakes up in the morning, Ray is already dressed, almost out the door.

"Where are you going?" Jeremy says. "Ray, we need to leave town. You haven't been listening to me. I'm in deep shit, man."

"I'm going to take care of things."

He's going to . . . what? *Take care of things?* Sid Schwartz is one of the most powerful men in Hollywood. Ray works for some two-bit mob guy in Vegas. How is Ray going to take care of things? He's going to get himself killed, and in the process, he's going to get *Jeremy* killed. Ray will lead Lung Cancer Carl straight back here. Is Ray really that dumb, that he thinks he can go up against someone like Sid Schwartz? Jesus. Jeremy knows Ray. He really is that dumb.

"No," Jeremy says. "No way. Listen. We have to go to Vegas. Today. *Now.*"

"I'll be back later."

Jeremy tries to catch him, but his feet get tangled in the sheets, he stumbles, the door *thunks* shut in his face. He grabs his pants, his shirt. Barefoot he sprints down the empty hallway. What's he going to do if he catches Ray? He'll be like a dog catching a car, like a dog catching a semitruck.

It doesn't matter. The elevator doors have already closed. Ray is gone.

Jeremy returns to the room. He can't live like this! Everything going wrong, everything collapsing around him. An hour goes by. Two, three, four. By the time dusk falls, Jeremy has stopped pacing and is curled in a fetal position. Will Carl torture him first? A bullet to the brain will be quick, painless. Instant emptiness. That won't be so bad. But Sid Schwartz will want to make him suffer. Jeremy knows it.

He should have stuck with Cushing. Is it too late? Jeremy could hitch a ride back to the Capri Motel. He still has the room key on the cracked plastic fob. Number 13.

Or Cushing is setting him up, selling him out. Giving up Jeremy would get Cushing back in Anna's good graces.

Should Jeremy try calling Penelope? He could tell her everything. She'll talk to her son and get Jeremy off the hook with Sid.

Or calling Penelope might make things even worse. Though Jeremy's not sure how things could get worse. Jeremy says a prayer. His first one since . . . forever.

God, please. Get me out of this, God. Get me out of this and I will change. All this was my fault. I know, God, I know. Get me out of this and I will become a better person. I swear.

The least original prayer ever. Probably the first ever prayer, the prayer that invented the idea of God in the first place. But Jeremy means it with all his fucking heart.

Just before midnight a key turns in the lock. Jeremy, pacing again, freezes. The door opens. God, please. Get me out of this and I will—

It's Ray. He yawns and loosens his tie. "I'm hungry," he says. "You eat already?"

"Where the fuck have you been, Ray? We have to go *now*. Can you not understand that? They're going to murder me. I'm serious, Ray."

Ray shakes his head. "It's okay now. I took care of it."

He tosses his tie and suit coat on the bed. He unbuttons the top few buttons of his shirt, picks up the phone, and orders two steaks, two beers, two slices of apple pie.

When Ray puts the phone down, Jeremy reaches up and grabs his shoulders. He shakes as hard as he can, but Ray doesn't budge. Doesn't even blink. Mom has always been convinced that Dad or some teenage babysitter dropped Ray on his head when he was a baby. Somebody did, that's clear.

"Ray, focus for a minute," Jeremy says, very slowly. "And tell me exactly what you mean, you took care of it."

"I went to see Schwartz. Schwartz won't bother you anymore. You just have to leave town. That's the deal we made."

Jeremy searches Ray's face. Is Ray messing around with him? Why would Schwartz agree to a deal like that? Why would he let Jeremy off the hook so easily?

"You can't trust him, Ray. What about Carl? He's a psycho. He'll—"

"Schwartz's guy?" Ray says. "No. I went to see him first. He's out of the picture now."

"He's . . . what?"

"And the girl's fine. I checked on her."

"Who?" And then Jeremy remembers. "Dawn. Thank god. Yes."

"Schwartz will stick to the deal. You're okay now."

"But . . ."

The room starts to spin around Jeremy—but in a good way, like it's been stuck and now is moving again, working the way it's supposed to. Ray isn't messing with him. Jeremy's prayer was answered. He's okay. And Dawn too. Jeremy's lungs fill. He can breathe again.

He notices a couple of dark spots on the white wing of Ray's collar. Jeremy, inches shorter than Ray, is eye to eye with them.

Dark *red* spots. Blood.

Ray glances down to see what Jeremy is staring at. "Don't worry," he says. "It's not mine."

CHAPTER 32

LAX hums and bustles. Jeremy checks the board. His flight to San Francisco is on time. He finds a seat by the gate. He doesn't want to miss the first call for boarding.

He's in good shape. Great shape. Some new clothes, two nights of sound, solid sleep. Before Ray drove back to Vegas, he loaned Jeremy a thousand bucks. That's almost exactly the amount of money Jeremy had when he arrived in LA.

A thousand bucks, a new city. You could argue he's back where he started, but not really. Jeremy is older now, a lot wiser. He's learned so much over the past year in LA. The most important lesson? Or maybe it was just a strong reminder: he can handle whatever the world throws at him. It—life, *his* life—will always work out.

A chick sits down next to him. She's pretty, probably an actress. Jeremy smiles at her. She smiles back. Jeremy doesn't rush into a conversation with her. There will be time for that. The chick will be sitting next to him on the plane, or they'll find themselves in line together at baggage claim in San Francisco or waiting for a cab. Jeremy can count on it.

He's jazzed to explore a brand-new city. San Francisco! The Golden Gate Bridge, Haight-Ashbury, the cable cars from the Rice-a-Roni commercials. New friends, new experiences. Jeremy is ready for anything.

PART IV

Tallulah
1994

CHAPTER 33

Tallulah flies through the air. Up, up, up. Is there a better rush than this? Tallulah is something of an expert on the subject and no, there is no better rush than this. For a few seconds time slows, the petals of a flower unfolding, and the laws of physics are suspended. The chandelier above Tallulah glitters. It's colossal, a million crystals, a dozen grasping tentacles, grotesquely and wonderfully excessive. Tallulah stretches her arms, reaching . . . she can almost touch it.

She plunges. That's almost as much fun as the flying. Tolstoy and Chekhov catch her in the basket of their muscled arms and flip her back up and out. Somersault, twist. She sticks the landing. *Ta-da!*

A few polite claps. Most of the partygoers aren't paying any attention to the entertainment. They knock back vodka and compare chunky watches trimmed with diamonds, purses plated with precious metals. They dance/dry hump as the DJ spins the latest New Kids on the Block.

Lev eats fire and blows it back out. *Whoomp!* Boyle clowns and Eva juggles. Waiters wheel out more vodka and caviar, more lobster tails, a fresh ice sculpture to replace the one that's begun to melt. A man beats his chest and howls.

This is nothing, though. This is a slow night in Moscow, a Tuesday. Just wait till the weekend.

Tallulah still has her eye on that chandelier. A second-floor mezzanine runs the length of the ballroom. Can Tallulah make the leap from the mezzanine to the chandelier? It's a long way. And the chandelier might not be able to bear her weight. The whole ceiling could come crashing down.

Lev, watching her, shakes his head. He knows what Tallulah is thinking. *Don't do it. I am serious.*

Tallulah turns her palms up. *Who me?* While Tolstoy and Chekhov are popping off some aerial walkovers, she slips through the crowd. At the foot of the staircase, a security guard stops her. Even the scar-faced security guards at these things wear beautiful Italian suits.

He takes in her bare feet, the sequined leotard that Lev insists they all wear for gigs. "Only guests are authorized," he says.

"Do you think I can jump from there to there?" Tallulah says, pointing. After a year of living in Moscow, her Russian is decent. She doesn't know the words for *mezzanine* or *chandelier*, though.

The security guard cracks half a smile. "Are you a lunatic? It's impossible."

That's all she needs to hear. That's all she *ever* needs to hear, since she was a little girl, her very earliest memories. *That tree is too big for you to climb, Lulu. Impossible.* She smiles back and the security guard blinks, and she's gone, halfway up the stairs before he can turn his head. She's half his size and ten times as quick. A breath, a breeze, just a memory.

She springs onto the marble balustrade. It's a *long* way to the chandelier. An impossible, some might say, leap.

Down below a couple of partygoers have noticed her. One by one more faces turn up toward the mezzanine. Conversations sputter. Dry humpers hesitate. Tallulah's heart hums along, fast but not too fast, just the right speed. She snorted some coke before the party, and took a couple of the pills Eva offered her and drank some champagne the host left out in the kitchen for them, but otherwise she's sharp, sober, and clearheaded.

And having the time of her life.

Ta-da!

• • •

So how did a runty adopted Choctaw girl from Oklahoma City (of all places) end up in Moscow, Russia (of all places)? Who knows? Who cares? Tallulah goes with the flow. She takes every leap.

She hit San Francisco first, straight out of high school. Those were some fun years. Life on the Oklahoma prairie had not prepared her for such ridiculous hills. She got a job as a bike messenger. Imagine the fastest, steepest roller coaster ever. Imagine the gnarliest obstacle course. Cable cars and junkies and jaywalking tourists, speeders and swervers, car doors springing open with no warning at all. Each and every job was impossible. Get this packet of lawyer bullshit across town by two! Go go go! She shared a grungy warehouse loft in grungy China Basin with a stripper/poet, a drug dealer/bassist, and a gay docent at the Legion of Honor. Ted, the gay docent, was so young, even younger than her, sweet and shy and loony. When he got sick, Tallulah quit her job to take care of him. It wrecked her. Ted's parents refused to attend the funeral. The next day Tallulah got on a bus. She couldn't get out of San Francisco fast enough.

Next stop: Orlando, Florida. Orlando was wild. For real! Thousands of young theme park employees bursting with hormones and good drugs. When Cinderella clocks out, she wants to rage! Tallulah landed at a second-tier park, Festival World. Her boss, a gruff Russian bear with a limp in both legs, gave Tallulah thirty minutes of training on the trapeze and three rules: pay attention, never hesitate, don't die. Got it! She had a couple of close calls—almost missing the safety net once, a midair collision another time—but picked up the routine quickly. She'd always been a natural.

Orlando was a blast until Tallulah had a bad experience with a guy she met, a guy who seemed nice but turned blank-faced and crazy and put her in a choke hold. If it hadn't been for Tallulah's roommate coming home early, unexpected . . . Tallulah doesn't want to think about what would have happened. She doesn't *have* to think about it. Because here's what Tallulah has learned over the years: when bad shit happens, move on and leave it in the dust behind you.

Her boss at Festival World, the gruff Russian bear, suggested she give post-communist Moscow a try. This was two years ago, 1992. Actually, what he said was "Don't go to Russia, *zayka*. Trust me. Is craziness over there right now. Is—how do you say?—wild and woolly."

And now here she is, hanging one-armed from a chandelier thirty feet above the ballroom floor. The crowd cheers. Tallulah hasn't thought about how she'll get down. Chekhov and Tolstoy grab a big tablecloth. Lev and

Boyle take the other corners. That'll work. Down Tallulah drops. Lev, smiling, makes her take a bow. He is so pissed at her. Members of Carnival Uncommon are supposed to stick to the script, whether they're performing at a fancy mansion or robbing it.

A sweaty red-faced partygoer hands Tallulah a glass of champagne and she downs it in one gulp.

God, she loves her wild and woolly life.

CHAPTER 34

After the party, Lev collects their fee. They change into street clothes and head to a bar called Sheriff, on Novy Arbat. Sheriff is the American West imagined by Russians who've never traveled farther west than Kiev: stuffed boar heads and an old cannon, a bartender in a sombrero.

Lev splits up the cash and passes it around. He is so, so pissed at Tallulah, but he won't say anything in front of the others. He needs them to believe that Tallulah and the chandelier was part of his plan. He needs them to believe that everything is part of his plan.

"So," he says. "What illuminating facts have we discovered this evening?"

First up, Chekhov and Tolstoy. Those are Tallulah's nicknames for them (Chekhov: terse and wry; Tolstoy: melodramatic and morose). Nice guys with great bods, legitimate gymnasts, willing and able when Tallulah is in the mood for a roll in the hay (Chekhov: deft and efficient; Tolstoy: passionate and exhausting). Chekhov sketches a floor plan of the Stepanov mansion. Tolstoy sketches the grounds. Boyle reports that, according to a guard he chatted up, security is light when the Stepanovs are out of town: just one man walking the perimeter and a second man inside. Eva says the alarm system is first-class, but the third-floor windows aren't wired. Why would they be?

"Piece of cake," Tallulah says. Well, the Russian version of "piece of cake," which Chekhov taught her: *proschche parenoi repi*. Simple as a boiled turnip.

"Better fucking be," Boyle says, glaring across the booth at her. Boyle, her fellow American in the group, has disliked Tallulah from the moment they met. Because she's brown and he's white? It happens. She's used to it.

Lev strokes his goatee. He dyes it silvery-gray to add gravitas. "Eva, see if you can persuade one of the guards to assist us."

Eva, cat-eyed East German beauty (with a degree in electrical engineering), nods. "I'll need a name. An address."

"You shall have it," Lev says. "Now let's get smashed."

They get smashed. Tallulah experiences the rest of the night as a series of quick cuts and snippets, time jumps, crazy camera angles. Chekhov tipping a bottle of vodka into Tolstoy's mouth. Lev kissing a stuffed boar on the mouth. Tallulah teaching Tolstoy how to do the Hustle.

"You should have seen my brother," she says, feeling a twinge of homesickness.

Now Tallulah dances with some hot, broad-shouldered Russian dude. Now he's naked and she's on top of him and they're both laughing. His flat smells like wet wool and old tea bags and pickled apples, like Russia.

Now Tallulah is walking down the street where she lives, the setting sun in her eyes, sweet spring on the breeze, gray lumps of snow dwindling. The *setting* sun? How many hours has she lost? She pauses to barf. An old woman scowls scornfully. Nobody can scowl as scornfully as an old Russian woman. She's selling Soviet medals and ribbons, spread out on a wool blanket. A woman next to her is selling porcelain teacups. Capitalism!

Tallulah loves her ramshackle old apartment building. It's ornate and whimsical, stone the color of a bruised peach, a glimpse of how Moscow must have looked long ago, before the communists turned everything to gray concrete blocks. Sure, her flat needs new paint and plumbing and electric. So what?

Tallulah searches for her keys. The pockets of her jacket, the pockets of her pants, her duffel bag. She finds her wallet, her sequined leotard, one wool glove, half a pint of cheap Zhuravli vodka, wooden matches, used tissues, bent bobby pins, two unidentified pills Eva gave her, and a set of matryoshka nesting dolls Tallulah could swear she's never seen before in her life. No keys. She tries the lobby doors, just in case. Locked, as usual.

It's not the first time Tallulah has lost her keys after a night (and day?) on the town. She eyes the fire escape—she keeps her bedroom window unlocked in case of situations like this—but the climb seems like a lot of effort. There are sixteen flats in her building, only one or two of them unoccupied. Someone will be along soon to let her inside.

Dusk now. She buttons up her jacket, turns up the collar, makes herself comfortable on the front steps. April in Moscow, when the sun goes down, is January in Oklahoma City. She takes Eva's pills and washes them down with a swig of the Zhuravli. Almost instantly she feels warmer. You see? These Russians have it all figured out.

Snowflakes, fat and wet. They melt on her eyelashes. She feels like running, leaping, flying. When doesn't she? But she's also content to just stay curled here on the steps. The neighborhood is relatively safe. She's nice and warm. One more sip of Zhuravli. All gone.

CHAPTER 35

Tallulah opens her eyes. She's been having the same nightmare all her life: she can't move, she's frozen, the light dims, her mother—her biological mother, whoever that might be—is just a receding shadow.

"You must come inside now, please," a voice says.

A little girl props the lobby door open with a book and steps outside. Blond braids, thick sweater, grave expression. And she's speaking English. It takes Tallulah a moment to realize.

"Must I?" Tallulah says. She's cold but comfortable.

"My name is Darya Nikolaevna Vasiliev," the girl says. "I am enchanted to make your acquaintance. You may call me Dasha."

"I know you." Tallulah has seen the girl around once or twice. She's not sure which family she belongs to, the one on the third floor or the one on the fifth. "Hi."

"You must come inside now, please."

The girl holds out her hand and helps Tallulah up. Good thing Tallulah is so small, five-two, barely a hundred pounds. The girl is maybe half that. Maybe nine or ten years old?

The warmth of the lobby closes around Tallulah like a hug. Ah. Nice. The girl tries to lead her to the elevator.

"I'm okay now," Tallulah says. "Thank you. You can fuck off now. I'm going to take the stairs."

"You are very drunk."

"Not really." Yes, the floor pitches and rolls beneath Tallulah's feet, but she's been a lot drunker than this. This isn't even close to what Tallulah would call "very drunk."

"I will see you safely to your flat," the girl says. She's so grave, so serious. Is it possible she's not actually a nine- or ten-year-old, but really just a very small adult person?

"I'm taking the stairs."

"Whatever you wish. I will see you safely to your flat."

Tallulah does just fine on the stairs, only a minor wobble or two. The girl keeps her hand resting on the small of Tallulah's back. "Are you a child or just a very small adult person?" For some reason Tallulah finds her own question hilarious. She starts laughing and can't stop.

"Careful, please."

"I'm an acrobat, you know. I perform acts of great daring."

"I know."

She knows? How does she know? Tallulah doesn't think she's ever had a conversation with the little girl, but maybe she just doesn't remember. She's not sure she'll remember *this* conversation.

"Here we are," the girl says.

"I'll prove it." Tallulah digs into her bag and pulls out the sequined leotard. Something clatters against the tile floor. Tallulah bends down to look. Her keys! She cracks up again.

The girl picks up the keys, finds the right ones, and unlocks the door of Tallulah's apartment. Tallulah makes it to the bathroom and barfs again. That's better. She swallows a Vicodin to head off tomorrow's hangover and tumbles into bed. The girl is still there, unlacing Tallulah's Doc Martens and tugging them off her feet.

"I'm enchanted to make your acquaintance," Tallulah starts to say, but she only gets partway through the sentence before she settles to the bottom of a soft, warm darkness.

I'm enchanted . . .

CHAPTER 36

Tallulah remembers nothing of her life before she became a Mercurio. She was only a baby, after all. Every now and then a fragment from a dream will linger after she wakes up—a woman's laugh, high-pitched and panicked; the taste of strong cheese; dust billowing from a beaten rug. The hint of a whisper of a rumor of a memory? Probably not. Probably just a dream.

Her first real memory, also just a fragment but solid, vivid, permanent: she sits on her brother Ray's broad shoulders, her fists clutching his hair, the world far below. Drops from a lawn sprinkler drum against her. A dog barks happily.

When she was six, first grade, Tallulah discovered she was different from her brothers and sister. It was brought to her attention by a couple of girls on the playground. Tallulah was *brown* and *dirty* and probably an *Eskimo*. The girls, her friends, came to this conclusion matter-of-factly, not unkindly. Tallulah didn't know what an Eskimo was. "I'm a Mercurio," she said.

But that planted the seed. She'd look at Jeremy and see their mom's eyes. She'd look at Alice and see Jeremy. Ray resembled their dad, just a lot, lot bigger. The nose, the heavy brow. Their dad smiled a lot. Did Tallulah have their dad's smile? She studied herself in the mirror. Hard to tell. She *did* look brown and dirty compared to the rest of the family. More of a reddish-brown, like the clay soil in Oklahoma City. Her eyes were tipped up at the corners, her nose and cheeks kind of squashed.

"You're not an Eskimo," Dad said. "Jesus Christ. Tell those kids at school to mind their own goddamn business."

"I'm a Mercurio."

"You're goddamn right you are."

By the time she was ten, Tallulah was used to people being surprised when Alice said, "She's my sister, why?" She was used to people asking her if she came over from Vietnam in a boat. "I came from Las Vegas. In a car. We all did." Mean kids at school called her names she didn't really understand. Nice kids called her names too but in a joking sort of way.

"Ain't nobody ever really joking," said Warren, who worked with their dad at the club. "Don't forget it."

In sixth grade, their class did a unit on Oklahoma history. The teacher explained that the word *Oklahoma* was the Indian word for "Land of the Red Man." She wrote it on the board in very pretty cursive, *Land of the Red Man*, then turned to smile at Tallulah. The whole class turned to stare at her too. She hated that.

In books, in movies, there were only two kinds of Indians, the poor pitiful ones on the Trail of Tears and the scary ones ambushing settlers and scalping soldiers. Tallulah knew she was different. A lot of people, though, didn't understand that.

Once, at North Park Mall, two teenage boys put their hands to their mouths and *whoop-whoop-whooped* at her. Tallulah's mom went over to them. Tallulah couldn't hear what she said to the boys, but their grins froze. They turned and walked away so quickly they clunked into each other.

Tallulah doesn't remember exactly when she figured out she was adopted. It was right around then, age ten or eleven. An ABC *Afterschool Special* may have been involved.

It kind of fucked Tallulah up for a while. Her mom and dad weren't her real mom and dad. Her real mom and dad had abandoned her. Think about it: you have to really be at the end of your rope to abandon your own baby; you have to really be sick of that kid.

She tried once, when she was living in San Francisco, to find out more about her real mom. Dead end. She didn't really try *that* hard. Tallulah already knows everything she needs to know about her real mom, doesn't she?

• • •

Sharp *rap-rap-rap* on the door. Tallulah spills out of bed, but lands on her feet. Hangovers never slow her down. The rapping continues, rhythmic and unrelenting. Tallulah opens the door. Irina, the building manager, scowls at her. Behind Irina, smiling, stands Ivan, her muscle, her *gopnik*. Ivan works for whatever mafia guy "privatized" the building.

"Good *afternoon*," Irina says, scornfully eyeing Tallulah's robe, her smeared mascara, her bedhead. Irina is stocky, strapping, with a pewter tooth and a bowl of gray hair. Tallulah can imagine her in charge of a Soviet gulag or winning a bronze medal in Greco-Roman wrestling at the Olympics. A widow with no children, Irina blames Gorbachev for the collapse of the empire. She despises capitalism, free speech, and the spread of degenerate Western values. Needless to say, she's not a big fan of Tallulah.

"Irina, what's the little blond girl's name?" Try as she might, Tallulah can't recall it. Maybe hangovers do slow her down just a bit. "Her family lives on the fifth floor."

"Who? There is no female child on the fifth floor."

"Or maybe the third floor. The little blond girl with the braids? She saved my bacon last night."

"I do not have time for this conversation," Irina says, scowling.

Oh, well. Tallulah hands over the rent. Irina counts the money slowly, *slowly*, licking her thumb after every single bill and shooting Tallulah suspicious glances. Ivan just smiles. Tallulah knows he carries a gun—she's caught a glimpse a couple of times, when he's left his black leather jacket unzipped. Not a big deal. This is Moscow. Every other guy on the street has a black leather jacket and a gun.

"Very well." Irina stuffs the money in the pocket of her housecoat. She always seems disappointed that Tallulah hasn't tried to cheat her.

CHAPTER 37

It's going to be a slow week or two. Tallulah and the others have to wait for Lev to find an inside man for the Stepanov job. Then they'll have to wait for Eva to insinuate herself into the guy's life and work her magic.

Tallulah—surprise—doesn't enjoy slow weeks. So she zips around Moscow on her noisy little Minsk MMVZ motorcycle, weaving through traffic at ridiculous velocities and popping wheelies. When she gets bored with that, she skateboards and smokes hash with the feral teen punks who lurk on the grounds of the abandoned biscuit factory.

Evenings, she hits the town with Eva. There's not much of a club scene in Moscow yet, but the underground parties are epic. A lot of times they're literally underground: basements, tunnels, crumbling bomb shelters, secret decommissioned Metro stations. One time a pipe burst and slowly filled the tunnel with water. Everyone just laughed and splashed and danced until the last possible moment. So much fun.

"You've got a screw loose, you know," Alice says.

"Maybe I do," Tallulah says. She honestly wouldn't want it any other way.

Tallulah and Alice talk on the phone every month or two. Tallulah tries to stay in touch with the family too. She sends postcards on a semi-regular basis to Mom and Dad, Jeremy, Ray, and Piggy.

Jeremy hardly ever writes back. His letters are impersonal and upbeat, like a report for investors, like a fan club newsletter. He moves around even more than Tallulah does—California for the first year or so after he left home, then Miami, Dallas, Puerto Rico. As of last December, he was back in Dallas, fired up by all the incredible opportunities in commercial real estate development there and engaged to be engaged to a former Miss Texas. This is—Tallulah has to stop to count—Jeremy's third engaged-to-be engagement.

Dad sends brief, occasional notes scribbled on the back of a losing tri-fecta ticket from Remington Park. "Heart fine." "Weather hot." Occasion-ally he calls to ask if Tallulah wants to get in on the ground floor of his latest venture. "Let me think about it, Dad." Mom sends greeting cards with pre-printed sentiments. "You are the light of my life." She never bothers to sign them.

Mom and Dad are still together after all these years. Tallulah isn't sur-prised. She vividly remembers that moment on the icy train tracks, the two of them kissing. It was so thrilling, so romantic.

Piggy, a student at OU, writes her two or three or even four times a week, a blizzard of letters. *Long* letters. Piggy wants to be a creative writer someday, a novelist. Tallulah doesn't know if he's any good at creative writ-ing, but he definitely puts a lot of effort into it, with sentences that make you dizzy they're so complicated and fancy words instead of normal ones.

His life is . . . Tallulah hates to say it, but Piggy's life at college seems extremely dull. He spends a full paragraph describing the sound of the fluo-rescent lights in the library. He spends a full paragraph detailing the route he takes from his dorm to the Student Union. He spends two paragraphs summarizing the plot of a Polish movie he saw.

Shouldn't Piggy, like, go to an occasional keg party? Or fall in love with some girl who already has a boyfriend? Or kidnap the mascot from some other school's football team?

In his letters, Piggy asks Tallulah a lot of questions about her life. She keeps it short and sweet, vague and G-rated. Piggy is the white sheep of the Mercurio family. Tallulah doesn't want to give him a heart attack.

Piggy is always trying to get her to start calling him Paul, not Piggy. Good luck with that, baby brother!

You know who writes good letters? Ray, believe it or not. He knows what details will make Tallulah smile. The Filipino Elvis impersonator at the El Marrakech Casino, for example. The Clark County Bureau of Records at three in the morning, crowded with drunk brides and grooms lined up to get marriage licenses.

Tonight, Friday, Tallulah is meeting Eva at nine. She rides her Minsk home to change. Outside her apartment building stands an Afghan vet with only one eye, palm out. Tallulah digs in the pocket of her coat and gives away all the cash she has with her, two crumpled 5,000-ruble bills. How much is that American? A couple of dollars? Inflation here is so crazy she's stopped keeping track.

Inside, sitting cross-legged in the hallway outside of Tallulah's flat and reading a book, is the little girl with French braids. She looks up and regards Tallulah gravely.

"You are late, Tallulah," she says.

"I am?"

"Since seven o'clock. One hour ago."

Tallulah has no idea what the girl is talking about. "Tell me your name again?"

"My name is Darya Nikolaevna Vasiliev. You may call me Dasha."

Right. "Dasha, I have no idea what you're talking about."

"We are watching a movie together on your videocassette player. *Citizen Kane.* You invited me. We made this arrangement when I helped you to your home."

"What?"

"Yes. I assure you."

Tallulah was admittedly trashed the night Dasha let her into the building. But wouldn't she remember asking a little girl to come over and watch *Citizen Kane*? Tallulah has no burning desire to watch *Citizen Kane*, a birthday present from Piggy, especially during prime party hours.

But . . . Dasha has closed her book, *The Sound and the Fury* by William Faulkner, and climbed to her feet. She waits. Big gray eyes, a grave, steady gaze. She's adorable but also just a tiny bit creepy—like a doll come to life, or an adult vampire in a child's body. Sober Tallulah wouldn't invite Dasha over to watch *Citizen Kane*, but Trashed Tallulah might have. It's plausible.

"Fine. Okay." Tallulah stops to think. Is this a responsible thing for her to do? Is she supposed to check with Dasha's parents first? Tallulah has no idea. "What about your parents? Are they cool with this?"

"They are cool. Yes. I assure you."

Good enough. Tallulah calls Eva to say she'll catch up with her later. She digs up a package of stale cookies for Dasha and pours a few fingers of vodka for herself. Dasha takes a seat, prim and perfect posture, on the middle cushion of the couch. Where is Tallulah supposed to sit? She has to pick a side.

Fifteen minutes into *Citizen Kane*, the lights wobble and the power dies. Not unusual for Moscow in general or Tallulah's apartment building in particular. Dasha helps her light candles.

"Shouldn't you go home?" Tallulah says. "I've got a flashlight somewhere. You can borrow it."

"My parents are not there. They have a function tonight."

Dasha bites into a cookie. She has sharp little vampire teeth—or maybe the candlelight just makes them seem that way.

"You have two boyfriends," she tells Tallulah. "I've seen them with you. They look very similar, but one is pragmatic and one is foolish."

Tallulah laughs. Dasha has Chekhov and Tolstoy down cold. "They're not my boyfriends."

"But they are both in love with you. I can see." Dasha frowns. "You must choose one."

"No, I mustn't. You'll see. How old are you?"

"I am ten years old."

When Tallulah was ten . . . well, she had very little adult supervision at that age too. She was hardly ever alone, though. Every time Tallulah has seen Dasha, she's been alone.

"Do you have brothers or sisters?"

"I do not."

In the flickering candlelight Dasha tells Tallulah about her parents. Her father is an engineer, "rather famous," who helped design and build the Mir Space Station. Her mother, "also rather famous," played cello in the State Academic Symphony Orchestra.

"Do you have brothers or sisters?" Dasha says.

"Boy, do I."

The phone rings. It's Eva. Tallulah can barely hear her over the din of music.

"Tallulah, *du musst jetzt kommen. Es ist die beste Party aller Zeiten!*"

When Eva is smashed, *really* smashed, she can only speak German. It doesn't matter. Tallulah gets the gist.

"Go home," Tallulah tells Dasha. "You've got your key?"

"Of course."

Tallulah pours herself another finger of vodka and wonders if she should walk the little girl back to her flat. Too late. When she turns back around, Dasha is already gone.

CHAPTER 38

She finds Eva around two in the morning, in a warehouse heaving with dancers. After a few hours of rejuvenating debauchery, Tallulah splits and takes a cab to Joe's apartment. He opens the door, groggy from sleep. She leaps into his arms and wraps her legs around his waist.

"Ready or not," she says.

Joe is American, works in economic development at the State Department, is possibly CIA. If Chekhov is Chekhov and Tolstoy is Tolstoy, that makes Joe . . . Tallulah needs to ask Piggy. Which author's writing is cynical and devious and charming? That's Joe. He, like Tallulah, doesn't see the appeal of traditional romantic relationships.

In the morning Tallulah brushes her teeth while Joe shaves.

"What will the CIA do now that there's not a Cold War anymore?" Tallulah asks.

"I'm not CIA," Joe says.

"It would suck if you were."

He makes a rueful face in the mirror.

Tallulah takes a cab home. As she's filling a glass full of water at the kitchen sink, she glances over and almost has a heart attack. There's the little girl with the blond French braids, Dasha, standing in Tallulah's kitchen and calmly observing her.

"How did you get in?" Tallulah says.

"You left your door open."

"I did?" Tallulah does leave her door open, occasionally, it's true.

"Shall I make toast for breakfast?" Dasha says.

"I don't have any bread."

"Tea?"

"Nope." *Go home*, Tallulah starts to tell her, but then changes her mind. All this talk of toast and tea has made her hungry. "Come on."

Down the block Tallulah buys two greasy kabobs from a street vendor. She and Dasha eat in front of the TV—a few more minutes of *Citizen Kane* and then, when that proves too placid for Tallulah, *Teenage Mutant Ninja Turtles* dubbed into Russian on Channel 2x2.

"Shouldn't you be in school?" Tallulah says.

"It is a holiday this month," Dasha says.

"Finish your goat on a stick and go home. I'm going to bed."

Dasha makes a face at the quality of Tallulah's humor. "It is not goat."

"Says you."

The next afternoon, Tallulah steps out of the shower and finds Dasha on the sofa, reading her battered paperback copy of *The Sound and the Fury*.

So, is this going to be a thing now? Dasha popping up out of nowhere and making herself at home?

"Where did you get that?" Tallulah says. "Isn't that, like, for adults?"

"It is quite amusing," Dasha says. "I am learning much about America."

"I doubt it."

When Tallulah finishes getting dressed, Dasha is still there. "I'm going for a ride," Tallulah says. "Hint, hint."

Dasha finishes the sentence she's reading before she closes her book. "Very well." She sighs, as if Tallulah has been down on her knees, begging her to come along. "I suppose I shall join you."

Tallulah, who apparently has no choice in this matter, shows Dasha how to hold tight, arms around Tallulah's waist. "Don't fall off until we find a helmet for you," Tallulah says.

They zoom across the city to the massive secondhand market at Luzhniki Stadium. You can find anything at the Luzhniki market, except a kid-sized motorcycle helmet. Tallulah has to settle for a dinged-up Dallas Cowboys souvenir football helmet, face mask missing. Good enough.

On the way back home, they stop at a kiosk on the street that rents pirated VHS tapes of American movies. Dasha picks out *A League of Their Own*, starring Tom Hanks and Madonna. Tallulah wonders how she'll be able to explain baseball to Dasha. How she'll be able to explain Madonna.

In the lobby, Irina the building manager scowls at Tallulah. She steps away and gives Tallulah a wide berth, as if capitalism is contagious. She might not be wrong about that, Tallulah supposes.

"See you later, alligator," Tallulah tells Dasha when the elevator doors open on the fourth floor.

"Shall we not watch our new movie?"

"Some other time. You're supposed to say 'After a while, crocodile.'"

"What?"

"You're supposed to say 'After a while, crocodile.'"

Dasha regards Tallulah with her grave, gray eyes. "I will not, thank you."

That's Sunday. On Monday they cross the river to Gorky. By American standards it's a grim and seedy park, with broken concrete and wind-blown trash and drunken soldiers staggering around, but the sun is shining and spring feels, finally, like the real deal and not just a trick winter is playing on you.

Wandering around, Tallulah and Dasha catch a few puzzled glances, a couple of sour frowns. It happened at the market too.

"Why do people stare at us?" Dasha asks Tallulah.

"People think I'm your mother and you're my kid," Tallulah says. "But you're white and I'm brown. Some Russians find that weird and disturbing."

"But Americans do not."

"Ha. No. Lots of Americans find it weird and disturbing too."

"Is your mother brown or white?"

"My mom is white. My real mother is brown, I guess."

"What is a real mother?"

"Why are we talking," Tallulah says, "when we could be riding something fast and dangerous?"

On the rickety roller coaster they both scream as the car plummets and twists. Tallulah throws her hands in the air. After a beat Dasha, smiling her sharp-toothed smile, does too.

CHAPTER 39

Tallulah doesn't mind this new wrinkle to her routine. A neighbor kid is less trouble than a cat or a dog. Tallulah can always kick Dasha out, back upstairs to her family, whenever she wants.

She and Dasha watch movies. They zip around town on the Minsk, Dasha's hot little face pressed between Tallulah's shoulder blades. Dasha teaches Tallulah about Russian history, the czars, all that. Dasha is pro-czar, anti-communist, agnostic at the moment on Yeltsin. That's actually the word Dasha uses: "agnostic." She reads the newspaper cover to cover, every day. But her favorite movie they watch is *It's a Mad, Mad, Mad, Mad World*, the dumbest movie ever, the silliest.

Tallulah still hasn't met or spoken to Dasha's parents, but Dasha says they know all about her—and they want Tallulah to come over for dinner. The problem is scheduling.

"They have many engagements, I am afraid," Dasha explains. "Next week, for an example, my father will play chess with Oleg Valerianovich Basilashvili. Do you know him? He is an actor, quite famous, and a politician as well."

Meanwhile, the rest of Tallulah's life continues to bubble happily along. After Dasha goes home, Tallulah hits the town with Eva. The nights roar past, a smear of bright colors outside the window of a bullet train. One night Tallulah finds herself riding a donkey down a street. Where did the donkey come from? Why are people cheering? Who knows?

This morning, Tallulah makes it home a little after nine. She collapses into bed. No Dasha yet. She's learned that Tallulah is more sociable after noon.

Knuckles *rap-rap-rap* against the door. Tallulah drags herself back out of bed. It's Irina. Tallulah is perplexed. Irina never appears unless the rent is due.

"I already paid you this month," Tallulah says.

Irina's eyes fire darts of disapproval at the shocking display of degenerate Western capitalism in Tallulah's flat—the Frida Kahlo print on the wall, the stack of VHS tapes on the coffee table, the empty Coke can on the TV.

"I will show you something in the basement," Irina says. "Come with me."

"The basement?" Tallulah says. "Enticing, but I'm going back to bed. I spent last night corrupting the morals of nice communist boys."

She tries to shut the door. Irina moves fast and gets her big block of a shoe in the way. "You must come with me immediately," Irina says.

Fuck it. Tallulah is too tired to put up a fight. She and Irina take the elevator to the basement. The basement is what you'd expect: dark and creepy and cobwebby, a low-ceilinged labyrinth of junk and junk and more junk, a century's worth of cracked toilets and moldering curtains.

They walk and walk, turning and turning. Finally, Irina stops. She points. "Do you see?" she says.

See what? A patch of concrete floor bordered on three sides by stacked boxes and some junk. An old blanket and a pillow. A hairbrush, a tin cup with a toothbrush.

Someone, Tallulah realizes, must be squatting in the basement. So? Squatters are more common than mice in Moscow. This is Irina's problem to deal with, not Tallulah's.

"Your new friend," Irina says. "You told me she lives here in the building. I investigate, thanks to you. And you are correct."

It takes Tallulah a second to connect the various dots. Wait. *What?* "Dasha?" Tallulah says. "She's living down here?"

That can't be possible. Dasha's family has a flat. They live on the third or fifth floor. Dasha's parents are rather famous, remember? An engineer and a cello player . . .

Oh, god. Tallulah can't believe how oblivious she's been. This is why Dasha's parents are always canceling dinner plans. This is why Tallulah's never met them or been to the flat. Of course. And the school holiday . . .

"For months, perhaps." Irina nods. "Very sneaky, this child. But now I have a proposition for you."

"A proposition?" Tallulah kneels to touch a corner of the thin blanket. She wonders how Dasha can possibly stay warm. And how does Dasha manage to fall asleep in such a creepy, cobwebby place?

"The girl will bring a very nice sum of money," Irina says. "We will divide it equally. I know someone who can arrange everything. Quickly and discreetly. I promise. You will not lift a finger."

"*What?*" Tallulah says.

Irina just smiles. She never smiles. Tallulah can't remember a single time. It's ghastly, a smile with no humor or warmth, Irina's teeth like the broken gray blocks of concrete in Gorky Park.

"You want to . . ." Tallulah says. Her stomach is a knot on top of a knot, a dirty broken shoelace. Irina is joking. Surely, Irina is joking. "You want to *sell* her?"

"The market will be very strong," Irina says, still smiling that ghastly smile. "Think how many men will treasure such a beautiful girl as this."

CHAPTER 40

Back upstairs, in her flat, Tallulah takes a swig of vodka. It shouldn't shock her that Moscow is the kind of place where you can buy or sell a ten-year-old girl like she's a pair of jeans, but . . .

"Consider my proposition," Irina said in the basement, walking away before Tallulah, dazed, could think of anything to say. "The girl trusts you. We will make a pretty penny."

Tallulah has to find Dasha. That, clearly, is her first order of business. Find Dasha and keep her safe from Irina. *Immediately.*

But where should Tallulah start looking? She has no idea. She corks the vodka and suddenly there stands Dasha, helping herself to a stick of Tallulah's sour Russian chewing gum.

"Shit!" Tallulah almost drops the vodka bottle. She's relieved to see Dasha, but the kid's vampire stealth isn't great for Tallulah's current state of mind.

Dasha shrugs off her knapsack and drops it at her feet. She's always carrying that knapsack, another clue that blew right past Tallulah. The knapsack must be holding everything she owns.

"Shall we go to the park?" Dasha says. "The weather today is quite pleasant."

"You're living alone in the basement?" Tallulah says. "You've been lying to me all this time about your flat and your parents?"

If Dasha is flustered or disconcerted by being caught dead to rights, she sure doesn't show it. "Yes, you are correct," she says. "I created a fiction for you."

"A *fiction*? You lied! And . . ." Tallulah wants to be angry, furious, but she can't shake the image of the basement from her mind. Dasha is only *ten years old*. And she's been living down there, alone, for *months*. Not to mention . . .

"Yes?" Dasha asks.

"I'll be back in two minutes," Tallulah says. "Lock the door behind me and don't leave. Do not let *anyone* in. Understand?"

"Very well."

On the first floor, Tallulah pounds on Irina's door. Irina cracks it.

"Good," Irina says. "You have acted with alacrity. We must not delay."

With the steel toe of her Doc Martens boot, Tallulah kicks the door all the way open. Irina jumps back with a bark of alarm and affront.

"Listen to me," Tallulah says. *Now* she has no problem getting, and staying, furious. It doesn't help her mood that she's the reason Irina knows about Dasha in the first place. If Dasha ends up a sex slave in some perverted oligarch's dacha, Tallulah will be the one to blame.

"Keep away from the girl. You're not going to sell her. You're not going to touch her. You're not even going to *look* at her."

Irina blinks and blinks. Her eyes are the same dull, Soviet gray as her dishwater hair, her pewter tooth. "How dare you!" she says.

"Me?"

"I would never suggest such a thing," Irina says. "Sell a child? Bah!"

"Yeah, right," Tallulah says. "You need to understand me. If you even *look* at her, I swear I will . . ."

Tallulah is too worked up to think of a vivid and terrifying threat. She's never been good at threats anyway. Her sister, Alice, was an artist, devastatingly surgical. Tallulah remembers the boy at Baskin-Robbins who refused to let the Mercurio kids have more than one ice cream sample per day. Alice found out he was giving free scoops to his friends and used that information to . . .

"Leave her alone," Tallulah says. "Or I'll tell the people you work for how much I'm paying for rent. Let's find out if it's what they *think* I'm paying for rent."

Bingo. Irina takes a sharp breath. Her hatred of Tallulah radiates like a fever. Finally, she nods.

"Good," Tallulah says.

• • •

"Start talking," Tallulah tells Dasha. "And no more lies. No more *fiction*."

"My mother and father are dead," Dasha says. "It happened quite long ago—an automobile accident, on Zhivopisny Bridge. A rainy evening, a sleepy man in his truck. You know how these things are."

Dasha sits, posture perfect, on the sofa. Her tone is casual, matter-of-fact, as if she's relating a ho-hum plot of a forgettable movie.

Tallulah's chest tightens. She rubs her nose hard, so she won't start crying. "I'm so sorry," she says.

Dasha eyes her with curiosity. "It happened quite long ago, as I said. I was six years old."

And now she's living, alone, in a basement. Tallulah goes to the kitchen and returns with the vodka. "Keep going."

"I went to stay with my uncle," Dasha says. "Anatoly Viktorovich Balikin. He is a bachelor but an excellent guardian. I have a nanny when he is at his office. When he comes home, we eat dinner together, we discuss the events of the day. He taught me to play chess and to speak English. He taught me to never fear wolves."

"Wolves?" Tallulah says. "Where did you live?"

"No," Dasha says slowly, patiently. "It is merely a parable. A rule to live by? 'You must explore the forest. You must not fear the wolves.'"

"Your uncle, where is he now?"

"He is gone. Since five months ago now."

Fuck! Could the little girl's story get any darker? Tallulah pours herself another shot. "I'm so sorry."

"No, no," Dasha says. "You misunderstand once again. My uncle is not dead, only gone. He has disappeared."

"Disappeared?"

For the first time during her story, Dasha hesitates. "I can trust you."

"Yes, of course."

Dasha considers, then nods solemnly. "Five months ago, late in the night, my uncle wakes me."

He tells Dasha to get dressed, quickly, to ask no questions. He kisses the tip of her nose, then looks into her eyes.

"I must go away for a time," he says. "You will go with Svetlana now. You will be safe with her. I will return for you."

The uncle drives away, into the moonless night. Dasha and Svetlana, the nanny, take a taxi to a tourist hotel near Red Square. A day passes. A week. Svetlana begins to pace, to chew her fingernails.

Another week passes. Dasha overhears Svetlana, on the phone, whispering. "I don't fucking know," Svetlana whispers. "How long can I risk my life?"

The next morning, Svetlana hugs Dasha. "Goodbye," she says. She presses a crumpled wad of ruble notes into Dasha's hand. "Good fortune."

Two days later, the hotel manager informs Dasha that she must vacate the room. New guests have arrived. So Dasha leaves. She doesn't know what to do, where to go. She and her uncle have no other relatives in Russia. Eventually Dasha finds the basement of Tallulah's building, where it is dry and quiet and safe.

Dasha finishes her story and plugs a pirated copy of *Back to School* into the VCR. Tallulah absorbs everything Dasha has told her. Dasha's uncle, it's pretty clear, must be on the run—from the Russian mafia, Tallulah bets. CIA Joe says every successful businessman in Moscow has to deal with the mafia. Loans, protection, money laundering. The mafia in Russia is like the Chamber of Commerce in America.

That fucking nanny! She was supposed to protect Dasha. Though Tallulah can't be too pissed off at Svetlana. She's probably only nineteen or twenty, overwhelmed. She didn't sign up for this.

Tallulah is feeling a little overwhelmed herself, a bit dizzy—and not in a fun way. But it's okay. Probably the uncle is desperately searching for Dasha right now, right at this moment.

"Does your uncle have any close friends?" Tallulah says. "Someone he trusts. Someone, you know . . ."

Dasha, engrossed by Rodney Dangerfield, doesn't answer.

If the uncle had close friends he could trust, Tallulah realizes, he would have left Dasha with one of them.

But it's okay. Dasha can stay here, safe with Tallulah for a couple of days, until Tallulah can find someone who can handle this situation—someone who can take Dasha off her hands, find the uncle, and restore their happy family. It will be okay.

CHAPTER 41

Tallulah wakes a little after six in the evening. A sweet spring breeze stirs the curtains. She yawns, stretches. For a moment it's just Friday, any Friday. Then it all comes back to her, piece by piece, like birds settling one by one onto a telephone wire. Ominous birds, Hitchcock birds. Irina, the basement, Dasha, the missing uncle.

In the bathroom, Tallulah applies her stage makeup. She waits for inspiration to strike, for a solution to the Dasha problem to present itself.

Nothing. Not yet.

Dasha sits curled in a chair, reading. Tallulah laces up her Doc Martens and pulls on her leather jacket.

"I have to work tonight," Tallulah says. "You can sleep on the couch. There's an extra pillow and blankets in the closet."

"May I bathe?"

"Sure. I guess. Can you, by yourself?"

Dasha looks up from her book and regards Tallulah evenly, icily.

"Fine, you can bathe yourself," Tallulah says. "Just lock the door the second I leave and don't open it for *any*one."

"You have explained this to me already."

"I'm reminding you." What else? Tallulah thinks. "Are you hungry?"

"Yes."

"Help yourself to anything you want." Anything being, Tallulah realizes, basically nothing. The remainder of the stale cookies, an antique jar of pickled anchovies that came with the flat. In the fridge, a few cans of Fruktoviy

Sad, the sad Russian version of V8 juice. "I'll pick something up on my way home. Some delicious goat on a stick."

"Goodbye."

...

The gig tonight is legit, some fat cat's birthday, too much security to even ever dream about robbing his mansion. Carnival Uncommon puts on the usual show. Eva juggles, Boyle clowns, Lev eats fire. Tolstoy and Chekhov fling Tallulah into the air. Up, up, up. She spins and relaxes, back in her natural habitat.

But she can't help thinking about Dasha. Balancing one-legged on Tolstoy's palm, Tallulah scans the fat cat's ballroom. Usually, Tallulah enjoys the spectacle. Tonight, though, see notices more sharply how young all the "dates" are, the mistresses and escorts. They wobble on stiletto heels, in cocktail dresses that barely cover their butts. Some of them can't be more than sixteen, seventeen years old. They're laughing, dancing, snorting coke. And desperately wishing—you can see it in their eyes—they were anywhere but here.

Is this the terrible future that awaits Dasha? This might not even be the worst possible outcome for her.

Tolstoy glances up at her, feeling the extra tension in Tallulah's muscles. She takes a deep breath and returns to her body. Muscle, tendon, skin, and pulse. She leaps, she soars.

After their last set, they head to Sheriff. Lev gathers everyone in a booth. The big news: Lev has finally found a security guard for Eva to charm. The Stepanov job is on.

"I'll need a few weeks," Eva says.

Lev strokes his dyed-gray goatee. "I am afraid not, my dear. You must accelerate the process. In ten days, the Stepanov family returns from their vacation in Hurghada."

"No, Lev," Eva says. "Ten days! No, I can't rush it. This is a dance."

"And the music ends in ten days."

Tallulah isn't really paying attention. Her mind has drifted back to Dasha. It's one in the morning. Tallulah's flat is a lot less scary than the basement, but still . . . Dasha is ten years old, she shouldn't be alone in the middle of the night.

Boyle glares across the table at Tallulah, waiting for her to say something so he can disagree with whatever position she takes.

"I'm with Eva," Tallulah says.

"Of fucking course," Boyle says, disgusted.

"I have already decided," Lev says. "*Fin.*"

He orders another bottle of vodka for the table. Tallulah follows Eva to the ladies' room, which at Sheriff is also the men's room—a single sink, a single toilet, a grimy mirror. Tolstoy squeezes in behind them. "Forgive me," he says, "I need to piss like a horse."

Tallulah swears them both to secrecy. Lev can't know about this conversation. It's easy to forget sometimes, because he looks like a rumpled university professor, but Lev is stone cold. This is his crew, his livelihood. Tallulah is good at what she does, but not good enough not to give Lev heartburn. If Lev thinks she's distracted . . .

While Eva swipes lipstick and dabs concealer, while Tolstoy pisses like a horse, Tallulah fills them in on Dasha.

"I don't understand," Eva says when Tallulah finishes.

"Her parents are dead," Tallulah explains again. "Her uncle, who was raising her, is on the run. She was living alone in the basement of the building and the landlord wants to sell her and she's only ten fucking years old!"

"She understands all that," Tolstoy says.

"I understand all that," Eva says. "Why is it your concern? That, I don't understand. The child is not your problem."

"In Russia," Tolstoy explains to Tallulah, "we worry for ourselves. Life is hard. Does a man ask another man if he can carry his burden? No! The man will be insulted by this offer."

"She's not a *man*. She's a little girl!"

Eva puts her hand over Tolstoy's mouth to keep him quiet. "Tallulah," she says, "what can you do, even if you wished?"

"I need to find someone who can find her uncle."

"You can't go to the police, of course," Eva says.

Tallulah knows. The chances of finding an honest cop in Moscow are vanishingly slim. "But what about social services? Whatever it's called here. Or like some charity?"

Tolstoy shakes his head dolefully. "She is safer on the streets than in a Russian orphanage."

"He's right," Eva says. "My god. They are like a nightmare."

"There has to be *someone* who can help her," Tallulah says.

Tolstoy shrugs. Eva shrugs.

"She is not your problem," Eva says again, her voice low and soothing.

After one more drink, Tallulah slips out of Sheriff early and calls CIA Joe from a pay phone. He remembers the Balikin disappearance. The story made all the newspapers and scared the shit out of every businessman doing business with the Russian mafia.

"Who should I talk to?" Tallulah says.

"Nobody. Do not get yourself involved in this situation. That's the best advice you'll ever get in your life. You're welcome."

"Fuck you, Joe."

"I'm serious. Whoever's after Balikin is bad news. Bad, scary news. The guy might already be dead, you know."

"He might not be."

"And Russia might one day rise from the ashes of the Soviet Union and become a functioning democracy with Western values."

"Come on. There's nothing you can do? Nothing, like, the State Department can do?"

"You overestimate my influence, babe. I'm a nobody. I transcribe interviews with wheat farmers. I file them."

"Oh, bullshit. You have to know somebody who knows somebody."

She hears ice clinking in a glass, Joe taking a sip of his good, imported bourbon.

"Let me think about it," he says. "In the meantime, why don't you come over? We can talk about all this in the morning."

Tallulah is more tempted than she'd like to admit. She can almost taste his good bourbon, can almost feel his hands on her hips. Her mind empty, clear, free.

"Fuck you, Joe," she says, and hangs up.

CHAPTER 42

Tallulah doesn't sleep well. She's in bed too early and her internal clock is off. Her body can't understand why it's not dancing, fucking, speeding through the darkness.

But in the morning, she has an idea. She'll track down one of the reporters who wrote about Balikin's disappearance. Maybe the reporter has some clue about where Dasha's uncle might be.

"I shall come with you," Dasha announces after they finish a breakfast of boiled sausage from a kiosk down the block.

"You shall not," Tallulah says. "I don't know how long I'll be gone. And you'll slow me down."

"It is my uncle we search for."

This is new. Dasha, jaw set stubbornly and brow bristling, has never seemed more Russian. Tallulah doesn't know if she can win this battle.

"Fuck."

"You should not curse," Dasha says. "It is a low habit."

"Fuck, fuck, fuckity fuck," Tallulah says. "Come on. Let's go."

Her best bet, Tallulah decides, is the *Moscow Times*, a newspaper geared toward expats that's printed in both Russian and English. The offices are in the old *Pravda* building. Tallulah knows this because she and Eva once attended a rave at a shooting range down the block. They drank *samogon*, Russian moonshine, and got to fire old machine guns from World War II.

Tallulah and Dasha climb the stairs, following the sound of a typewriter. *Clack-clack-clack DING*. In a small office they find a woman furiously smoking, typing, and drinking coffee all at the same time. She pauses none of it while Tallulah asks about the Balikin article.

"That was December 16 or 17." The *Moscow Times* woman is a few years older than Tallulah, American, with long bangs that she has to keep huffing out of her eyes. "Check the morgue."

"The morgue?"

She whips the sheet of paper from the typewriter, stubs out her cigarette, tips back her head to get the very last drop of coffee from the mug. "Where are you from?"

"Oklahoma. You?"

"Jersey. Come on. I'll show you the morgue."

The morgue, to Tallulah's relief, is not an actual morgue, but a room where past issues of the newspaper are stored.

The woman digs around until she finds the *Moscow Times* from December 17, 1993. The Balikin disappearance is on the front page, down in the bottom corner. "Moscow Businessman Reported Missing." No photo. Tallulah skims the article. Not much she doesn't already know. Balikin's secretary notified the police when Balikin didn't show up for work. He had a big meeting scheduled with a company called the Petrov Group.

Balikin's neighbors claim to know nothing. The police suspect foul play. Tallulah gets the sense, from the tone and brevity of the article, that a Moscow businessman disappearing isn't exactly man bites dog.

The byline on the article is Liz McLaughlin.

"You?" Tallulah asks the woman from Jersey.

"How'd you guess? I'm the copy editor too. And the staff photographer."

Tallulah asks if there's anything she might have left out of the article. "I'm trying to find him."

"Balikin?"

"He is my uncle," Dasha says.

Liz McLaughlin studies Dasha for a beat. "Hey, kid," she says. "You know how to work a Xerox machine? Go upstairs, the office down from mine, and make a copy of this."

Dasha, affronted by the presumption she might not know how to work a Xerox machine, marches away.

"Dude is probably in small pieces somewhere," Liz says when she's sure Dasha is gone. "It's been almost six months."

Tallulah ignores that. "Did you talk to the secretary? Do you know her name?"

Liz lights a fresh cigarette and blows smoke at the ceiling. "The secretary moved to Yakutsk before I could talk to her. About as far as you can get from Moscow. I doubt it was a coincidence."

And the company, she says, the Petrov Group, is a shell within a shell within a shell. Tallulah will have better luck trying to find the secretary in Yakutsk.

Dasha returns with the copy of the article, sheet of paper still warm from the Xerox machine. Tallulah folds it up and sticks it in the back pocket of her jeans. Her head aches and she isn't even hungover.

"Be careful," Liz says.

CHAPTER 43

On the way home they stop by the Luzhniki market again. Tallulah searches and searches until she finally finds a proper motorcycle helmet that fits Dasha's head.

"I prefer this one," Dasha says, refusing to surrender her Dallas Cowboys helmet.

"It's not safe," Tallulah says. "You need a safe one."

"As do you, then. You do not even have a helmet."

"I don't need one." But Tallulah sees the look on Dasha's face, the argument forming, Dasha preparing to step before the Supreme Court, or whatever it's called in Russia. "But okay, yeah, okay." Tallulah forks over another three thousand rubles for an adult-sized helmet, stickered with naked women and patriotic bears. Jesus.

Everything Dasha owns, Tallulah remembers, is stuffed into her knapsack. How has she been keeping her clothes clean? Tallulah buys her a few T-shirts, a pair of jeans, a couple of sweaters. They hit GUM, the big department store, for two three-packs of genuine Fruit of the Loom, one in pink and one in blue. Come on, Tallulah's not *that* bad, she's not going to buy Dasha underwear from a flea market.

Last stop is Eliseevsky on Tverskaya Street, a former palace the Soviets turned into a grocery store. Under the vaulted ceiling and crystal chandeliers, Tallulah stocks up. Bread, cheese, apples, pears. Healthier for a kid than goat kebabs or donuts sold out of the trunk of a Lada. Milk, eggs. Dasha insists on inspecting and approving everything, every single item, before Tallulah drops it in the basket.

Back home, Dasha reads and Tallulah sits out on the rickety fire escape.

The fresh air helps her, sort of, not freak out. This isn't going to be as simple or as easy as she imagined. *Tallulah* will have to find Dasha's uncle—somehow. And until then, *Tallulah* has sole responsibility for the health and well-being of a ten-year-old child. Tallulah wonders if there is anyone, *anyone*, less qualified for either job.

What if Anatoly Balikin really *is* dead? Then what?

She hears the phone ring. Tallulah crawls back through the window and into the flat. Dasha holds the receiver to her ear. "One moment, please." She turns to Tallulah. "A man named Paul."

"Who?" Tallulah takes the receiver. "Who's this?"

"Tallulah?"

"Oh. Piggy."

"Who was that?" he says. "Who answered the phone?"

"One of the other sisters. Here at the convent."

"What! One of the *other*..." He finally gets the joke. "Very funny. And can you please, please call me Paul? Do you have any idea what it's like to go through life with a nickname like Piggy?"

"Tough titties, baby brother," Tallulah says. "How's it going? What time is it there?"

"A little after seven."

"In the morning? Oh, Piggy, please tell me you've been up all night. Please tell me you've been to a keg party or something."

"Speaking of parties," Piggy says, "it's Mom's birthday next month, right? I have it on good authority that Jeremy might be in town. So, if there's any way you could fly home for a week or so, and we can get Ray and Alice on board..."

Piggy is always, *always* trying to orchestrate a family reunion. Tallulah feels sorry for him. He's the youngest in the family by a good chunk of years. By the time he was five or six, the other Mercurio kids were in junior high and high school. Piggy was practically an only child.

"I don't know, Piggy," Tallulah says. "It might be kind of tough for me to get home right now."

"Well, then, I don't know. I mean ... I've got summer break coming up. By the way."

He's also always angling—subtly, he thinks—for an invitation to visit her. Can you imagine Piggy in Moscow? He wouldn't last five minutes in Tallulah's world. Even Eva would eat him alive. *Especially* Eva.

"I've got to bounce, Piggy," Tallulah says. "Talk to you later."

For dinner Tallulah scrambles eggs, the one thing she knows how to cook. Around eight, Eva calls. She tells Tallulah to meet her at the Hermitage Garden. From there they'll go to a bash the Night Wolves, Moscow's version of the Hells Angels, are throwing.

"Mick Jagger will be there," Eva says. "That is the rumor."

That's always the rumor. Still, Tallulah feels a pang. Bashes thrown by the Night Wolves are never anything less than memorable.

But she can't leave Dasha alone all night again. At least not two nights in a row. And if Tallulah does go out, she can't get smashed. What if she gets home after a night out and Dasha is, like, sick? And needs a doctor? And Tallulah is too smashed to find her keys again?

"Well?" Eva says.

"Next time," Tallulah forces herself to say.

In the middle of the night a barking dog wakes Tallulah. *Yip, yip, yip.* A tiny frantic barking dog, in Tallulah's flat. What? Tallulah shuffles into the living room. Dasha is asleep on the couch, blanket kicked off and one arm flung to the side. The *yipping* is coming from her. Her Russian beetle-brows are knitted, and a fat teardrop is squeezing out from the corner of her eye. A dream, a bad one.

Tallulah places a palm against Dasha's cheek. With her other palm—this is a trick Tallulah remembers Alice used on her whenever she had a bad dream—she presses lightly but firmly on Dasha's sternum.

"You're okay," Tallulah says, "you're okay, you're okay."

After a few seconds, Dasha stops yipping and her breathing steadies. She lets out a peaceful snort and smacks her lips. Tallulah smiles. She's okay.

CHAPTER 44

The next morning Tallulah is rereading the *Moscow Times* article when she lands on the address, Balikin's home address, where he and Dasha lived. What if . . . no, that would be too easy, so obvious. But what if Balikin has returned home? Maybe—it's possible!—he's not even missing anymore, but just keeping a low profile as he searches for Dasha.

The odds that Balikin is still alive *and* back home are astronomically long, the length of the expanding universe. It's worth a shot, though. It's better than sitting around, doing nothing.

Dasha, again, insists on coming along. She also insists on expressing her opinion about the idea. "It is unlikely he has returned home," she says.

"I *know* that," Tallulah says.

She digs up her tattered map of Moscow and pinpoints Balikin's address. Tallulah knows the area, Rublyovka, the leafy western suburbs outside the Rings, along the bank of the river. Carnival Uncommon has played parties out there, in newly built mansions designed to look like Disney castles.

Tallulah squeezes into her new helmet. The ride out to the suburbs takes about forty-five minutes. She's getting used to having Dasha plastered to her. The extra weight on the bike makes cornering a snap.

Dasha's street is Mikhaylov Lane. And it is kind of a lane, winding and quaint, the houses nice but not over-the-top. No gates, no Disney castles. Tallulah stops at the corner and checks the address she's jotted down. The Minsk, idling, throbs and belches. A lady steps out of her house to water the flowers. She gives Tallulah a brisk nod, the Russian equivalent of a big friendly smile.

"That's the one?" Tallulah asks Dasha, pointing. Brick, two stories, ringed by budding beeches. "The gray house with the yellow shutters?"

For a second Dasha doesn't answer. She's just gazing, her visor flipped up, taking it all in. Tallulah wonders what she must be feeling, back home after so many months away.

"That is correct," Dasha says.

"Let's check it out."

Tallulah parks her bike. She and Dasha walk up the flagstone pathway. It's a sunny day, the air out here in the suburbs less burnt and grimy than in the city. But Tallulah also starts to feel . . . what? A stillness, a faint vibration, a static charge in the air. She stops.

"Trust your instincts," her dad used to say. "God gave the Mercurios a head start, but only if we're smart enough to use it."

Once, at a jewelry store, Tallulah watched her mom examine a bracelet. When the clerk turned his back, her mom started to slip the bracelet into her pocket . . . but didn't. She placed the bracelet back on the counter. On their way out, Tallulah saw that a second clerk had emerged from a back room. Tallulah's mom, her back turned, couldn't have seen him. How did she know he was there?

"Put your helmet back on," Tallulah tells Dasha. "Let's go."

Dasha frowns. "Already?"

Tallulah takes Dasha by the shoulders and steers her into a sharp U-turn, away from the house. That's when she sees the car—a black Mercedes-Benz, parked down the street. So what, right? If Tallulah had a ruble for every black Mercedes-Benz in Moscow . . .

Two guys sit in the Benz. Thick necks, slicked-back hair, Ray-Bans. If Tallulah had a ruble for every thick-necked guy in Russia with slicked-back hair and Ray-Bans . . .

"Yes, already," Tallulah says. "Let's get out of here."

They climb back onto the bike. Tallulah kicks it to life. One of the guys in the Benz has picked up a car phone. He's speaking into it, rapidly. *Fuck.* How could Tallulah be so dumb? The guys in the Benz are the people who want to kill Dasha's uncle. Of course they'd be staking out his house in case he returns. And now Tallulah has la-di-da'd right into their crosshairs.

Tallulah putters past the Benz. Nice and easy, no need for hysterics. Because she reminds herself, the guys in the Benz want to kill *Anatoly Balikin*. They're not interested in some random brown chick and a random blond kid on an old motorcycle.

Left turn, right turn, nice and easy. Tallulah is just starting to relax when the Benz swims into her mirror, a block behind them. Following them, no question about it.

But why? The answer comes quickly. Too quickly. The guys in the Benz are very *much* interested in a little blond girl returning to the house on Mikhaylov Lane. They know she's Anatoly Balikin's beloved niece. And Anatoly Balikin's beloved niece will give them valuable leverage—a hostage who might flush Balikin out of hiding.

Fuck. Images flash through her mind as Tallulah imagines the worst: a bloody finger in a box, a severed ear.

Left turn. Tallulah opens the throttle a little, but she knows she won't be able to outrun the Benz, not on the Minsk, not on these stupid *lanes*. The Mercedes pops back into her mirror, closer now.

Tallulah feels Dasha's arms tighten around her waist. Maybe Dasha has that Mercurio spidey-sense too. Well, no way will Tallulah let these assholes get their hands on her.

Right turn. Tallulah guns it, hits the next turn before the Benz can make the previous one. She spots a pile of firewood stacked head-high next to a house. That will have to do. She parks the Minsk behind the firewood, the bike hidden—she hopes!—from the street.

"Let's play a game," Tallulah says.

"What game?" Dasha says.

"Like hide-and-seek, but just the hide part. We're going to hide somewhere and be very quiet."

"That's all?" Dasha says, dubious.

"Come on."

They have, at best, three seconds. Behind the house is a big lawn and a small shed. Unlocked, thank god. Tallulah and Dasha slip inside. It's dark. Tallulah wishes the shed was darker, and bigger.

She points Dasha into the space beneath a workbench and squeezes in behind her. There's just barely enough room for one small child and one small woman, behind a wooden crate of tools.

"And now?" Dasha says. "This seems a very simple and insipid game."

"I told you," Tallulah says. "*Quiet*. Don't even breathe."

Tallulah waits. Maybe the Benz missed the first turn. Maybe the Benz made the first turn but didn't see the motorcycle behind the firewood and sped right past. Maybe . . .

She hears the faint, throaty purr of German engineering. Brakes squeak. A moment passes, and then a car door slams shut. A second car door slams shut. Shoes scrape on the driveway.

Tallulah hates herself. How could she be so dumb, so *reckless*, putting Dasha in this situation? The shed is a terrible hiding place, the first place the two guys will look. They'll grab Dasha and drag her away by her blond braids. They'll kill Tallulah. They'll *have* to kill Tallulah, before she lets them drag Dasha away.

Silence. Footsteps on a grass lawn don't make noise. Tallulah truly isn't breathing at this point. She eyes the crate of tools. What will make a better weapon? The belt sander or the stud finder? Neither.

The two guys are silent too. No talking. They're communicating with hand signals, probably. Professionals. One will go to the door of the shed, the other will cover the . . .

A dog barks. What sounds like a big, aggravated dog.

"Hey, you!" a man says in Russian. "What are you doing back here?"

"Calm down, old man," another voice says. One of the guys from the Benz. "Take it easy with that toy."

"Toy? Let me put a bullet in your gut and you tell me then, this is a toy."

"Hey, hey, hey," says the second guy from the Benz. "Just . . ."

"I am GRU," the man, the homeowner with the gun and the dog, says. "You know what that means? I hope you do, for your sake."

Tallulah isn't sure what GRU means, only that it has something to do with the Russian military. Whatever the case, it shuts up the two guys from the Benz.

"Good boys," the homeowner says. "Now drive away. I'm going to go make a call now, in case you decide to turn around."

Car doors slam. Tallulah hears the Benz's engine purr and fade. She hears dog nails click on wooden steps. The back door of the house opens and closes.

"And now," Tallulah whispers to Dasha, "we sneak out and get on the bike and go."

Traffic is a mess on the Ring Road. Tallulah whips between the creeping, honking cars. Like her old days as a bike messenger. Like the old days on the dance floor of Club Mercurio. Tallulah, free and clear, should be elated. But something is different now. The kid with her face pressed against Tallulah's back, the one she almost got killed or worse, makes everything different.

CHAPTER 45

Tuesday, Wednesday, Thursday. Each morning Tallulah wakes with zero new ideas. Each night, when she goes to bed, the same.

At least she's certain now, pretty much so, that Dasha's uncle is still alive. Otherwise, the guys in the Benz wouldn't be watching his house, wouldn't have gone after Dasha.

But if those guys can't find Anatoly Balikin, how will Tallulah? And what happens to her the next time she gets in their way? What happens to Dasha if something happens to Tallulah?

After dinner they walk down the block to the VHS kiosk. Out of the blue Dasha takes Tallulah's hand. Tallulah, surprised, doesn't know what to do. Dasha's hand is small, warm, a little sticky. Tallulah honestly can't remember the last time she held a kid's hand. Ever? Not since she was a kid herself. A memory flickers: sunny summer day, Memorial Park in Oklahoma City, Alice grabbing her hand, or maybe it was Jeremy, grabbing her hand and dragging Tallulah, barely able to walk yet, toward some family adventure.

Tallulah hates being responsible for another human being, a kid. Also, she doesn't hate it. That's the confusing part. It's an exhausting *weight*, for example, to always keep an eye on Dasha—to make sure she doesn't fall into an open manhole or disappear in a jostling crowd at the Metro station or step in front of a speeding, weaving drunk driver. Moscow is full of crowds and open manhole covers and drunk drivers. Tallulah never realized how full until now.

But always keeping an eye on Dasha—it's kind of a nice weight too, like a heavy blanket on top of you at night, like the ballast in the hold of a ship that keeps it steady.

Dasha herself is a pain in the ass. She's bossy and doesn't seem to understand that she's only ten years old and Tallulah, an actual adult, is in charge of *her*. Dasha, for example, is full of unsolicited pronouncements.

"You drink too much," she pronounced this morning when Tallulah splashed her knockoff V8 with a little vodka.

"It's none of your business how much I drink," Tallulah says, who—the irony!—has been drinking hardly anything since Dasha exploded like a depth charge into her life.

"Yes, that is your business," Dasha says. "It is my point precisely."

But Tallulah kind of likes that Dasha is a bossy, opinionated pain in the ass. Tallulah wouldn't know what to do with a typical boring ten-year-old. A typical ten-year-old Russian girl plays with dolls, Tallulah guesses, and invents voices for the dolls so they can talk to each other, and pretends she's, like, the czarina or whatever of the dolls. Boring.

At the kiosk, they buy a copy of *The Blues Brothers*. They both love the movie, especially the song Aretha Franklin sings. They rewind and watch that part twice. Dasha falls asleep with her head on Tallulah's lap.

Tallulah wonders if she ever fell asleep with her head on her biological mother's lap. She must have. Tallulah doesn't miss her biological mother. Does she? You can't miss someone you never knew. Dasha knew her parents, knew her uncle. She never shows it, but Tallulah can't imagine how deep the ache must be.

Friday, Lev summons her to lunch. "Three more days," Lev says after the waiter brings their soup. "Eva says she will be ready."

"Cool," Tallulah says. "Let's get this show on the road."

Tallulah has barely given the Stepanov job a thought. Lev does not, obviously and emphatically, need to know this.

But she senses, the way Lev gazes at her, it may be too late. The thick lenses of his rimless glasses add a glaze of light to his eyes, like a layer of ice on a pond. Except with Lev what lies beneath the ice is just more ice.

"So," he says. "A child?"

Tallulah's fingers lock on her spoon. How did he find out about Dasha? Her visit to the restroom at Sheriff with Eva and Tolstoy, she guesses, didn't go unnoticed. Lev grilled Tolstoy afterward. It had to be Tolstoy. Eva would never crack.

Lev will know if she's lying, so Tallulah tells him the shortest possible version of the story. Never give Lev any extra reasons to be pissed off.

"A little girl was squatting in the basement of my building," Tallulah says. "So I took her in for a few days. She's no trouble."

Lev dips a spoon into his soup. On the not-happy scale, Tallulah calculates he's about a six out of ten, maybe a seven.

"You were bored, my dear?" he says. "You thought to yourself, 'Why, what I need in my life is a problem to occupy myself.'"

"I didn't go looking for this, Lev."

"When you have a problem in your life, when it becomes a distraction for you, this is a problem for *me*."

Tallulah readjusts her estimate. Lev seems closer to an eight or nine on the not-happy scale. Yikes. She remembers one of the very first things Eva said when Tallulah joined Carnival Uncommon. "Never be a problem for Lev," Eva said, drawing a finger across her throat.

"I'm going to do my job, Lev," Tallulah says. "I won't be distracted. I always do my job, don't I?"

He twists and twists the end of his goatee until it's as sharp as a knifepoint. "Get rid of the child, my dear."

"I will, I promise. I just need a few more days. Till I find someone to take her. A few days. She's not a problem for me or you."

The waiter stops by the table to pour more wine. Lev says something to him in Russian far too rapid for Tallulah to understand. The waiter glances at Tallulah and roars with laughter.

Lev reaches across the table to pat Tallulah's cheek. His fire-eater fingertips are hard and calloused. They smell like camping fuel and burnt sulfur.

"Get rid of the child now, my dear," he says, "or I will do it for you."

• • •

When Tallulah returns to the flat, Dasha is in the tub and the telephone is ringing. Tallulah answers it.

"Hey, Oklahoma."

It's the chick from the *Moscow Times*, Liz. Tallulah can hear her smoking and typing. "Hey, Jersey."

"I asked around and a name popped up. A guy who might know what's up with Balikin."

Tallulah grabs a pen and the closest piece of paper, her map of Moscow. "Thank you, thank you, thank you."

CHAPTER 46

Tallulah sneaks out while Dasha is napping. Dasha rarely goes down, but when she does, she's *out*. Tallulah should have a couple of hours to roam on her own, till at least four o'clock.

Gennady Gusev. That's the name of the guy. According to the *Moscow Times* reporter, Gusev is a medium-sized piranha in the big swampy pond of the Russian underworld. He runs his own operation—his own *masterskaya*, or "shop"—out of Burning Love, a casino in the Stalin skyscraper on Kutuzovsky Prospekt.

Is Gusev the same guy trying to kill Balikin? Is he the guy keeping watch on the house? Tallulah recognizes the very real possibility, the very real danger of knocking on Gusev's door, but this is her only lead. She doesn't have another choice.

Tallulah takes the Metro to the Kievskaya station, the one with the marble arches and glorious chandeliers. From the outside, Burning Love seems marginally classier than other casinos in town, which is to say not classy at all. There's a shitload of gold, a shitload of tinted glass, so much buzzing neon it's like staring into the sun. Who was it, somebody's wife, who disobeyed God and was turned into salt when she couldn't resist one last peek at Sodom and Gomorrah? Tallulah gets it. How could you not resist one last peek at Sodom and Gomorrah?

Inside, it's dark, claustrophobic, noisy, and crowded, fogged with perfume and cigar smoke. Tallulah spots a big, thick-necked man with slicked-back hair standing in front of a velvet rope. He's watching the crowd, hands clasped behind his back. Tallulah threads her way through the crowd. She feels eyes on her—other big, thick-necked men with slicked-back hair, positioned at various points in the room.

"Hi," Tallulah says to the man in front of the velvet rope. Was he one of the goons in the Benz? Will he recognize her? Maybe, maybe not. She had her helmet on most of the time. *Most* of the time. "Can you help me?"

He gives Tallulah a glance, then ignores her. Behind the rope is a dark hallway that must lead to a VIP area.

"I'd like to speak with Gennady Gusev," Tallulah says.

"Go away." He flicks a hand at her. She notes the size of the hand, the nicks and scars, the crude gulag tattoos. A hand like that gives her a chill, more than any knife or gun would.

"I'm told he's the owner of this lovely establishment."

"Go away. I have never heard of him. What American newspaper do you write for? Do you know what happens to journalists who annoy me?"

"I'm not a journalist."

He stares down at her. "I can show you," he says, softly, "what happens to journalists who annoy me."

"What is this?" A gruff voice from the hallway jerks the VIP bouncer to attention. Here comes yet another heavy-browed hulker in an expensive Italian suit, his hair slicked back.

"Sir," the first guy says. "I will take care of this."

"Idiot," the new guy, his boss, says. He grins at Tallulah. "Do you not know who she is?"

Not good. Tallulah has been recognized, exactly as she feared. The entrance to Burning Love is miles behind her. She's fast, but there are the other thugs to contend with between here and there.

"*Ptichka!* I knew it was you." The boss man grins at her. "I saw you on the security camera. My name is Dmitri. It is an honor to meet you. *Ptichka!*"

Ptichka? Tallulah doesn't understand the Russian. The boss man, Dmitri, mimes flapping, soaring, swooping. He has surprisingly small, graceful hands. Tallulah gets it now. *Ptitsa* means bird, so *ptichka* must mean something like "little bird." Oh! She really gets it now: the parties, Carnival Uncommon.

"You've seen me perform?" Tallulah says. Knees really can, she discovers, go weak with relief.

"Three times! You are magnificent. Even lighter and more graceful than a bird, more willful. Like . . . a *feather*. A feather with consciousness, with a soul, with an intuitive understanding of the entire universe."

Russians: wow. The other guy is beaming now too. He holds up two fingers. "Twice I have seen you," he says. "Please forgive my rudeness."

"Is it possible for me to speak with Gennady Gusev?" Tallulah asks Dmitri. "Do you know him?"

"Yes, yes, yes." He laughs and unhooks the velvet rope. "Come, come, come. You must drink champagne with us. You must allow us this honor."

She follows him down the hallway to a smaller, quieter room. No slot machines or wailing Guns N' Roses here, just craps, blackjack, and some Russian crooning from the speakers. A man sits in a booth. He's tiny, not much taller than Tallulah, though in every other way—suit, slicked-back hair—he resembles his goons. He reminds Tallulah of the *semya*, the seed, the smallest figurine in a set of nesting dolls. Gusev.

"*Ptichka!*" Gusev says. He grabs a bottle of champagne from the bucket. "Sit! Drink!"

She sits. She drinks. You can't rush Russians. Tallulah listens to a blow-by-blow, flip-by-flip description of her performance last February 9, Gusev and Dmitri, back and forth. "And then, do you remember?" "Yes! The grand finale!" Dmitri, it turns out, was at the recent Stepanov gig. Gusev, green with envy (his words), demands a full accounting of Tallulah's chandelier stunt.

Finally, after three glasses of champagne, Tallulah is able to squeeze into the conversation.

"Milostivy Gosudar," Tallulah says to Gusev, using the most formal Russian honorific she knows. *Kind sir.* "Can you help me with a problem? I'm trying to find a certain man. A child's missing uncle."

This sparks a round of vows, pledges, champagne toasts, and hands pressed to hearts. "Whatever you desire!" "Nothing shall stand in our way!" "We will scour the earth until we find him!"

"Tell us his name," Gusev asks. "Tell us the name of this man and we will bring him to you."

"Anatoly Balikin," she says.

Abruptly, the whole VIP room goes silent. That's what it seems like. Even the Russian crooner on CD seems to pause, startled, in the middle of a chorus.

Gusev clears his throat. Dmitri studies his fingernails.

"Guys?" Tallulah says. This isn't one of the reactions she expected. She's not sure what to make of it.

Gusev clears his throat again. For the first time, Dmitri does not refill Tallulah's glass the instant she empties it. She realizes: they're *scared*.

But why? Of what? She doesn't get it.

"*Ptichka*," Gusev says, "you must be very, very careful. Anatoly Balikin is a powerful man. A very dangerous man."

What? There's been some kind of mix-up, a misunderstanding. And . . . isn't *Gusev* supposed to be the dangerous man here?

"No," Tallulah says, "this is a different Anatoly Balikin. This Anatoly Balikin is a businessman. He disappeared in December. The story was in all the newspapers."

Gusev nods. "A story. Yes."

"So . . ." Tallulah tries to wrap her head around this development. Gusev and Dmitri are really, truly talking about Dasha's uncle? But how is that possible? "So you're saying he's, like, some kind of gangster?"

Gusev shakes his head. "Oh, no."

"Okay," Tallulah says. That's a relief. "Good."

Gusev shakes his head again. "Oh, no," he says mournfully. "No, no, no. He is much worse."

CHAPTER 47

Anatoly Balikin is former KGB. A master of the low profile, the anonymous existence, he wields high-level influence in industry, government, the military, even the Russian Orthodox Church. Millions of dollars have been funneled to his offshore accounts. A dozen of his enemies have succumbed to mysterious ailments and unfortunate accidents. A few of his friends too. Tallulah, Gusev says, should not even allow Balikin's name to pass her lips. And then Gusev personally escorts her out of Burning Love. He politely tells her to never return, thank you very much.

No, this isn't great news. But by the time she gets home Tallulah has convinced herself it's not bad news either. Balikin may be a ruthless, shadowy, dangerous power broker, but he's still alive, he's still Dasha's uncle, he still loves her, he'll still be thrilled to see her. And Tallulah still has to *find* him. That still won't be easy, especially if every person Tallulah asks about him instantly shits their pants with terror.

Over the next couple of days Tallulah and Dasha see some sights. Dasha finds it outrageous that Tallulah has never been inside St. Basil's Cathedral or properly toured the Alexander Garden. Okay, Tallulah has to admit, not too shabby.

On Monday she takes Dasha to the McDonald's on Pushkin Square, Dasha's first ever Big Mac and fries. Dasha eats the fries, takes only a single dubious bite of her Big Mac. Tallulah remembers the 1976 Olympics. That summer McDonald's handed out promotional cards with each purchase. If the USA won a gold medal in the event on the card (rowing, judo, or whatever), you won a free hamburger. Silver was fries, bronze a small drink. Each customer was supposed to get only one card per day, but Alice—of course—devised a plan. The Mercurio kids scammed enough cards to feed, literally, a small army.

Dasha is intrigued. She wants all the details. She can't get enough of the stories about Tallulah's family.

"You are bribing me," Dasha realizes when they get back to the flat.

"No shit, Sherlock." Tallulah has already used all the other tactics she can think of. Tonight is the Stepanov job, and she can't, obviously, bring Dasha along. "I have to go out tonight."

"Where?"

"None of your business. Just some party. I'll be very, very late, but you can't be mad. I took you to McDonald's. We went to that church."

"It is a cathedral! The most glorious in all of Europe!"

"We'll do anything you want tomorrow. You name it."

Dasha stews, but finally accepts these terms. She seems particularly intrigued by the idea of "anything." Tallulah wonders what she's gotten herself into.

"Go to bed by nine," she says. "Or ten. Or at some point, okay? I probably won't be home till morning."

"Please be careful," Dasha says.

That stops Tallulah. How does Dasha know Tallulah is lying about the party? Probably Dasha is just remembering that first night, when Tallulah was stuck outside in the snow, so wasted she couldn't find her keys.

"I'll be careful," Tallulah says, then realizes that's a lie too.

Everyone meets at Lev's place. Chekhov: calm. Tolstoy: gloomy. Boyle: surly. Eva: inscrutable. And Tallulah? She lives for this shit, for shimmying three stories up a stone chimney in the pitch black, two armed security guards patrolling below. Tonight, though, she's weirdly on edge, jumpy.

Lev goes over the plan one last time. "Plan" is a stretch. This isn't exactly the heist of the century. Alice, at age eleven, would have been appalled. It's basically just a smash-and-grab burglary. Tallulah has the top floors. Chekhov and Tolstoy will position themselves in back, Eva and Boyle on the sides. At one a.m. on the dot, everyone moves in. Once the alarm system is triggered, they'll have only five to seven minutes to score what they can score before security shows up—that's why they're each covering a different part of the house. Tallulah has the riskiest assignment, as usual, both the entering (the chimney) and the exiting (she'll be the last one out).

After the briefing, Lev leans close and whispers into Tallulah's ear.

"She's gone?" he says.

"Yep," Tallulah says.

"Good."

A little after midnight they drink a round of shots, then pile into Lev's van. It has special diplomatic plates of some kind. Lev can park wherever he wants, and no cops should—*should*—fuck with him.

The Stepanov mansion is dark, quiet. Tallulah goes over the wall first. Quickly and silently, she crosses the grounds. Eva's security guard will stay in his little booth at the head of the driveway, as instructed, until the alarms go off. After that, Tallulah—last one out—will be on her own.

Finally, she starts to feel like herself again. A tingle spreads through her like an electrical current. Her mind eases into a soft idle and her senses rev up. She has complete understanding of her physical body—the location of every molecule in relation to every other molecule. Calf muscle, knee joint, hamstring. Ears, eyes, the whirring gyroscope at the base of her spine. Balance and acceleration.

The chimney is made of stacked stone, with uneven shelves and ledges wide enough for Tallulah's toes and fingertips. A dark, cloudy night, perfect. She makes her way up the chimney by feel. Higher, higher. Absolutely *nothing* feels better than this.

And yet . . .

Tallulah pictures Dasha back at the flat, curled under a blanket, drifting off to sleep. Dasha will wake up in the morning, smell sizzling butter, see Tallulah scrambling some eggs in the kitchen. She'll feel safe and settled. Everything will be okay.

Unless something happens to Tallulah. She's always taken every risk, without a second thought. But now . . .

She glances down. She's twenty feet up. Her eyes have adjusted to the darkness, and she can see Boyle crouched next to a ground-floor window. It's a long way down and Tallulah's fingertips cling to half an inch of stone. And wait till the alarms start blaring.

Tallulah can't keep doing this. She can't keep climbing chimneys and robbing mansions and eluding security guards with guns—not if she's going to take care of Dasha. But she's *not* going to take care of Dasha. She can't. She just can't. To take care of Dasha, permanently, Tallulah would have to become a different person, and that terrifies her. Is it even possible?

Stop thinking, she tells herself. She's thinking too much at a time when she shouldn't be thinking *at all*. She'll find Balikin and there will be a happy ending for everyone involved. She climbs higher, higher. Molecules and muscles, blood thumping in a perfectly even rhythm, plenty of time . . .

Her pinkie slips. That puts pressure on her ring finger, which pops loose too. Tallulah digs in with her index and middle fingers, but now her weight is shifting, rippling to all the wrong places, and her right toe gives. She loses her right hand, her left foot. She dangles by a single hand.

Hold on, hold on. Her shoulder burns. Her bicep burns. Her fingertips start to go numb. Tallulah's had close calls before, so she keeps her cool. She's strong. She's not letting go. Gravity will have to rip the arm out of its socket. If she falls, she knows how to land.

Her right hand, clawing at the chimney, finally finds the barest smidgen of protruding stone. She clamps down. Her toe finds a crack. She starts climbing. She wants to laugh. Talk about a *rush*. But then she thinks again about Dasha, alone in the flat, waking up to . . . nothing, nobody.

Don't think! As Tallulah is pulling herself onto the roof, she hears a crash of glass from below. Alarms begin to *whoop-whoop-whoop*, deafening. What? It's not one o'clock yet. Is it?

She darts across the roof to the first dormer window. She smashes the glass with her crowbar, flips the locks, raises the sash, slides inside. She won't have enough time now.

This is how it always begins: the shit going sideways.

CHAPTER 48

But guess what? The shit doesn't go sideways. Life can surprise you. That's something Tallulah has learned over the years. Life surprises you.

The rest of the Stepanov job goes off without a hitch. Tallulah moves room to room, walk-in closet to walk-in closet, stuffing a silk pillowcase with Swiss watches, French jewelry, stacks of American hundred-dollar bills. *Whoop-whoop-whoop*. It's a Chinese security system, according to Eva.

And then Tallulah is out the back door, flying through the woods, literally *flying*, as the first security vehicle fishtails to a stop in the porte cochere. Another night, in a different universe, there's a shout, a gunshot, a bullet that drills Tallulah between the shoulders, but not this night, not this universe. She hops in the van and Lev hits the gas.

They celebrate. Tallulah refills her glass after every sip, so it looks like she's drinking more than she is. She sees Boyle, across the room, talking to Lev. Did Boyle see Tallulah lose her grip, temporarily, on the chimney? Boyle, the jerk, will rat her out at the first opportunity.

"Drink!" Eva says, and Tallulah pretends to drink. She can't risk slipping out early. Lev will be watching, waiting.

The party breaks up just after sunrise. Tallulah takes a taxi most of the way home. She has the driver drop her at a bakery a few blocks from her building, so she can pick up some fresh *ponchiki*, Russian donut holes, for breakfast.

She's turning the corner onto her street when a Jeep Cherokee eases up next to her. Tallulah stops. The back door of the Jeep opens, and a man leans out.

"Hello, Tallulah Mercurio," he says in excellent, barely accented English.

He's lean, dark-eyed, his salt-and-pepper hair shaved close. "Please join me for a drive, will you?"

Under normal circumstances, a Jeep Cherokee pulling up next to her and some strange guy ordering her to get in, some strange guy who somehow knows her name, Tallulah would drop her damn *ponchiki* and hightail it out of there. But Tallulah, even through a fog of exhaustion and vodka, immediately recognizes what's happening here.

The man slides over. Tallulah gets into the back seat next to him. The Jeep Cherokee pulls away.

"You're Anatoly Balikin," Tallulah says.

He shrugs. Yes, of course. He's around forty-five years old. Or maybe fifty-five, maybe thirty-five. He has a mild, forgettable face. A glass of milk, an empty sky. He's amused. Or bored. Or annoyed. Or . . . nothing at all.

"I have learned you have an interest in my affairs," he says.

Gusev, that sly dog, must have tipped him off, covering his own ass. Good! Tallulah feels suddenly weightless with relief. Dasha's uncle is alive, he's right here next to her, and Tallulah is about to be liberated. In five seconds, she will have her life back. She's going to have so much fun tonight. She's going to drink all the booze and do all the drugs and pick out some hot guy at random from the crowd and do him too. She'll speed on her motorcycle through the predawn streets of Moscow, without a helmet.

So why, then, does Tallulah burst into tears? Tallulah hardly ever even, like, *gently* weeps. This—her entire face wet, honking snot into a cocktail napkin—is ridiculous. Being so torn up about a kid she's known for less than a month is ridiculous!

Balikin sighs. With impatience? With sympathy? "Please," he says. "Answer my questions and you will not be harmed."

"Dasha is with me." Tallulah blows her nose one last time. She rubs her eyes dry with the heel of her palm. "She's okay. She's safe. She's been staying with me. She's going to be so happy to see you."

They cruise down the street. The radio plays softly, something lugubrious and lofty, something Russian. Balikin doesn't say anything. For the first time his expression is unambiguous: he's surprised.

Tallulah waits for him to recover from the electric jolt of her news.

Finally, she gives his shoulder a poke. "Hey," she says. "It's okay. Dasha is safe."

He turns to her. He's not just surprised now, but also totally confused. "Who?" he says. "What are you talking about?"

• • •

Tallulah is so mad at Dasha she's about to burst into flames. That little sociopath! Has she ever told the truth in her life? Anatoly Balikin isn't Dasha's uncle. He's not *anyone's* uncle, in fact—he's an only child.

Dasha must have read about him in the newspaper and appropriated his story for her own purposes. Of course. Tallulah is so mad at *herself* she's about to burst into flames. How could she be so gullible?

On the way back to Tallulah's building, she tells Balikin the whole story. She thinks she sees a twinkle in his eye and suspects that if Balikin *did* have a niece or a daughter—he has two sons, both in college in England—he'd probably want one like Dasha.

"Would you like my advice?" Balikin says as Tallulah starts to climb out of the Jeep.

She already knows what he's going to say. "Go ahead."

"Do not get involved with this child," he says. "No good will come from it."

You think? Tallulah doesn't want to wait for the elevator, so she stomps up the stairs. The little sociopath, she decides, gets one last chance and one last chance only. Either she tells Tallulah the truth, the whole truth, or Tallulah is done with her forever.

"Good morning," Dasha says. She's in the kitchen, in her pajamas, searching the fridge. "What shall we plan for today? You have visited Lenin's Mausoleum, I presume? If not, we must do so at once."

Tallulah discovers she's not so mad anymore, just extremely weary. She flops onto the sofa. "Anatoly Balikin isn't your uncle," Tallulah says.

"He is," Dasha says from the kitchen.

"Stop lying, please. I met him. He's never heard of you. He doesn't have a niece."

"Would you prefer toast or an apple first for breakfast? I will cast my vote for an apple."

"Will you just tell me the truth?"

"Yes, of course."

Tallulah closes her eyes. "Why do you keep lying to me?"

Why, why, why? Tallulah would honestly love to know. Dasha doesn't say anything. Tallulah keeps her eyes closed. The sofa cushion shifts as Dasha sits next to her, the skin of her arm against the skin of Tallulah's. She places an apple in Tallulah's hand.

Dasha keeps lying, Tallulah realizes, because the truth is unbearable. And the truth doesn't change anything, does it? Dasha is all alone. She has nobody.

"Let's go out for breakfast," Tallulah says. "Let's go to a restaurant and have a feast. Get dressed. I'm going down to get my mail."

Tallulah opens the door. Irina, fist raised, is about to knock. Behind her stands a red-nosed man with a thick mustache. He's wearing a ushanka hat with the fur earflaps buttoned up, epaulets on the sleeves of his shirt, a red-and-gold badge above his heart. Tallulah is so, so weary. Her mind isn't yet moving at full speed. What does Irina want now? Why has she brought a police officer to Tallulah's flat?

Irina lowers her fist. She smiles her gray, ghastly tombstone smile. "I have brought the authorities," she says. "To take custody of the child."

CHAPTER 49

In the space between heartbeats—that quickly, but also way too late—Tallulah understands what's happening. When Tallulah wouldn't help her sell Dasha, Irina went and found a different, even better business partner.

That's a real badge the red-nosed man is wearing, a real gun on his hip.

Irina glows with joy. She's won. She's crushed the impertinent imperialist Yankee whore. *Did you think you could outsmart a Russian, you Yankee whore?*

"Okay," Tallulah says. "Give me five minutes to get her dressed and you can have her."

She shuts and locks the door before Irina can say anything. Irina will give her the five minutes, Tallulah predicts. Five minutes is a reasonable request, and Irina won't want to make a commotion. She won't tell her drunken, crooked cop to break down the door unless it's absolutely necessary. And where will Tallulah and Dasha go anyway? They can't escape. They're four stories up and the fire escape is a skeleton missing most of its bones.

Tallulah darts to the bathroom. Dasha is half-dressed: T-shirt and sweater up top, but pajama pants still down below. She's deliberating between two different pairs of acid-washed jeans.

"Put your shoes on, right now," Tallulah says. "Let's play another game."

Dasha crosses her arms. "I am not stupid, you know."

"Fine. It's not a game. It's we need to get out of here right *now* or we're in big, big trouble. Okay? Put your shoes on."

Tallulah darts to the kitchen and grabs the cereal box where she hides her cash and passport. Irina raps on the door.

"Do you understand?" Irina says. "You must cooperate, or you will be arrested."

Tallulah darts to the window and yanks it open. She looks down. Oh, boy. What's left of the fire escape—not much!—barely clings to the side of the building. Just one hot heavy breath and the rusting, rotting tangle of iron will probably go crashing down to the alley below.

Dasha, tiny Doc Martens on and laced, stands next to Tallulah. She stares down at the fire escape too. Tallulah can guess what she's thinking. *Nope.*

"What was it your imaginary uncle said to you?" Tallulah says. "You know, about the wolves?"

"You must never go in fear of wolves."

"Did you just make that up, or did you hear it somewhere?"

"We cannot go this way," Dasha says, still staring down at the fire escape. "It is ridiculous."

"Be light," Tallulah says. "Be light as a feather. That's going to be the trick. Take off again before you even land."

"This makes no sense."

Irina knocks more insistently. Tallulah hears her grumble and curse. How much time will it take the red-nosed cop to kick down the door?

"Follow me exactly," Tallulah says. "Grab exactly what I grab. It *can* be a game."

Dasha looks up at her with her grave, gray eyes. Tallulah swings herself over the window ledge. She grabs a rail attached to the brick by one small bolt, then quickly drops to a narrow balcony platform slanted at a forty-five-degree angle. From there, taking off before she even lands, Tallulah works her way down a broken piece of ladder until she can drop to what's left of the next balcony, a single broken bracket with just enough room for the side of one foot.

This isn't the craziest thing Tallulah has ever done, but it's close. She's fizzing, her blood is carbonated. Dasha must be terrified. Tallulah knows she's following behind—she can hear Dasha breathing, can hear that first small bolt creaking and groaning. Tallulah resists the urge to look up. An encouraging smile might distract Dasha, might do more harm than good.

Third floor to second floor. It takes forever. Or maybe that's time playing its usual tricks? The final drop is a long one, around eight feet to the alley pavement. Tallulah knows how to land. *Now* she looks back up. Dasha is right behind her, perched on the last rusted bracket. Eight feet is a long drop if you're Dasha's size, if you've probably never dropped eight or six or even four feet before.

"I've got you," Tallulah says.

She's expecting that Dasha will need some coaxing, but no, Dasha immediately launches herself straight at her. Tallulah manages to brace herself an instant before Dasha hits her like a ton of bricks. They go down, hitting the pavement like another ton of bricks. A second later the struggling bolt outside Tallulah's window gives out and the lethal iron railing plummets four stories, missing Tallulah's head by about a foot.

"Are you okay?" she asks Dasha.

"I am. Yes. Are you okay?"

Tallulah climbs to her feet and pulls Dasha up. "Run," she says.

They run. Tallulah has to abandon her little Minsk, parked out front. They run and run and run, sticking to alleys and cutting diagonally across vacant lots and construction sites. They run for ten, fifteen minutes, until Tallulah is sure nobody is chasing them. They're free. Either Irina didn't pay for a second crooked cop or he was covering the lobby, the front of the building, and not the fire-escape side.

Tallulah wheels slowly around, taking in the buildings and billboards and street signs, getting her bearings. How far is the nearest Metro station? Dasha is doubled over, hands on her knees. It takes Tallulah a second to realize Dasha's not out of breath from their escape—she's giggling uncontrollably.

• • •

Tallulah can't ask Eva for a place to stay. Eva is sensible. If forced to choose between a friend and Lev, her livelihood, Eva will choose Lev. Same deal with Chekhov and Tolstoy. Every person who knows both Tallulah and Lev is off the table.

Balikin? Tallulah actually considers it for a second. He seems nice for a shadowy ruthless ex-KGB power broker! But no. Of course not.

They could check into a hotel. Tallulah has plenty of cash. But someone in Lev's network—a desk clerk or bellhop—might spot them. She and Dasha aren't exactly inconspicuous. The Moscow police might be asking around about them too, if Irina's crooked cop is still on the job. Don't underestimate Irina. Tallulah won't do that again.

She'll have to try CIA Joe, Tallulah decides, as she and Dasha ride the Arbatsko line across town. Joe won't be thrilled to see her, not when he learns why she's there. Joe values, above all else, a personal life that's simple, uncomplicated, and hassle-free. It's why he and Tallulah are—or used to be, she guesses—such a good match.

Joe isn't thrilled to see her. Tallulah doesn't have to say a word. Joe, one look at her and at Dasha, gets the situation—that this *is* a situation.

"Come on in," he says tightly.

Tallulah parks Dasha in the living room with Joe's chess set. She and Joe go out onto his spacious, un-collapsing balcony. He shuts the sliding door behind them and lights a cigarette. He blows out a long, long, long stream of smoke.

"You could have called first," he says.

"I knew you'd say no. I just need a week or two. Till I figure shit out."

He passes her the cigarette. He doesn't tell her *I told you so*, which she appreciates.

They watch the slow, sluggish pulse of the Moscow River down below, the gridlock of black luxury sedans inching around the Kremlin. Finally, Joe runs his fingers through his hair, squeezing a handful of it hard, yanking it around.

"Look," he says. "I can ask around. I can try to find a place that won't be so bad for her."

"Encouraging. A *nice* Russian orphanage."

"It's either that or you adopt her. Take her back to the United States."

Tallulah's heart hiccups, her face starts to flush. Is this what a panic attack feels like? The blood crashing through your body like waves against the rocks?

"What?" she says. "No. No way. Adopt her? I can't . . . are you kidding me?"

He nods. "You can stay here for a week. I'm leaving for St. Petersburg this afternoon and I'll be back Wednesday night."

"We'll be gone. Thank you."

Joe flicks the butt out into nothingness and lights another cigarette. "You've got to untangle yourself from all this," he says. "You know that, right?"

Tallulah watches the river. She remembers something her dad used to say, a typical nugget of Mercurio wisdom. Amateurs spend all their time figuring out a way in; professionals always make sure they know how to get out.

CHAPTER 50

"How long will we stay here?" Dasha asks every morning at breakfast. Every day at lunch. Two or three times every afternoon and evening. Every night, last thing, when Tallulah tucks her in. "How long will we stay here?"

"Long enough," Tallulah says.

"And then?"

"Eat your eggs," Tallulah says. Or "Eat your sandwich." "Play some chess." "Go to sleep."

It's already Monday. How did five days pass so quickly? And how, after five days, has Tallulah made exactly zero progress in figuring this shit out? This is what crazy people must feel like: having the same conversation with themselves over and over and over again, desperately searching for some way out, some way to change the topic.

She steps out onto the balcony and closes the door behind her. Joe left behind most of a carton of Marlboro Reds and Tallulah has smoked more cigarettes in five days than she has in the previous five months. Dasha sternly disapproves. She wrinkles her nose and fans her face whenever Tallulah gets within sniffing distance.

Maybe Joe *can* find a nice place for Dasha to live. Tallulah has a certain image in her mind when she thinks "Russian orphanage," but what does she know? Maybe there are homes for kids that aren't actually called "orphanages." Tallulah tries picturing a sprawling sunlit dacha by the shores of a pretty lake. Pine trees, deep blue water, kids laughing and shouting on the pebbled beach. Big steaming bowls of stew, a warm fire in the winter.

Tallulah manages to sustain that fantasy for approximately two drags.

An orphanage is an orphanage. It might be clean, the food might be fine, the people working there might be humane, but Dasha will still be alone. People won't tell stories about her. She won't have a place in anyone's memory. Every day that goes by she'll drift farther and farther from shore, until it will be like she never existed.

What if Tallulah's mom and dad had taken one look at the little Indian baby sucking its thumb and shrugged? What if they'd said, *not my problem*.

Sure, growing up a Mercurio wasn't always a picnic. But Tallulah had a family. She had a *place*. She'll always be part of a story bigger than just her own. That's deeply comforting, somehow.

Joe is willing to make some calls, pull some strings. It's probably tricky for an American citizen to adopt a Russian kid, tons of paperwork, but this is Moscow. Money is all that counts, and Tallulah has plenty of that.

She'll buy two plane tickets back to the United States. She and Dasha can move in for a while with Ray or Alice or even Jeremy, wherever he happens to be at the moment. Mom and Dad won't be thrilled, but they won't turn Tallulah away either. Nobody will. Tallulah is one of them, a Mercurio, and now Dasha will be too.

Tallulah is having a hard time catching her breath. The smoke filling her lungs doesn't help. Her head has been aching for days. She's going to *adopt* Dasha? She can't. She truly can't. Tallulah isn't fit to be a parent. Are you kidding? She would have to change her life. She'd have to change her very own *self*. That's impossible. And if it's not impossible, it's deeply terrifying. Tallulah loves her life! She loves her own self! She loves how uncertain her future is, how wild with different possibilities.

And she loves Dasha too. It's true. Tallulah wishes it wasn't. Her decision would be a lot easier.

She hasn't bothered calling Alice. Tallulah knows exactly what Alice will say. She'll be furious that Tallulah is even considering the possibility of adopting a ten-year-old Russian girl. Alice will want to have her committed. Ray won't be any help either. He'll be supportive but as indecisive as Tallulah. "Do what you think is right," he'll say.

So...

Maybe Joe *can* find a nice place for Dasha to live.

Tallulah lights another cigarette and starts the whole conversation over again. Again.

Back inside, Tallulah hesitates before pouring herself a shot of vodka.

"Don't silently judge me," she tells Dasha.

Dasha pretends she's studying the chessboard and not judging Tallulah. "You may do as you wish, of course," she says.

Tallulah pours a double shot to demonstrate that yes, she may in fact do as she wishes. She flops down on the sofa next to Dasha, who wrinkles her nose.

"I don't know what to do," Tallulah says.

"I understand," Dasha says.

"I don't know what to do about *you*."

"Yes, of course. I understand."

"You do?" Tallulah supposes she shouldn't be surprised that Dasha is a step ahead of her. She's been a step ahead of Tallulah from the beginning.

Dasha moves a rook and turns to regard Tallulah. "You would like my advice?" she says.

No, not really. What Tallulah would like is the ability to unzip her heart and display the contents for Dasha, so that Dasha might really, truly understand why Tallulah doesn't know what to do about her. Because words by themselves will fail her. So will no words at all. Anything Tallulah says or doesn't say, Dasha will just hear the same thing: *I'm not sure I want you.*

"In all decisions one must be quick and firm," Dasha says. "One must stride into the future and never look back. That is my advice."

"Where do you come up with this shit?"

"You do not agree?"

"What if it's the wrong decision? What if you make a quick and firm *wrong* decision?"

"This is why," Dasha says, slowly and patiently, pained by how dense Tallulah can be, "one must never look back."

CHAPTER 51

Dasha goes to bed. Tallulah steps out onto the balcony to smoke one last cigarette and beg for a sign. What kind of a sign? Anything, really, as long as its meaning is unmistakable. A comet streaking through the night sky at precisely the same moment Tallulah whispers *I can do this*. Or a comet streaking through the night sky at precisely the same moment Tallulah whispers *I can't do this*.

"I can do this," she whispers.

"I can't do this," she whispers.

Would Tallulah even see a comet if one streaked past? The lights of the city blaze so brightly that the stars are faint and almost invisible.

She remembers that first snowy dawn, the flakes floating onto her eyelashes, Dasha's face blurry above her, slowly coming into focus. Tallulah was so drunk. She couldn't even make it up the steps of the apartment building by herself. Was that night the omen she's looking for?

The lights of the city begin to blaze even brighter. A wave of dizziness gently lifts Tallulah off her feet and gently sets her back down. For the first time in days her head has stopped pounding.

The lights of the city shouldn't be this bright, Tallulah realizes. Why is she so dizzy? She grabs for the balcony railing but misses it. She's falling. Falling or flying? She's too dizzy. The light blinds. It's like looking directly at the sun.

CHAPTER 52

You are a very lucky girl," a man's voice says.

Tallulah opens her eyes. Where is she? A room. A bed. She's dying of thirst. An overhead tube light buzzes and flickers. An IV bag hangs on a pole. A hospital room. A hospital bed. Why? She's dying of thirst. The back of her hand aches, where an IV needle is stabbed into a vein.

"A very lucky girl."

Is the man speaking English? Or Russian? English, Tallulah decides, with a heavy Russian accent. He makes a note on his clipboard.

"Thirsty," she manages to say. "Please."

A woman, a nurse, holds a plastic cup to Tallulah's cracked lips. The water is warm, slightly sour, and heavenly, the best thing Tallulah has ever tasted in her life.

"You speak Russian," the doctor says. "Not too badly either."

"What happened?" Tallulah says.

"You have experienced a ruptured intercranial aneurysm. For how long you've had this aneurysm, I do not know. An aneurysm is an assassin, lurking in the shadows, waiting, waiting."

What? Is he speaking Russian or English now? Both? "Thirsty," Tallulah says. "Please."

The nurse gives her another sip of water. The doctor keeps talking. Tallulah tries to follow. He placed a clip in her head to repair the aneurysm and prevent rerupture. A clip or a grip? "You are a bionic woman now!" Tallulah is young and healthy. She should, in the doctor's estimation, recover fully.

"But I must emphasize that you came this close to death." He holds his thumb and middle finger an inch apart, then moves them slowly, dramatically closer and closer, until they're almost touching. "If the ambulance had not been called at once . . ." He snaps his fingers.

The moment on the balcony comes back to Tallulah. The smoke in her lungs, the city lights, the stairs so faint they were almost invisible. The decision she was trying to make.

The decision she *did* make, in her heart, days ago. She realizes that now. Of course Tallulah can do this. Of course she'll adopt Dasha.

"Where is she?" Tallulah says.

"Who?" the doctor says.

"The girl. Dasha. The little girl who called the ambulance."

The doctor fiddles with the IV bag. "I have no idea. I have seen no little girl, I'm afraid."

"Nor I," the nurse says.

Oh, god. Tallulah remembers what Dasha said. *In all decisions one must be quick and firm.* Dasha understood the decision Tallulah was struggling with. Dasha was trying to make it, the decision, easy for her.

"No," Tallulah says. "No, no. I have to find her."

"Shhh, dear." The nurse dabs Tallulah's forehead with a cool cloth. "You are safe now."

"You must rest now," the doctor says.

"Please, no, you have to let me . . . I have to . . ."

Tallulah feels the new drugs kick in. The world softens. She's a feather on a breeze. "I can do this."

• • •

The next time Tallulah wakes up, it's a different doctor and a different nurse. They too know nothing about a little girl. They're confused when Tallulah tries to explain—is this mysterious child Tallulah's daughter or not?

Tallulah calls Joe from the hospital. "Is she there?"

"Hey. Where are you? I just got home."

Tallulah already knows the answer. "Is she there?"

Dasha isn't there. Tallulah, voice shaking, her whole body shaking, presses him. What about the clothes she bought Dasha when they first got to Joe's place? What about the new knapsack?

"No," Joe says. Clothes and knapsack and Dasha, all gone.

• • •

After she's released from the hospital, Tallulah goes straight to Lev's place. Will he cut her throat when he sees her? Tallulah doesn't care. She has to take the risk. He's her best chance of finding Dasha.

Lev doesn't cut her throat. He forgives Tallulah for her sins against him, accepts the ten thousand American dollars she's saved up, and agrees to look for Dasha. And he really does look for her—Tallulah's pain, her guilt and regret, stirs something in his tiny black heart. He puts out the word, far and wide.

But nobody has seen her. Nobody has seen Dasha.

A bitter autumn scours away the summer. Tallulah moves in with Eva. Every day, all day, Tallulah roams the streets of Moscow, the streets and alleys and parks and subway stations, the flea markets and kiosks and department stores and churches, searching and searching—every child, every face. She starts to wonder if she's going crazy. Did Dasha ever really exist? By the time Tallulah snuck back into her old flat, Irina had already cleared it out.

"I've lost everything," Tallulah says.

"Not your life," Lev says.

"I've lost everything else."

He strokes her cheek with his sulfur-scented fingers. "Now you understand. Now you are a real Russian."

PART V

Ray
1996–1997

CHAPTER 53

It's just mud at first. No big deal. You keep walking.

Step by step, the mud thicker and thicker. After a minute you're up to your ankles. The mud sucks away a shoe. You keep walking.

Now you're breathing hard. Your legs weigh a thousand pounds each. Lift, lift. The ache in your back, the ache in your thighs.

When it can't get any worse, when you're buried to your chest, when every inch forward is a fight, the mud starts to dry, to harden around you.

The ancient Egyptians, Ray heard someone say once, baked mud into bricks. They stacked the bricks into pyramids. The guys who made the bricks, who did all the work, got sealed up in the pyramids, deep down inside.

What do you do when the mud turns to brick, and you've got a whole pyramid on top of you? It's too late to do anything. Maybe it was always too late, from the minute you were born.

• • •

Ray sits in back. Mr. P. never lets him drive the Cadillac. "Not if my life depended on it," Mr. P. says. "I'd sooner put the damn monkey behind the wheel."

The monkey is a real monkey, a small gray one, the mascot at the El Marrakech. Mr. P. owns the El Marrakech, a lounge on the Strip, one of the oldest.

The Mexican sits up front in the passenger seat. He has long hair, down past his collar, and wears gold-rimmed sunglasses at night. His cologne fills the Cadillac. It's not any worse than the cologne Mr. P. wears.

"I'm telling you what, Mr. Pappalardo," the Mexican says. That's an English phrase he picked up somewhere. *I'm telling you what.* He uses it a lot. "This is a business opportunity of a lifetime."

Mr. P. hates long-hairs, Mexicans, and people who tell him what. That's three strikes for the Mexican. But Mr. P. has to play nice because the Mexican is connected. That's the word from LA yesterday. Ray overheard Mr. P.'s side of the conversation on the phone.

"You're gonna dig this joint," Mr. P. says, ignoring the Mexican. "The Golden Steer, best steakhouse in town. It's been around longer than me, and I've been in Vegas since '59."

They pass the Mirage. Mr. P. points. "A damn volcano. For the kids, for the families. Since when was Vegas for the families? They're turning this city into damn Disneyland. You think I'm joking? The MGM Grand is building an amusement park. You know who's rolling over in his grave right now?"

Sam Giancana, Ray thinks.

"Sam Giancana," Mr. P. says.

Sam Giancana and Moe Dalitz. Big Ed Zingel and Handsome Johnny Roselli. Ray knows this speech by heart. He knows all of Mr. P.'s speeches by heart. He's worked for Mr. P. for almost fifteen years, since Ray was eighteen years old.

"Sam Giancana and Moe Dalitz. Big Ed Zingel and Handsome Johnny Roselli," Mr. P. says. "They understood that Vegas was where you could get *away* from your fucking family."

The Mexican fiddles with the Cadillac's electric door locks, flipping them up and down, up and down. He's impatient. He just wants to take care of business and go home to Mexico.

Ray doesn't point this out to Mr. P. "When I need an opinion," Mr. P. always says, "I'll ask the damn monkey before I ask you."

Fifteen years. Ray is tired just thinking about it. He's tired of Mr. P. and the El Marrakech and Vegas. He's tired of himself.

That doesn't make sense, Ray understands. How can you be tired of your own *self*? But he isn't smart enough to explain it any better than that.

"We have a new way of doing business, Mr. Pappalardo," the Mexican is saying. "Producing the product, moving the product. If you come with us, you will make more money than your wild dreams, I'm telling you what."

They move through the intersection. Mr. P. points to the east side of the Strip. "See that?" he says. "The Sands. It was a palace. People came from LA, New York, all over the world. Ann-Margret shooting craps. Dino used to deal blackjack for a goof. It's a damn shame."

It's a shame, Mr. P. means, that the Sands is closed now and scheduled to come down next week, a couple of days before Thanksgiving. Ray doesn't know what will replace the Sands. Whatever does, he's sure he'll hear a lot about it from Mr. P.

Ray rehearses it in his head. "Mr. P., respectfully, I'm done. I need to make a change." Sure, Mr. P. will blow his top. He'll ooze lava like the volcano at the Mirage. But he won't be able to stop Ray from walking out the door. Ray is the one, in Mr. P.'s crew, who stops people from walking out the door.

So why is Ray still here, still sitting in the back seat of the Cadillac, still listening to the same stories? Because he doesn't know *how* to make a change. He doesn't know what to do after he walks out the door.

All his life, Ray has let other people tell him what to do. His brothers and sisters, his mom and dad, now Mr. P. and Slick. It's one of the reasons Ray is so tired of himself.

"We gotta take one last look," Mr. P. tells the Mexican, cutting the wheel and pulling into the deserted parking lot of the Sands. "You're going to dig this."

CHAPTER 54

The security booth in the parking lot is empty. The guard must be on his break. Lucky for them, Mr. P. tells the Mexican.

Inside, the casino floor has been stripped to the studs. The slot machines are gone, the tables, the carpet, all the fixtures, even the wiring. Moonlight filters in through the front glass doors.

"What are we doing here?" the Mexican says.

"Keep your damn pants on," Mr. P. says. "The Sands is a piece of history. Ray, I ever tell you about the time I punched Sinatra and knocked his tooth out?"

Yes.

"No," Ray says.

The Mexican taps his foot impatiently. He wears black cowboy boots with sharp silver toe-tips. The toe-tip of his right boot goes *click click click click* against the concrete.

"Okay," the Mexican says. "We happy now? We can do some business now, please, Mr. Pappalardo?"

"Will you shut the fuck up?" Mr. P. says. "Just give me five damn minutes, then we'll eat a steak and you can talk till the cows come home."

Ray watches the Mexican's hands, his feet. If you can't see a guy's eyes, because he's wearing sunglasses, watch his hands and his feet—his hands and feet will tell you if he's about to try something. Ray doesn't remember when he learned that. A long time ago. Maybe he just always knew it.

But the Mexican won't try anything. He doesn't have a gun. He's half Ray's size. He wants to do business with Mr. P.

"Sinatra was plastered, in one of his moods, cussing out the dealer, the waitresses. I don't care who you were, back in the day, you didn't cause a scene in one of our joints."

Mr. P. tells his story. Sinatra didn't hold a grudge. He sent Mr. P. a silk tie for Christmas.

Click click click. The Mexican's silver toe-tip catches the moonlight. Mr. P. is getting madder and madder at him, his face an unhealthy shade of tomato.

"*Now* we happy?" the Mexican says.

"Ray," Mr. P. says. "Shoot this greasy cocksucker."

The Mexican laughs. Ray tries to work out if Mr. P. is joking or serious. Usually Ray can tell, but not this time. Mr. P. is interested in doing business with the Mexican. Ray heard him say so to Slick. And usually, Mr. P. tells Ray in advance if Ray is going to do a piece of work. Usually, but not always.

"Ray!" Mr. P. says, snapping his fingers. "I said shoot this greasy cocksucker in his head. Paw the ground once if you understand me."

When Mr. P. snaps his fingers, he's always serious. Ray takes out his gun, his Ruger P90. The Mexican is still laughing, louder and louder, his neck slick and sweating in the moonlight. Ray thinks maybe the Mexican understood that Mr. P. was serious from the very beginning.

Ray points the gun at the Mexican. The Mexican is about ten feet away. At ten feet, Ray couldn't miss if he tried.

"Let me apologize, Mr. Pappalardo," the Mexican says. "Please. This is a terrible misunderstanding, I'm telling you what. I work for important people."

"Damnit, Ray," Mr. P. says, "what the fuck are you waiting for?"

Ray doesn't really know the answer to that question. He's never not followed an order before. He's never not pulled a trigger. Pulling a trigger has always been easy for him, even the very first time. That's another part of what makes him so sick and tired of himself, that pulling a trigger had always been easy.

The Mexican takes off running. He heads toward the inky darkness at the far end of the casino floor. If he can make it to the stairs, he can disappear up into the hotel tower. The Sands has hundreds of hotel rooms where he can hide.

212 · LOU BERNEY

But he won't make it. The Mexican can't run very fast in cowboy boots. He's only fifty feet away. Fifty feet for the Ruger, for Ray, is still nothing.

"Ray! Ray! Jesus fucking Christ! I told you to shoot the cocksucker!"

Ray watches the Mexican disappear into the inky darkness. He hears the *clickety-click* of his silver toes fade.

Mr. P. grabs his ears like he wants to rip his own head off his neck and throw it at Ray. He's mad, even for him. Ray has never not done something Mr. P. told him to do. Ray feels a little off-balance, like his foot reached for the rung of the ladder but didn't find it. Is it a good feeling or a bad feeling? Ray's not sure.

"Mr. P., respectfully," Ray says, "I'm done. I need to make a change."

"What?"

"I need to make a change."

"I heard you. What are you talking about? Change? What the fuck do you want to change?"

Ray hasn't rehearsed anything past this first part of the conversation. "All this," he tries to explain. He nods at the inky darkness on the other side of the casino floor. He nods at Mr. P. He taps the barrel of the Ruger against his own chest. "Me."

Mr. P. stares at Ray, his eyes bugged. He's really going to blow up now. Ray is glad he's the one with the gun and not Mr. P.

But then Mr. P. doesn't blow up. He takes a deep breath. He sinks back down into himself. He looks small and old and tired in the moonlight, like somebody's grandpa, which he is.

He walks over to Ray. He puts his hand on Ray's shoulder. "Ray," he says, his voice quiet, or at least quiet for him, "listen to me."

"Okay."

"What the fuck are you gonna do, you don't do all this? Who the fuck are you gonna be, you're not you?"

Ray doesn't answer. Mr. P. is right. He's hit the nail on the head.

"I thought so, you brick-headed moron," Mr. P. finally says. He reaches up to give Ray's cheek a pat. "Go find that greasy cocksucker and shoot him in the head. Then take the day off tomorrow. Take two days off, if you want.

We're not having this fucking conversation again. I'm gonna go wait in the car."

He walks away. The wind blows through the cracks of the Sands, and it sounds like voices murmuring. Memories. They follow Ray wherever he goes, more vivid and present than memories should be. Their sweat smells like vinegar. They swallow hard before they try to say one last thing.

Mr. P. is right. Ray has no idea how to be anyone but himself. All he can do is give it a try. Today, he decides, is the day he finally gives it a try.

Ray points his gun at Mr. P. and—for the last time ever, he tells himself—pulls the trigger.

CHAPTER 55

Ray puts Mr. P.'s body in a gap between walls where a ventilation duct used to be. The security guard isn't back yet. Ray drives away in Mr. P.'s Cadillac. He's not worried about the Mexican. The Mexican won't go to the police. He'll run back to Mexico as fast as he can.

That night Ray sleeps okay. The minute he wakes up, though, his mind starts buzzing. What now? He makes coffee in the microwave and eats his usual for breakfast—runny fried eggs on white toast, a lot of pepper. What now? He brushes his teeth and shaves. What now? He moves his bowels. He takes a shower. He gets dressed, sits on the edge of his bed, and studies the blank white wall of his apartment. What now? A person less dumb than Ray would have already figured it out.

Ray's sister Tallulah says he's not dumb. She says he's just smart in a slow and steady way, like the tortoise who beat the rabbit in the race. Nobody but Tallulah has ever had this opinion, that Ray's not dumb, so it's hard for him to believe. Besides, the tortoise doesn't win that race in real life. Never happens. The tortoise is dumb for ever thinking he could beat a rabbit in a race.

Ray feels edgy, a little uneasy, his chest tight. What now? Outside, in the courtyard, there's a commotion. Ray steps out onto the breezeway. Two guys are shoving around a third guy. *You stole our shit!* And *I never even saw your shit!* There's some commotion at Ray's apartment complex two or three times a day. Normally Ray doesn't mind, but right now he's trying to think.

He walks the three blocks to his gym. A couple of working girls are still out on the corner, or already out on the corner, Ray isn't sure which. They stop chattering at each other as Ray passes.

The gym used to be a Midas Oil-Change. It still smells like grease and wiper fluid. On the cinder-block wall is stenciled Octavio's one main rule: *Please Do Not Bleed On The Floor Gentleman!*

Ray's buddy Purdy and another guy are in the ring, sparring. Octavio sits on his stool, reading the *Review-Journal*. Ray hits the free weights, then skips rope for a while and works the speed bag. Purdy gets out of the ring and comes over to Ray. He's holding a towel to his nose to catch the blood. Octavio is serious about his one rule.

"I'm feelin' enchiladas today, brother man," Purdy says. He's black and from East Texas, from a farm on the border with Louisiana, and his accent is like three or four different accents mashed together into a thick paste. The first time they met, Ray thought Purdy was speaking a foreign language. Now, after ten years, Ray is fairly fluent in Purdy.

"Enchiladas are good," Ray says.

At Casa Don Juan on Main Street, they sit at a table because the booths are too tight for them. Purdy is almost as big as Ray, only an inch or so shorter, ten or so pounds lighter.

Ray thinks about asking Purdy for advice. The problem with asking Purdy for advice, though, is that Purdy isn't any smarter than Ray.

"I need to make a change," Ray says, deciding to take a shot. "In my life, I mean. I don't know what to do next. I'm done with Mr. P., but I don't know what to do next."

"All right, I got you," Purdy says. "Come on down to the Nugget tomorrow. I got you."

Purdy says he'll set Ray up with a job at the Golden Nugget downtown, where Purdy works security. Ray eats his enchiladas and thinks it over. A job working security at the Golden Nugget would be legal, and Ray probably wouldn't have to shoot anyone. But he'd still be muscle, still be busting heads. Some guy in a suit would still be telling him where to go, where to stand, which heads to bust.

"No," Ray says. "I need to make a big change. Not just my job."

"All right. All right. I got you." Purdy concentrates hard, puzzling it out. "You need to mix up your workout. That's what you do. Start on the bag, you know what I'm saying? Do your legs last."

Ray nods. This is what he means about Purdy not being any smarter than him.

The waitress clears their plates. When she leaves, Purdy leans in close. "Check this shit out," he says, lowering his voice.

He slides a small square envelope across the table. Ray picks it up. Inside is one of those new silver discs they put music on now—a CD disc. Purdy says it's not music, though, it's for something called America Online, AOL. Purdy tries to explain what AOL is, but he doesn't make any sense at all, and Ray loses him in a hurry.

"Just get you a computer and check this shit out," Purdy says. "All you got to do is put it in a computer and hit a button or two."

"I don't have a computer," Ray says.

"That's why you got to get you one. What'd I just say?"

Purdy gives Ray a lift back to his apartment. Ray sits on the edge of his bed and stares at the wall. What now? He's still tense, uneasy. His stomach is uneasy, and he has to move his bowels again. A little before four he gets in his truck and drives to the El Marrakech. He doesn't know what else to do. And it's probably better if he shows up for work like he always does, at least for a week or two. He might not be smart, but he knows how to be careful.

• • •

The El Marrakech is dead. It always is. There are too many newer lounges on the Strip, too many nicer ones. Every lounge on the Strip is newer and nicer than the El Marrakech.

Paz is working the bar today, both making the drinks and delivering them. Ray takes a seat at the rail. The monkey slouches in his cage and intently watches Paz mix drinks, like one day he, the monkey, might have to mix drinks and needs to be prepared.

• • •

Paz pours Ray a cup of coffee, black. Ray wants to ask if Slick is in yet, but that's not something Ray usually asks, so he doesn't.

"Do you ever forget what day of the week it is?" Paz says. "What month of the year?"

Ray nods. Paz has worked at the El Marrakech almost as long as Ray. She's a couple of years older than him. Slick mentioned once that Paz used to be a showgirl at Bally's. She still has the legs for it. Mr. P. makes her and Claire, who works the other shift, wear uniforms they hate—too-short leopard-print hot pants, too-tight leopard-print bikini tops, too-tall high-heel shoes. Paz and Claire are always having to tug the hot pants out of their butt cracks. Their feet ache after a shift in those heels.

"Here he comes," Paz says now, pouring herself a cup of coffee. "God help us."

Ulan takes the stage in the lounge and starts his act by swiveling his hips and singing "All Shook Up." The first half of his act is Early Elvis. The second half of his act, after a costume change, is Late Elvis. Ulan is from the Philippines. Ray wonders if Ulan has ever actually listened to an Elvis record. Mr. P. doesn't care. He says why pay for a good Elvis when you don't need a good Elvis.

"Sometimes I forget what *year* it is," Paz says.

Slick emerges from the office. He drums his way down the bar, using his index fingers for drumsticks, and takes the stool next to Ray. "Give us a minute," he tells Paz.

Paz heads out onto the floor. Slick reaches over the bar and pours himself bourbon on the rocks. "Where's the old man?" he says. "He should have been here three hours ago."

Ray takes a second to consider the question, because that's what he'd usually do. He has to be extra careful right now. Slick is smart. Slick, Ray suspects, might be even smarter than Mr. P.

"I don't know," Ray says.

"Everything go all right last night?" Slick pops a few peanuts in his mouth. "Mr. P. told Delgado we might be interested?"

"Yeah."

"And then what? After dinner?"

Ray's not a good liar when he's not prepared, but he's prepared for this. "He took a cab back to the airport."

"Delgado did?"

"Yeah."

"And you drove Mr. P. back here?"

Ray doesn't think this is a trap. Slick is just thinking out loud. But Ray is careful anyway. "Mr. P. always drives," he says.

"Because the old man should have been here three hours ago," Slick says. "I went by his house. Caddy's gone; nobody answers the door. I let myself in with my key, nobody's home. Where is he?"

The Caddy is long gone at the bottom of Lake Mead. There's a ramp there nobody but Ray knows about. Not an official ramp, but a slope with a steep drop about twenty feet in.

"I don't know," he says.

Slick tosses a peanut at the monkey. The monkey snatches the peanut out of the air one-handed, like a pitcher getting the ball back from the catcher. Slick believes that Ray doesn't know anything because Slick is used to Ray not knowing anything.

"Well, fuck me." Slick finishes his drink, then slides off the stool. "Like I don't already have enough to worry about. He probably drove to LA for the weekend. He'll be in touch."

Slick goes back to the office. Paz returns. Ulan sings "Heartbreak Hotel." A middle-aged couple gets up and leaves. Later, during Late Elvis, during "Suspicious Minds," a different middle-aged couple walks into the lounge, hears Ulan, and makes a U-turn without even slowing down.

"You know what he said the other day?" Paz asks Ray.

"Ulan?"

"He said the problem is the production design. He said the lounge décor is dated and tacky. That's why he doesn't draw a bigger crowd."

Ulan has told Ray the same thing. "That must be it," Ray says.

Paz smiles. "No doubt."

CHAPTER 56

Another commotion in the courtyard, barely eight o'clock in the morning. Ray steps out onto the breezeway. A working girl from down the block is screaming at a guy. She holds a sparkly red shoe in one hand and a wig in the other. The guy, screaming back, holds a wig in his hand too. His wig is red, hers is blond.

Ray watches the screaming girl and the screaming guy down below and imagines how a person walking by would picture this. The person would see the girl and the guy and the wigs. And the person would see Ray, standing on the breezeway in his boxer shorts. The person would probably assume Ray was part of the picture too.

An idea creeps toward him. A tortoise. Maybe changing who you are, Ray thinks, starts with changing *where* you are.

He gets dressed and drives over to Beverly Green. He tries to find the house where his family used to live. Ray was only eight years old when they moved to Oklahoma, so he doesn't remember the house in Vegas very well. He remembers the white carpet in the living room. He remembers Jeremy telling him to grab the raspberry and coconut Zingers off the shelf in the kitchen, too high for Jeremy to reach.

Ray can't find the house, or even one he thinks might be it. And he doesn't see any FOR RENT signs. He tries the Scotch 80s next. No FOR RENT signs here either, just one FOR SALE on Shadow Lane. Ray pulls over to the curb. For sale or for rent—he decides it doesn't really matter to him. The house on Shadow is long and low, spotless white stucco and red tile roof, an arched and shaded porch. The person who lives in a house like that is nothing like Ray.

Ray memorizes the name on the FOR SALE sign—Jacob Bickham,

Cannon Realty—and his phone number. When he gets back to his apartment, he calls the guy. The secretary puts Ray through.

"Jacob Bickham," the guy says. "At your service."

"I want to look at the house on Shadow," Ray says.

"Wonderful. Mandy can schedule a time for you next week. I—"

"What's wrong with now?"

"Now?" Bickham chuckles. "You're eager. I like that. But I'm booked solid today. Give me your name and number and I'll see what I can do about tomorrow. This property is hot, I've got everybody in town—"

Ray hangs up. Bullshitters like Jacob Bickham give him a headache. Bullshitters like, if Ray is honest, his own dad, his own brother. Ray gets back in his truck and drives over to Cannon Realty. He memorized the address for that too.

Bickham gives Ray the same runaround in person, with extra exasperation and every now and then a sarcastic roll of his eyes. Ray supposes he doesn't look like one of Bickham's usual customers.

"So, let's try this again," Bickham said. "Make an appointment with Mandy out front and we'll take it from there."

What Ray would normally do, what Ray almost starts to do, is put his hand around Bickham's throat and lift Bickham up out of his chair and thump Bickham once against the wall and tell him again, "I want to look at that house on Shadow."

Ray concentrates hard and lets that urge pass. It's not easy. That's the old Ray and he's been the old Ray all his life.

And now what does the new Ray do? Figuring that out isn't easy either. What does a person who lives in the house on Shadow do in a situation like this? Ray feels himself tense again, his stomach uneasy. He hopes he can get the hang of the new Ray soon.

"Fine," Bickham finally sighs, exasperated, while Ray is trying to think. "It's on the way to my next showing. I can give you a quick look. A *quick* look. Okay?"

The house on Shadow is fine. There's a pool in back. There's plenty of space on each side of the house. The neighbors can cause all the commotion they want. But Ray bets they hardly ever do.

He tells Bickham he'll take it. Bickham smiles like Ray is joking. Ray waits. Bickham rolls his eyes and starts talking fast—bullshitting. Asking price is one-sixty and Ray will have to come in fairly close to that. He'll also need to get preapproved for a loan before Bickham can take an offer to the sellers. Just let Mandy know when . . . bullshit, bullshit, bullshit.

Ray lets it pass again, the urge to pick Bickham up and thump him against a wall. One good thump and guys usually stop bullshitting and start paying attention.

"All right, one-sixty," Ray says.

Never take the first offer, Ray hears his dad instructing Alice when they were kids, *never ever ever.* But Ray can afford the one-sixty with no problem, and he wants to wrap this up. Letting his urges pass, not being Old Ray, is wearing him out.

"I pay you now?" Ray says.

"What?" Bickham says.

Ray walks out to his truck and comes back with the garbage bag. He counts out sixteen bundles of cash, ten grand each, onto the kitchen counter. Bickham stares at the money. A hundred and sixty grand in cash, it turns out, works a lot like a good thump against the wall.

"House keys," Ray says, and holds out his hand.

Bickham forgets to take the FOR SALE sign with him when he leaves. Ray is pulling the sign out of the ground when his new next-door neighbor turns into her driveway. She gets out of her car, sees Ray, stops.

She's a nice-looking lady, in a nice skirt and blouse, carrying a purse that's not flashy but probably expensive. Ray can already tell she'll be an improvement over his previous neighbors.

He nods at her to be polite. Probably he should be friendly instead of just polite. Wave? That might be too friendly.

The lady keeps watching him. Ray's probably not the new neighbor she expected. He can see her taking deep breaths through her nostrils. In, in, in . . . out. In, in, in . . . out. Ray nods again, in case she missed the first one, but she just turns and hurries up the walkway to her house.

CHAPTER 57

Saturday. Sunday. By Monday Slick knows Mr. P. won't be walking through the doors of the El Marrakech ever again. Slick is a little bit panicked. Was it LA who popped Mr. P. and Slick is next on their list? Slick is also a little bit hopeful. Was it LA who popped Mr. P. and now they want Slick to take over Vegas for them?

It might not have been LA. It might have been . . . who knows? Gangbangers? Crackheads? Maybe Mr. P. got carjacked. The Mexicans didn't pop Mr. P. That wouldn't make any sense.

Slick explains all this to Ray, though really, he's just talking to himself.

"What do you want me to do?" Ray says.

"Nothing. Sit tight. I've got to think this through."

One thing for sure Slick won't do is call the police. Sooner or later, he'll have to call LA. Slick starts changing his tie three or four times every day, either because he's panicked or because he's hopeful or both. He takes a long time with the knot, getting it perfect. He switches out his cuff links to match the new tie.

Tuesday night after Ulan finishes his set, Paz turns on the TV and the three of them, Paz and Ray and Ulan, watch the news. First there are speeches and music and fireworks. Finally, the Sands comes down. The windows flash and wink when the explosives go off, then a few seconds later the tower slumps sideways and collapses like a drunk stepping off a curb. Dust billows and the crowd cheers like crazy. Ray thinks about how Mr. P. would hate this, the celebration. It's a good thing he's not around. He'd give Ray an earful.

Ulan wanders off, complaining about his crap audiences and the crap stage design and how he's sick of the crap. Slick zips by from the other direction, on his way to the office, pausing just long enough to grab a bottle of bourbon. "Shit, shit, shit," they hear him hiss under his breath.

"Hey," Paz says when it's just her and Ray and the monkey at the bar, and the monkey curled up asleep. She clicks off the TV and sneaks herself a shot of vodka. "I noticed you've been awfully imperturbable."

"I'm what?"

"You always are. True. But Mr. P. disappearing, I thought you'd be at least a little perturbed."

"Upset, you mean."

"Upset or worried or sad or thrilled. Or puzzled. I'll go with puzzled. You don't wonder what happened to him?"

She's not suspicious. Ray doesn't think so. She's just bored. She just wishes she had someone more interesting than Ray to talk to. If Paz *is* suspicious, she won't do anything about it. She likes Ray better than Slick. She likes Ray way, way better than Mr. P. She definitely won't call the cops.

"I forgot," she says, "you got mail today."

Ray has his mail sent to the El Marrakech because someone is always breaking into the mailboxes at his apartment complex. He supposes now he can change his address. He doubts the lady with the expensive purse, or anyone on Shadow Lane, will steal his mail.

Paz finds what she's looking for under the bar. She slides a postcard across to Ray. The postcard has a picture of a gorilla on the front. Ever since she left Russia, Ray's sister Tallulah has been in Africa, in Rwanda, working for a charity that helps kids. Tallulah has even adopted one of the kids, a little girl named Ingabire. Ray worries it's not safe in Africa for Tallulah, but he also knows she can take care of herself. So can Ingabire, probably, now that she's a Mercurio. *You don't fuck with a Mercurio*, their dad used to always say. *Fuck with a Mercurio at your own peril.*

The monkey is awake now. Ray shows it the picture of the gorilla. The monkey pretends to be unimpressed and goes back to sleep.

"You always smile when you get a postcard from your sister," Paz says.

"I do?"

"Well, what we'll call a smile for you, Ray. A Ray smile. You're not much of a smiler, Ray."

"Okay."

"I'm so fucking bored."

November is a dark month in Vegas, which means the El Marrakech is even more dead than usual. Ray tries to decide how long he should stick around. Another week? Two weeks? He's probably already safe, but the truth is he doesn't have anything better to do. *What now?*

At the end of his set, Ulan asks the audience for feedback. He asks which they like better, his Early Elvis or his Late Elvis. Tonight, the audience is only four people, two elderly couples sitting together. The two elderly men wear cowboy hats, and the two elderly women have their hair in buns.

"Just be yourself!" one of the men advises Ulan.

"Good advice," Paz mutters under her breath.

Ray wonders, again, if that's all you *can* be. Yourself. You're born a certain way; you're raised a certain way. That's a lot of forward momentum. Like a rocket blasting off into the sky. Rockets don't make a sharp left turn all of a sudden, do they? They can't. Ray wonders if his plan to change his *self* is doomed from the very beginning.

CHAPTER 58

Ray knocks on the office door and steps inside. It's strange to see Slick sitting behind Mr. P.'s big wooden desk. Slick seems a little uneasy about it himself. Ray notices that Slick hasn't touched or moved any of Mr. P.'s knickknacks—a frosted shot glass from Lido de Paris, a pair of ruby-red dice, a framed photo of Mr. P. with Elvis Presley's manager.

"Yeah?" Slick says.

"Busy?"

"Am I busy? What do you think, Ray?"

Ray sits down. He doesn't say anything. He knows Slick isn't really asking him a question.

"Somebody popped Mr. P.," Slick says, thinking out loud. "Who? Why? It's very concerning. At the same time, you could also say it's an opportunity. Fortune favors the bold. You understand what I'm saying, Ray? With Mr. P. gone, we have to be bold. We have to show LA that the El Marrakech is in good hands."

Fortune favors the bold means, Ray supposes, that you'll make your own luck if you take risks. Maybe it's true. But the thing about famous sayings, Ray has noticed, is that there's always one with the opposite message. Like, in this case, good things come to those who wait.

"So, first thing, we need to get our house in order and pull some weeds," Slick says. "You understand what I'm saying? Over on Sangallo Street."

Sangallo Street is where Nealy lives. Slick wants Ray to shoot him. Nealy is a guy with, according to Slick, a poor work ethic.

Ray shakes his head.

"No?" Slick says. "No, you don't understand, or . . ."

"No," Ray says. "I'm not pulling any more weeds."

"What?"

Ray's already been over all this once already, with Mr. P. He doesn't feel like going over it all again. "No," he says.

Slick tugs his tie loose, then knots it back up. "Fuck, Ray," he says. "You know how many headaches I have right now? I don't need another headache. It's extremely, extremely important we show LA that the El Marrakech is in good hands."

Slick's hands. But why? Ray has been thinking about this for a couple of days now, ever since the postcard from Tallulah. The gorilla on the postcard made Ray remember the costume his dad made him wear that one Halloween, which made him remember his dad's disco in Oklahoma City, which made Ray remember the music, the crowds, the chips of light from the disco balls like schools of fish swimming across the ceiling. Everyone was always in a good mood. Ray, who worked the door, hardly ever had to get rough.

Ray learned a lot about running a club from his dad. He's learned a lot about running a joint from Mr. P. too. Ray might not be smart, but he pays attention. He's learned a lot about how *not* to run a joint.

That's when Ray has the idea. It's a crazy idea. It's an idea that belongs in somebody smarter's head but accidentally ended up in Ray's, a red card in a blue deck.

"Ray?" Slick says. "Hello? Are you listening to me?"

"I'm taking over," Ray says.

"What? Take over what?"

"I'm taking over the El Marrakech."

Slick goes blank, then blinks and laughs. "Stop fucking around, Ray. I don't have time for you to fuck around. Get over to Sangallo Street and pull those weeds, like I told you."

"You're still general manager," Ray says. "Don't worry. But we're going legit. One hundred percent."

No more running dope or cleaning money for LA. And definitely no more pulling weeds. That's the biggest thing Ray has to change about his life. All those people he hurt without thinking twice about it. What kind of person hurts all those people without thinking twice about it?

"You want to take over the El Marrakech?" Slick says slowly, once he realizes Ray is serious, once that soaks through the surface of his brain. "You want *me* to work for *you*?"

"And the El Marrakech is a normal joint now," Ray reminds him. "Everything legit."

"What the fuck, Ray? What the fuck are you fucking talking about?" Slick is furious. He just about strangles himself with his tie, he knots and reknots it so tightly. "You're out of your fucking, fucking mind. You want me to tell LA we're going *legit*?"

He goes on like that for a minute. Ray lets him get it out of his system. Finally Slick calms down. He's not cursing or strangling himself anymore. He's calm, reasonable. "Ray," he says, "listen to me as a friend. Okay? Ray. The El Marrakech, it's not worth a dime. Not by itself, not legit. You understand that, right? How are we supposed to make money? A busy night, we sell fifty bucks' worth of booze."

Ray feels his chest tighten, his stomach get uneasy. He doesn't know yet how the El Marrakech will make money. But he can't worry about that right now. He has to take one step at a time. That's just how he takes steps.

"And LA, Ray. What am I supposed to tell LA? Sorry, fellas, we're legit now. You'll have to find somebody else."

"Tell them what you need to tell them," Ray says. His mind is made up.

Slick gets mad again. He goes on for another minute. Ray waits again. A quicker option would be to shoot Slick in the head. But shooting Slick in the head, Ray reminds himself, would defeat the whole purpose of what he's trying to do. And the El Marrakech needs a general manager.

In the middle of a sentence, Slick suddenly stops talking. He calms down. He's looking at Ray in a new way now. Like he's realizing for the first time that Ray has a mind of his own, and with a mind of his own Ray could decide to shoot him in the head.

"We good?" Ray says.

"Okay," Slick says. "Sure, Ray. Whatever you say."

CHAPTER 59

Ray has plenty of furniture. He has a table, a chair, a futon frame, a futon. He's never needed more than that. His new house, though, needs more than that. His new house is the wrong kind of quiet—an empty quiet, an unsettling quiet, all those bare hardwood floors. At night, Ray hears his memories walking around, sighing.

So, he's got to buy some furniture, some furniture that will match his new house and the new self that Ray is trying to become.

But he doesn't know where to start. Big things, little things—every day is some new thing, and Ray doesn't know where to start. That's the problem with making your own decisions.

He drives to the Fashion Show mall and walks around until he finds a store that sells furniture. Pottery Barn. He's relieved. The people shopping at Pottery Barn look more or less like the neighbor lady next door, so Ray knows he's on the right track.

All the salesgirls at Pottery Barn are too busy to help him. They scoot away whenever he gets too close. Ray guesses he doesn't look like a guy who buys furniture at Pottery Barn, the same way he doesn't look like a guy who buys a house on Shadow Lane. But he can't change how he looks. Different clothes? Maybe. But Ray is always going to look like a big hulking low-brow Neanderthal. That's what Alice used to call him, among other things. Ray is always going to look like the guy he used to be.

Finally, a salesgirl, the only black salesgirl, spots Ray and comes over. She asks him what he's looking for. Ray shows her a diagram he drew on a cocktail napkin, a floor plan of his new house: blank squares for the living room, for what he guesses is the other living room, for a dining room, for three bedrooms. "Everything," he says.

The salesgirl's name is Jazzy. She's only a sophomore at UNLV but she calls Ray "hon" like she's sixty years old. She takes charge of the cocktail napkin and fires questions at him. Napoleon chairs in antiqued natural or whitewashed? Stewart sleeper sofa in dark brown or moss green? Ray doesn't have an opinion. He tells her to ring up whatever's in stock, whatever can be delivered as soon as possible. Still, though, she deliberates about every detail. She takes her job seriously. Ray appreciates that.

"Rugs too?" she says.

Ray forgot about rugs. Rugs should have been the first thing he bought. A smart person—rugs would have been the first thing they bought.

After the rugs, Jazzy the salesgirl shows him sheets and towels, cups and dishes, flatware. Ray doesn't need any of that—he'll never see it hidden away inside the cupboards and drawers. But he wonders if maybe part of what makes a house sound normal and nonempty is what's in the cupboards and drawers. He tells Jazzy to go ahead and pick out sheets and towels, cups and dishes, flatware. Can't hurt.

Jazzy rings up his order. She makes a list for him on the flip side of the cocktail napkin: pillows, shower curtains, lightbulbs for the Pottery Barn lamps he bought, felt pads for the feet of the tables and chairs, rubber pads for the rugs. "There's a Sears at the other end of the mall, hon," she tells him. Ray thanks her and tips her a hundred bucks. She doesn't want to take the money, but Ray just waits until she has to give in.

On the way out of Sears, Ray sees a display for computers. Computers are in color now, he learns. He remembers the CD disc Purdy gave him and buys a Macintosh Performa. In a day or two he'll have a farmhouse desk to put the Performa on. He'll have a farmhouse chair that matches the desk.

CHAPTER 60

Ray takes his usual seat at the bar. Paz pours him coffee. The monkey yawns. Ray writes a postcard to Tallulah. He tells her he bought a house. He tells her he's taking over the El Marrakech. He tells her about the old cowboy advising Ulan to be himself. He tells her he's worried he's not smart enough to run the El Marrakech. He thinks he can imagine what she'll say. She'll say: *Only dumb people don't worry if they're smart enough.*

Paz, Ray realizes, has been staring at him. "What?" he says.

She shakes her head. "Nothing. Slick was just fucking with us. Claire and me, earlier."

"Okay."

"He said you're taking over," Paz says. "I know that can't possibly be true, but he was adamant."

"It's true," Ray says.

"Why did you let him talk you into that?"

Ray finishes writing the postcard and signs it. *Love, Ray Mercurio.* Tallulah gave him shit for signing his full name, the first time he wrote her years ago, so he's done it ever since.

"I talked *him* into it," he says.

"What?"

A customer wanders up to the bar and orders a margarita. It turns out he was looking for a different lounge, across the street, and accidentally wandered in here. He doesn't look too happy about it.

"Listen to me, Ray," Paz says after the customer heads off to the slots with his margarita. "I don't know what's going on, but you can't trust Slick. You understand that, right?"

Ray understands that. But he has to take the chance if he's going to take over. Fortune favors the bold. Ray hopes so. "I'm good," he says.

Pottery Barn delivers the order to his house. Ray screws in lightbulbs and sticks on felt pads. He rolls out rugs and positions the furniture in each room using a Pottery Barn catalogue for a guide. When he's finished, his new house looks and sounds less empty, but still not quite right. Ray decides he'll give it a day or two, to see if he gets used to it, before he heads back to the mall.

He takes the Performa out of the box, plugs it in, turns it on. That's about all Ray knows how to do with a computer. Luckily, though, when he slides in the CD disc that Purdy gave him, some friendly and simple instructions pop up on the screen. Ray connects the telephone line to the Performa and clicks the mouse. The Performa makes a terrible screeching and beeping and squawking sound. Ray wonders if he got a bum Performa or if somehow, he already busted it. He unplugs it, connects the telephone line back to the telephone, and calls Purdy. Purdy doesn't answer, so Ray calls Piggy next. Piggy's in his last year of college at OU. He should know if Ray busted the Performa or not.

"Hey, Piggy."

"Ray! Hi. But . . ."

"Sorry. Paul."

"It's fine. To what do I owe the pleasure? How are the bright lights, big city? Finals are next week. It's like *Wuthering Heights* here on campus, a tense and desperate gloom. 'A range of gaunt thorns all stretching their limbs one way, as if craving alms from the sun.'"

"Okay," Ray says.

"I finished sending in all my applications. For graduate school? I'm applying to both MFA and PhD programs. I want to focus on my novel, but there are more job opportunities for PhDs."

"Okay."

"What's new in Vegas?" Piggy says. "Any exciting developments?"

"Not really."

"Ray, c'mon, give me *something*."

Ray considers. He can't tell Piggy that he's making a big change in his life, because Piggy will ask what the big change is and why Ray is making it. His little brother doesn't need to know anything about that.

"I went to the mall," Ray says.

"Ray, hey, I've been toying with an idea."

"Okay."

"I graduate in May of next year," Piggy says, "the same week as Mom and Dad's anniversary, the day they met. It's a perfect time to get everyone together. It's a long trip for Tallulah, but my powers of persuasion are formidable. And I know we can convince Alice to fly in too. She can take a weekend off, once in her life. What do you think?"

May of next year? Ray can't think that far ahead. He has to get through this month first. This week, this day.

"I bought a computer," Ray says.

"What? Really?"

Ray tells Piggy about the Performa. Piggy promises that the terrible sound means the computer is working properly. That seems crazy to Ray, but after he finishes talking to Piggy, Ray tries again. Eventually the terrible sound stops, like Piggy said it would, and Ray is on—or in?—America Online.

He clicks some buttons. They want him to pick a username. Ray doesn't know what that means, so he sticks with Ray. AOL turns Ray into Ray3298. Ray supposes that's okay. He clicks some more buttons and doesn't understand why Purdy is so fired up about AOL. The first of anything, Purdy gets fired up about it. Super Nintendo, the Walkman.

Ray clicks some more buttons. Somehow, he ends up clicking into what the top of his screen says is a "chat room." This is a weird deal. Ray watches for a while until he figures it out. Different people on different computers are "chatting" with each other by typing out what they want to say. Each person has a nickname. Are they all in Vegas? No, Ray realizes. A person called MaeFlower7 types that she's in snowy Western Mass, which Ray guesses must be Western Massachusetts. JimJim49 types, Brrr, Mae. You should come visit me in sunny CA!

Ray waits. He's curious how MaeFlower7 will answer JimJim49. Do these people in the chat room know each other? Ray thinks, judging by the questions they're asking each other, that they don't know each other—he thinks they might be meeting here for the first time, on or in AOL. This is a very weird deal, but also interesting.

Before Ray knows it, an hour has passed. He figures out part of the code. A/S/L means age/sex/location. People type that to break the ice. Ray follows a variety of different conversations. People talk about their Christmas vacation plans, their jobs, their pets, and—a lot—the weather where they live. Sometimes two people agree to "go private" and disappear from the chat list. Ray guesses the room he's in must be like the bar of a joint, and "private" is like a table in a corner where two people go to have a more personal conversation.

Ray's never been good at small talk, or really any kind of talk. But he's intrigued by how AOL lets you think about what you're going to say before you say it. No rush, no pressure. He hesitates, his fingers over the keyboard. Why not give it a try?

33/m/Vegas.

Almost immediately a response pops up. Hi Ray! And then another. Welcome, Ray! Then a whole swarm of greetings from people in the chat room. Ray feels a buzz of both alarm and pleasure.

Hi, Ray! I'm your neighbor! 28/f/Reno.

That's from charliegirl28. Ray feels another buzz, even stronger this time. He thinks about what he wants to say. He starts to type, "Hello, charliegirl," but then stops himself.

Hi neighbor, he types.

CHAPTER 61

Sunday, Ray's day off, is warm for Vegas in December, almost seventy degrees, so he calls Purdy and tells him to come over and swim. Purdy brings his boom box, pizzas with pineapple and ham, and a cooler full of Diet Cokes. Turns out the water in Ray's pool is too cold for swimming—Purdy discovers that with a shriek when he cannonballs in—but the stone patio is a good place to sit in the sun and eat the pizzas.

Purdy doesn't bring up the AOL disc. Ray is glad. He'd rather not discuss the conversation he had with charliegirl28. It was just a normal conversation—how do you like Reno, how do you like Vegas, what do you do for work, don't you hate the tourists—but that's what made it so strange for Ray. He's never in his life talked to a girl for forty minutes. Well, technically they were typing, not talking, but still. Forty minutes went by in a blink. Her name is Charlie. She told Ray she's usually on AOL most weekdays, before her shift at the Club Cal Neva. Evenings she deals blackjack there and mornings she works on her art. Ray was curious to know more about her art, but she had to leave for her shift.

Catch you later this week? she typed, and Ray felt another buzz, the most electrical one yet.

Ray does tell Purdy that he's taking over the El Marrakech. That fires Purdy up. Purdy wants to know about the moves Ray has planned, and Ray has to admit again he doesn't have any moves or plans yet.

"You need to get you some of them girls with feathers," Ray says with his thick paste of a black/Texas/Louisiana/farm-boy accent. "You know what I'm saying? Nothin' but feathers. Put them girls up on the stage there instead of that Elvis fella, what's his name, cain't sing worth a damn."

"I don't know," Ray says. The quality of topless showgirls the El Marrakech would be able to attract might make the place even sadder and more
depressing than it is already. And Ray's not sure he wants the El Marrakech
to be the kind of joint that has topless showgirls at all. Purdy has one thing
right, though. Ulan shouldn't be up on the stage.

Purdy forgets how cold the swimming pool was the first time and tries
another cannonball. Ray goes inside to get him a towel from Pottery Barn,
so Purdy doesn't freeze to death. While Ray is inside, the doorbell *ding-ding-
dong-dongs*. It means business, like the bells on a church. Ray opens the front
door. The lady from next door stands there. She's not wearing work clothes
today, a Sunday, but instead a pair of jeans and a sweatshirt. Still neat as a pin,
though. A ponytail without a single blond hair blowing loose.

"I'm going to have to ask you to turn down the music, please," she says.
But she's telling, not asking, her lips pursed so tight it's a miracle she can
squeeze any words out.

Ray realizes he can hear the O'Jays blasting all the way in here. He should
have been on that sooner. If he doesn't want his neighbors causing a commotion, he better not cause one himself.

"I'll take care of it," Ray says.

That just seems to make the lady from next door more annoyed, though.
She's like a bottle of carbonated beverage that's been shaken up hard. Ray can
practically hear the bubbles sizzling inside her.

"It's Sunday," she says. "I'm just trying to have a nice Sunday afternoon
working in my garden. I don't think that's too much to ask."

"It's not," Ray agrees. He hollers through the house until he gets Purdy's
attention. *Turn down the O'Jays*, Ray signals with his thumb. *Down*. After a
minute Purdy understands and turns down the O'Jays. "That all right?" Ray
asks the lady.

"That's fine. Thank you."

She seems surprised and suspicious and not really any less carbonated.
Ray guesses she's around . . . fifty or so years old? It could be the way she
purses her mouth so tight, which makes her look older than she is.

"My name's Ray," Ray says.

"Dianne Holloway," the lady says. Ray wonders if they're going to shake hands, but she keeps her arms folded tight across her chest. "Thank you. Have a nice day."

She marches off across the clean white gravel of Ray's yard, back to her place. He hears her front door swing shut with a boom that echoes down the block.

CHAPTER 62

Ulan bursts into tears when Ray fires him. Real tears, genuine nose blowing. Ray's ready for it. Ulan has always been dramatic and emotional. Ray's ready when Ulan stops crying and delivers a passionate speech about injustice and ignorance. Ray has no right to fire Ulan! How dare Ray, how dare he! Ulan demands to know upon what grounds Ray has made this decision.

Ray gives it to him straight. "You're a bad singer."

"You mean I'm a bad Elvis," Ulan says, searching for a loophole. "I can do Michael Jackson. I can do a *fantastic* Michael Jackson."

"No."

"I'm not a bad singer! Pinoys are the best singers in the world! Everybody knows!" He appeals to Paz. "It's true, isn't it? About Pinoys?"

"I don't know," she says. "You're the only Pinoy I know."

Slick strolls up to the bar. He doesn't say anything. Slick has been keeping his thoughts to himself ever since Ray took over.

"Slick! Slick!" Ulan swings around to appeal to Slick now. "Tell Ray he has no authority to fire me. Whatsoever!"

"Sorry, bud," Slick says. "Ray's in charge now."

Paz hands Ulan a Long Island Iced Tea. Ulan takes a sip, and Ray finally has a chance to explain to Ulan that he's only fired as a singer. Ray plans to redecorate the El Marrakech. Ulan is always talking about how bad the joint looks, so . . .

Ulan's eyes light up. "I would be the production designer. Yes. The art director."

Ray isn't sure that Ulan will be a better decorator than he is a singer. But he can't be any worse, and he's cheap.

"Great idea," Slick says. "Brilliant. What's the theme going to be?"

"The theme!" Ulan says. "It's midnight at the oasis. Colorful and exotic. Turbans and silks, lanterns and incense . . ."

Ray's been thinking about this. What made Club Mercurio so popular? What made joints like the Sands so popular back in Mr. P.'s day? Ray wants to attract a crowd like that, a serious crowd, with money to spend. So, no turbans, no volcanoes, no pirates. People filled Club Mercurio and the Sands so they could look good and feel special. The El Marrakech needs to look good and feel special.

"Vegas," Ray says. "That's the theme."

Slick laughs. "Vegas is the theme? A casino in Vegas where the theme is . . . Vegas?"

"Not Vegas now," Ray says.

"No? Vegas when?" Slick laughs again.

But Paz gets it. She's heard all of Mr. P.'s stories too. "Sinatra's Vegas," she says. "Classy and hip."

"That's it," Ray says. "Smooth."

"Yes," Ulan says. "I like it. An understated glamour. Sleek and refined. A crisp white shirt under a black tuxedo jacket. The golden flame of a candle."

Ray hopes he's making the right decision letting Ulan do the redecorating. "Smooth," Ray emphasizes again.

"Huh," Slick says.

"Not such a terrible idea, is it?" Paz asks him.

The monkey, who hasn't weighed in yet, grabs the bars of its cage and dances what looks like an Irish jig.

"You know how expensive it will be to redo this whole place?" Slick says. "Who'll pay for it? Have you thought about that, Ray?"

"We've got some dough." In the office, Ray knows, in Mr. P.'s safe. Mr. P. always kept forty or fifty grand on hand.

Slick knows Ray knows about the forty or fifty grand. "Whatever you say, Ray. You're in charge." Then Slick heads back to the office, shaking his head. Ray turns to Paz.

"The other day," he says. "You said you know a hundred singers."

"I might have been exaggerating, but yeah," Paz says. "I know some singers."

"Pick the three best. The three smoothest. Bring them in so I can hear them."

"Oh, Ray. You know this is going to end in disaster, don't you?"

"Bring them in."

She shrugs. Okay. Ulan is sketching, on a cocktail napkin, what looks like a chandelier. Ray's not about to buy a new chandelier for the El Marrakech—forty or fifty grand isn't much dough, and he needs to be smart with it—but Ulan is on the right track. Ray lets him do his thing.

CHAPTER 63

Ulan comes in the next day with more sketches, these done on real paper, with colored pencils and shading. Not bad.

Ray drives over to the Fashion Show mall and hires Jazzy, the salesgirl from Pottery Barn, to help Ulan. She's dubious at first that Ray actually runs a lounge on the Strip, but he offers her double what she makes now and already—she can't stop herself—she's spilling over with ways to save money. Garage sales, flea markets and pawnshops, the mom-and-pop secondhand stores far off the Strip. Ray thinks Jazzy and Ulan will make a solid team. She'll pay attention to details and get shit done.

A couple of days later, Paz brings in the first three singers. Ulan plays piano. The singers Paz brings in aren't bad, but they're not what Ray hears in his head when he imagines the new El Marrakech—the singers aren't *smooth* enough.

"What the hell does that *mean*?" Paz says, irritated, but Ray suspects she secretly agrees with him. She says she'll keep looking.

What about the monkey? He won't fit the new theme. Slick suggests they stick the monkey in a little tuxedo. Ray doesn't know if he's joking. He's probably joking. Ray doesn't like the monkey, and the monkey doesn't like him, but you can't just fire a monkey, you can't just kick him onto the street. The monkey never asked to be hired in the first place.

"What did LA say?" Ray asks Slick.

"About what?"

"When you told them we're legit now."

"What do you think they said? They're not happy about it, Ray. But what can they do? They have to live with it."

Good. That's one problem Ray can cross off his list.

Friday morning Ray goes to the gym—not his old gym, and not even a gym, but a health and fitness center located a few blocks from his new house. No boxing ring, but a brand-new speed bag and brand-new free weights and nobody has to be warned not to bleed on the floor. Mirrors everywhere, though. Ray could do without those.

He drives home, counting down to one o'clock. That's when he'll get on America Online and talk to Charlie. They've chatted three times this week, in a private room, and already Ray is getting to know her better than any girl he's known before. For example, Charlie has a mixture of feelings about Reno, where she was born and where she grew up. Reno feels like home to her, but home can feel claustrophobic the older you get, can't it? Ray left Oklahoma City when he was only eighteen, so he can't relate exactly. But he tells her about his life in general, feeling like he's been getting stuck deeper and deeper in the mud.

They talk about music. Charlie likes a very specific kind of country music, from Texas, not Nashville. She says she'll make a list of songs for him to try. Ray tells her he usually just listens to whatever somebody else has on.

They talk about their favorite foods to eat. They talk about if they think there is life on other planets. The one thing Charlie doesn't want to talk about: her family, her personal life. That's fine with Ray.

I like you, Ray, she typed yesterday afternoon. There, I said it.

He hesitated, tried to think. If it had been a conversation in person, the delay would have been awkward. Luckily it wasn't a conversation in person. I like you too, he typed back.

When Ray gets home from the gym, he sees his next-door neighbor, Dianne Holloway, standing in her driveway. She's staring at the flat back tire of her car like maybe she can reinflate it just using her mind.

Ray parks his truck. Stick to your own business. That's a rule he usually follows. What if the flat tire is a trick, a trap? What if Ray walks over to help and while he's bent down helping with the tire . . . pop? A bullet right behind his ear.

But that's crazy. Ray reminds himself where he lives now. The tire isn't a trick or a trap. The lady or boyfriend hidden in the bushes isn't going to pop him. That was his old life. He walks over.

"Dianne," he says.

She turns, sees him. Her small frown becomes a bigger frown. "What do you want?"

"I can help with that," he says, pointing to the tire.

"No. I don't need any help. Thank you."

Ray always tries to respect a person's privacy, because he expects people to respect his, but unless Dianne Holloway wants to get her skirt greasy and her face sweaty, unless she knows her way around a jack and a lug wrench, she could use some help. If she knew her way around a jack and a lug wrench, Ray suspects, she'd already be using them.

"You have a spare?" he says. "I'll change it out for you. Only take a couple of minutes."

"I said *no*," she says, cracking that *no* like a whip. "AAA is on their way. I'm *fine*." *Crack.*

"All right." Ray doesn't push. He guesses Dianne is still mad at him about the O'Jays on Sunday. Pushing won't make her get over it any faster. He turns to leave.

"Wait," she says. "They were supposed to be here half an hour ago. And I'm late for ... *damnit*. I should know how to change a tire."

That's true, but Ray doesn't say so. "Give me your keys."

She gives him her keys. He opens the trunk. Spare, jack, tire tool, everything he needs. He's done in a couple of minutes. He puts the flat tire in the trunk and tells her she should get it fixed as soon as possible—no telling what kind of shape the spare is in, though it looks like it's in pretty good shape.

"I've got to go," she says. She hands a five-dollar bill at him.

Ray looks down at the five, not understanding at first. Then he shakes his head and hands the five back to her. "I'm your neighbor," he says.

He doesn't know if she gets it. She just looks at him.

"I run the El Marrakech on the Strip," he says. "It's a hundred percent legit."

She just looks at him. Ray realizes maybe he's the one who doesn't get it.

"Well, okay," she says. She sticks the money back in her wallet, climbs into her car. "Thank you. I've got to go."

CHAPTER 64

Today Charlie can only chat for a few minutes. She's picking up a split shift at the Cal Neva. Ray asks if it's snowing up there in Reno. Charlie doesn't answer for a while. Maybe she's gone to look out the window and see.

Sunny and clear and cold, she types finally. High today is 41.

Have a good shift, he types back.

Ray's never been with a girl like Charlie. None of the girls he's been with up until now—not many, never for very long—had steady jobs, passions like painting and art, dreams for the future. And all the girls he's been with up until now had specific reasons for being with Ray. One got kicked out of her apartment and needed a place to crash. One needed to scare off her ex-boyfriend. One needed dope and thought Ray might help her rob Mr. P. Ray supposes that last one counts as a dream for the future, but not the kind he's talking about, not the kind Charlie has.

Charlie doesn't *need* anything from Ray, not as far as he can tell. She *wants* to spend time with him.

He eats lunch, leftover Chinese food from yesterday, at his farmhouse dining room table. The house still doesn't feel exactly right to Ray. Something is missing. Does he need more furniture? Any more furniture, though, and it would be hard for him to move around.

After lunch he takes a nap on one of the two different sofas. The doorbell wakes him up. *Ding-ding-dong-dong.* It's a lot of doorbell for one house.

The neighbor lady, Dianne, stands out front, holding a box in her hands.

"Ray," she says. "Hello."

"Hello."

She takes a deep breath. "I would like to apologize, Ray, for being such a . . . you know."

Ray's not sure if she wants him to fill in the blank or not. And he's not sure why she's apologizing. So he doesn't say anything.

"For being so unpleasant to you earlier," she says. "You were very helpful and I just . . . and I'm sorry for being so unpleasant on Sunday too. Your music wasn't that loud. I don't know what . . ."

She keeps starting sentences that she doesn't finish. But she doesn't seem angry like she did before. And she's holding out the box now like she wants Ray to take it. He does.

"I hope you like brownies," she says. "Freed's is my favorite bakery in town. I'm so sorry about the . . . you know. The tip. The money I offered you. I'm such a jackass."

Ray opens the box. The brownies look good. Freed's is Ray's favorite bakery too. But Ray is in uncharted territory again. What does a normal person do when your neighbor brings over a box of brownies to thank you for changing a tire?

"You want to come in?" he says. "I'm going to make some coffee."

"Oh, no. Thank you. No. I need to . . ." She stops herself again. She takes another deep breath. She's wondering, Ray thinks, if she's being a jackass again. "Sure, okay," she says. "I'd love to come in and have some coffee."

They drink their coffee and eat the brownies in the main living room, Ray sitting on one sofa and Dianne sitting on the other. Dianne keeps looking around.

"This is nice," she says, sounding surprised. She said the same thing, sounding the same way, when they came through the smaller living room, when she waited in the kitchen while Ray made the coffee.

"Pottery Barn," Ray says.

"Oh. Very nice."

Ray isn't used to expressing his true feelings to a stranger—he's not used to expressing his true feelings to anyone or having true feelings of his own to start with—but he decides to take a shot. He doesn't see the harm.

"There's still something not right about it," he says. "I can't put my finger on it. I want it to be a normal house. To feel like one."

She regards him over the lip of her coffee cup. "Oh. I see. Well, it really is . . . nice, I mean."

She asks him about the El Marrakech. He explains the new theme. She tells him she works for the city's tourism department, in charge of public relations. She's been there seven years.

"You like it?" Ray says.

"Gosh, yes. It's so rewarding to help shine a light on what makes the city so . . ." She stops, puts down her coffee cup, picks up another brownie. "No. I hate it. I hate everything about it. My boss is a major . . . you know."

Ray nods. "Yeah."

"You too?"

"Not anymore. I'm the boss now."

"Oh, good. I'm glad for you. I should quit. I should have quit six years and eleven months ago. I don't know why I'm telling you all this. My life at the moment is a disaster. That's why I was so unpleasant to you earlier. My husband, my *ex*-husband is a major you-know too. My kids are off in college and . . ."

She runs out of steam and flutters her fingers. The fluttering fingers say, Ray guesses, both *never mind* and *I don't know why I'm telling you all this*.

"Yeah."

She laughs. "You're like a therapist, Ray."

He doesn't know what she means by that. Nothing bad, he supposes. Her laugh seems loose and relaxed. She seems looser and more relaxed than she was before the coffee.

At the door, when she's about to leave, Dianne stops. "Could I make one suggestion?" she says.

"Okay."

"It might be the walls. What you can't put your finger on."

Ray looks around at the walls. She's right. It's the walls that are still wrong, long stretches of white and empty.

"You could put up some pictures," she says.

"Of what?"

"Whatever you like. Whatever makes you happy."

She makes the decision sound simple, easy. Ray supposes it should be.

CHAPTER 65

Jazzy finds a deal on some used carpet. Guess where it's from? The Sands. Ray's not superstitious. He doesn't believe in omens. But this might be a good omen. The carpet from the Sands looks good, looks right, with bold but smooth geometric shapes in tan and gold and burnt orange, a few stabs of black here and there. The El Marrakech only needs a fraction of what's left over from the Sands, so Jazzy picks out the cleanest, most pristine rolls, the carpet that was off on the untrodden edges of the casino floor.

In a forgotten corner of a forgotten warehouse out by the train tracks, Ulan finds wallpaper—the overage from the original high-roller room at the Dunes. Ulan sends Jazzy in to negotiate. The guy practically pays her to haul away ten thousand square feet. At an estate sale, Jazzy buys a big box of black-and-white eight-by-ten photos. The lady who died, the owner of the estate, worked for the Desert Inn as a roaming camera girl in the sixties. The photos in the box show couples laughing, dancing, kissing, rolling dice, toasting the New Year. The dead camera girl had a gift, Jazzy explains to Ray. She made everyone look like a star, made everyone sparkle. Ray thinks he knows what she means. He wonders if his mom and dad have a picture of themselves like this at home. Jazzy says she'll get the best photos matted and framed.

That works for the El Marrakech, but Ray doesn't want pictures of people on the walls of his house. All those eyes, watching him. But down at the bottom of the box he finds a dozen or so photos in color, without any people in them. The desert, the mountains, a residential street at sunrise.

"Put those in frames too," Ray tells Jazzy. "I'll take them home with me."

The remodel costs a lot. Slick hands over the cash from Mr. P.'s safe without making too much of a fuss. Ray is surprised Slick doesn't make more of a fuss. Slick, Ray supposes, finally recognizes the new theme has potential. Ray tells Slick he plans to have everything ready by the end of the year. New Year's Eve is the biggest night of the year in Vegas.

"Good idea, Ray," Slick says. "I have to admit. Very smart."

Paz brings in three more singers. The first two are just okay. But the third one . . . Ray sits up straight. He's a black guy with wavy hair, in a suit that fits him like a glove. Hard to tell from his face if he's an old forty or a young sixty-five. His voice is *smooth*. Even Ulan looks up from his piano keys to watch him, to listen better. The singer sings "Summer Wind" and sounds just like Sinatra. Then he sings "You Send Me" and sounds just like Sam Cooke. So not only is he one kind of smooth, he's all the kinds of smooth.

"Damn," says Purdy, who dropped by to say hello and stayed for the auditions.

"He's the one," Paz says.

The singer's name is Fox. "Why aren't you working somewhere better than this?" Ray asks him.

"None of your business, motherfucker."

"Heroin," Paz says. "Various minor felonies. No one else will let him near the silver."

"Been clean two years," Fox says. "More or less. Never missed a show in my life."

He's been clean for more or less two years? Or more or less clean for two years? Doesn't matter to Ray. This is the smooth singer the lounge needs. And Fox, Paz has already told Ray, will work cheap. Ray hires him on the spot. Fox will start at the end of December.

New Year's Eve is only three weeks away. Then only two weeks away. The lounge shapes up. Down go the El Marrakech's old brass pendant lights and the Moroccan arches and the dusty tapestries illustrated with scenes of camels and minarets. Out go the squat, square lounge tables and heavy chairs, the dark wood and the faded red cushions. In come sleek tables with slender gold-tipped legs, chairs with interesting curves, wood that's caramel-colored and glows in the candlelight.

If there's anywhere you can find a tuxedo that fits a capuchin monkey, it should be Las Vegas. No. Ulan comes up empty. Nobody knows what to do about the monkey. Keep it in back? Paz puts her foot down. The monkey would be too lonely in back. It's a social creature, she says. All Ray can think to do is not do anything. Maybe customers will think casinos back in the day all had pet monkeys behind the bar.

Ray's new house feels just about right now. Normal. The framed photos on the walls look good. Ray can sit for thirty minutes, even an hour, just staring at the clouds over Lake Mead or the empty windblown intersection of Las Vegas Boulevard and Tropicana Avenue. Pictures on the wall are like having extra windows in the house.

He invites Dianne over to see what she thinks about the framed photos. She says she loves them. They drink coffee and eat the chocolate chip cookies he bought from Freed's. They talk about where Ray should put a Christmas tree. Dianne's tree has been up since the day after Thanksgiving. She's in a good mood because all three of her kids are coming home for Christmas.

Ray is cautiously optimistic about his own life. He has a nice house with nice furniture in it and pictures on the wall. He has a nice neighbor lady who comes over to chat and drink coffee. He has a nice girl he's getting to know on America Online. He has a legit job where nobody tells him what to do, where Ray makes his own decisions. That's a lot of changes since the night at the Sands with Mr. P. and the Mexican.

But . . . has *he* changed? That's the worry that creeps in every now and then, when Ray lets it.

"What's on your mind, Ray?" Dianne says. "I see the wheels turning."

He doesn't know if he can explain. "What makes a person who they are?"

"Well . . ."

"The things they do?"

"Yes. I think that's right."

"And the things they've done."

"Sure. Yes."

"You can't ever change that part of you. What's already happened. That's you forever."

Her smile fades. Now it's both of them sitting there in silence, their wheels turning.

Most of the time, though, Ray is in a good mood. Getting the new El

Marrakech in shape puts him in a good mood. Paz and Jazzy and Ulan buzzing around, everyone with a purpose, a job, working together. Hand me that. No, try the red ones. On three, lift. Ray has always missed those days, way back when, with his brothers and sisters. When you grow up like that, crowded into every car and room and experience with your brothers and sisters, you never have to wonder where you fit in the world.

Ray's chats with Charlie put him in a good mood too. He wishes she lived in Vegas so they could meet and talk in person. Would that ruin everything between them, if they met in person, or would it make it even better? Charlie might take one look at Ray in the real world and run as fast as she can in the opposite direction. Ray wouldn't blame her. He's a menacing Neanderthal, no matter how many roll-neck sweaters and pleated khakis Jazzy picks out for him from J. Crew.

A few days ago, Charlie asked him to describe himself. Ray was honest, but he's not a writer like Piggy. He said he was tall and big, with a shaved head and a few tattoos. What else? Hound dog eyes. That's what Paz said about him once.

Charlie is pretty. That's the impression Ray draws from her description of herself. Auburn hair, curlier some days than others. Green eyes. Dimples when she smiles, which the other kids teased her about when she was little. She looks, if she had to pick one person, a little like Neve Campbell, the actress, if Neve Campbell had auburn hair and green eyes.

Ray's never heard of Neve Campbell, but he finds a photo of her on America Online. He's troubled. Charlie is much, much too pretty for him. She'd surely take one look at Ray in the real world and run away as fast as she could.

So, it's Charlie who makes the first move. Ray, she types one afternoon, don't you think it's time we went on an actual date?

Ray feels his heart beating. He stands up and gazes for a while at the soothing photograph of Lake Mead above the desk. He sits back down. He remembers something Tallulah told him in a postcard a long time ago. When it comes to her stunts and acrobatics, running through fire or jumping off the trapeze, she runs or jumps before she has a chance to get scared. That's the trick.

Come visit me in Vegas, Ray types before he's too scared to type it.

Excellent idea, Charlie types back.

She has some time off in early January. Ray says he'll book her a hotel room. They make plans to meet in front of the volcano at the Mirage. Charlie has always wanted to see it.

Can't wait! Charlie types, and Ray is cautiously, cautiously optimistic.

CHAPTER 66

The day before Christmas Eve, four guys deliver the . . . Ray's not sure what you would call it. Ulan calls it "a statement piece." Okay. It's seven feet high by twelve feet long, taking up almost the whole wall behind the stage, dozens of narrow metal strips, horizontal and vertical, supporting dozens and dozens of round winking mirrors.

"A mid-century masterpiece," Ulan says. Some guy Ulan knows in Chinatown welded it together for him, from a picture in an old issue of *Life* that Jazzy showed him.

The four delivery guys install the statement piece. Looks fine, Ray is relieved to discover. Classy but glamorous. Jazzy knew the exact right shade of reddish-brown to paint the wall behind it.

Ray goes to get the cash. One grand, payment on delivery. Slick counts ten hundred-dollar bills onto the desk and doesn't make too much of a fuss about it.

"What's next, Ray?" he says. "You gonna buy a . . . why not put in a balcony? Why not gold-plated toilets like Elvis had? It's only money, right?"

"We'll make it back," Ray says.

"It's an investment. Uh-huh. Whatever you say, Ray."

A knock on the door. Paz sticks her head into the office. "A guy wants to see you," she says.

"What guy?" Slick says.

"I'm not telling you. I'm telling Ray." Paz smiles sweetly at Slick. "The guy wants to see the *boss.*"

Slick gives her the finger. "What guy?" he says.

"*Yo no se,*" Paz says. "*Pero es un hombre muy guapo.*"

Ray knows that Paz speaks Spanish, but he doesn't understand why she's speaking it now. Slick seems to understand why. He slaps his palm on the desk.

"Come on," he tells Ray. "The fucking Mexicans are back."

Two Mexicans stand at the bar. One is a Mexican Slick—lean, good-looking, an easy, friendly smile, a nice suit. The other one is hunched and burly, with small black eyes and a face like a waffle iron. Neither is the Mexican Ray didn't shoot at the Sands.

"My friend! It is such a pleasure to finally meet you!" Mexican Slick spreads his arms wide and beams. Slick switches on his charm too. He clasps Mexican Slick's hand and pumps it up and down. "Welcome to Las Vegas, *amigo*!" Slick says. "*Mi casa*, et cetera."

Ray watches the burly Mexican, his hands and his black eyes. The burly Mexican is watching him. Ray has always had a sixth sense about these things. The burly Mexican is the real deal, the same way Ray is the real deal. No. The way Ray *used to be* the real deal.

Mexican Slick's name is Eduardo. His "associate," his muscle, is Lopez. They happened to be in town for the night, thought they'd drop by and say hello. A social call only, no business, let me buy you dinner, my treat and pleasure. No, no, no, my treat and pleasure, just let me get my coat.

"This is good," Slick tells Ray in the office. "They still need a partner up here."

He grabs Ray's sleeve as they're heading back out to the bar with their coats. He tells Ray it's a very delicate situation. He wants Ray to let him do all the talking at dinner. Ray is okay with that, as long as Slick is clear about the main thing.

"We're clean now," Ray says. "We're staying clean."

"One hundred percent," Slick says. "You bet."

They eat dinner on Fremont, downstairs at the Four Queens. Ravioli, chicken parmesan, spaghetti with meatballs. The Mexicans don't care for Italian food, Ray can tell. They push it around on their plates. It's not very good Italian food.

Eduardo tells Slick about the operation his people down in Mexico are running. It's a beautiful operation, says Eduardo. No risks, good product, profits you won't believe. Expansion, transportation, facilitation. Las Vegas can play a very important role. A smart man in Las Vegas can be very successful.

Ray waits for Slick to say, Sorry, we're out of your kind of business now, we're clean now. But Slick lets Eduardo talk. He asks questions about numbers, revenue streams. Ray gives Slick the benefit of the doubt. It's a delicate situation. Slick is being polite. He knows how to handle a delicate situation.

Dessert comes. Cheesecake. Lopez, the muscle, pokes at his slice with a fork. Eduardo sips his espresso, then turns to Ray and smiles. Eduardo has given Ray one, maybe two glances all night. That's it. Now he studies Ray like he's memorizing him.

"What is your name, my friend?" Eduardo says.

"Ray."

"Ray. Can you tell me why my associate has vanished? My associate, you recall, who came to visit Mr. Pappalardo last month? He never returned to us. Why is this, do you think?"

Slick shifts in his seat. "Eduardo, I don't know what you're—"

Lopez lifts his fork. He's watching Ray but the fork's for Slick. *Stop talking.* Slick stops talking.

"I don't know," Ray says.

It's the truth. Ray doesn't know what happened to the Mexican he didn't shoot. Why didn't the guy go back to Mexico? Ray tries to imagine the possibilities. One possibility: the guy was scared because he didn't close the deal with Mr. P., scared because he almost got himself shot. He was scared of what Eduardo, of what Eduardo's boss, would do to him.

Or . . . did the Mexican make it out of the Sands before the Sands came down? Surely, he made it out of the Sands. He wouldn't have spent five or six days hiding. He would have realized at some point the Sands was about to come down. Maybe he realized too late?

"I can see you are sincerely confused," Eduardo says. "Good. I am relieved. You do not know why Miguel has vanished. But you will permit us"— Eduardo is talking again now to Slick—"to further investigate the matter."

He folds up his napkin very neatly and places it carefully on the table. Slick is paler than Ray has ever seen him. Slick doesn't have anything to worry about, though. Eduardo isn't going to start a shoot-out in a public restaurant, around all these witnesses. That only happens in movies. Eduardo would wait until they're in the parking garage.

In the parking garage behind the Four Queens, Eduardo shakes Slick's hand. The Mexicans have their own car, a rental. "Thank you for dinner, my friend," Eduardo tells Slick. "We'll be seeing you soon."

"Safe travels," Slick says.

That's it. Ray doesn't know what Slick is waiting for. Ray isn't going to wait anymore.

"We're clean now," Ray says as the Mexicans start to get in their car. "We're staying clean now."

Eduardo stops. He looks genuinely confused. "Pardon me?"

"I run the El Marrakech now," Ray says. "And we're clean now. Everything legit. You need to find someone else to be partners with."

"Ray," Slick says. He's turned even paler than he was before.

Lopez stares at Ray. Not a dead stare like before, though. Lopez's black eyes flicker with . . . curiosity, maybe.

"*You* run the affairs now?" Eduardo asks Ray. Then he looks at Slick. He looks back at Ray. He looks at Slick again. "Are you amusing me?"

"No," Ray says. "I'm not amusing you. And the affairs I run is just the El Marrakech. That's all, the lounge. We don't have affairs anymore. You need to find somebody else."

"What Ray here is saying is, is let's not rush into anything." Slick is talking to Eduardo, but he's also, Ray can tell, sending hot, panicked brain waves at Ray. *Do you know how dangerous these people down in Mexico are, Ray?* "We'll continue to have discussions, is what Ray is saying."

Ray is already aware that the people down in Mexico are dangerous. That's why he's making himself clear to Eduardo now. He thinks Eduardo and Eduardo's bosses will be less mad if he doesn't waste their time.

"No," Ray says again. "No more discussions."

Eduardo smiles. "Tell me again, please. Your name."

"Ray."

Ray could end this conversation quickly and easily. The parking garage is deserted, and Lopez has made his first mistake of the night—he's half in the car, half out, one foot up, one foot down, off-balance. Ray just needs to give the car door a hard kick, put an elbow in Lopez's waffle-iron face, take his gun. Three seconds. Ray sees the scene play out in his head. He *feels* it. Everything feels right, like clothes that fit.

Ray makes himself let the moment go. A second later Lopez realizes his mistake. Both of his feet on the ground now, sliding away from the open door, his stare dead again.

"I'll look into your guy," Ray says. "Your associate who never turned up. I'll see if I can find anything out."

A car pulls into the garage, parks a few spaces away. Two young guys get out. They look like computer guys, though that convention isn't in town till January. "It's cheaper to pay the fine," one guy is saying to the other guy.

"Good night, Ray." Eduardo comes around the rented car and shakes Ray's hand. "We will be in touch."

CHAPTER 67

That night Ray doesn't sleep much. He tosses and turns. His mind tosses and turns. Something isn't right. He can't put his finger on it. The Mexicans? No, not the Mexicans. Something wasn't right even before they showed up. Ray was just too busy with picking wallpaper and finding a singer to notice.

At the El Marrakech, Ray sits at the bar. Three o'clock in the afternoon. The lounge has been closed all week so they can put the finishing touches on it. Ray and Paz and the monkey watch Jazzy hang the last of the old black-and-white photos on the wall. Fox rehearses a song, "A Fool in Love," while Ulan tinkles along on the piano.

"Something isn't right," Ray says.

"With Fox?" Paz says. "Sounds good to me. Or do you mean the pictures?"

Ray shakes his head. "I can't put my finger on it."

"Whatever you say, Ray."

Fox finishes the song and cusses out Ulan for some mistake he made on the piano. Ulan ignores him and starts the next song. Fox hits his cue, smooth as silk.

Ray thinks about dinner with the Mexicans last night. He thinks about Slick and Eduardo talking about revenue streams, distribution networks. Why didn't Slick just come right out and say it? That the El Marrakech is clean now? He was being polite.

Or he wasn't being polite. Ray starts to see another possibility. He starts to understand why Slick didn't put up more of a fight, that very first day, when Ray told him the El Marrakech was clean now.

"Ray," Paz says.

"What?"

"You okay?"

A smart person, Ray knows, would have figured this out a long time ago. He's frustrated. He's tired of being the tortoise. A tortoise never won a race against a rabbit. Slow and steady doesn't win a *race*.

"No," he says.

• • •

Slick doesn't get to work until four. Ray waits for him in the office. He sits in the visitor's chair and examines his hands. He makes two fists. He spreads his fingers out. He hasn't decided yet what he should do. He wonders if he'll ever get used to it, all the deciding he has to do now. It's exhausting.

Slick opens the door, shrugs off his overcoat, jumps. "Christ, Ray, where'd you come from? You almost gave me a heart attack."

"You didn't shut it down," Ray says. "You never called LA."

"What?" Slick says. "What are you talking about?"

"The El Marrakech. I told you. We're legit now."

Slick moves around behind the desk and drops into Mr. P.'s chair. "We are! Ray, I did exactly what you told me to do."

Ray examines his hands. "You never called LA," he says. "We're still washing their money."

"For the time being, Ray. Only for the time being." Slick sighs. "We have to do this in stages. Ray, it's a highly complex situation. It's a delicate situation. I'm protecting us, Ray. You and me. I'm protecting both of us. The plane is in the air. I can't just kill the engine. I have to land the plane."

That makes sense to Ray. But would it make sense to a smart person? Ray doesn't know.

He decides to trust Slick. But Slick needs to understand that Ray runs the El Marrakech. Ray runs the El Marrakech and he wants off the plane right now.

"Ray?" Slick says. "Say something, man. Let's talk."

"You have a week. Shut it all down. Call LA."

Slick grimaces. "You sure? Absolutely sure? Once we do this . . ."

"A week."

"Okay," Slick says. "A week."

• • •

After he leaves the El Marrakech, Ray heads to his new health and fitness center.

"Wipe down the bench, asshole," a guy tells Ray when Ray finishes his presses.

Ray was just about to wipe down the bench. The guy, a bodybuilder type, thinks he's bigger and badder than he really is. A month ago, Ray would've had to stop, concentrate, and fight off the urge to put the bodybuilder through the wall. He might even have put the bodybuilder through the wall before he could stop and concentrate.

Today, though, Ray sprays his bench and wipes it down. He walks away. He hardly has to think twice about it.

CHAPTER 68

On his way home, Ray stops at Target to buy an artificial Christmas tree and lights for it. His neighbor Dianne told him where to go and all the reasons why he should get an artificial tree instead of a real one (he doesn't want dead pine needles all over his rug, for example). Later that afternoon Dianne comes over with a pecan pie from Freed's. She helps Ray assemble the tree and string the lights. It's not hard work. They take a break to eat pie and drink coffee.

"Are you excited?" Dianne says.

"About the lounge opening back up?"

"About your friend coming to visit. It's not long now."

Ray has told Dianne about Charlie. He's told her that he worries Charlie is too pretty for him. "Sixteen days," he says.

"You'll be fine," Dianne says. "Listen to me. You've already hit it off, the two of you. That's the important thing. And you're not an unattractive man, Ray. You're not a monster."

"I'll be fine," he says. He wants to believe it. "You want some more coffee?"

She takes a packet of tissues out of her purse. At first Ray thinks she's blowing her nose, but then he realizes the steady honking sound is her crying. Tears spill out of her eyes and run down her cheeks.

"Dianne?" Ray says.

This can't be a normal neighbor thing, for your neighbor to just start crying, out of the blue. He thinks about the things she might be crying about. Her job, her dick of a boss? Her dick of an ex-husband?

"Sorry," she says between honks. "This is painfully awkward, isn't it?"

"Your kids?" he says.

She nods. She finishes honking and uses additional tissues from the packet to wipe the tears off her cheeks. "They're not coming home for Christmas."

Ray wonders if he should cut her another slice of pie. Or change the subject? Or put his hand on her shoulder to comfort her? His hand on her shoulder won't be much comfort. Ray is smart enough to know that. He goes into the half-bathroom off the living room and brings back the Pottery Barn woven trash basket, so Dianne will have somewhere to throw away her crumpled-up tissues, which rest like a bouquet of flowers in her lap.

"Of course they're not coming for Christmas," she says. "I shouldn't be surprised."

Did Ray's mom ever burst into tears because Ray and his brothers and sisters didn't come home for Christmas? Ray doubts it. He can't remember a single time, growing up, when he saw his mom cry about anything.

Piggy keeps trying every year, but the last time the whole Mercurio family was home together would have been the summer before Ray turned eighteen and moved to Las Vegas. He hasn't been back to Oklahoma City since, going on fifteen years now, though he calls his mom and dad every now and then. It's a short conversation. "Hey, Dad." "How the hell are you, Ray? Say hi to your mother." "Hello, Ray." "Hey, Mom." That's about it, unless his mom wants him to send some money to Jeremy.

Tallulah, Ray knows, has only been home a couple of times in the last fifteen years. Jeremy's probably been back a lot. He's been everywhere a lot, from what Ray knows. Alice? It's easier for Ray to imagine his mom crying than it is to imagine Alice ever going back to Oklahoma City.

"Why aren't you surprised your kids aren't coming home for Christmas?" Ray asks Dianne.

It's the dick of an ex-husband, she explains. He made the kind of move he likes to make: a last-minute surprise ski trip, luxury lodge, all expenses paid. Dianne's kids (two sons and a daughter) felt bad about bailing on her last minute, but . . . she understands it's not their fault. The dick of an ex-husband puts them in an impossible bind.

The sons and the daughter seem like they might be dicks too. Ray doesn't say so. And he doesn't say that if Dianne knew her ex-husband was going to make a move like this, she should have made her own move ahead of time.

"Always beat 'em to the punch, Ray," his dad said. Ray doesn't remember the exact circumstances. A deserted parking lot behind a warehouse, his dad buying something from a guy in a light blue Ford Pinto. Or maybe selling something to him. Ray was a junior or senior in high school. His dad gave the guy in the Pinto a duffel bag stuffed full of newspaper instead of cash. His dad must have been buying something.

"What's his name?" Ray asks Dianne.

"My ex? Eugene."

"Eugene Holloway."

"*Dr.* Eugene Holloway," she says. "He'll have you know, and trust me he will, that he has a PhD."

"He lives in Vegas?"

"Houston now. He got a new job there last year. Why do you want to know where he lives?"

Why? Because Ray could take care of Dianne's ex for her. No problem. Go see him, Dr. Eugene Holloway, and take him for a drive, and show him a peek into the future if he doesn't leave Dianne alone.

But that's Old Ray. New Ray just listens. He pours Dianne more coffee.

"I don't know how to help you," he says.

"Of course not." She sighs. "I have to help myself. But that's harder than it looks, isn't it? Helping yourself."

Ray agrees. "It's hard."

They string the last of the lights and turn them on. Ray's new Christmas tree looks good, looks right. Next year, Dianne tells him, he'll be able to start earlier and put up some lights outside too.

At the door, she gives him a quick hug. It's too quick and unexpected for him to hug back.

"Dianne," he says.

"What?"

Ray hesitates. He's the last person who should be giving advice to someone else. Except maybe in this case. In this case, he might have the right advice.

"You know your ex-husband is going to make a move," he says. "And you know what kind of move."

She sighs. "Yes."

"So, you need to make your own move. From now on you need to make your own move first. Beat him to the punch."

CHAPTER 69

The El Marrakech opens back up for business on Christmas Day. The new lounge is perfect. Ray has seen it come slowly together, but now—the full picture—it's something. Jazzy and Ulan are grinning. They know it's perfect. Light the candles on the table, turn down the houselights . . . Ray wishes Mr. P. were around to see it. Though if Mr. P. was still around, none of this would have ever happened.

Ray isn't expecting a miracle. He bought quarter-page ads in both the *Sun* and the *Review-Journal*, but it takes time for word of mouth to spread. That's what Jazzy and Ulan say.

Three solo customers wander in for Fox's first set. That's it. Two of them order soft drinks, the other one the cheapest beer on tap. Second set: it's just one of the couples from earlier that month, an elderly man with a cowboy hat, his wife with a bun. The man complains to Paz that "the colored boy" on-stage isn't singing any Christmas songs. Paz passes the word to Fox, who sings "Backdoor Santa." The elderly couple gets up halfway through and leaves.

Slick sits on a barstool and listens to the last couple of songs. When Fox wraps up, Ray expects Slick to say *I told you so*, or something smart-alecky that means *I told you so*. Instead Slick just downs his bourbon and walks back to the office.

• • •

Ray reserves a room with a view for Charlie at Caesars Palace. He makes dinner reservations for them at the Golden Steer. But the Golden Steer might be too old-fashioned for Charlie, so Ray changes the reservations to

Kokomo's, in the Mirage. He's heard Slick say it's the hottest restaurant on the Strip.

Night two, Fox puts on another good show, but the lounge is just as dead as night one. Night three isn't much better—a few more customers, one couple under sixty, but that's it. "Give it time," Ulan says. Word of mouth, et cetera. But now Ray isn't just worried that Charlie will be too pretty for him. He's worried Charlie will want to see the El Marrakech after they have dinner at Kokomo's. Once she sees how deserted and depressing the lounge is, her whole opinion of Ray will change. She'll get back on the plane to Reno and he'll never hear from her again.

He could ask Charlie to postpone her trip from January to February. But what if the lounge is still deserted and depressing in February? In March? Probably Ray won't be able to keep the El Marrakech going that long, even if he puts in his own money. What then? He's already put in a good chunk of the money he's saved. What if Ray, his first chance to make decisions of his own, has made all the wrong decisions? What does that say about him? It says, he can hear the ghost of Mr. P. whispering in his ear, that Ray shouldn't be making any damn decisions of his own.

Only three people in the lounge tonight, night four. Fox is smoother than ever, putting his heart and soul into every number. "I'm getting paid no matter how many motherfuckers in the audience," he told Ray.

Ray sits at the bar with Paz and Jazzy. Nobody has anything to say. Even the monkey seems morose and dejected as Fox sings "Merry Christmas, Baby."

A couple enters the lounge. They're young and stylish and dressed up for a night out. They listen to Fox sing. "He's fantastic," the man says after a minute.

"This *place* is fantastic," the woman says.

Paz looks at Ray and Ray looks at Jazzy and Jazzy looks at Paz. The monkey, who usually screeches if anyone gets too close to him, purrs like a cat.

"You guys want a table?" Paz asks the couple.

"Oh, for sure," the woman says.

CHAPTER 70

The young couple returns the next night, with a group of friends. They order cocktails that haven't been ordered at the El Marrakech in a long time. Old Fashioneds, Manhattans, gin fizzes. Paz stays busy all night.

Dianne, Ray's neighbor, shows up for Fox's second set. She brings Ray a wrapped present to celebrate the grand reopening.

"And to say thank you," she says.

"Thank you?"

"For the advice. I needed the kick in the butt, Ray. I've spent too much time feeling sorry for myself."

He's not sure what he said that might be considered a kick in the butt, but appreciates that she stopped by to support the El Marrakech. He unwraps the present. It's a watch.

"You've really done a marvelous job here, Ray," she says, looking around. "I've never seen anything like it. And the singer is perfect."

Ray takes off his old watch and puts on the new watch, which seems like the polite thing to do. He likes the new watch. It's heavy, solid. It fits his wrist just right.

"My ex-husband's favorite watch. Very expensive. I'm supposed to FedEx it to him." Dianne smiles. "I can't seem to find it, though."

The next night a few ladies from Dianne's work, the tourism department, come in. "Dianne insisted we check it out. Upon pain of death." It turns out that one of the ladies from the tourism department also freelances for the *Review-Journal*. Her review is published soon after. The headline says: "An Outta Sight Trip Back to Vegas's Swinging Past."

That brings in their best crowd yet. The lounge isn't completely full on

New Year's Eve, but it's close. Claire the day girl has to work a double and Slick helps out behind the bar. The most encouraging development: pretty good crowds during the first week of January. Ray is cautiously optimistic. Even Slick admits it. "This might actually work, Ray," he says.

Slick talked to LA. He says he thinks LA might—*might*—be willing to let Ray go his own way. They're coming to Vegas in a couple of weeks to sit down with Ray and Slick. Slick will have to talk his ass off. That's what Slick says. He'll have to convince LA that they should be satisfied with a legitimate piece of a legitimate business. Otherwise . . . Slick shakes his head and tightens the knot of his tie. Ray is cautiously optimistic. The one thing he knows about Slick is that Slick can talk his ass off.

Charlie can't wait to meet Ray in person. It will be strange, won't it? Yes, Ray agrees. But maybe just at first, Charlie says. Yes, Ray agrees. He hopes so. He hopes he can talk to Charlie in person like he talks to her on America Online. Alice used to say, when they were kids, that talking to Ray was liking talking to a tree stump. She used to say that a tree stump had more personality. But she said that about Jeremy too. She said that at least Ray knew he was a tree stump.

The second weekend of 1997: this is the real test for the El Marrakech. If the El Marrakech continues to draw a decent crowd this weekend, it should continue to draw a decent crowd. It will have, Slick says, legs. Slick and Ray discuss the numbers. If business drops off ten percent or less this weekend, they're in good shape. Fifteen to twenty percent is a problem. Any more than that . . .

Friday night, business is *up* ten percent. Around ten o'clock, for about half an hour, there's even a line to get in. Ray hasn't worked a door in years. He doesn't mind at all.

Another good review of the El Marrakech's lounge, this one in the *Sun*, comes out Saturday morning. Ray takes it over to show Dianne, with donuts from Freed's. Afterward he lifts some weights, then meets Purdy for lunch. Purdy gave Ray's new health and fitness center a try, but decided to stick with their old gym. He says he likes not having to see his big sweaty black ass reflected in all those mirrors all the time. Ray understands. He asks Purdy to come work at the El Marrakech. Head of security. Purdy whoops. Hell, yes! He'll have to give the Nugget his two weeks, though.

Saturday is the busiest night yet. Claire works another double and Jazzy pitches in by waiting tables. Ray, working the door again, knows he'll have to hire another bartender and a permanent server, soon.

They close down and lock up at two in the morning. Paz laughs at how much money she and Claire and Jazzy made in tips; the cash spread out the full length of the bar top. Ray guesses they beat Friday night's business by . . . another ten percent?

"Where's Slick?" Ray asks Paz. Slick should be in the office, already running numbers, but he's not.

"Who cares?" Paz says. She and Claire and Jazzy are drinking shots of something Paz poured for them. "We're going to Disneyland."

"You are?" Ray says.

"Oh, Ray," Paz says, and all three girls laugh good-naturedly.

Ray checks the men's room, the dressing room, the office again. It's not like Slick to just disappear. Ray sends Claire and Jazzy home. Paz starts cleaning up the bar, so she won't have to do it tomorrow. Ray gathers glasses and wipes down tables.

Something's not right. Again, Ray can't put his finger on it. He checks to make sure the front doors are locked. Yes. But through the glass he sees a car turn into the empty parking lot, its headlights off.

"Get down," he tells Paz.

"What?" Paz says.

Ray reaches over the rail for the Glock he keeps beneath the cash register. The Glock is gone.

"Get down now," Ray says. "On the floor, face down. Stay down."

He can't wait to make sure Paz does it. He kills the houselights and heads straight to the door marked EMPLOYEES ONLY. He knows they won't come through the front doors. They'll come through the employee entrance, at the end of the hallway, or they'll come through the emergency exit next to the stage. Fifty-fifty.

Ray flattens himself next to the hallway door. Claire hasn't snuffed the candles on the tables yet. That's the only light left in the lounge. A good thing or a bad thing? Fifty-fifty.

The employee door bangs open. A guy steps into the lounge—ski mask, pump-action shotgun. He's screaming. "Hands up, fuckers!" Et cetera. Ray doesn't rush. He's calm now. He waits until the guy takes a step past him. The guy doesn't see Ray. Ray, one smooth movement, grabs the shotgun and headbutts the guy. The guy staggers, a shotgun blast rips apart a pendant light fixture, the guy drops to the carpet. Ray flips the shotgun around and shoots him.

And then Ray is moving again. Keep moving. That's the key to a situation like this, when you're outnumbered. Three to one? Four to one? Ray can't see Paz. She must have listened to him. She's down on the floor, safe for the time being.

A second guy comes through the employee door, swinging his shotgun toward the spot where Ray used to be. Ray crouches low and slides through the maze of tables, from pool of shadow to pool of shadow. Footwork, just like in the boxing ring. The second guy edges toward the bar, peeking around the corner. Ray eases up behind the guy. Shoots him.

How many more? One or two. Ray keeps moving. Through the tables, across to the stage, to a spot where he can watch the employee door and the emergency exit. But not both at the same time. That's the problem. If there's a third guy in the hallway, he'll come through the door fast. He won't give Ray a clear shot.

The monkey shrieks. Ray jerks to his right—the emergency exit—and pulls the trigger. The third guy slams against the wall. A photo, a happy couple on New Year's Eve at the Dunes, 1963, jumps off a hook and dangles crooked. Ray is glad they kept the monkey around.

There's one last guy. Ray caught him from the corner of his eye, coming in through the employee door the same time his buddy came through the emergency exit. Smart. Now the last guy is crouched and silent and invisible too. Now it's a fair fight.

Boom! A shotgun blast. Ray peers into the smoke, the flickering shadows. A figure holding a shotgun stands near the bar. Who?

Paz. The last guy never saw her coming.

Ray walks over. Paz is shaking so hard Ray thinks she might break. He gently pries her finger off the trigger of the second guy's shotgun. He gently pries the shotgun out of her hands. She grabs his forearm and digs her nails in. But she can't stop shaking.

It's all over in . . . what? A minute, sixty seconds. Ray's ears are ringing but he can almost still hear the last notes of Fox's last song. "Another Saturday Night."

"Close your eyes," Ray tells Paz. "Take a deep breath."

CHAPTER 71

They wait fifteen minutes, Ray listening for sirens. Nothing. Ray doesn't think the police will be a problem, even if they show up. Attempted robbery, self-defense. Ray's record is clean. He'd rather not deal with it, though. The police, at best, will be a hassle. They'll ask a lot of questions. And if what happened at the El Marrakech tonight gets out, that's bad for business.

He calls for a cab to take Paz home. "You'll be all right?" he says.

She's still shaking, but not as much. She's tough as nails. "Yeah."

"You have something at home?"

"Valium. Yeah." Then: "I better get a fucking raise."

After she's gone, Ray calls Purdy to help him. The dead guys parked in back, an Oldsmobile with California plates. Ray finds the keys on the first guy and pulls the Olds up close to the back entrance. He and Purdy load the bodies—one in the trunk, two in the back, one in the passenger seat strapped in place with the seat belt. Nobody sees Ray and Purdy. The back lot is too dark. And who's going to be gazing down at the back parking lot of the El Marrakech at three thirty in the morning from their suite on the fortieth floor of a luxury hotel?

Ray drives the Olds and Purdy follows in Ray's truck. Lake Mead. Ray lines the Olds up on the unofficial ramp he knows about. Don't forget to roll down the car windows. Ray and Purdy finish sinking the Olds and the bodies and all the guns just as the sky to the east starts to glow. They drive back to Vegas in Ray's truck.

The El Marrakech is dark Sunday and Monday, so that'll give Ray two full days to get it back in shape, clean up. Lucky for him, there are a couple of extra rolls of fresh carpet in the storage room. First, though, Ray has to run an errand. Purdy says he'll get started on the mess.

"I appreciate it," Ray says. "Everything."

"Shit. It's my job. Head of security."

Ray stops by his house and picks up his Ruger. He drives out to Slick's place, a glass and concrete split-level out in the middle of the desert. Slick's place used to belong to a famous Vegas headliner, a magician, and before that in the sixties to Big Ed Zingel. Big Ed, rumor has it, got popped right in his own living room. Slick tells that story to every girl he brings home.

Ray parks half a mile from Slick's property and hikes the rest of the way, approaching the house from the rear. If Slick is already awake, eight o'clock in the morning, Ray will know for sure what right now he only suspects. Slick never gets up before noon.

Slick is wide awake in the kitchen, sitting next to his phone on the table, a glass of ice and bourbon in his hand. Ray watches him through the window for a minute, then tests the back door. Locked. Ray kicks it open. Slick jerks around. A look flashes across his face. Astonished.

"They're not going to call," Ray says.

"Listen to me, Ray. Please." Slick isn't wearing a suit, which makes him look naked. He's wearing a T-shirt, drawstring sweatpants, fuzzy slippers. "I can explain."

"That's all right." Ray doesn't need him to explain. He's had time to figure it out for himself. Slick cut a deal with LA. They send hitters to pop Ray, Slick takes over, back to business as usual.

Slick lifts the glass in his hand. "Can I finish my drink?"

"They were going to kill Paz too."

"No! Ray, fuck no! Only you. I swear to God."

And what if Ray hadn't sent Claire and Jazzy home? He doesn't know if Slick is telling the truth or not. The hitters from LA wore ski masks. They didn't want anyone seeing their faces. Maybe Slick is telling the truth, that only Ray was supposed to be popped.

"You put me in a difficult position, Ray," Slick says. "What was I supposed to do? I was supposed to tell LA to go fuck themselves? Then it's you and me both. We're both dead."

"I'm not dead," Ray says.

"Right. You're right. So now we talk. Now we discuss the situation, all our cards on the table. You can shoot me. That's why you're here. And no hard feelings if you do. You have every right. But let's consider, just for the hell of it, what happens if you don't shoot me."

Ray lets him talk. Why? Ray should have pulled the trigger already, before Slick ever opened his mouth. But Ray doesn't *want* to pull the trigger. That's why he lets Slick talk. The hitters at the El Marrakech—that was one thing, that was Ray reacting and not thinking, Ray trying to stay alive and keep Paz alive. This is different. If Ray pulls the trigger now, he's the old Ray again. The last month and a half becomes . . . nothing. A daydream. The old Ray is the only Ray.

"You need me, Ray," Slick is saying. "I'm just being honest. If you're going to take the El Marrakech legit, you need someone who knows numbers inside and out. A few weeks ago, I thought you were crazy. I admit. I never thought . . . you know what I'm saying. But this might work after all. But you need me for the numbers, the money. Permits, taxes. Ray, are you gonna handle all that? And what about LA? That's still . . . I don't know what we're going to do about that. But I'm your best chance to make peace with them. To figure it out."

The ghost of Mr. P. whispers in Ray's ear, exasperated. "You fucking moron. Shoot that rat between his damn eyes."

"Ray, think about it. You kill me, what do you gain? How do you profit? If you *don't* kill me, think about that. I'm indebted to you for the rest of my life. I'm your blood brother."

The clock on the counter *tick-tick-ticks*. Slick still hasn't finished his drink. Most of the ice has melted. He's been taking very small sips. He's breathing slowly and carefully, waiting. Looking Ray right in the eye.

Ray doesn't pull the trigger. He lowers the gun. How does all this end? Ray can't say for sure. Is the old Ray the only Ray? Maybe, but Ray wants to give his new life a fighting chance.

"Thank you for trusting me, Ray," Slick says. "You won't regret it."

CHAPTER 72

Halfway back to his truck, Ray stops. Clouds have rolled in and tiny snowflakes feather down. It doesn't snow that often in Las Vegas. Once in a while. Piggy told him once, Ray remembers, that in ancient times the Greeks took changes in the weather very seriously. A thunderclap was a sign from the gods. That sort of thing. Ray wishes you could look at the sky and it would tell you the right thing to do.

Slick has poured himself a fresh drink when Ray walks back in. He sees Ray and his hand goes to his throat, where the knot of his tie would be if he was wearing a tie. Ray pulls the trigger. This time, he tells himself, is the last time.

CHAPTER 73

Look at you," Paz says.

Ray is wearing a new suit, new tie, new shoes. He bought the suit at Mastroianni Fashions, which specializes in big and tall. Old man Mastroianni himself put the pins in Ray, to show the tailor where to snip and stitch.

Paz sits at the rail with him. She's not behind the bar because she's the general manager now. Ray asked her if she was any good with numbers. "I can add them together," she said. "I can hire an accountant."

The new girl, Candy, is behind the bar. She's also a pretty good singer. Ray is thinking about staying open on Sunday nights, letting Candy do a couple of sets.

"Call Kokomo's if you need me," Ray tells Paz.

"I won't need you."

"Don't make a big deal of it." His shoes are shined. He's got plenty of cash. What else? He's nervous he'll forget something small but important. "When we come back here after dinner."

"Ray."

"What?"

"Don't get your hopes too high. You've never even met this girl. Who knows, you know?"

"I'm good," he says. He's talking to Paz. He's talking to himself. *I'm good.* Except he's not. His hopes *are* too high. Ray knows it. He's never felt about a girl the way he feels about Charlie. And there's a chance—there is—she's never felt the way she feels about him.

Jazzy sits down. "You tell him about the avocados?" she says.

Paz shakes her head. "Not yet."

"A crate of avocados was delivered this morning," Jazzy tells Ray.

"Avocados," Ray says.

"From Mexico. Did you order them? Who are they from?"

Ray didn't order a crate of avocados from Mexico. He can guess who they're from. But what do the avocados mean? Ray forgot all about the Mexicans. He was supposed to help find their guy for them, if their guy isn't buried deep beneath the rubble of the Sands.

The avocados could mean anything. A warning. A threat. A thank-you for dinner when the Mexicans were in Vegas. Ray doesn't know. Slick might, but he's not around anymore to ask.

Candy, the new girl, makes her way down the rail. "I forgot to ask," she says, "what's his name?"

"Who?" Paz says. Ray wonders the same thing.

"The monkey. What's his name?"

Paz turns to Ray. "My first act of business."

He shrugs. She's right. The monkey should have a name.

"Handsome Johnny," Paz says. "You remember, Ray? The stories Mr. P. used to tell?"

Ray remembers. He shrugs again. Handsome Johnny is fine with him.

He drives down to the Mirage twenty minutes early, so he has plenty of time to park in the garage and make his way through the sprawling casino. Seven o'clock on the dot, he's standing at the volcano. A crowd has gathered. The volcano begins to rumble and seethe.

One woman is watching Ray, not the volcano. She's lanky, a head taller than anyone around her. She smiles at Ray. She wears a long coat and earmuffs. She looks just like Neve Campbell.

PART VI

Alice
2006

CHAPTER 74

The scales fell from her eyes. The blind could see.

That's how Alice came to regard what happened to her in 1978. She watched her father drag the suitcase full of money from the trunk of the Buick. She watched her mother squeeze the trigger of the gun. She watched the two of them embrace as the sleet needled down around them.

At the time, age eleven, Alice wasn't familiar with the story of Saul on the road to Damascus. But she knew she'd been struck by lightning. She would never be the same again. A sudden, shattering truth had set her free.

The family legend, the family religion, it was all bullshit. The Mercurios weren't dashing outlaws or rakish pirates. They didn't live lives of daring adventure and bold defiance. Alice's mother and father were crooks, plain and simple—*petty* crooks, grasping and fumbling, selfish and duplicitous, full of half-baked schemes and cheap dodges, the sort of people who pedaled coke and fudged numbers, who double-crossed each other at the drop of a hat, who almost *killed* each other but then decided on a whim to forgive and forget.

And they were raising their children, raising Alice, to be just like them.

Oh, my god. The engine of her father's idling Camaro chugged. Piggy squirmed in Alice's arms. Alice burst into tears. How could she have been so stupid? She was too smart to be this stupid. It was like still believing in the Easter Bunny. No, this, Alice believing in her parents all these years, was far worse, much more humiliating.

As a mournful whistle grew louder and louder (her parents were the sort of people who left their cars on train tracks, *who left their kids in cars on train tracks!*), Alice made a vow to herself. She would *not* follow in the family footsteps. She would not be *anything* like her parents, her brothers, her sister. No. No way. Never. Cross her heart and hope to die.

Alice's dad jumped back in the Camaro and gunned it off the train tracks with about two seconds to spare. He grinned. "That was a close one!" he said. "Now let's get some ice cream to celebrate."

To celebrate? To celebrate *what*? And *ice cream*? Are you kidding? It was thirty degrees outside and sleeting. Alice couldn't believe she'd been so stupid. She'd actually been proud to be a Mercurio.

"Take me home."

"What?" her dad said. "What's the matter with you, sourpuss?"

From that day on, Alice refused to participate in whatever scheme her dad or mom cooked up. The bogus title company after Club Mercurio went bust? Nope. A door-to-door magazine subscription scam? No way. Even sneaking into movie theaters through the back exit, a family tradition? Never again.

Her dad was confused at first, then exasperated, then deeply wounded by Alice's betrayal. "Deeply wounded." So he claimed. Alice would never again believe a word that came out of his mouth. For a couple of years, until she started high school, he kept trying to lure her back into the fold. But he was no match for Alice's iron will, not even close.

Alice's mom didn't really care what Alice did or didn't do. Alice's mom had Jeremy, and in a pinch Tallulah. She'd never been that interested in Alice. Now, even less.

Alice turned the sharp, whirring blades of her mind toward academics. She channeled her talents for plotting and planning, for research and assessment, into high school debate and advanced calculus. Her ambition remained ferocious; she worked her ass off; teachers quailed when she raised her hand.

"You're no fun anymore," Jeremy groused when Alice wouldn't help him cheat his way to a B in Oklahoma History or refused to figure out a way to get them good-quality fake IDs. Alice ignored him in the halls of Northeast High School. She told her nerd friends in chess club that she and Jeremy weren't related.

She and Tallulah grew apart too. Tallulah was wild and Alice didn't drink or smoke, didn't skip a single homeroom period. She dressed in baggy sweaters and wide-wale cords to forestall any boys foolish enough to approach her. No makeup, hair in a bun smooth as a bullet. Every night Alice was in bed by ten o'clock, hours before Tallulah usually came dragging back to their bedroom, hair smelling like cigarettes and airplane glue.

"Let's go to Frontier America and hang out," Tallulah would say. Or "Let's go see a band at the Land Run."

"I have to study," Alice would say.

"I'll study with you, then."

But poor Tallulah, try as she might, couldn't sit still for fifteen minutes. If that.

"I'm sorry, Al," she'd say, giving Alice a hug before she flew off. "Love you!"

"Be safe, Lulu."

On the SAT, Alice scored a 1,590, only ten points shy of perfect. With that, a stellar grade point average, two years as editor in chief of the school newspaper, and a full slate of strategically chosen community service activities, she had her pick of colleges. She chose Dartmouth. It offered her a full scholarship and, most importantly, was the Ivy League school most geographically distant from Oklahoma City.

In New Hampshire she flourished among fellow students who were almost—*almost*—as smart, driven, and uninterested in a social life as Alice was. Holidays and summer breaks she stayed in Hanover—ha, right, like she was ever going back to Oklahoma City, to the Mercurios, to all *that*.

God, what a relief it was, a joy—to be a productive member of society, a net benefit to the world, a clean and shining part of the solution and not the grubby problem itself. Alice considered legally changing her last name but decided that would be a tacit sign of defeat. Screw that. She planned to give the Mercurio name new meaning.

Columbia Law. Editor in chief of the *Law Review*. Federal circuit court clerkship. Fast-tracked partner at a white-shoe Manhattan firm.

And now here she is, New York City, May of 2006, on her way to work.

Alice knifes a straight line through the gridlocked sidewalks and heaving masses, the finance bros and dumbstruck tourists. At every red light she stops, waits, even as all around her pedestrians spill into the empty intersection. Why? Because every game has rules. *Life* has rules. What's the point of playing if you're going to ignore the rules? Alice can't deal with people who feel entitled to do whatever they want, whenever they want.

CHAPTER 75

A paralegal brings Alice the first box of documents. Alice knows little about her new case, which is how she prefers it. Fresh eyes, blank slate. This is a dispute about a parcel of property just across the Harlem River, a decommissioned train repair yard. Who's involved? A better question: who isn't? The state of New York, the city of New York, the Port Authority, the EPA, various developers, various groups of concerned citizens. Alice sees a satisfying few months ahead of her—a steep but steady climb, signposted by clear precedent, by statute and code and law.

She eats lunch at her desk, highlighter in one hand and sandwich in the other. Bill calls, as he does every day, precisely at two. He's in an office almost identical to this one, eleven blocks away, eating lunch at his desk too. They chat for a minute. "How's the new case?" "Fine. Made any progress with yours?" Bill suggests the trattoria on the Upper West Side for dinner, their traditional Monday spot. Alice concurs.

"Love you," he says, and she hears the squeak of his highlighter.

The two of them, Alice and Bill, are a good fit. Alice isn't quite ready to discuss marriage yet—they've been dating for two years—but she'll turn forty next month, the point at which an unmarried, childless lawyer, at least one with ambition, becomes suspect in certain circles. Alice is confident that Bill has made the same calculations.

"Love you too," she says, flipping through a survey of land use planning and regulations.

The afternoon passes peacefully, a low pleasant hum, a single unwavering chord. A little before five, Alice's assistant buzzes. Patricia would like to see her.

Alice hops to. Patricia is one of the firm's senior partners, Alice's boss, her supportive but (and) demanding mentor. One day Patricia will be on the US Supreme Court and Alice, if all goes according to plan, will be Patricia.

"Come in," Patricia says.

Alice takes a seat. The office is as strategically composed as a Rembrandt— law books and vintage typewriters, fresh flowers and Jets memorabilia, a photo of Patricia with her husband and kids, a photo of Patricia with the Clintons.

"Have you started on the Devlin Depot case?" Patricia says. She's a Rembrandt herself, the light and shadow in any given room always arranging itself to best suit her.

"This morning," Alice says.

"Stop."

"Stop?"

Patricia gets up, crosses the room. She shuts the door and locks it. "This stays between us," she says.

Alice wonders. Is Patricia making the jump to circuit court? But the timing doesn't make sense. And circuit court would be good news. Why would Patricia, whose usual demeanor is one of smooth, serene rumination, seem so . . . grim?

Patricia returns to her desk and stares silently, grimly, at the photo of Bill and Hillary. "I'm being blackmailed," she says.

"What?" Alice says, startled.

Patricia gathers herself and presents the facts of the case the way she always does, in concise, well-ordered bullet points.

- It's January of 1973, New Orleans, Patricia a freshman at Tulane University.
- Her mother and father divorce unexpectedly.
- Patricia is shocked, unmoored.
- A semester of abandon follows. Patricia does a lot of drugs. She has a lot of risky and random sex.

- Eventually the world rights itself. Patricia returns to herself.
- What happened in the spring of 1973 fades away. It disappears.
- Until now.

Alice has an almost impossible time imagining it. Patricia—sleek torpedo of purpose and propriety, her temperature never dipping or rising more than a degree or two—doing drugs and having random sex? Patricia's reputation is spotless, her integrity unquestioned. It was her character, as much as her intellect, that drew Alice to the firm in the first place. Patricia is the last person on earth, after Alice, who would put herself in a position to be blackmailed.

Patricia slides an opened envelope across the desk. *Patricia Campbell, 80 Mallard Drive, Greenwich, CT.* Her home address. There's no return address, just the postmark: Phoenix, Arizona, three days ago.

"Read," Patricia says.

Alice removes a single sheet of paper from the envelope. The handwriting is loopy and exuberant, like something you'd find in a note passed between seventh graders.

Greetings from Nowhere!

Hi there Dish. It's been too long!
We had some fun times didn't we Dish?
Let's catch up soon and break out those old photos!
You know the ones tee hee!

Your old pal Moon

Dish? And then it clicks: Patricia is Trisha. Trisha is Trish. Trish the Dish. That anyone, anywhere once called Patricia Campbell, *the* Patricia Campbell, *Trish the Dish* shocks Alice almost more than the sex and drugs.

"Don't judge me, Alice."

Alice can't help it. She feels awful about Patricia's predicament, but this is a mess of Patricia's own making. No one forced her to do what she did back in 1973. She knew, or had to know, she was making bad choices. All she had to do was stick to the path! Life isn't that complicated. Follow the rules!

Alice shifts back into lawyer mode and scans the letter again, this time with a neutral and objective eye. "How can you be sure it's blackmail? There's nothing explicit here."

"I'm sure. His full name is Seaver Moon. I know him. I haven't seen or talked to him in thirty years, but I know him."

"So the photos he mentions . . ."

Patricia nods—well, more of a quick, pained twitch than a nod. "Polaroids. Three of them. Compromising. Moon swore he burned them the next day. The pictures."

Alice doesn't bother asking how bad the photos are. It's obvious Patricia isn't talking about a few innocent nudie shots. *What in the world were you thinking?* That's the answer Alice really wants from Patricia.

"Have you gone to the police yet?" Alice took only a couple of criminal law courses back at Columbia. If she recalls correctly, extortion—how blackmail is codified in the New York penal code—is automatically a Class E felony.

"I can't," Patricia says.

"What do you mean?"

"I can't go to the police, Alice. This will leak. Rumors about the photos will leak. It'll be on Page Six before I even hang up the phone. People won't even need to actually *see* the photos. When this comes out, my career will be over."

Yes, potentially true, but . . . Patricia *has* to go to the police. What other option does she have? Paying off the blackmailer, engaging with him in any way, is a terrible idea. Patricia would be putting herself in an even more vulnerable, and potentially dangerous, position.

Stick to the path! It's there for a reason!

"Patricia . . ."

"I've already decided. I'm going to pay Moon and get those photos back. And I need you to take care of this for me."

Alice, whose mind never goes blank, finds herself floating in space. Is she upside down? Right-side up? She has no idea.

"What?" she says. "*Me?*"

"Talk to Moon," Patricia says. "Find out how much he wants. I'm a public figure. This has to be done completely off the books."

Patricia can't be serious. There are sleazy lawyers who specialize in things like this, professional fixers who get paid a lot of money to navigate the gray areas between legal and illegal. Alice, of course, goes nowhere *near* gray or sleazy. How can Patricia think she'd even consider it?

"You're the smartest, most capable person I know," Patricia says. "And the most principled. I know you won't betray me."

"Patricia, I can't even . . ."

A tear squeezes free from the corner of Patricia's eye. "You're the only person I can trust, Alice."

"No!" Alice says when she can finally form a clear thought. "I can't do it, Patricia. No, absolutely not. I'm sorry. No, no, no."

After a moment, Patricia sighs and wipes the tear from her cheek. Instantly she's composed again, her expression pleasant and impregnable.

"Don't be naïve, Alice," she says, "I'm not asking."

CHAPTER 76

Alice orders her usual, the cacio e pepe. Bill orders his usual, the spaghetti with clams. A walk-in at the maître d' stand complains loudly about the forty-five-minute wait for a table.

"Make a reservation, for god's sake," Bill says under his breath.

"Life isn't that hard," Alice agrees. "Just follow the instructions."

The waiter brings two glasses of their usual Pinot Grigio. The first familiar sip, the familiar rhythm of their Monday-evening routine, steadies Alice—a bit, at least. She's still reeling from her conversation with Patricia.

"You need to have my best interests at heart," Patricia said. "My best interests are *your* best interests."

Alice kicked herself for not connecting the dots sooner. Patricia doesn't trust Alice because—or not just because—Alice is smart, capable, and principled. She trusts her because Alice is ambitious, and Patricia is her most powerful advocate and ally. Patricia, if she's so inclined, can strike a match—a conversation or two with the right people, an aside at a cocktail party—and it's *Alice's* career that goes up in flames. *Alice* will have to start all over again, from ashes.

Patricia, satisfied that Alice grasped the big picture, nodded. "It's a simple errand, Alice. One conversation, a wire transfer, and then it's done. And you're on the side of the angels here, don't forget. I was single. All parties were consenting adults. No laws were broken. But guess what? I'm a woman."

Alice can't dispute that. A man in Patricia's position would laugh off a couple of X-rated Polaroids. And he'd have no idea in the first place what it cost Patricia, or Alice, to get where they are. Alice thought of all the men over the years who'd ignored her, who'd undermined her, who'd held her to impossible standards because she didn't have a cock, who'd handed a choice assignment or case to the dumbshit son of a frat buddy.

Still, though, Alice was furious that Patricia had put her in this position. She stood.

"No," she said.

Patricia smiled. "Call me later. When you've had a chance to think about it."

The waiter asks Alice if she'd like another glass of wine. She's surprised to discover her first glass is empty. She hesitates, then shakes her head. "No, thank you."

"You seem distracted," Bill says.

"Do I?" Alice says.

"Objection."

"The witness is evasive?"

"Exactly. Work?"

"Yes," Alice says. It's not a lie.

Here's the diabolical rub: Patricia might be bluffing, might not really turn against Alice, but Alice's career still remains at grave risk. If the Polaroids come out, Alice becomes collateral damage. She works so closely with Patricia, she'll be smeared by association.

Can Alice afford to put her fate in the hands of some professional fixer, most likely a man, who through greed or incompetence might screw Patricia over? Who through greed or incompetence might screw over Alice as well?

Alice excuses herself from the table. After she uses the ladies' room, she steps outside the restaurant and calls Patricia. "How would I find him?" she says.

"Don't you remember the letter? Moon's not trying to hide."

The letter Moon sent Patricia was postmarked Phoenix. *Greetings from Nowhere.* "Nowhere, Arizona?" Alice says. "It's a real place?"

"Two hours west of civilization. You fly out day after tomorrow. My assistant made all the arrangements. As far as she knows, you're meeting a potential client to discuss trust obligations and water rights. As far as *anyone* knows."

Already Alice feels tainted by her involvement in this sleazy affair, and she hasn't even *done* anything yet. She feels . . . *gross*. Like she's stepped into a packed subway car without air-conditioning, the heat and the sweat-stink settling onto her.

Alice is so furious at Patricia, so furious at the blackmailer, so furious at everybody and everything that has brought her to this moment in her life.

"I owe you one, Alice," Patricia says. "A big one. I hope you know that."

When Alice returns to the table, their entrees have arrived, and Bill is frowning at his spaghetti.

"Everything okay?" Alice says.

"It's good," Bill says, "but different. More garlicky."

"A different cook tonight?"

He nods, frowns again.

Alice orders another glass of wine. "I have to fly to Phoenix Wednesday," she tells Bill. "On business. For a couple of days."

Bill, still preoccupied with his spaghetti, doesn't pursue the subject. Alice is relieved, but she knows half-truths aren't any better than lies.

Gross.

CHAPTER 77

Patricia can't involve the firm's private investigator, obviously, so Alice has to do her own digging, on her own personal laptop.

Seaver James Moon. Alice doesn't find much about him. His most recent appearance in a local, state, or federal database is from seven years ago, an Oregon driver's license issued in 1999. Date of birth: June 12, 1952, which would make him a few years older than Patricia, fifty-three years old now. Hair: black. Eyes: blue. Height: five feet eleven. Weight: 170 pounds. There's no photo of the license, just the information, so Alice can't tell what Moon really looks like. Or looked like, back in '99.

What else? Moon's criminal record. Arrested in 1972 for misdemeanor possession, charges dismissed (Louisiana). Arrested in 1974 for misdemeanor theft, a $250 fine and time served (Louisiana). Arrested in 1976 for felony possession with intent to distribute, sentenced to two years at Brushy Mountain State Penitentiary (Tennessee). After that, Moon either cleaned up his act—unlikely, given the current blackmail attempt—or got better at hiding his crimes.

Seaver Moon isn't on Facebook. A Google search returns zero hits for him.

Google and JSTOR searches return only a single hit for "Nowhere, Arizona." According to a short feature in the *Los Angeles Times*, six years old, Nowhere is five hundred unincorporated acres on the site of an old army base abandoned in the 1950s. The reporter calls the place a "colorful mélange of artists, retirees, hippies, assorted eccentrics, and hardcore off-the-gridders." No photos, at least online.

At the airport, Alice's head pounds. A mental picture of Seaver Moon forms. A greasy loser, a slippery lowlife, criminal to the bone. And here's

Alice, sneaking around too, forced to meet Moon on his terms, down in the muck.

She observes the mad scramble around her, the wild-eyed passengers with overstuffed roller bags sprinting toward their gates. Alice doesn't understand. *Arrive two hours before your domestic flight.* Every idiot knows that rule. It's not some closely guarded secret.

She swallows a couple of Tylenol and reframes. It's *good* that Seaver Moon is a greasy loser, et cetera. He won't draw this out. He'll take the money and run. Alice's headache begins to ease. Remember what Patricia said: this is a simple errand, point A to point B. Find out how much money Moon wants, pay him, destroy the three Polaroids. In a couple of days Alice will be back home, scrubbing herself clean in a hot shower, forgetting she was ever a part of something like this.

Her flight lands just after three o'clock in Phoenix. She leaves her watch set to Eastern Daylight Time—symbolic act of resistance—and picks up her car from Hertz.

Her hotel is in Scottsdale, the Canyon Oasis, a five-star resort, the lobby hushed and chilly. The receptionist runs through the various spa packages. Hydration wraps, ginger scrubs, thermal mud treatments. Alice has been here before, for various legal conferences over the years. Not *here* here, but nearly identical resorts in San Diego, Tampa, Savannah, Austin. The only difference, Alice notes, is the artwork on the walls: desert sunsets here in Scottsdale, regal horses with manes flowing. She appreciates places like this, the order and familiarity, everything exactly where it should be.

Alice eats dinner in the bar. She doesn't call Patricia. They're keeping contact, while Alice is in Arizona, to an absolute minimum.

The bartender, like the receptionist, is in her early twenties, unreasonably fit and healthy and wholesome. Alice asks if she's ever heard of Nowhere, Arizona.

The bartender cocks her head. "I don't think so?" she says.

It drives Alice a little crazy that she's so unprepared for her meeting with Seaver Moon. She's never been this unprepared in her life—not for a test, an interview, a debate, a deposition, not for *anything*.

But that's fine, she reminds herself. Get in, get out. Find out how much money Moon wants, pay him, destroy the three Polaroids. Patricia has authorized a hundred thousand dollars, the amount she can swing without having to explain anything to her husband. Alice thinks Moon will jump at half that much.

Her phone buzzes. Her brother Piggy. Alice answers. Piggy will just keep hounding her if she doesn't. She might as well get this over with.

"Piggy, I'm busy," she says.

"You always say that."

"It's always true."

"How's everything? How are you?"

What's that old joke? *The longest week of my life was the night I spent in Cleveland.* Well, the longest hour of Alice's life is the five minutes she spends talking to Piggy every few weeks.

"I'm fine," she says. "How are you?"

"I know that tactic, Alice. You're trying to change the subject."

"Never. I'm just eager to hear about . . . Velvet?"

"Her name is Vivian. My daughter's not a stripper, Alice."

"Fingers crossed."

"She's wonderful, thank you for asking. We had her third birthday party last week. Guess what the theme was?"

This is why Alice changes the subject—because the tactic, with Piggy, works. He relates Vivian's latest exploits and details of a contemporary fiction course he's teaching on Dark Side of the American Dream. Alice wonders how his students manage to stay awake.

"Your turn now," Piggy says. "You have only delayed the inevitable."

"I'm fine. Working." She knows she'll have to throw him a bone. "I'm in Arizona for a couple of days. Scottsdale."

"Are you kidding?"

Alice doesn't like the sound of that. "Why?" she asks warily.

"Jeremy's in Scottsdale! He lives there now!"

Oh, god. It's even worse than Alice feared. Piggy might be boring, but Jeremy is—as he was when they were kids, as he will ever be—insufferable. The last time Alice saw him, Jeremy bragged about his various business enterprises (all of them wildly successful) while at the very same time trying to squeeze her for money ("Trust me, Alice, this is an investment of a lifetime. I'm doing *you* a favor").

"This is fantastic!" Piggy says. "You and Jeremy can get together, have dinner."

"Nope," Alice says.

"Or coffee at least," Piggy says. "Wait. We can all meet in Scottsdale this weekend! The flight's only a couple of hours, nonstop from Oklahoma City. I can talk Mom and Dad into—"

"Nope."

"And Tallulah's a nonstop flight too."

"I have to go. Bye, Piggy."

"Okay, okay. I give up. How's Scottsdale? Where are you staying?"

Alice hangs up—does Piggy really think she'll fall for that?—and motions for the check.

CHAPTER 78

Alice wakes before dawn. She orders coffee and toast from room service, then puts on her sneakers and gets in some exercise. With the first light of day bleeding into the sky, she walks quick laps around the resort, past the fire pits and the cactus garden and the multiple pools. The grounds are huge and sprawling, but there's no risk of getting lost. The stone paths always loop around to the beginning.

When she gets back to her room, she showers and dresses. She opens her laptop. Piggy has emailed photos of his three-year-old, as threatened. Alice scrolls. She's caught off guard by how much the little girl, Vivian, resembles Piggy at that age. A memory sneaks up on Alice: the clean, powdery smell of Piggy's head as she holds him on her hip; the slap of bare feet on scorching summer asphalt. Who had they been running away from? Why? Alice can't remember. They did a lot of running away when they were kids. Tallulah is in the lead, Alice and Piggy next, the older boys behind—wild laughter ringing out.

Alice wishes she knew more about Moon. Will he, in fact, settle for a hundred thousand dollars? Is he in this just for the money, or does he get off on having power over a powerful woman? Probably he made photocopies of the three Polaroids, but neither Patricia nor Alice are too concerned about that. The originals—Patricia remembers them vividly—are poorly lit and slightly blurry. A reproduction would just degrade the quality even more. And photocopies in general can be easily faked and manipulated. Moon has to know that photocopies are worthless.

Blazer, blouse, skirt, heels. Alice regards herself in the mirror and considers the affect. Her usual business attire might signal to Moon that she's serious, formidable, and not to be fucked with. Or looking like this, like the expensive Manhattan lawyer she is, might encourage Moon to squeeze Patricia for even more money. What's the right approach to take?

She decides it's a long drive to Nowhere and she might as well be as comfortable as possible. Alice changes out of her Ralph Lauren and leaves her gold watch in the safe. She puts on yesterday's travel clothes: blouse, stretchy slacks, flats. She pops off the rubber band and liberates her ponytail.

The first hour of the drive is interstate, smooth and swift and dull, through a bleached, featureless desert landscape. Finally, a cluster of mountains appears on the horizon and Alice exits onto a two-lane state highway. The blacktop frays like a string, gradually cracking and buckling, one mile at a time. After about twenty minutes of that, she turns onto an even smaller road. She begins to climb.

Her rental, an anonymous American midsize sedan, strains, huffing and puffing. Every time the wind gusts, Alice feels like she's being lifted up, plucked off the earth like a fleck of dandruff off a shoulder.

The road narrows the higher it goes. Hairpin turns and blind corners, sagging guardrails. Alice grips the wheel and tries not to blink. For a short stretch the road is just a single lane, with room for only one car and barely that. Alice creeps around a bend. Her right front tire is only a foot or so from the crumbling edge of the cliff.

After that, thank god, the road levels off, widens. Alice spots a handful of buildings up ahead. That can't be Nowhere, not yet. She passes a sign: WELCOME TO RINGO, ARIZONA!

She pulls to a stop and checks her map. There it is: *Ringo*, in tiny print. Nowhere isn't even on the map, but Alice has marked the general vicinity with a felt-tip *X*. According to the *LA Times* article, Nowhere exists somewhere in the desert valley between here and, twenty miles farther north, another state highway.

Alice hasn't encountered another car since she exited the interstate. In Ringo, as she rolls down the one main street, she sees no signs of life whatsoever. It's a ghost town, she quickly gathers, the original frontier Victorians half-collapsed and the more modern additions—a gas station, a diner—boarded up. An old, rust-blistered car abandoned half on and half off the cracked sidewalk. It's a Buick Regal from the 1970s, a gas-guzzling tank like the one Alice's mom used to drive way back when.

The place gives Alice the creeps. She's relieved when she's left Ringo behind and is speeding across a wide, flat plateau. This is high desert, and the scenery is an improvement—spring wildflowers everywhere and rose-colored boulders, some the size of houses, strewn across the sand. Alice guesses she must be getting close to Nowhere when graffiti art begins to blanket the boulders. Peace signs and lizards with lolling tongues, psychedelic sunsets and hearts bursting apart like fireworks.

Up ahead, two old yellow school buses frame the road. Painted in big, sloppy letters on the left bus: *NO*. Painted on the right bus: *WHERE*. The missing hyphen irritates Alice. Really? Would a hyphen take that much more thought or effort?

Here we go, she thinks. She steels herself. Get in, get out, get this over with.

She parks and climbs out of her car. Nowhere sprawls before her. The place is sheer chaos. Campers, trailers, mobile homes, pickup trucks and vans, tents and more tents, lean-tos and yurts, cargo containers and plywood shacks, all of it just . . . heaved up and spewed out onto a series of big concrete slabs. There's no hint of an organizing principle, no trace of a right angle or straight line. Even the slabs, which must have been rectangles once, foundations for buildings when this was the old army base, have cracked apart over the years into jagged, wonky shapes.

Smoke rises from charcoal grills and various campfires. Generators cough and chug. The graffiti "art" climbs like ivy, spreading and suffocating everything.

Alice doesn't understand, genuinely, how someone could live like this. She doesn't understand why someone would *want* to.

CHAPTER 79

Alice descends. How, in this chaos, will she be able to locate Moon? The search might take hours, days. She approaches a couple on the edge of the encampment, a man and a woman in their sixties. They could be twins: gray ponytails, wraparound sunglasses, sleeveless Black Sabbath T-shirts. They're sitting in lawn chairs outside a structure (Alice uses the term loosely) assembled from packing pallets, sheet metal, old tires filled with sand, and a camper shell.

"Welcome to our world!" the woman says. She introduces herself as Cheetah. Her "fella" is Dale. Without prompting, Cheetah explains that she and Dale have been together fourteen years but never married, the institution of marriage being, of course, an egregious example of oppressive—and illegal!—government overreach. Cheetah, by the way, was originally in love with Dale's better-looking brother, Tim, but Tim's wandering eye and the motorcycle accident put an end to all that. Dale is a diamond in the rough, though.

"A diamond in the rough!" Cheetah repeats for emphasis. Dale nods and cackles.

"Hi," Alice says, and then before she can manage a second word, Cheetah is off to the races again.

"Let me guess, you heard about Nowhere and you thought, *well, well, well, now that's a place I am curious to experience.* Best decision of your life. Because you do, you need to *experience* a place like this. That's what's wrong with the world today. It's delivered secondhand to your doorstep. But here, oh my goodness, every day is one hundred percent *authentic.* One hundred and eighty proof!"

Dale cackles. "One hundred and eighty proof!"

"You know how many people live here? I bet you can't even guess. More than two hundred folks. All colors, all creeds. Not counting the dogs and the goats and that damn donkey. Two hundred folks! That's not some fad, that's a revolution! We've got gardens. We've got a reservoir for the rain, for the gardens and washing and so forth. You know how much money the government spends killing folks in Iraq and Afghanistan? Don't get me started on 9/11, honey, who's behind all that. We truck in the drinking water. Other than that, though, one hundred percent self-sufficient."

Alice isn't sure the need to truck in drinking water meets any definition of self-sufficiency, but she's not about to quibble with Cheetah, and eager to not get her started on 9/11. "That's wonderful."

"Solar. We got some of that. Everyone here's an individual, like America's supposed to be, but we're neighbors too. Seaver! Make sure you talk to him."

Alice perks up. First spin of the wheel and she hits the jackpot. "Seaver?"

"He'll explain it better than me. Seaver understands what makes this place special. It's not a fad at all. It's a revolution."

"A revolution of the heart!" Dale says.

"Do you know where he is?" Alice says. "Seaver? Do you know where I can find him?"

"Well, sure. He lives on the other side of things, just past the reservoir. A bright blue trailer, can't miss it. If he's not home, just ask around. Ask anyone! Everybody knows Seaver."

Alice sets off into the maze of vans and tents and makeshift shanties. The citizens of Nowhere are out and about in the warm spring sunshine, some just lazing but others hammering nails into boards, weeding gardens, creating "art." Mannequin heads with stained glass eyes, a Stonehenge made from old refrigerators. Some of the "art" isn't terrible, actually.

The demographic in Nowhere is mostly white, uniformly weathered, and a mix of all ages. Alice passes elderly retirees, middle-aged couples, hippies in their teens and twenties, a handful of children, a toddler in a diaper attempting to ride a world-weary yellow Lab.

Alice prepares herself. She's decided on the simplest, most straightforward strategy. She'll offer Moon the full one hundred thousand, right off the bat. Take it or leave it.

If Moon doesn't take it? Alice and Patricia haven't discussed that possibility. There's nothing, in that case, either of them can do.

A hippie boy waves Alice over and asks if she wants to do some mushrooms.

"No, thank you," Alice says.

"Hi!" he says. "My name's Zed. This is Bree."

Bree, the hippie girlfriend, doesn't look up from the Monopoly board she's studying. It appears, from the cash and deeds in front of her, that she's kicking Zed's ass.

"I'm Alice."

"Hi!"

Their canvas teepee is covered with an elaborate and colorful mural: angels and devils, dancing together, snuggling on heavenly clouds, surfing a wave of fire. It's better than not terrible.

Zed sees her admiring it. "Bree rocked that," the hippie boy says. "She's an awesome artist."

Bree doffs an invisible hat but still doesn't look up from the Monopoly board. The boy crawls into the teepee and then back out with an empty Folgers coffee can. Alice gets the hint. She takes out her wallet and drops a five-dollar bill in the can.

"Did you know this place used to be, like, an army base?" Zed says. "I'm serious! Like way back in one of the world wars."

Alice asks a question she's been wondering about. "Who owns the land now?"

"Oh, Arizona does, officially. The state. But they don't care what happens way out here. The closest town with police is, like, an hour north. So, we just do our thing. Did I ask if you want some mushrooms?"

"You did."

"Nowhere is all about *freedom*," Zed says. "If someone somewhere makes some, like, frivolous law, why do we have to follow it? That's what Seaver says."

Moon again. Apparently, everyone here does know him. Alice's curiosity is piqued. Before she can ask Zed to elaborate, though, Bree finally looks up from the Monopoly board. She's freckled and fox-faced and not smiling. "Zed."

"What?" he says. "She's cool."

"Zed."

He shrugs. "I better get back to the game, Alice. Take it easy!"

CHAPTER 80

Finally, after a lot more zigging and zagging, Alice reaches the reservoir, a concrete basin the size of a swimming pool. A few naked people splash around. Bathing? Alice cringes. Not for all the tea in China would she dip a toe in that soup of bacteria.

Moon's trailer should be close by, but it's been almost three hours since Alice left Scottsdale, and she badly needs to pee.

A woman chuckles when Alice asks where she can find a restroom. "It's the desert!" the woman says. She's carving faces into an old telephone pole. "Go out there, pick a rock, and get 'er done. If it's number two, you can borrow my cat hole trowel."

Alice politely declines the cat hole trowel, whatever that might be, and heads out into the desert, a hundred or so yards from the edge of Nowhere. She squats behind, yes, a rock, and for a moment has a true out-of-body experience.

What in the world is she doing here? But Alice *isn't* really here. She can't be. She's in her office in Manhattan, slowly and steadily scrolling through the requirements for initiating review of real estate tax assessment, soothed by the familiar sound of soft voices, shoes clicking, the familiar *hussssh* of her laptop fan.

The sky is a dazzling, dizzying blue. Alice thinks about her conversation with the hippie boy, Zed, how the girlfriend cut him off when he started to tell Alice about Moon. What should Alice make of that? What should Alice make of the fact that Moon is such a celebrity in camp?

She dries herself with a Kleenex from her purse. As she's pulling up her pants, she notices what looks like an alien spaceship a few hundred yards farther out. That's how disorienting and strange this place is, that her first thought is *alien spaceship*. It's just an old army Quonset hut, of course.

Alice walks closer and shades her eyes against the glare. Other than splotches of rust, the corrugated steel shell is bare—the only inch of Nowhere not covered with graffiti or art. And, even more interesting, the Quonset hut is surrounded by a tall chain-link fence.

Dust blooms to the north. Alice watches a white minivan approach the Quonset hut. The minivan stops at the fence and a man in the front passenger seat hops out. He unlocks a gate, motions the driver through, then relocks the gate behind them.

The back of Alice's neck warms and tingles. That's how her body reacts—how it's always reacted, since she was a child—to an unexpected rush of adrenaline. When is the last time Alice's neck tingled like this? She can't remember.

Something strange is going on here. Which seems silly to think, of course, since *everything* here is strange. But Alice is absolutely certain now—that tingle—there's more to Nowhere than meets the eye.

"What are you doing?" a voice says.

Alice turns, startled. A man stands a few yards away from her. He's tall, lanky, with mirrored sunglasses that hide his eyes, and a beard twisted into dirty black dreadlocks. There's an embroidered patch on the chest of his leather biker vest: a snake uncoiling from the empty eye socket of a skull.

Nowhere is grungy and chaotic, but this is the first moment Alice has felt . . . *uneasy*. And that's before she notices the holster on the man's hip, the gun in the holster.

"Hi," she says, keeping her tone light. "My name's Alice. I'm just having a look around. Nice to meet you."

The wind gusts and the man's beard tinkles. It's braided, Alice sees, with tiny bells. This makes her more uneasy, not less. And the gun: a big, heavy pistol with a well-worn wooden grip.

"Nothing to see out here," the man says.

Alice disagrees but decides to keep that opinion to herself. "It's a beautiful day," she says. "What's your name?"

"Come with me," he says. "Come meet Seaver."

CHAPTER 81

Alice doesn't bother attempting, as she follows the bearded biker back to Nowhere proper, any more small talk. She knows a lost cause when she sees one.

Just as well. She can use a moment alone with all her whirling thoughts. The Quonset hut and the fence, the white minivan and the locked gate, Zed's hippie girlfriend shutting him down when he started to share too much information. The pistol on the biker's hip.

Drugs. That's the conclusion Alice reaches, the only logical one. Moon must be transporting drugs up from Mexico, then moving them along to points north, west, and east. Nowhere is truly *nowhere*, safely removed from the authorities, but also well-positioned for relatively easy access to major interstate highways. And what better cover for illegal activity than some kookie artist's commune?

"Here," the biker says.

Moon's trailer, as promised, is painted a bright blue, almost the exact same shade as the sky behind it. That creates, for an instant, an unsettling optical illusion: the trailer vanishes, the trailer appears, the trailer vanishes.

And then a man steps outside and walks over to them. He's in his fifties, his black hair gathered up into a messy bun.

"Howdy," he says to Alice. "Thanks for stopping by."

Moon. He's more or less exactly what Alice expected. The cutoff jeans and unbuttoned aloha shirt; the three-day salt-and-pepper scruff; the sly, snaggletoothed smile of a lifelong hustler. The only feature at odds with the rest of him: his eyes, a gaze that's intense but warm, as if the rest of the world has fallen away and Moon has no interest in anyone but you.

It's just an act, that gaze, as artificially manufactured as the fabric of his aloha shirt. But Alice better understands now why Patricia, age eighteen and emotionally broken, might have trusted a lizard like this.

"Did I have a choice?" Alice glances over at the biker's pistol.

"Oh." Moon giggles. "Don't worry about Skin. He just uses that to scare off the javelinas. Like wild pigs, kind of? They love to get in the gardens and act like assholes."

Sure they do, Alice thinks. "I haven't seen any javelinas."

"Exactly! That's my point. My name's Seaver."

"Alice."

"You want a pop, Alice?"

"A pop?"

"I've got Coke, Pepsi, Seven-Up, Dr Pepper. You name it. Come on in."

The biker, Skin, melts away, his beard tinkling. Alice hesitates, just for a moment, then follows Moon into the trailer. It's as cluttered and chaotic as the rest of Nowhere. Alice would have an easier time listing what's *not* crammed inside his living area. The couch alone accommodates a microwave oven, a million rusty screws in Mason jars, two guitars, a boat's outboard motor, and a milk crate full of old *Playboy* magazines.

A haze of sepia-tinted cigarette smoke, a layer of dust, windows so grimy they suck the light out of the room instead of letting it in.

Moon lugs the microwave off the sofa, making a place for her to sit. "Sorry about all this," he says. He seems slightly, though genuinely, abashed by the state of the trailer. "So? What'll you have to drink?"

"Anything's fine."

He returns from the kitchen with two cans of Barq's root beer. He hands one to Alice, then takes a seat on the outboard motor. "I'm like the welcome wagon around here," he says. "We don't get many visitors. I like to meet the new faces, get to know everyone."

Alice bets he does. Moon probably screens every stranger to make sure they're not law enforcement. She's even more certain now that Moon is running drugs through Nowhere.

But so what? Whatever else Moon is up to, other than blackmail, is irrelevant. The focus of Alice's mission is narrow and sharply defined. How much does Moon want for the Polaroids? How much will he take? How quickly can Alice destroy the Polaroids and be on her way home? Nothing else matters.

"So, tell me about yourself, Alice," Moon says.

My name is Alice Mercurio. I represent Patricia Campbell. I'm here to discuss the three Polaroids.

A few short, simple sentences. So why doesn't Alice say them?

What if, Alice considers, Moon's drug operation *isn't* irrelevant? Right now, he has all the leverage in the situation—the three Polaroids, the power to destroy Patricia's professional future, and by extension Alice's. Alice *might* have the opportunity here to balance the scales. Moon's operation is a potential vulnerability that Alice *might* be able to use for Patricia's advantage, a way to ensure he accepts the hundred thousand dollars without any argument.

Moon smiles his sly, snaggletoothed smile, waiting.

But Alice needs to know more, a lot more, before she can even think about balancing scales or exploiting vulnerabilities. She needs to slow down and approach this new twist in the road carefully.

The idea takes her by the hand and tugs gently. An extra few hours, an extra day—what's the harm? Alice will become acquainted with Moon. She'll gather, if she can, a bit more information about him and Nowhere.

The back of her neck tingles.

"There's not much to tell," Alice says. "I've got two kids, a boy and a girl, Mack and Jenny, eight and nine. Irish twins. My ex-husband shares custody. I do medical billing and coding in Point Pleasant, New Jersey, which is just as boring as it sounds. The job and the place, both. It pays the bills, though, most of them. Actually, the job and the place are even more boring than they sound."

Medical billing and coding? Mack and Jenny? Where did that come from? Snippets of conversation overheard at the airport or a restaurant, a day or a decade ago, subconsciously filed away? Alice is one hundred percent certain she's never been to Point Pleasant, nor had any reason to think of it. This is how it used to be, she remembers, when she was a child. Her lies, magically, had a life of their own.

Moon smiles, studying her. "And what breeze blows you to our little corner of the desert?"

"I'm visiting a girlfriend from high school. She lives in Phoenix now. We
were having drinks last night, and the bartender told us he'd heard about
this place. I thought it sounded intriguing, and I have the day to myself while
April's at work, so I thought . . . you know."

"What does she do?"

"Who? April? She's a stylist. The hair kind, not the kind that picks out
clothes for celebrities. Why? That's kind of a random question."

Alice knows exactly why he asked it—Moon is testing for holes in her
story—but a divorced medical records coder from New Jersey would be
puzzled.

He laughs. "I can be random. Guilty. But tell me. You thought Nowhere
sounded intriguing how?"

"I don't know," she says. "I like the idea of a place where you can stop
and . . . *breathe*. Do you know what I mean? A place where tomorrow might
be anything. Who knows? The future isn't already decided for you."

"You can't breathe back in New York?"

Nice try, Alice thinks. He's not going to trip her up. "New Jersey."

"Right."

"My life back home is fine. It's just . . ." The character Alice is playing is
open-minded but not naïve. She's been around the block. "Excuse me, but are
you in charge here? Is that why you're asking me all these questions?"

The movement is subtle, almost imperceptible, but Alice catches it:
Moon's shoulder softens, his fingers on the Barq's can relax. He's satisfied
she's not a DEA agent.

"Let me tell you something," he says, and his voice has changed now too.
It's softer, but also more urgent.

"Okay."

"No, first of all, I'm not in charge," he says. "Nobody is. That's the whole
point. Because you're right, Alice. This is a place where everyone should be
able to breathe. Everyone should be able to *be*."

Alice resists the temptation to roll her eyes. "Be what?"

"The full version of ourselves. Alice, before I came here, I thought I understood who I was. But really, I only understood a part of myself. It was like my life was a house and I was holed up in one little room of it, never coming out. I'd convinced myself the room *was* the house. You know what I mean?"

"Maybe. I think so."

Here it is again, that signature gaze of his, warm but intense. "It's like you said, Alice. Here you can *breathe*."

A cell phone chirrups. Moon takes it out of his pocket, checks the number, and stands. Alice takes that as her cue to stand too.

"How long are you going to be here?" Moon says. "In Arizona?"

"A few more days."

"Come back tomorrow afternoon," he says. "Okay? It's the first of the month and we have a cookout for the whole community. You'll love it. You'll get a better feel for us. For me."

"Tomorrow, sure," Alice says. "Sounds perfect."

CHAPTER 82

On the drive down the mountain, wind buffets the rental car and regret buffets Alice.

What in the world was she thinking? Lying to Moon, pretending to be someone she's not, scheming to gain advantage—Alice has made a sleazy situation even sleazier. She's made *herself* sleazier!

No, technically, Alice did nothing wrong. And she acted on behalf of a wronged party, the victim of a blackmailer. Doesn't the end justify the means?

But those rationalizations provide no comfort. The first refuge of an unscrupulous mind, for god's sake, are the words *"Technically*, I did nothing wrong." And "The end justifies the means."

A gust wallops her. She grips the wheel of the car more tightly. It's not just regret. It's guilt too. She hates how easily the lying and scheming came to her, how it felt so . . . *natural*. A relief, a release, a current bearing her away.

It's in your blood, her dad used to say.

Bullshit! The biggest lie of all! No one is born crooked. It's a choice. It's a choice that people like Moon make. It's a choice that people like Alice refuse to make.

She also—oh, by the way—needs to consider the wisdom of attempting to hoodwink armed drug dealers. The pistol on Skin's hip, the well-worn wooden grip, is definitely not just for show. His gaze was empty, indifferent. Alice doubts very much that he'd hesitate if Moon ordered him to shoot her. She doubts very much he'd give it a second thought afterward.

And Alice isn't in Manhattan anymore, is she? A vast, empty desert surrounds Nowhere. They could bury Alice anywhere, a quick and shallow grave, and she'd never be found.

So what in the world, in other words, was Alice thinking?

She tries calling Bill. She wants to hear the sound of his voice, steady and familiar—a horn in the fog, guiding her back to port. There's no cell service, though, between the ghost town and valley. Her phone beeps twice and goes silent.

By the time she reaches the valley and turns onto the state highway, Alice's nerves have settled. She made a mistake, a distressing error of judgment, but no irreparable damage was done. And the past is the past. The important thing: Alice is back on track now and is absolutely clear about what she needs to do tomorrow. No more delays. No more detours. She'll tell Moon why she's here and finish this business as quickly and simply, as safely and *cleanly*, as possible.

Back at the resort, she orders dinner at the bar and calls Bill. As he updates her on his day, Alice watches a succession of men try, and fail, to charm the female bartender. It's mildly diverting. The lobby of the Canyon Oasis is freezing, the air brittle and artificially aseptic. It's a beautiful spring evening. Why not turn off the AC and open a few windows?

Bill goes on. He's representing a chain of grocery stores being sued for breach of fiduciary duty because the board didn't terminate the company president for cause. Alice loses the thread. It's not that the case is boring . . . okay, yes, Bill's case is a bit boring. But delightfully, wonderfully boring! This is exactly what Alice needs right now. She's glad she can't talk to him about Patricia and the blackmail, about Moon and Nowhere. She just wants to forget about all that right now.

Because there's nothing to think about! Even if Moon is running a drug operation, that by itself isn't a useful bargaining chip. Alice can threaten to alert law enforcement and Moon will just shrug. He'll threaten to release the Polaroids the minute he's arrested. Alice can't use Moon's crimes against him without also destroying Patricia's reputation, the one and only thing she's been tasked to protect.

"Okay, then," Bill says. "Love you."

"Love you too."

Alice puts her phone away. A grinning man strides toward her. Alice doesn't know him, or why he's grinning. He's forty or forty-five, excessively tan and meticulously coiffed, his teeth a blinding, unnatural white. Once upon a time he must have been lean and mean, movie-star handsome, but now his jowls droop, his belly bounces, all his seams show. And yet, Alice has to admit, he still has a certain . . .

"Oh, for fuck's sake," she says, realizing.

"Baby sister!" Jeremy says.

CHAPTER 83

Jeremy opens his arms wide and snares Alice in a hug before she can evade it. He smells like English Leather. After all these years, the idiot still wears the same cologne he wore in high school.

When he finishes squeezing her to death, he helps himself to the stool next to her.

"Did I say you could join me?" Alice says.

"You look wonderful, Alice," he says, ignoring the question. He turns his smile on the female bartender. "Gin on the rocks, please. Just a whisper of tonic. A mere suggestion."

"How did you find me?"

"Piggy called and said you were in Scottsdale. I know the kind of places you stay. I'm your brother, Alice! I know everything about you!"

That couldn't be less true, but Alice still hates that Jeremy knows *anything* about her, and that he was so easily able to track her down. Alice is going to murder Piggy for this. She's going to make him suffer.

Or maybe all this is her fault. Maybe Jeremy is punishment sent from the gods—what Alice gets for only *technically* doing nothing wrong in Nowhere, for letting herself enjoy it.

The bartender brings Jeremy's drink. He interrogates her about multiple items on the dinner menu and suddenly the bartender is a purring cat, delighted to assist. For god's sake.

"I'll have that right out for you," the bartender says when Jeremy finally makes a decision.

Alice pushes away her plate of mediocre pasta primavera. She's lost her appetite. Another glass of Sauvignon Blanc might ease the pressure building behind her eyes, but she'd rather get this family reunion over with as soon as possible.

"What do you want?" she asks Jeremy.

"What do I want? Jesus, Alice, can't we just have a conversation? We haven't seen in each other in, like, two years."

"Five."

"Really?" He turns to look at her. For the first time, Jeremy seems to actually *see* Alice. That lasts about a second. "Everything is great with me. Better than great. This place, Scottsdale, Phoenix in general, you wouldn't believe the opportunities. They're out of this world. Real estate, tech. Indian casinos! I'm putting together two, three deals a week."

"So, I guess San Diego didn't work out?" she asks. "Because five years ago didn't you say the opportunities there were out of this world? And before San Diego, wasn't it Houston?"

He's either oblivious to the jab or unfazed by it. "Phoenix is the future. The desert is blooming. Last week I met with some investors from Oman. The week before some guys from Germany."

"What do you want, Jeremy?"

"I want to catch up with my sister. Piggy says you're out here for business. Give me some details."

"Not in a million years."

"C'mon. Anything I can help with? I'm happy to lend a hand. We were a good team when we were little, remember? You were always the mastermind. The brains of the operation."

The nostalgia angle seasoned with flattery. Good luck with that, Jeremy. He definitely doesn't know Alice as well as he thinks. "What do you want?"

He shrugs, squeezes a lime wedge into his gin, and lights up like an idea has just occurred to him. *Well, now that you mention it . . .*

"I *could* use a favor," Jeremy says. "A tiny one, and entirely painless."

Alice can't get over how different Jeremy looks since the last time she saw him, but also how much the same—how much the same as he did when he was eleven and she was ten. Alice has known him her entire life, which equips her with a weird kind of X-ray vision. It's like being able to see all the way through a book, every chapter and page of a life all at once.

"Really? A favor?" she says. "I would never have guessed."

"I miss you, believe it or not," he says. "Sometimes I do. I miss everyone."

"You miss Mom and Dad?"

"Jesus. Like a hole in the head."

At least they can agree on that. "What's the favor? The answer is no, by the way."

"Have dinner with us tomorrow night. I'd love for you to meet my girlfriend. She's a special lady and we're getting serious. I know, look at me, acting like a kid again. But I'm over the moon, Alice. When Piggy called and I found out you were in town . . . it's perfect. I want to show Beverly who I am. I want her to know everything about me."

Uh-huh. Alice uses her X-ray vision again. Let's see. The girlfriend is rich. Obviously. Jeremy has an angle on her money. Obviously. And Alice is supposed to . . . vouch for Jeremy? Corroborate all the stories about his successful entrepreneurial ventures? Demonstrate how Jeremy is such a good guy, close to his loving family?

Alice shares her observations. Jeremy doesn't answer. He pouts, the same poor wounded sparrow he played as a kid, until the bartender delivers his steak and retreats again. "You think you're so smart," he finally says.

"Am I right?" Alice asks.

"Will you do it?"

"What makes you think I'd ever help you with one of your scams?"

"What makes you think it's a scam?"

"Are you kidding me?"

"I genuinely love her, Alice. And c'mon. It's one dinner, a couple of hours. It's one small favor. You and me, we're family."

She grimaces. Her headache pounds. She can think of only one way to get rid of him. "You won't leave me alone until I say yes, will you?"

He starts to go in for another hug. Alice fends him off with a fork. "Seven o'clock tomorrow evening," he says. "We live just a hop and a skip from here. You'll love the place. You'll love Beverly. This is what family is all about, Alice."

Jeremy writes an address on a cocktail napkin. *9335 E. Adobe Drive.*

"And that's it?" Alice says. "You promise? One dinner, then you'll leave me alone for the next five years?"

"I promise. Cross my heart and hope to die."

Just look at that face, the aching sincerity in those eyes. Jeremy means what he's saying, which means of course he's lying. But that's just fine, because Alice won't be anywhere near 9335 E. Adobe Drive tomorrow at seven. That she can promise.

CHAPTER 84

The next morning Alice power walks the resort grounds in the gray, predawn glow. She showers, drinks her room-service coffee, and gets dressed. The same casual outfit she wore on the plane, in the interest of comfort, but otherwise she's all business. Crisp, focused.

She leaves Scottsdale a little after ten. By eleven thirty she's climbing into the mountains. The road tightens like the aperture of a camera slowly closing. Alice, for the second day in a row, doesn't see another car. What happens when—if—two vehicles meet on this stretch? She wonders if the white minivan is still in Nowhere, or if it's already on its way to Mexico.

The road widens just before she reaches the ghost town. Alice rolls through. One day some entrepreneur might turn Ringo into a tourist draw, but she doubts it. No one is going to drive two hours from Phoenix to marvel at heaps of bleached and splintered wood, at a stripped video rental store, at a broken-down 1978 Buick Regal.

She taps her brakes and jolts to a stop. This is strange. Alice could swear, she *would* swear, that yesterday the Buick had been abandoned with one tire propped up on the curb. Today, though, all four tires rest level on the street. Which must mean, unless some supernaturally strong wind blew through town, someone has moved the car. It's not in fact broken-down. It's not in fact abandoned.

But that can't be right. Someone actually lives here? The Buick is parked in front of a two-story Victorian wreck. Alice examines the house more closely. It's relatively sound, she realizes, at least by the standards of the ghost town—merely on the *verge* of collapse.

Alice finds herself turning off the ignition, climbing out of her car. Why?

She can't really say. She has no reason to investigate the mystery of the Buick Regal. She has every reason to *avoid* a building on the verge of collapse.

She knocks on the front door. She waits, then knocks again. Only one of the big bay windows on the ground floor isn't boarded up with plywood sheets. Alice cups her hands and peers inside. She sees gray walls, a gray rug, a gray couch. And, she realizes after a moment, the almost invisible figure of an old man in a gray suit, sitting on the couch and gazing straight back at her.

Her heart jumps. The old man doesn't move, doesn't blink. Can he see her? It's possible he's blind. Finally, just as Alice begins to worry that he's dead, mummified by the dry desert air, he slowly, slowly lifts his arm. Slowly, slowly he crooks a finger.

Come in.

Alice, who's never believed in ghosts, concedes this might be an excellent time to start. On the other hand, she's fairly confident that ghosts, if they do exist, don't drive 1978 Buick Regals. She walks back to the front door and tries the knob. Unlocked. She tests, with one foot, the floor of the foyer. The oak groans like it's been punched but seems relatively solid.

Relatively solid! Bill would be horrified by what Alice is doing. He'd be baffled.

Down a short hallway to her right is another door. Alice opens it. The old man turns his head. Slowly, slowly. He's not just old but *old*, a wisp of smoke, a trace of gray ash that might blow away if Alice sneezes. But he's dressed impeccably—suit and tie, crisp white shirt and gleaming black dress shoes. A few strands of hair left on his liver-spotted head have been neatly oiled, parted, combed.

He examines Alice. His dark, hooded eyes weigh more than the rest of him combined. "Well," he says, "you found me."

"Pardon me?" Alice says.

"It's fine. It's time. But they send a goddamn girl." His voice is as insubstantial as he is, just dust and smoke. "The world turns, I suppose."

That's a lot to unpack. Alice has no idea where to even begin, so she takes a seat in the chair across from him. The floor groans again. Above her, the old house pops and creaks.

"My name is Alice," she says. "It's nice to meet you."

"How the hell did you find me? Who sent you?"

"Nobody sent me. I promise. I was just passing through."

The dark eyes narrow. "Baloney. I saw you yesterday. Saw you drive past."

"Yes. I'm staying in Scottsdale. I've been visiting Nowhere. The art community on the old army base."

The old man sighs. "It's fine. I'm tired of running. I've been running since 1974."

Since 1974! Alice wants to reassure him that he can relax. Whoever he's running from is probably dead or in a nursing home by now.

"I stopped to admire your car. My mother used to drive one just like it."

A long moment passes. His stare shifts away from Alice, back to the window behind her. "Well, hell."

"What is it?" Alice says.

"You're telling the truth."

"Yes. I promise. What's your name?"

"Call me Ned."

"Ned, do you live here all by yourself?"

His fingers twitch impatiently. "Of course I do. Now go make us some coffee, why don't you? Kitchen's in back."

Alice considers her legal responsibility here. Her *moral* responsibility. The old man is ancient, and probably addled. He shouldn't be living alone here in an abandoned town, in a collapsing house. He shouldn't be living alone *anywhere*. Alice should find out if he has any relatives, should contact the state's social services department . . .

"Any day now," the old man says. "Jesus Christ."

Alice finds the kitchen. To her surprise, the cupboards are neatly stocked with cornflakes, cans of Campbell's chicken soup, instant coffee. The refrigerator hums, which means the house must be drawing power from somewhere, and inside is milk, cheese, packages of salami, a six-pack of Coke. A microwave on the counter looks almost brand new.

Somebody must be looking after the old man. That's a relief, though it still doesn't explain why he's living *here* of all places.

She heats two mugs of Folgers in the microwave and takes them back to the parlor. The old man takes a careful, dubious sip of his coffee and then, after a pause, nods his grudging approval.

"Smart lady," he says.

"Me?"

"Your mother. A Caddy is too flashy. Draws too much attention. And I wouldn't piss on a Ford or a Chevy. But a Buick. There you go."

He's looking out the window again. Alice guesses that might be how he spends the better part of his day.

The question slips away from her almost before she's had a chance to form it in her mind. "Ned, have you ever seen a white minivan drive by?"

"A what?"

"A white minivan. I don't know the make or the model."

"See for yourself," he says.

Alice doesn't understand. She turns to look out the window. Nothing, of course. She would have heard the engine. Ned, she suspects, might be further gone than she thought. But then she sees him rummaging beneath one of the couch cushions.

He sets a small, pocket-sized New Testament on the coffee table. Alice still doesn't understand, but she picks the book up and opens it to a random page. She lands on Mark 13:

Therefore, stay awake—for you do not know when the master of the house will come, in the evening, or at midnight, or when the rooster crows, or in the morning—lest he come suddenly and find you asleep.

There's also writing in the margins, tiny block letters that Alice assumes at first glance are glosses on various chapters and verses. It's not.

Monday 7/13/98 4:08 p.m. tan Ford Taurus
Wednesday 7/15/98 9:15 a.m. white Nissan Stanza
Tuesday 7/21/98 3:34 p.m. red Jeep Cherokee

Alice turns to the next page. Those margins too are filled with dates, times, makes and models. He's been keeping a record, the paranoid old ghost, of every vehicle that passes through town, circling the ones that appear more than once. She flips forward, through the gospel of Luke and into John— through 1998, 1999, 2000 . . . all the way up to now, 2006. The last entry is today, twenty minutes ago, with Alice's rented silver Nissan Altima, circled.

She flips back to the previous page. Alice's car again—noted twice yesterday, her first pass through and coming back from Nowhere. And then, four days before that:

Sunday 4/30/06 11:45 a.m. white Dodge Caravan

Just before that:

Monday 4/24/06 1:08 p.m. white Dodge Caravan

The white Dodge Caravan again on Sunday, March 26, 11:45 a.m., and Monday, March 20, 1:14 p.m.; on Sunday, March 12, 11:45 a.m., and Monday, March 6, 1:05 p.m. And so on and so on, month after month, every two weeks like clockwork, the white minivan making the roundtrip from Nowhere, heading south and then returning five days later.

"See for yourself," the old man says.

Alice nods. She does see for herself.

CHAPTER 85

When Alice arrives in Nowhere, the festivities Moon promised are in full swing. What seems like the entire population of the place is milling around on and spilling off a pair of empty concrete slabs near the reservoir. Card tables are loaded with platters of food and six-packs of sweating Budweiser cans. Jimmy Buffett blasts and the donkey wanders around, sporting a red fez.

Alice doesn't see Moon. What she can just glimpse, as she circles the periphery of the crowd, is the Quonset hut, a knuckle of corrugated steel out among the rose-colored boulders. No sign of the white minivan, which must still be inside the hut. According to old Ned's meticulous notes, the Dodge Caravan should be making the trip south—through the ghost town and down the mountain—Sunday morning, the day after tomorrow.

That's merely an observation. Alice remains on task. When it comes to Moon's drug business, she's a disinterested party. No, make that an *un*interested party. Moon can bring whatever he wants up from Mexico. She's here for the Polaroids, and those alone.

She spots familiar faces: Cheetah and Dale, the woman who offered her the cat trowel, Zed the hippie boy. Zed waves to her. Alice waves back and he makes his way over. The funk of pot smoke reaches her a few seconds before he does.

"You're back!" he says.

"I'm back."

"Did you try the spinach and mushroom salad? That's what I made. Don't worry, they're just regular mushrooms."

Alice isn't worried. She won't be going anywhere near any salad served in this place. "Do you know where Moon is?"

"Seaver? He's around somewhere. Yeah. I saw him with Skin a while ago. Seaver's always around somewhere."

A couple of children are setting off fireworks. A bottle rocket explodes directly overhead and Alice flinches. A full second later, Zed flinches.

"Whoa," he says.

"Yesterday," Alice says, "you mentioned Seaver does some interesting business down south."

"I did?" He thinks hard. "I guess so. Yeah."

"Do you ever help out? Do you ever make the trip down in the minivan?"

"Me? No way. That's all Mitch and Tammy, nobody else, ever. Tammy is Seaver's cousin. Or maybe like a niece? They're related some way. Mitch and Tammy, they look like they're people who drive a minivan. That's the main thing, Seaver says."

And an innocent family minivan, of course, is less likely than other vehicles to be stopped and searched at the border.

Moon is smart. But he's also, Alice recognizes, not *that* smart. If he were, he wouldn't be using the same minivan for every run. Maybe he's switching out the license plates—Alice gives him the benefit of the doubt there—but he should be switching out the vehicles themselves on a regular basis and rotating the upstanding citizen drivers too. He shouldn't be sticking to such a regular schedule either.

"But I've helped load it up before they head down," Zed says. "A couple of times. It can take, like, a whole night. You kind of almost have to take apart the whole minivan."

That makes sense, hiding the drugs, but the timing perplexes Alice. Moon wouldn't be sending drugs down *to* Mexico. She turns to Zed. "Before they went *down*?" she says. "What were you loading?"

He hesitates. He seems to realize, finally, that it might not be wise to spill so many incriminating secrets to a complete stranger. But he's already spilled enough. Alice, after a moment of thought, understands. It's *cash* that Zed loaded. The minivan brings drugs up and sends proceeds from the sale, minus Moon's cut, back down.

"Um," Zed says.

These are just observations Alice is making. She is, she reminds herself, *uninterested* in Moon's drug operation.

Except the pieces of the puzzle do tempt her, drawing her closer, closer. She can see the corners of the big picture, the edges. With a little time, a little effort...

It infuriates Alice. She's never tempted! She never wavers! But the thought of matching wits with Moon, of cutting that sleazy fucker down to size, makes her mind hum.

One of her dad's favorite movies, Alice remembers, was an old comedy short called *The Fatal Glass of Beer*. W. C. Fields plays a father whose naïve son descends into a life of crime after succumbing to that first, "fatal" glass of beer

That's Alice. She should never have taken the first, fatal step down this crooked path. In Patricia's office—Alice should have stood up and walked out the moment she understood what was being asked of her.

"I don't know if I should really say," Zed says. "But I guess if you swear to be really chill about it."

Alice sees Moon, making his way from his trailer to the party. He's walking with a clean-cut couple who could have just stepped out of Whole Foods. Mitch and Tammy, undoubtedly. At the same time here comes Bree, the unfriendly fox-faced girlfriend, marching over to shut Zed up—and save Alice from herself.

"Never mind," she tells Zed. "I need to have a word with Moon."

CHAPTER 86

itch and Tammy have peeled away by the time Alice maneuvers her way to the other side of the crowd. Moon stands by himself, hands on hips and chin lifted, a pose that suggests a benevolent monarch surveying his kingdom. Alice sees no sign of Skin, the armed biker, which is a relief.

"Alice!" Moon says. "What do you think? You can feel it, can't you? The love. The energy. The *freedom*."

She wonders if Moon, like her brother Jeremy, believes his own crap. Maybe the drug operation is merely a secondary interest, and Moon is establishing his own little cult up here in the high desert. Maybe the Quonset hut stores not only drugs and money, but Moon's multiple wives too.

"I'm an attorney with the firm of Bergen, Baker, and Tatum," Alice says. "Patricia Campbell sent me to discuss the letter you sent her."

For a moment Moon continues to smile. His eyes dance with confusion. And then his whole face tightens into an ugly little knot of anger. Alice hasn't met many men in her life, or perhaps even any at all, who enjoy discovering that a woman is a step ahead of them.

"Can we speak privately?" Alice says.

In his trailer, Alice takes her usual seat on the couch. Moon doesn't offer her a soft drink, but he's cooled down. His smile has returned, only slightly worse for wear, a bird nursing a damaged wing.

"Alice!" he says. "I have to give it to you. Is that even your real name? Very sly, very crafty."

"Yes. It's my real name. And I apologize for misrepresenting myself."

"Why apologize? That's your job, isn't it? The rich and powerful pay you to grub around and bury their scandals."

Moon is a drug dealer, a blackmailer, a rotten egg of a human being. It shouldn't sting Alice that someone like him has such a false impression of her true profession and character, but it does.

"This isn't my job," she says. "Patricia isn't paying me. She's my friend and colleague. I'm here as a personal favor."

"Uh-huh. Whatever you say. But now you've got dirt on me, right? You figured out about my business ventures, I assume, so now you think you've got me by the balls."

"I don't have you by the balls," Alice says.

"No, you don't. You don't. Because guess what?"

"If Patricia tells law enforcement that you're distributing drugs, you'll release the Polaroids."

His face knots again. Alice has spoiled his big checkmate. "That's right," he says. "I will *crush* her."

"Can we discuss the Polaroids?" Alice says.

"Sure. Let's do that."

"May I see them, please?"

"You think I'm bluffing?"

No, Alice doesn't think he's bluffing. But she's going to make damn sure of it. "You know I'll need to see them before we go any further."

Moon shrugs. He goes down the hall, past the kitchen, and through a door that must lead to the trailer's bedroom. Alice listens for a hint of where he's keeping the photos—the squeak of a closet door, the beep of a safe's keypad—but there's nothing. Moon returns with a manila envelope.

"No touching," he says.

"Understood."

"Sit right there and don't move."

He drags over a guitar amp. On top of the amp he places, one by one, slowly and dramatically, the three Polaroids.

Alice leans in. Eyes, mouths, bare legs twined together. A penis that, because of the angle and the unflattering flash, looks like a blanched root vegetable. An arched stomach, sweat on an upper lip. The images are less pornographic than Cubist, parts and pieces instead of wholes. In only a single photo can you really, truly tell that one of the participants is Patricia.

That's the good news. The bad news is that in the single photo you *can* really, truly tell that Patricia is in bed with two, no three, other people. Two men, one woman. The worse news is the expression on Patricia's face: dreamy, dizzy, blissful. Zoom, crop, print. Every newspaper in the country, every website, will run that photo. A woman of Patricia's standing *might* be forgiven for sex with multiple partners of various genders, but definitely not for enjoying it.

Moon isn't checking Alice's reaction. He's studying the photos too. "You wouldn't believe it," he says, a gentleness in his voice that surprises Alice. "How much fun Dish could be."

"Why are you doing this?" Alice says. "What did she ever do to you?"

He looks up at her, perplexed. "Nothing. What do you mean? I thought these pictures were long gone. I didn't even remember them. And then I saw Dish on TV, a month or so ago, and she's this big-deal lawyer now. And the next day, literally, I'm going through some old boxes and I find these. Pure luck."

Pure luck. Alice wants to punch him. Punch him, take the photos, run. But how far would she get? She wouldn't get out of the trailer. She hasn't thrown a punch in her life.

He slips the Polaroids back in the manila envelope and flops back down in his La-Z-Boy. "Satisfied?"

"Patricia can pay you a hundred thousand dollars for the photos," Alice says. "That's her best and final offer. Yes, she's well off, but she can only access a certain amount of cash before she creates even bigger problems for herself."

"A hundred thousand dollars?"

"You can believe that's best and final now, or you can believe it after you've wasted a lot of time."

Moon laughs. "I don't want money, Alice. I'm offended you'd think that."

So, he's going to drag this out. Alice needs fresh air. The trailer is growing smaller and more cluttered by the second, the stacks of old newspapers multiplying like loaves and fishes. Moon has kicked off his huarache sandals and propped his bare feet on the amp. His dirty soles are much closer to Alice than she can really tolerate.

"A hundred thousand dollars," she says. "Best and final offer."

"Hand me that guitar. I want to play you a song."

"Over my dead body."

"Alice, did you read the letter I sent? Dish must have shown it to you."

Stop calling her Dish, you lizard. "A hundred thousand dollars. Best and final offer."

"I don't want money. You're not hearing me. I never mentioned anything about money in the letter, did I? Not once. I just want to be *friends* again. I want Dish to be my *friend*."

Where is he going with this? He's toying with Alice, that much is clear, but it's strange he hasn't made some outlandish counteroffer. *I'll take a million cash.* And it's strange how dead serious he seems right now, as if he's not toying with Alice at all.

Finally, Alice understands. He's *not* demanding money for the Polaroids. He's after something much more valuable, something that will come at a far greater cost to Patricia.

"You get it now?" he says. "I just want Dish to have my back. That's all. Maybe down the line I need a little favor. Maybe I need some information. I'm in a very competitive industry, you know what I mean? Dish knows a lot of important people. Dish can protect me."

Alice feels her stomach twist. *Friends.* Moon wants access, influence. Which means he'll never give up the Polaroids, never let Patricia off the hook. Either she refuses his terms and her career is over, or she corrupts herself utterly by serving Moon. She'll *wish* her career was over.

Now it's Alice who has to work hard to keep her cool. Moon picks at one of his crumbling yellow toenails. "It's funny how everything works out for the best," he says. "You just have to trust it. Life, I mean. You just have to go with the flow."

CHAPTER 87

Alice dreads what she has to do now, but delaying the inevitable won't make it any more pleasant. As soon as she's back in her car, driving away from Nowhere, she calls Patricia.

"Well?" Patricia says.

"He doesn't want money," Alice says.

"I don't understand."

Alice tells her about Moon's drug-running operation. She explains how he wants to use Patricia's influence and connections.

Silence. Patricia processes. "He's not bluffing? He's not just trying to . . ."

"No," Alice says. "I don't think so."

"What if . . ." Patricia's voice trails off again.

"He wants your answer in forty-eight hours."

Silence again. "I've worked so hard. And I still have so much to accomplish."

"Let him release the photos," Alice says. "It's 2006. Attitudes toward women have changed. Scandals burn out quickly. It will be painful, but you'll get past this."

"Do you really believe that, Alice?"

Alice doesn't, not really. She passes through the ghost town. The '78 Buick Regal has both passenger-side tires up on the curb this afternoon. She pictures old Ned on his sofa, growing fainter and fainter as the years pass, slowly disappearing.

This will be Patricia if the Polaroids come out. There's absolutely no chance she'll ever be appointed to a federal circuit court or granted tenure at a top law school. She'll never raise a dime for a congressional run. Alice understands exactly what that would mean to someone as driven and ambitious as Patricia.

Alice understands too what it will mean for *her* career. But it's the only option Patricia has.

"You have to let him release the photos and live with it," Alice says. "Paying him money is one thing but giving into him like this . . . you'd sacrifice every shred of your integrity. And Moon would *own* you."

"Not necessarily. I could manage the situation. I could find a way to manage him without really . . . without really compromising myself."

Alice can't believe what she's hearing. Patricia, she tells herself, is still in shock. "Take the forty-eight hours to think about this, Patricia."

"I can't let him win."

"You can send him to prison."

"But he still *wins*. Don't you understand?"

"Please take the forty-eight hours."

"I will. But how can . . ."

The cell reception cuts out. Alice has started the steep, winding descent down the mountain.

• • •

Phoenix rush-hour traffic is hellish. Time slows, heat builds, the smell of exhaust and baking asphalt overwhelms. Alice doesn't get back to her resort until a little after six thirty. She's stiff, exhausted. She needs a drink, a shower, a handful of Advil.

Patricia's mind is made up, Alice knows. The next forty-eight hours aren't going to change it. Alice can't blame her—not for surrendering to Moon, not for making that first, innocent mistake thirty years ago. Moon is the only person to blame in this situation, and it infuriates Alice that he'll end up with exactly what he wants.

As for Alice herself . . . she's screwed either way. If Patricia gives in to Moon, Alice will have to protect *her* integrity by distancing herself from Patricia. She'll have to leave her job and start over from square one, essentially, at a new firm. Just the thought of it exhausts Alice.

Alice drags herself across the lobby. Near the elevators, a man springs suddenly out of a chair and directly into her path. She's startled and then, when she realizes who it is, horrified.

"Baby sister!" Jeremy says.

What is her stupid brother doing here? It's six thirty. He should be at his lady friend's house, not yet wondering why Alice hasn't arrived for dinner.

His satisfied smile explains it. He's guessed, correctly, that Alice never had any intention of showing up. He's been waiting to ambush her.

"I thought I'd swing by and give you a lift to the house," he says. "That way you don't have to bother with a cab."

"Screw you, Jeremy."

"You promised, Alice."

Asshole. When has a promise ever meant anything to him? But she's mostly angry at herself. Jeremy would never have outsmarted her if she hadn't been so distracted.

"I've had a hard day," she says. "Why don't we reschedule for tomorrow night?"

"Funny. C'mon, Alice. A couple of hours won't kill you."

Only probably. Alice makes a rapid calculation. It will take more effort to fend Jeremy off than it will to have dinner with him and his lady friend. Even if she locks herself in her room and unplugs the phone, there's a decent chance Jeremy will call down to the desk, report an emergency, and have security break down her door.

"I need to take a shower first," she says.

"No, you don't."

"Let me change, at least. And wash my face."

"I'm coming with you. But hurry."

While Alice gets ready, Jeremy drinks a mini-bottle of Jack Daniel's from her minibar and watches *Entertainment Tonight*. During the walk to the parking lot, he sticks close to her, as if he's afraid she might suddenly bolt. The thought does occur to her.

He points out what looks like a brand-new Cadillac. "How do you like my wheels?" he says. "Not too bad, is it."

His wheels? Right. Alice opens the center console compartment. Inside is a tube of Estée Lauder rose-scented hand cream, a pair of bejeweled sunglasses, a prescription bottle of cephalexin.

"How's your bladder infection?" she says.

Jeremy slams the compartment shut. "Remember, okay, family is important to Bev. She's tight with her brothers, their kids, her parents."

"Got it."

"I mean it, Alice. Just . . . help me out here, okay?"

She closes her eyes and leans her head back. It would never occur to Jeremy that she might have more on her mind than this dinner, his problems, *him*. Alice just wants to get this over with.

"Okay, okay, okay," she says.

A few minutes later they pull into a long, smooth loop of driveway. The house—Beverly's house—is a vast, interlocking series of postmodern cubes, glass, and faux adobe. Lanterns glow, fairy lights drape the cacti.

Beverly meets them at the front door. She's late fifties or early sixties, at least fifteen years older than Jeremy, a slight woman with unnaturally smooth skin and expensive perfume, slightly cross-eyed. Her diamond bracelet cost more than Alice's paralegal makes in a year. Alice gets why Jeremy needs tonight to go well.

"Alice!" Beverly says. "Jeremy has told me so much about you."

"I'm sure he has," Alice says, smiling back.

CHAPTER 88

At dinner, prepared by a private chef and served by a young Latina who doesn't make eye contact, Beverly gushes about her brothers, how close the three of them have all remained over the years, and isn't family such a *gift*? Her brother Ronald named one of his daughters after Beverly, and Beverly named one of her sons after her brother Jim, and for decades now they've all summered together every year on Cape Cod, three and now four generations of Munsons.

"It's one of the reasons I was so drawn to Jer so quickly," Beverly says, "because family is so important to both of us."

Jeremy is nodding along and smiling. Alice nods and smiles too. "You can't escape your family, can you?" she says. "You can't run, and you can't hide."

Beverly laughs uncertainly. Jeremy shoots Alice a look. She lifts innocent eyebrows. *What?*

But then she shapes up. She plays her part. Why, yes, Alice and Jeremy have always been close. Why, yes, "Jer" does visit her in New York every year, like clockwork. They try the newest restaurants, take in the latest Broadway musicals. (Broadway musicals? Are you *kidding*?) And, absolutely, it's really quite impressive, how Jer's been in on the ground floor of so many successful Silicon Valley start-ups. But, no, the money's not what matters to him—it's the opportunity to make the world a better, greener, more compassionate place.

Beverly eats it up. Or Alice should say, Beverly eats *Jeremy* up. Her adoring gaze rarely leaves him. The house could be on fire, Alice could be on fire, and Beverly would never notice. Beverly's *hands* rarely leave Jeremy. She strokes, she paws, she practically jerks him off right there at the table.

Alice can tell Beverly isn't a stupid woman. Jeremy *makes* her stupid. His dark magic, after all these years (and despite that new paunch), is still potent. Alice has never understood it.

Beverly's husband, a real estate developer, passed away four years ago. Beverly never *dreamed* she'd meet another man who could ever . . .

Alice tunes out. She thinks about Moon. She thinks about Patricia. At least, some consolation, this ugly affair is about to end. Alice will prove herself to a new group of senior partners, will find new influential advocates and allies. Her career trajectory will be delayed, but her life in New York won't change. She and Bill will get married, as planned. Moving to a new firm might make the timing even more straightforward.

"We had such good times growing up, didn't we?" Jeremy says, kicking Alice's foot under the table. "We did everything as a family. Card games, camping, you name it. Right, Al?"

Card games? Camping? And when in his life has Jeremy ever called Alice *Al.* For god's sake.

"Our mom and dad owned a disco," Alice tells Beverly. "They put all of us to work there when we were just kids. I mean, *kids* kids. I was ten or eleven."

"Oh?" Beverly says. Alice has her attention. "Jer didn't mention a disco. And you *worked* there? When you were just children?"

Jeremy squirms. His hand tightens on the butter knife he'd like to stab Alice with right about now. "Well," he says, "it was just for a couple of years. And Al, Mom and Dad didn't 'put us to work.' You make it sound like the salt mines. We had fun!"

"True," Alice says. "It was wild. It was the seventies! Sex and drugs, all that. Remember, Jer, how Dad kept two sets of books? I was the smartest kid in the family, so I helped him with the business."

"That's not true," Jeremy says, taking the bait. "You had the best grades in school. You read the most. That didn't make you the *smartest.*"

Beverly is frowning. "When you say your father kept two sets of books, do you mean . . ."

Jeremy strains to chuckle and shakes his head. *No, no, no.* Alice considers starting with Chapter 1 and regaling Beverly with the full Mercurio story. Dad working for the mob, swooning as Mom pilfers cash from a purse! The family fleeing Vegas in the middle of the night! Tallulah and Jeremy delivering coke at the Mercurio Club, Ray cracking heads at the door! Mom, skimmed money stuffed in her car trunk, firing a gun at Dad while the kids wait in the cars! The cars parked on icy railroad tracks!

Oh, how Alice would enjoy the look on Jeremy's face as she sets Beverly straight. It would be her good deed for the day. *He's after your money, sister. You shouldn't trust him to pass the salt. Get a restraining order and block his number.* Honestly, is Jeremy any different from Moon?

"Sex and drugs?" Beverly says. "While you kids were around?"

The temptation to drop a bomb on Jeremy passes. He's not Moon. He's not breaking laws and ruining lives. It may be inexplicable, unfathomable, but he seems to make Beverly happy.

And . . . he's Alice's brother. As much as she wishes it didn't, that counts for something. What was it Paul McCartney said once? Or maybe it was John Lennon. There are only four people on earth who know what it was like to be a Beatle. Well, there are only four people on earth who know what it was like to be raised a Mercurio. Piggy, arriving so late to the party, doesn't really count.

On the practical side of the ledger, if she does expose Jeremy's true character to Beverly, Jeremy will find a way to get back at Alice. She doesn't need the headache. She needs him to disappear and leave her alone for another five years.

"I'm just joking," Alice says. "There was no second set of books. We weren't around anything inappropriate. And we did have fun as kids. We were always having some kind of adventure."

Jeremy nods cautiously. "Right."

"The five of us were inseparable. In the summer we went everywhere together. We traveled as a pack. Remember how we used to swim in the creek behind the park?" Alice doesn't mention the NO TRESPASSING sign, the eight-foot fence Alice had to figure out a way past, the park maintenance guy she had to outwit and elude. "We made a rope swing."

"I forgot about that." Jeremy laughs. "Right. None of us really knew how to tie a knot. We were all scared to do the first jump."

"Except Tallulah."

"Except Tallulah."

Beverly beams. Now *these* are the family stories that warm her heart. The shy Latina serves dessert. Jeremy shows off his new phone, a Nokia. He makes Alice show him hers. She has a Nokia too! Jeremy and Alice can electronically text photos back and forth to each other now! Their brother Ray claims that Apple will release something called a ground-breaking "smart phone" next year. But of course, Ray of all people, Jeremy scoffs, doesn't know the first thing about technology.

After dinner, Jeremy calls Alice a cab. Beverly hugs her goodbye with one arm—she keeps her other hand gripped tight to Jeremy's wrist.

"Great to see you, Al," Jeremy says. "As always."

CHAPTER 89

The cabdriver confirms that Alice is headed to the Canyon Oasis. As he's pulling out of Beverly's driveway, though, Alice asks him to wait. She's tired, not sleepy, and could use a drink stiffer than the expensively bland rosé Beverly served with dinner. The prospect of the resort's bar, all those golfers and spa wives, the generic corporate artwork of desert landscapes, makes her grimace.

"Is there a bar around here that's more . . ." She's not sure how to describe it since she's not sure what she's looking for. "Interesting?"

The driver nods. "Coming up."

He drops her in Old Town Scottsdale, outside a time-capsule relic wedged between an art gallery and a boutique. The neon sign hums and flickers: THE SORRY JACKALOPE.

Inside, Alice takes a seat at the bar and orders a Scotch, neat. Without asking the bartender reaches for the Cutty Sark. It's that kind of place. Mismatched barstools, a wall of signed headshots from long-ago B-list celebrities. Charlene Tilton. Hal Linden. Adrienne Barbeau and Charles Nelson Reilly. The customers scattered around the room are a mixed bag—a few grizzled old coots who'd be right at home in Nowhere, a couple of Latino guys in muddy work boots, a rumpled and weary public defender (Alice's guess) watching CNN. Alice doesn't fit in, but she doesn't stand out either.

The bartender is generous with the pour. Alice's glass is more or less clean. The Cutty Sark tastes like gasoline. Alice gets it down in a hurry.

That creek on the edge of the park, back when they were kids. She hasn't thought about that iffy rope swing in a hundred years. It proved shockingly durable.

That would have been . . . 1976? The same year as the Olympics in Montreal. The McDonald's promotion! Alice hasn't thought about their summer of Big Macs and fries in a hundred years either. It was a truly elegant scheme Alice came up with, if she does say so herself.

You see, McDonald's kept the one-a-visit promotional cards stacked next to the registers. That was the vulnerability Alice exploited. Piggy created a diversion—he would howl like a banshee, for example, if you pinched him just right. Jeremy would distract a female cashier while Ray, a wall, blocked the view of customers in line. Tallulah darted in and out, snagging the cards. Alice had Tallulah steal only five or ten cards at a time. That way the cashiers were none the wiser and the Mercurios could return a day or two later, employing of course a different diversion.

Alice can't let Moon, that fucker, win. He's not afraid of Patricia or the cops, but he has to have *some* weakness, *some* vulnerability. If Alice had more time, she might be able to persuade Skin, Moon's biker henchman, to get his hands on the Polaroids. Maybe *he* wouldn't turn up his nose at a hundred thousand dollars.

But she doesn't have more time. She's all out of it.

Her cell phone rings. Bill. Alice lets it go to voicemail. Now that she thinks about it, she can guess what probably scares Moon: the people down in Mexico he's doing business with. She's no expert on the cartels, but Alice is confident they'd be much more forceful and persistent than the DEA.

Okay. So? Alice would need to convince Moon that she has the power to turn the cartel from his friend to his enemy. What if . . . what if Alice arranged to have someone steal one of Moon's shipments? He'd be desperate to get the money or the drugs back. He'd hand over the Polaroids immediately.

But of course, Alice is not about to hijack one of Moon's shipments. It's a ludicrous notion. She'd need time she doesn't have, connections she could trust, and—oh, yes, last but not least—a willingness to commit multiple felonies.

A man takes the stool next to her. He's a few years younger than Alice, his jeans splattered with paint. Hair down almost to his shoulders, but inked on his forearm is a tattoo of the Marine Corps: eagle, globe, and anchor.

"Want another one?" he says, nodding at Alice's empty glass.

Odd question. "If I want another one," Alice says, "I'll order it."

He winces. "Right."

"It's fine."

"I'm Max," he says.

Is he hitting on her? Alice needs a beat to process the possibility. It's not that she doesn't get hit on occasionally, she does, but only occasionally and never by men like this. She's never even around men like this.

"Alice."

The bartender pours Max a beer. Max plays with the cardboard coaster, tapping the edge of it against the counter. His hands, like his jeans, are spotted with paint.

"I'm trying to think of what to say next," Max says. He's got a shy, sideways smile.

He *is* hitting on her. Alice doesn't know what to say next either. Well, she knows what she *should* say. She should tell this man she's in a relationship, not interested. She should pay her bill and head back to the resort.

"The Sorry Jackalope," Alice says. She points to the name of the bar, stenciled on the brick wall. It curves around a scrawny cartoon creature with drooping ears. "In what way?"

"In what way?"

"Is the jackalope sorry as in apologetic or sorry as in pitiful?"

Max taps his coaster and considers. "He looks pitiful, but maybe he's also filled with regrets, haunted by the various choices he's made in life that have led him to this sorry bar."

Alice motions to the bartender for another two fingers of gasoline. "Just who exactly are we talking about now?"

"Not me. I may be filled with regrets, but I like this bar just fine."

It's happening to Alice again, the same kind of dizzy, shimmering moment she experienced that first day in Nowhere, when she went to pee behind a boulder. *Where am I? What am I doing here?* She's herself but also not, fundamentally, the same; informed and shaped by a multitude of different decisions that led her here, to this sorry bar.

"You're a painter?" she says.

"Yep."

"Houses or . . ."

"Houses for a living. My own stuff for me."

On CNN, a jittery handheld shot shows Baghdad, black smoke pumping from a building like blood from an artery, the aftermath of a bomb. How fragile an artifice is civilization. How fragile an artifice are we ourselves. One breath here, the next breath gone. We don't have a say in the matter.

Alice thinks about the Marine tattoo on Max's arm. She wants to ask him, but won't, what he's seen and what he's done and how it changed him. If he was his true self before or after.

As if he can read her mind, Max gets up and turns the TV from CNN to a baseball game.

"Do you know about this place called Nowhere?" Alice says when he sits back down.

"I went up there once. Yeah. Some cool work happening, but . . ." He shakes his head. "The scene is a little too much for me."

The bad Scotch has gone to Alice's head. Not only is she waxing philosophical, she feels her cheeks flush when Max gives her his shy, sideways smile. She imagines the first rough kiss, his skin against hers, paint-splattered hand locked around her wrist.

She should be ashamed of herself. She *is* ashamed of herself. If you want to do something badly enough, she reminds herself, that can be as much a sin as actually doing it.

Alice remembers another twist to her McDonald's scheme back in 1976. After Tallulah stole the promo cards, she'd quickly pass them off to Alice. That way if the manager busted Tallulah, she wouldn't have the evidence on her. He'd have to let Tallulah go.

"It's not what you do," Dad used to say, "it's what people *think* you do."

The whole family watched Doug Henning's TV special *World of Magic*. That was 1976 too, or maybe 1975? Jeremy liked the glittery costumes, the beautiful female assistants. Tallulah did somersaults and handsprings between illusions. Ray (probably) thought magic was real.

"See that?" Dad said.

"Smart," Mom said.

Alice moved closer to the TV. She watched every move.

It's not what you do, it's what people think you do.

Max clears his throat. "So, okay, I'm not good at this. At all. But maybe if you're around tomorrow and want to get dinner. With me, I mean. Or even, I don't know . . ." He stops. "You okay?" he asks Alice.

Alice nods. She guesses her eyes have gone glassy. Because she's just realized—a bottle rocket exploding directly overhead—that she doesn't need to actually *steal* one of Moon's shipments, she just has to figure out how to make it, for a couple of hours, disappear.

CHAPTER 90

Alice bundles up—the desert, at midnight, is unexpectedly cold—and finds a bench in the most secluded corner of the resort grounds. Alice tucks her knees under her chin. She needs silence to do her best planning. Silence and a sky patterned with stars. When she was a little girl, she'd remove the screen from her bedroom window, hers and Tallulah's, and crawl out onto the roof.

She returns to her room just before sunrise and sleeps for a few hours. After coffee and a shower, her first stop is a Best Buy on the other side of Old Town. Alice's cell phone uses Sprint, so she buys prepaid phones that work on the other two major networks, Verizon and T-Mobile. By eleven o'clock her car is laboring up the mountain toward Nowhere. When the road narrows to a single lane, at the crook of a hairpin turn, Alice stops. She checks her phone. No signal. She tests the prepaid phones. Verizon: no signal. T-Mobile: no signal.

There's always the possibility that Mitch and Tammy in the minivan use a different, obscure carrier, that this won't be a dead spot for their phones, but it's unlikely. Alice will have to take the chance.

In the ghost town, the 1978 Buick Regal is in the same spot as yesterday. So is Ned, resident ghost, sitting on the sofa and staring out the window. If not for his tie—sky blue stripes on navy today, red stripes on navy yesterday—she might suspect he hasn't budged in the past twenty-four hours. Alice taps on the glass. He motions her inside.

"You found me," he says. He sighs, with either relief or defeat, Alice still can't tell which.

"It's me, Ned. My name's Alice. My mom used to drive a Buick Regal."

"Bullshit. How the hell did you find me? Who sent you?"

"They wouldn't send a girl, Ned."

His eyes drift, then narrow. "You're right."

Alice makes them coffee. Ned stirs his with the wrong end of the spoon. Her plan, Alice recognizes, is absurdly ill-advised. She remembers a piece of wisdom her dad imparted to her in the manager's office of Club Mercurio. *Do what you can, with what you've got, where you are.* He claimed the quote belonged to Theodore Roosevelt, though more likely he just pulled it out of his own ass.

"Ned?"

"Hmm."

"I'd like to borrow your car for an hour or two tomorrow. Your Buick."

His eyes narrow again. "Like hell you will."

Alice is prepared for this. Has Ned really been on the run for thirty-two years? Maybe, maybe not. Either way, he must have some reason to *believe* he's been on the run for fifteen years.

"You're no choir boy are you, Ned?" Alice says.

"I don't know what you're talking about."

"I'll make it worth your while. You'll get a piece of the action."

He pinches the crease of his slacks and crosses his legs. It might be just her imagination, but Alice could swear he suddenly seems less gray, less ghostlike and more substantial. His skin warms, blood stirs.

"I don't get out of bed in the morning for less than thirty percent," he says.

"Ten percent. I'm doing all the heavy lifting, Ned."

"Twenty-five."

"Twenty, but you give me the keys now." Alice won't have time to have this whole conversation again. Plus, she's already taking too many risks. She can't take the risk that Ned will decide to go for a drive at exactly the wrong time tomorrow. "I hold on to them until I'm done."

Ned holds out his hand. Alice shakes it. His grip is iron. "You get nabbed," he says, "I never heard of you."

On the way back to her car, Alice stops to inspect Ned's Buick. The tires are bald but serviceable. She climbs inside and turns the key in the ignition.

The engine roars to life, shaking Alice so forcefully she can barely keep her hands on the wheel. The gas gauge shows half a tank of gas.

Would Alice trust the Buick for more than a mile or so? No. But she only needs it for a mile or so.

She drives back to Scottsdale in her rented Altima. So far so good. Well, relatively speaking. Alice tries to ignore the fact that her plan is woefully precarious. She is Ned, sitting in the middle of a derelict house, surviving at the whim of rusted nails and rotten planks.

If she goes through with this, Moon will take the gloves off. Alice will be interfering with his livelihood, his *life*, and he'll come at her with everything he's got. If Alice goes through with this and can't pull it off, there's a very good chance she *will* end up buried in the desert.

At a Bank of America branch, she withdraws a thousand dollars, cash, from her account. "Use it for something fun!" the chatty teller says.

"You betcha," Alice says.

Jeremy opens the front door of his lady friend's mansion and blinks with surprise. Jeremy, now that he doesn't need Alice's help, has forgotten she exists.

"I'm your baby sister," she reminds him. She opens her arms for a hug.

"What are you doing here?" he says.

If Alice's shaky plan is Ned's house, then Jeremy is the rustiest nail in it, the rottenest plank. But you do what you can, with what you have, where you are. No one else Alice knows in Arizona, probably no one else she knows *anywhere*, would agree to do what she's asking.

"You owe me a favor, big brother," Alice says.

CHAPTER 91

The next morning Alice leaves the resort at seven and makes it to the ghost town by nine—three hours before the white minivan loaded with cash will pass through.

That's *if* Ned's notes are correct. *If* Moon hasn't changed the schedule. *If* Mitch and Tammy didn't leave Nowhere early and aren't already down in the valley, on their way to the border.

For the fourth or fifth time already today, Alice reminds herself of Teddy Roosevelt's and Buddy Mercurio's immortal words: *You do what you can, with what you have, where you are.* She tries not to picture the biker henchman's big, heavy pistol, the hammer cocked back.

The Buick balks when Alice turns the key—a rough, halting chuckle, *huh huh huh.* She doesn't panic, though, and on the third try the big engine thunders. She wrestles the gear shift from park to drive and creeps slowly down the mountain. When the road narrows, Alice eases to a stop. It's a perfect fit: the Buick blocks the road completely, like a cork wedged into the neck of a bottle. Alice opens her door. She has barely enough room to squeeze her way between the car and the sheer drop-off.

Mitch and Tammy, when they find the abandoned Buick blocking their way, will leave the minivan here and walk back up to the ghost town. They'll find Ned, get the keys to the Buick from him, return to the bottleneck, and move the Buick out of the way. That should give Alice plenty of time in Nowhere.

Should. And only *if* Mitch and Tammy don't just put the Buick in neutral and use the minivan to shove it off the edge of the cliff. *If* they've noticed the Buick during their trips through town and know where to find Ned. *If* they do the safe, sensible thing and walk back up, instead of trying to navigate the twisty road in reverse.

"You found me," Ned tells Alice.

She doesn't bother to argue. She hands him the keys to the Buick and an envelope with ten crisp, brand-new hundred-dollar bills. "As promised," she says. "You don't get out of bed for less than thirty percent."

His eyes brighten. "Like hell I don't."

Five minutes outside the ghost town, almost to Nowhere, Alice picks up a signal. Her phone shows one flickering bar, then two. She calls Jeremy.

"Are you ready?" she says.

"Where do you think I should pop the question to Beverly?" he says. "Here or when we're in Carmel this summer? Never mind. Carmel, definitely."

"Jeremy. Are you ready? Do you understand what I need you to do?"

"Relax, Alice. I'm ready."

She has to believe him. What else can she do? He's the most untrustworthy, unreliable person Alice has ever known in her life, but also the most self-interested. He understands the value of having Alice in his debt.

She *hopes*.

"Eleven thirty, Jeremy. Eleven thirty, *sharp*. Okay?"

"Relax!"

Here's the strange thing: Alice *is* relaxed. She's put herself in the most dangerous position of her entire life, and yet she feels . . . well, she feels pretty fantastic, actually. Wide awake, bare feet slapping against hot asphalt, laughter. She looks at herself in the rearview mirror. There's more color in her cheeks. Blood swirls through her body. Like old Ned, Alice isn't a ghost after all.

Just this once, she tells herself. Just the one glass of beer.

Five minutes from Nowhere, the white minivan zooms past in the opposite lane, headed toward the ghost town, Mitch behind the wheel and Tammy in the passenger seat next to him. Right on schedule. Start the clock.

Alice passes the scatter of graffiti boulders, the peace signs and psychedelic sunsets, then the two old school buses. *NO* and *WHERE*. She finds a place to park close to the road and backs her car in, nose pointing out. When is the last time she had to think about making a quick getaway? Such a long, long time ago.

She waves to Cheetah and Dale. They stare puzzled at Alice in her all-business Ralph Lauren. When they finally recognize her, they wave back uncertainly.

Moon and his biker henchman, Skin, are standing outside the bright blue trailer. Moon smirks at Alice and, without a word, points her inside. Skin stays outside, guarding the door. The only way in, the only way out. Skin's gaze is as empty and indifferent as ever, terrifying.

And yet . . . this is the best part, Alice remembers. When you release your plan into the world. When you cross your fingers and hope it will flap its wings and fly.

Moon's trailer seems even more crammed with junk, the porthole glass even grimier. Alice squeezes onto the sofa, between a new tangle of Christmas lights and the milk crate full of old *Playboys*.

"I've got a proposition for you," Moon says.

"Oh?"

"Come join us, once all this is settled. You're welcome here, Alice."

Is he serious? Alice thinks he might actually be. "No, thank you."

"You want to be somewhere you can breathe, don't you? I know you were lying about the other stuff. New Jersey, medical records. But you weren't lying about how you *feel*, were you?"

She glances at her watch. The minivan should have reached the bottleneck a few minutes ago. Mitch and Tammy should have started the hike back up the mountain. It's time. "I have a proposition for *you*," she says.

Moon's cult-leader gaze cools and hardens. Now it's just a plain old-fashioned glare. "No," he says. "Either Dish takes my deal, or she doesn't. End of discussion."

"Just one more option. Give me the Polaroids and you can have your minivan back."

"What? What are you talking about?"

"Your business partners in Mexico are going to be upset if their money never arrives."

It takes Moon a moment to fully process this information, the implications. And then his face curdles, his body clenches. He's a submarine crumpling beneath the pressure of a deep black ocean.

"You're bluffing," he says.

"If you want your minivan back, give me the Polaroids. It's simple. You have five minutes to decide."

"You're bluffing." He takes out his phone and dials.

Alice picks up the July 1983 issue of *Playboy* and, as casually as she can manage, thumbs through it. What if Mitch and Tammy rolled the Buick off the edge of the cliff? What if they're already down the mountain, out of the dead spot, their cell phone ringing?

Moon kills the call and tries again. "Fucking hell, Alice," he says. "Do not fuck around here. The people I'm dealing with, they're serious."

"So am I. You have four minutes."

"Fucking hell! I know you're bluffing. You didn't hijack my van. Skin!"

Alice hears the door open. Skin's beard, braided with bells, tinkles. He walks over to stand directly behind her.

"Alice," Moon says, "do you want to know why they call him Skin? Do you know what he's going to do if you don't stop fucking around?"

"Three minutes," Alice says.

"You see the gun and you think, oh, he might shoot me. He's got a knife too, Alice. The gun is for business, the knife for pleasure."

Alice grips her Nokia. Jeremy will come through. He *has* to come through.

If this were one of the short stories Piggy writes, the next thirty seconds would take three pages to describe. Internal monologues, flashbacks shrouded in mist, lots of strained metaphors. In real life, the temperature in the trailer feels like it increases by about twenty degrees. Moon is seething, sweating, losing his patience. Bells tinkle and Skin moves even closer. Alice feels a dirty tendril of his beard brush the top of her scalp. Her heart tumbles down an endless flight of stairs.

Where the fuck is the text from Jeremy?

Moon tries calling Mitch and Tammy again. Sooner, not later, he'll get through. How could Jeremy botch something so simple? Drive up the mountain to the bottleneck. Take a photo of the minivan's license plate. Drive back down the mountain and text the photo of the license plate to Alice. That's it! That's all he has to do!

Jeremy took the wrong exit. He lost track of time. He forgot to charge his phone. He refused to flee the alley behind TG&Y without the stupid bicycle.

Alice's phone dings. A photo slowly unfurls down her screen, one line of pixels at a time.

A close-up shot, the back of a white Dodge Caravan. A license plate, the sun rising behind a mountain. Arizona, P-53136. *The Grand Canyon State.*

She holds up her phone and shows the photo to Moon. "You have one minute to give me the Polaroids."

He squints at the picture and then stands, stiffly. His walks to the back room of the trailer like a Great Dane with bad hips. His feline grace has deserted him.

Alice doesn't celebrate yet. She should still have ten minutes or so. But if Moon's phone rings now, if Mitch or Tammy reports that no, of course the minivan hasn't been hijacked, just delayed . . .

Skin's beard tinkles behind her. He's breathing slow and steady. Finally, Moon returns and hands Alice the manila envelope. Alice opens it. Polaroids are difficult to burn, she learned last night on the Internet, so this morning she borrowed scissors from housekeeping at the resort. She quickly but carefully cuts up the photos, into pieces so tiny they'll be impossible to reassemble. Not that she'll give Moon the chance. She pours the pieces back into the envelope.

"I'll make a call once I'm gone," she tells Moon. "Your delivery will be back on its way in fifteen minutes."

She moves toward the door. Skin steps in front of her. Alice stares up into his mirrored sunglasses and pictures—*becomes*—her brother. Ray, the mountain. Ray, immutable and immovable. Ray, never backing down.

"Pardon me, Skin," she says evenly. "But you're in my way."

Skin shifts to his back foot. He looks over at Moon. Moon picks up a guitar and raises it above his head. Alice thinks he'll smash the guitar to pieces, but after a moment he lowers it and strums a morose minor chord.

Skin steps aside to let Alice pass.

"You lied," Moon says. "You cheated."

Alice pauses at the door of the trailer. Looking innocent is an art all Mercurio kids master at an early age. "Did I?" she says.

CHAPTER 92

It's the longest walk of Alice's life, from Moon's trailer back to her car. She hauls ass as nonchalantly as she can. She's ready at any moment for the tinkle of bells, for the barrel of a gun pressed against the back of her head.

She makes it to her car. As she leaves Nowhere, she keeps an eye on the rearview mirror to make sure no one follows her. So far so good. Once past the school buses, she turns north instead of south, away from the ghost town. This alternate route will add almost an hour to her trip back to Scottsdale, but it's safer. Moon might tell Mitch and Tammy, once he can get through to them, to double black and intercept Alice.

Once she's off the gravel and back on state highway asphalt, Alice pushes her rented car to seventy-five. *Now* she can celebrate. She rolls down her window, opens the manila envelope, gives it a good shake. The pounding wind lifts and scatters the confetti of Patricia's secret past far and wide.

Order has been restored to the universe. Tomorrow Alice will fly back to New York, and she will return to her normal routine. Office, case files, Bill. Alice's relief will be immeasurable. All of this, Moon and Nowhere, will sink like a stone to the bottom of a lake. It will be as if the past week never even happened.

Or . . .

Alice lets herself imagine, just for the sake of argument, a life without routine, without *normal*. What if every week were as volatile and high-risk as this one? A series of unexpected puzzles, each without map or precedent, that would stretch Alice's talents and skills to the very limit. *All* of Alice's talents and skills.

There's no reason she would have to be either crooked or sleazy. She might bend the law at times, but she'd never break it. And, crucially, Alice would only take cases on behalf of clients like Patricia. She'd only represent the wronged, the exploited, the innocent.

But of course, Alice isn't going to quit the firm, put out her own shingle, and become a fixer, a professional problem-solver.

Right?

The highway curves west, away from Alice's destination. She won't hit the interstate and start circling back for another twenty miles. That's fine with her. She's in no hurry. She doesn't mind taking the long way home.

PART VII

Piggy
2015

CHAPTER 93

The point of Paul's pen rests against the blank page. It's December and his Moleskine notebook remains overwhelmingly empty. Don't let anyone tell you that writer's block is a myth, that a writer just needs to sit down and write, one word after another. Writer's block is a tumor, a thick hairy lump in the pit of the stomach that grows larger with every heartbeat, with every tap of the pen against a blank page.

Paul's notebook has been empty since December of *last* year. That's twelve months of struggle, fifty-two weeks of trying to come up with one decent idea for a new novel, approximately twenty emails from the assistant dean and his department chair, reminding Paul that his tenure and promotion review process begins next fall.

A man, he writes, *discovers that*

He tears out the page, balls it up, tosses it in the trash.

"Writer's block is a myth," he always tells his Intro to Creative Writing class at the beginning of the semester, "you just have to sit down and write, one word after another."

He gazes out his window. The skeletal trees of December in Oklahoma City.

A squirrel flows through the grid of bare branches, like a packet
of digital information pulsing through a . . .

He tears out the page, closes the notebook.

Okay, fuck it. No more gloom today, no more doom. Other than the hairy tumorous writing block in his gut, Paul is in excellent spirits. For the first time in decades, after years of Paul begging and cajoling and guilt-tripping, the entire Mercurio clan is finally, finally back together. Can you believe it? A Christmas miracle. Well, a week-before-Christmas miracle.

Ray got in last night, with his wife and two kids, Tallulah and four of her kids the day before, Jeremy and his fiancée last week. The last piece of the puzzle is Alice, whose flight lands in an hour. Paul doesn't know if Alice's husband is coming with her. Alice's texts, as always, are terse and cryptic.

On the way to the airport, Paul picks up his daughter from school. This was Viv's last day of classes before the break and she's in an exuberant mood, which for a twelve-year-old girl means she's slightly less surly, sulky, and snarky than usual.

"Can't you just drop me off at home first?" she groans. "Dad! For the love of God, please."

"Aren't you excited to see Aunt Alice?" They haven't seen Alice since a spring break trip to New York two years ago.

"I'm *so* excited. I'm impressed you saw right through my attempt to disguise my excitement."

Paul smiles. Other parents, friends of his, bemoan the tween years. But he and Kelly don't mind this iteration of Viv. Sure, she's a pain. Sure, she can drive them crazy. But she's their daughter, endlessly fascinating, resolutely original, relentlessly lovable.

"You know what gave it away?" he says. "You pulling your stocking cap down over your face and trying, apparently, to suffocate yourself."

"Remind me why all this is happening? All these aunts and uncles suddenly coming out of the cracks?"

"I told you."

"Some wedding. Yadda yadda. I know. But who is this Warren person anyway?"

"He's an old friend of your granddad's. He's an old friend of the family. Your granddad and grandma owned a nightclub way back when. Warren worked there. Or worked with them. I'm not sure."

"A nightclub?" Viv says, perking up. "More information, please."

Paul doesn't have more information, or at least not much. He was too young and doesn't remember Club Mercurio at all. Well, a flash of a memory here and there, but nothing that makes sense. A blue silk turban?

Dad just waves away questions about back then. "Ancient history," he'll say. Mom shrugs. "That was all your father's business," she'll say. "I didn't have anything to do with that."

"Warren has been with Curtis for almost thirty-five years," Paul tells Viv. "They can finally get married, now that the bill passed last year. It's a big deal."

It *is* a big deal. And Paul couldn't be happier for Warren and Curtis. But . . . he still feels a pang of jealousy. No one, not one sibling, came home to Oklahoma City for Paul's own wedding fifteen years ago. Ray was in Mexico, negotiating with an artisanal tequila maker who supplied his bar in Las Vegas. Really, Ray? You couldn't reschedule that? Tallulah claimed her invitation got lost in the mail. At least they provided excuses. Alice just RSVP'd *No*. Jeremy never even responded to the invitation. Only Ray sent a gift.

But forget about that! Paul reminds himself that what matters is *now*, today, this weekend, the whole gang back together again.

"Dad!"

"What?"

"Music! But not Bruce Springsteen or I actually *will* try to suffocate myself."

Alice is waiting outside the terminal at Will Rogers, alone in the chilly wind with her carry-on. She's spotted Paul before he's spotted her. That's Alice. She's the most alert person Paul has ever known. He pictures the inside of Alice's mind as a control room filled with a dozen tiny Alices, each behind her own computer monitor and radar screen, processing information at an exponential rate.

He puts the car in park and hops out to hug her.

"Okay," Alice says when, very quickly, she's had enough. "Hi, Piggy."

Viv, who's slunk grudgingly out of the car, snorts with amusement. Paul ignores her.

"Hi, Vivian."

"Hi."

"Just you?" Paul says.

"Just me," Alice says. "Steve's in the middle of a big project. Life-and-death stakes."

Steve, Alice's husband, restores vintage jukeboxes and sells them to rich collectors. He's shaggy and amiable, just about the last person Paul ever imagined Alice would end up with.

"Ray got in last night," Paul says as they drive past the fairgrounds. "Ray and Charlie and their kids. Tallulah brought four of hers. Ang and Marjani, Sol. And . . ."

"Kervens," Vivian reminds him.

"Kervens. Guess what? Ingabire is pregnant. Tallulah's going to be a grandmother, if you can believe that. Jeremy and Gloria have been here since last week. You're the missing piece. Can you believe it? Everyone back together again finally."

"Dad, settle down."

"Do you have any Tylenol?" Alice says.

"Check the glove box. And no, Viv, I will not settle down. I will remain effervescent with joy."

Alice dry swallows a couple of Tylenol. She looks tired but tan.

"You've been traveling for work?" Paul says.

Alice was a lawyer until eight or nine years ago, when she quit her Manhattan firm. Paul isn't exactly sure what she's done for work since then. Some kind of corporate consulting. Probably some Kafka-esque, Coen-esque series of endless, interlocking cubicles, meeting after meeting, Alice digging her way through layer after layer of middle management.

"Cincinnati this week." Alice scrolls through her phone.

"I would love a bit of elaboration," Paul says.

"I don't want to bore you. How are Mom and Dad?"

Their health, she means. Every conversation about Mom and Dad starts there. Mom is seventy-three, Dad seventy-seven.

"They're good," Paul says. "Dad will need a new knee in the next year or two. But he's getting around okay. Mom has more energy than me. She's in two different book clubs and chairs a committee at church and has taken up beading. She's been baking like crazy this week. Right, Viv? She's made fudge. She's made cookies. Brownies, Hello Dollies. She's making the wedding cake. You know Mom and her baking."

Alice smiles.

"What's funny?" Paul says. "Mom's always loved to bake."

Alice turns back to her phone. "Right," she says.

CHAPTER 94

Alice is sharing Paul's old room with Tallulah. Though actually, Alice reminds him as he carries her bags upstairs, it was her room long before it was his.

By the time Paul was old enough to form real memories, by the time he was a real *person*, Ray had already left for Vegas and the others were in high school. They had no interest in a six-year-old kid. Alice was always locked in her room, studying. Jeremy and Tallulah were rarely even home. And then they were all gone, flung to the far corners of the map. Paul, for all intents and purposes, was an only child.

"I've got to make a couple of calls," Alice says. "I'll be down in a minute."

Downstairs, Viv has disappeared, probably off somewhere conspiring with her various cousins. Paul wanders into the living room, where Mom and Tallulah are trimming the Christmas tree. It amuses Paul how much they resemble one another: both round and rosy-cheeked, both in reading glasses and novelty sweatshirts (reindeer dancing in a chorus line for Mom, a mug shot of the Grinch for Tallulah).

"Hold that pose for Norman Rockwell, please," Paul says.

"Isn't this one adorable?" Mom says, displaying an ornament for him to inspect. "Tallulah and I found it at TJ Maxx today."

A folk-arty Santa Claus dangling from a striped parachute. "I defer to your expertise," Paul says.

"Piggy," Tallulah says, "what time is it?"

"Almost five thirty."

"I need to pick up the pizza."

"I'll go with you," Paul says.

"That's okay. I can handle it by myself, no problem."

"I just mean . . ."

Tallulah eyes him over the rims of her reading glasses. "Sure," she says after a moment. "Let's roll."

At the pizza place, waiting for their order, Tallulah gives Paul the latest on Ingabire, Kervens, Ang, Marjani, and Sol. The tale of Tallulah's family is an overstuffed Dickens novel—so many personalities and subplots and character arcs. Paul doesn't know how Tallulah has managed to raise five adopted children (from five different countries!), all by herself, while also serving as executive director of a nonprofit that feeds the homeless. It's like she can juggle basketballs while riding a unicycle—on a tightrope.

"Does Ingabire know if she's having a girl or a boy yet?" Paul says.

"Girl. And she gave me the naming rights, since all my kids came prelabeled."

"Have you decided yet? The name?"

Tallulah nods, but then puts a finger to her lips. "It's my secret for now."

Six extra-large pizzas. Yes, Tallulah can indeed handle it by herself. Paul tries to stay out of her way.

"Tallulah," he says on the way home, "what were Mom and Dad like when you guys were growing up?"

"What? Why are you asking a weird question like that?"

"Mom always liked to bake, right? And Dad coached Little League. I know people evolve over time, but I wish—"

"Oh, I forgot to tell you," Tallulah says. "Kervens is going to live in Bulgaria next year."

"Bulgaria?"

"Right? He's going to study ethnomusicology. Do you think that's a made-up subject? It kind of sounds like a made-up subject."

Paul thinks about Viv. She's not even in high school yet, but already determined to spend her junior year in college abroad. Barcelona, Tokyo, Buenos Aires. "Somewhere," she's explained to Paul and Kelly, "exceptional."

"Remember when I was going to visit you in Moscow?" Paul asks Tallulah. "I wish that had worked out."

Why didn't it? Paul was too much of a coward. That's the honest answer. He kept waiting for Tallulah to formally invite him, to arrange everything, when he could have easily hopped on a plane and shown up at her door. *Surprise!*

"You didn't miss much," Tallulah says. "Russia was a yawn."

Paul doubts that, but he'll never know now.

CHAPTER 95

Paul wants to pinch himself. This is perfect. Dad in his chair, Mom in hers. Tallulah passing a slice of pizza to Ray. Alice rolling her eyes as Jeremy talks about his new job. The living room of the house on NW 34th Street filled, once again, with all the Mercurios.

"But Jeremy," says Charlie, Ray's wife, "you don't think he can actually win the nomination, do you?"

"I most certainly do," Jeremy says. He's lost some weight since Paul saw him last summer and positively bubbles with energy, as if he could hop off the couch right now and run a marathon. "And he's going to win the general election too. Mark my words. This will be the earthquake no one sees coming."

"No way," Tallulah says. "Not in a million years."

Paul agrees with Tallulah. Of course Trump can't win, he'll be out of the race by the New Hampshire primary. Still, though, Paul is happy for Jeremy. After years as a successful venture capitalist, he's now made an impressive entrance into the political sphere. A top fundraiser for a major presidential campaign—who knows where that might lead?

"Alice," Tallulah says, "please tell Jeremy he's full of you-know-what."

Alice rolls her eyes. "He's full of you-know-what. But he might be right about this. You know what they say about broken clocks."

Cincinnati in December—wait, why is Alice's nose sunburned? Paul doesn't have time to wonder. Viv, seated on the floor next to Paul's chair, tugs at the cuff of his chinos. "Dad," she whispers, "is that really Uncle Jeremy's fiancée?"

Paul can understand why she might be bewildered. Gloria seems like a lovely person, but she's easily twenty-five years older than Jeremy, Mom and Dad's age.

But, hey. What's that line from Shakespeare?

"'Love looks not with the eyes, but with the mind,'" Paul whispers back to Viv. "'And therefore, is winged Cupid painted blind.'"

His daughter groans. "Whatever."

Tallulah asks Jeremy if, as part of his campaign duties, he'll be doing the Electric Slide. Jeremy and Alice laugh, Mom and Dad too. Even Ray cracks a smile. Paul joins in on the merriment, a beat too late. He has no idea what an Electric Slide is, or what it has to do with Jeremy.

Paul, who's been basking in the warmth of family, feels the temperature change, cool. Melancholy settles over him. The irony doesn't escape him: it's here, now, that he feels the most connected to his brothers and sisters, part of the pack; but it's also here, now, that he's sharply reminded again that he's just a distant moon orbiting the planet they share.

He takes out his phone and jots a note into Notes.

he's just a distant moon orbiting the planet they share

Not bad, right? After a moment's consideration, he grimaces and erases it.

"Dad," Viv says, "what's wrong?"

"Not a thing." He gives her a light punch on the shoulder. "I'm just going to get some air."

Paul grabs his coat and relocates to the front porch steps. This would be the time to smoke pensively if he smoked, but he doesn't, so he gazes at the stars instead. He's such a fucking cliché. "Write what you know," he tells his students. Good advice if what you know is in the least bit compelling.

He hears the door open and shut behind him. Ray. He lowers himself slowly, carefully to the top step. Cartilage pops, bones groan. Piggy always forgets just how massive Ray is—a house, a tank, the mountain that refused to go to Mohammed.

"Hey, Piggy."

"Hi, Ray."

They sit in silence. Paul knows, from experience, that Ray can sit in silence for a long time. Nobody can compete with Ray when it comes to sitting in silence.

"I'm fine," Paul says. "It's just . . . it's writer's block. I'm trying to come up with something to write about for my next novel. And I've got bupkus, basically."

Ray nods. They sit in silence.

"Also, it's stupid, I know," Paul says. "I love this, everyone back together. But it also reminds me I'm not really part of the pack. I'm not one of you guys. I don't really even *know* you guys, your stories."

Ray nods. They sit in silence.

"My story is so dull. I'm happy! I am. But my story isn't a novel. You know?"

Ray nods. They sit in silence.

CHAPTER 96

After dinner, the kids scatter, and the adults pair off. Tallulah drags Alice over to the Christmas tree, Mom and Charlie turn on the Thunder game, Kelly makes polite conversation with Gloria, and Jeremy discusses electoral math with Ray (i.e., Jeremy talks, Ray listens).

Paul floats from group to group. Eventually he makes his way to the kitchen, where Dad is playing chess with Ray's youngest. She's ten, with Charlie's dimples and Ray's implacable gaze.

"Ellie here is already beating my pants off," Dad says. "Can you believe it?"

Paul grabs a Coke from the fridge, pulls up a chair, and watches the game for a while. Dad is a good teacher, congratulating Ellie on every successful move she makes and patiently explaining her mistakes.

"You never lose a game," Dad tells her, "if you have fun along the way."

Kelly and Viv enter the kitchen, in their coats. "Bye, Dad," Viv says.

"I'm coming," Paul says, standing. "Cool your jets."

"You're going with Alice, I thought," Kelly says. "She said they'd drop you off at our place after."

"Who? She did? After what?"

"See you at home, Dad," Viv says. "Please make responsible decisions."

Kelly and Viv leave. Paul searches the house for Alice but can't find her. He can't find Jeremy or Ray or Tallulah either. Perplexed, he grabs his coat and steps outside. His brothers and sisters are gathered around Jeremy's rented car, their breath billowing in the frosty night.

"Finally," Tallulah says when she sees Paul.

"What . . . what's going on?" he says.

"We're getting a beer," Jeremy says. "Maybe two. Is the Sipango still in business? I loved that place. Or Cock of the Walk."

Paul looks over at Ray. Ray looks impassively back.

"You guys," Paul says, "you don't have to do this. I'm fine, honestly. I don't want to be a fifth wheel."

"We need a lookout," Tallulah says. "Get in."

"No time to waste," Alice says. "Jeremy has to get back and help his girl-friend with her dentures."

They climb into the car, Paul squeezed between Ray and Tallulah in the back seat. Jeremy fiddles with the radio till he lands on a classic rock station.

Alice turns to regard Paul. "Ray says you need some ideas for a novel."

"Maybe we can help with that," Tallulah says as the radio blasts some old funk song.

ACKNOWLEDGMENTS

Huge thanks to my agent, Shane Salerno, who can do it all—and then some. And thanks to everyone at the Story Factory, especially the inimitable Ryan Coleman.

Emily Krump is one helluva editor. I owe so much to her and the other good folks at William Morrow and HarperCollins, including Liate Stehlik, Jennifer Hart, Paige Meintzer, Kaitlin Harri, Danielle Bartlett, Carla Parker, Chris Connolly, Virginia Stanley, Lainey Mays, Shelby Peak, Jane Herman, and Joe Jasko.

There are, and have been, so many excellent people in my life. I don't deserve them. To name just a handful: Ellen, Adam, Jake, Sam, Davis, Carson, Andy, Ryan, Mason, Cookie, Thomas Cooney, Laura Moon, Misa Shuford, Rene Sanchez and Kerri Westenberg, Martha Sanchez, Scott and Jennifer Booker, Alicia and Chris Milum, Chris and Elizabeth Borders, Janice Dillon Himegarner, Kristen Cole, Sheila Prosser, Jay Neugeboren, Susan Berney, Vicki Berney, Joe and Nan Hight, and Nick Zarbano.

The best part about being a crime writer is that you become part of the crime-writing community. I've met some of my absolute favorite people in the world here (they know who they are, I hope), and I'm so grateful for all the writers, readers, reviewers, bloggers, marketers, and booksellers I've had the good fortune to know.

My wife, Christine, is responsible for every (good) thing in this book and in all my books.

ABOUT THE AUTHOR

LOU BERNEY is the multiple award–winning author of *November Road*, *The Long and Faraway Gone*, *Double Barrel Bluff*, and *Dark Ride*, as well as *Gutshot Straight* and *Whiplash River*. His short fiction has appeared in *The New Yorker*, *Ploughshares*, and the Pushcart Prize anthology. He lives in Oklahoma City.